his tenth dance

A HAMMOND FAMILY FARM NOVEL

IVORY PEAKS ROMANCE
BOOK 10

LIZ ISAACSON

feel good fiction

LIANA JOHNSON

one

Mission Redbay left his cabin, already too hot in the navy blue suit coat. One, he never wore clothes like this. Certainly not in the summer, and never around the farm. Maybe to church for a wedding.

And today, Mission wasn't attending a wedding.

"Feels like my own funeral," he muttered as he went down the steps of the new cabin where he'd moved last night.

The foreman's cabin.

Mission didn't have to share as the foreman, and the cabin had been designed and built specifically for a career cowboy and his family. He supposed he had one of those, and blast everything to the stars, an image of the pretty blonde veterinarian he'd once fed a turkey sandwich to entered his mind as his boots touched gravel.

1

Kristie Higgins.

He'd seen her around the farm, of course. She came at least once a week, but Mission wasn't the one who had to deal with her.

Until today, he thought as the enormity of the farm spread before him. The foreman's cabin sat down at the end of cabin row, where all the cowboys lived. The equipment shed sat across from the last one, and way down by the homestead stood the generational house, where Deacon Hammond, Mission's boss, lived.

Behind the homestead sat the family barn and buildings, and Hunter Hammond and his family took care of that part of the farm.

Other than that family land, the farm looked to Mission for guidance. They had pastures and paddocks for horses and cattle, a large amount of alfalfa acreage, and a dozen commercial buildings for the children's equine therapy unit Molly Hammond administered.

The farm did horseback riding lessons too, and while Mission didn't have to take care of every horse personally, every responsibility of the farm now sat on his shoulders.

No wonder he could barely take the first step across his front lawn and toward the south side of the farm, where the big red barn welcomed students and riders. He had to get over there, though, because the retirement party for Matthew Whettstein, who'd been acting as the foreman for the past twenty-five years, had already begun.

"Such big boots to fill," he murmured to himself, imagining himself to be talking to his grandfather. A rare smile touched his lips then, for Granddad should be waiting for him at the party.

A friendly face.

Of course, everyone at the Hammond Family Farm had been nothing but congratulatory and supportive of Mission moving into the foreman position. Deacon had announced it a couple of months ago, and Mission had been meeting with Matt and his teams since then.

He'd already learned far more than he'd even realized he didn't know.

He tugged at the end of his jacket sleeves, half-wanting to go home and throw the jacket in the trashcan. He wouldn't, of course. Because this jacket had come from his grandfather, and Mission loved it beyond measure.

Still, something felt off. Maybe it was the way he'd trimmed his beard this morning. Or the fresh polish on his best boots.

Or maybe it's the jacket.

You have to wear the jacket, he argued with himself. *You're becoming the foreman today.*

And there it sat. The reason the world felt like it had been knocked another twenty-three degrees off center was because Mission was willingly stepping into the spotlight.

Nervous energy thrummed through his veins, and he fisted his fingers to contain the shaking. "It's just a party," he told himself, though Mission couldn't remember the last party he'd been happy to attend.

Which so wasn't true, and Mission pushed against the false narrative happening inside his head. He loved the Hammond family parties around the fire pit in the backyard, for every holiday, for birthdays, and sometimes just because it was Taco Tuesday, and Molly didn't want to cook.

You're ready for this, he told himself as he made it past the buildings and onto the dirt path that led in front of the generational house. Then he just had to walk past the counselor cabins and between the pastures, and he'd be at the stables. The administration barn stood in front of that, and the party had been set up on the south side, where trees provided shade for bigger outdoor parties such as this one.

Mission breathed in deeply as he took in the pretty blue sky above him, and he tipped his head back and prayed. "Lord." His mind stilled for a moment, and while Mission had known his past indiscretions had been forgiven, he once again felt that cleansing power of God in his life.

"Thank You for this amazing opportunity. Bless me to have a level head and clear thoughts to make good decisions."

It wasn't just him who would pay this time, and Mission's chest threatened to collapse in on itself, trap the breath there, and prevent Mission from ever breathing again.

A bolt of terror moved through him as his swallow reflex abandoned him. Then, his regular faculties returned, and he could exhale and swallow, and everything normalized.

You've got this, boy. You were meant for more than hiding in the shadows.

Granddad's words further buoyed him, and Mission released the tension in his hands in an attempt to find a better way to deal with his nerves. His grandfather had always believed in him, even when Mission himself didn't. Even when his past mistakes haunted him, threatening to drag him back down.

The June first breeze carried the scent of alfalfa, wildflowers, and something barbecued through the air. As he started down the fences between two pastures, the distant sound of music came from the direction of the big red barn.

His steps slowed as he approached, the knot in his stomach tightening. Only the width of the barn, and the turning of a corner, and Mission would arrive at his own party. Or rather, Matt's party.

He fully committed by striding over the remaining distance and turning the corner before allowing himself to stop. Tents had been erected, with strings of twinkling lights crisscrossing through the rafters. Tables adorned with checkered cloths filled the space, and a long row of tables holding more food than Mission had ever seen stood against the far wall of the tent.

The Hammonds had gone all out for this celebration, and the thought only added to Mission's anxiety. No one had seen him yet, and he took the moment to collect himself. Deacon stood with Hunter and Mike, two of the most powerful men Mission had ever met. Both Hunt and Mike had stood at the helm of a multi-billion-dollar company, with thousands and thousands of employees, and somehow knowing they'd done that and now stood wearing cowboy hats and laughing with loved ones gave Mission confidence that he could do this job.

Travis Thatcher had brought his whole family, and Tucker, Bobbie Jo, and Tarr had come from the farm where they'd been living and working for the past six months.

Gerty Hammond walked super-slowly beside her toddler, who bent down every other step to exclaim over something, and she chatted with Opal and Taggart Crow, whose clasped hands only reminded Mission of how alone he stood.

Boone and Cosette Whettstein stood with Gloria, but Mission didn't see Matt anywhere. His eyes landed on the other cowboys and cowgirls who worked the farm, as well as several of the counselors at Pony Power.

And then the lovely Kristie Higgins. She wore a pair of blue jeans and a short-sleeved sweater the color of bright purple grapes. Very sensible shoes for a farm, too.

Mission's mouth watered slightly, and he told himself it was because he'd loved his grandmother's grape juice growing up.

Not because of Kristie's curves in those clothes.

"You can't go in either?"

The familiar voice made Mission turn. Matt, his mentor and soon-to-be predecessor, stood a few feet away, a knowing smile on his weathered face. The older man was dressed similarly to Mission, though his jacket was made of crushed brown corduroy.

"Just taking it all in," Mission said, working to keep his voice steady.

Matt moved to stand beside him. "It's a lot, isn't it? All this fuss."

"Yeah." Mission let out a breath that had felt trapped. "Matt, I don't know—"

"Don't you dare try to back out now," Matt interrupted, his tone light but with an underlying firmness. "You're ready for this, Mission. More than ready."

Mission met the older man's gaze, seeing the confidence there that he wished he felt himself. "Yeah." He nodded, trying to switch his thoughts again. Why was it so hard to think good things about himself? Other people didn't seem to have the same struggles he did when it came to self-confidence. "You're right."

"I sure am." Matt clapped him on the shoulder. "Now come on. Let's get this show on the road before Deacon sends out a search party."

With a nod, Mission walked with Matt further under the tent and into the party. The noise level increased tenfold as they entered, and it seemed like every eye turned toward them. Mission resisted the urge to rip his jacket off, despite the added heat it brought, and he forced a smile to his face as he approached Deac, Hunt, and Mike.

"Hey," he said.

"There you are." Deacon flashed a quick smile at him, and thankfully, Deacon wasn't one to wear smiles for miles either.

"Hey, Mish." Hunter pulled him into a quick hug, and Mission did the same with Mike, who'd once worked the farm before becoming a CEO and moving to the place he'd bought for his wife. "You ready for this?"

"Ready," Mission said, because he'd been given this role, this promotion. People assumed he deserved it, because it had been given to him. He didn't have to make excuses or be self-depreciating. He was the foreman.

"Hey, man." Tuck arrived and shook his hand, pulling him into a hug as he laughed. "You're going to be so amazing at this."

"Thank you," Mission said, starting to feel a little robotic in his movements and what he said. "Have you seen my granddad?"

"Yeah, I saw him," Tuck said as he turned to survey the crowd gathered under the tent. "I think he asked Cosette for something to drink."

Concern spiked through Mission, but he told himself worrying over his grandfather wouldn't make anyone happy. Granddad didn't need Mission to come pick him up; he could still drive himself. Granddad didn't want to order his groceries online and have them delivered; he wanted to pick out his own bananas and pork chops.

Mission couldn't help worrying over him as he aged, so he looked around, hoping he'd come out of the barn with Cosette, something cold to drink in his hand.

"I could use something to drink too."

"Cosette set up the drinks right around the corner," Matt said. "I could use something too." He met Mission's eyes, and a swell of gratitude moved through him, because Matt wasn't going to leave Mission alone tonight.

He led the way toward the front corner of the barn, where Kristie happened to be standing. Her golden hair cascaded over her shoulders in soft waves, and she looked his way as he neared.

She smiled, and oh, that rivaled the glory of the early evening sun. Mission wasn't sure if it was the uneven ground or if he'd temporarily gone blind at the nearness of Kristie's beauty, but he stumbled.

Jolt after jolt of electricity struck through him, and he managed to throw out his hand, hoping to find something to grab onto.

His hand landed on Matt, and his friend said, "Whoa, there," as if Mission were a horse who'd been spooked. Maybe he had been.

His granddad came around the corner then, and Mission detoured toward him when he wanted to go over to Kristie and talk to her. *About what?* he asked himself as he said, "Hey, Granddad."

"There he is." His grandfather's face lit up, and he handed his cup of drink to Matt, who took it like he'd expected to play Mission's butler that evening. "How are you, my boy?"

"I'm great, Granddad." Mission hugged him, leaning and sinking into the embrace. "The drive was okay?"

"Fine."

"I can take you home if it gets too dark."

"I'll be fine." Granddad stepped back, his smile very nearly lifting all the wrinkles in his forehead. "This jacket looks mighty fine on you."

Mission grinned down at the navy blue blazer. "Thanks, Granddad." He looked past him to the corner of the barn. "What do they have to drink over there?"

"Lemonade, ice tea, water, soda pops, all kinds of stuff." He stepped over to Matt and took his drink, then asked him something.

That left Mission to continue to the drink counter by himself. Fine by him. He needed a moment alone right now anyway, after that stumble where he'd nearly gone down in front of Kristie—and everyone else at the party.

He'd barely picked up a red plastic cup when the scent of flowery, fruity perfume met his nose.

"Hey, Mission."

He looked over to Kristie, so many things running through his head. "Hey." Always the example of loquacious.

"I like your jacket."

"Thank you. I—it's my granddad's."

Her face lit up. "Yes, I met him. Very nice guy."

"Yeah." Mission smiled, mostly at the way she'd come to life while talking to him. "He's great."

"Are your parents coming?"

Mission's jaw tightened, and he moved down the table to fill his cup with half lemonade and half iced tea. He could brush off her question, avoid it the way he had for the past thirty years of his life. But something about her made him want to tell her.

"Hey, are you okay?"

Mission lifted his cup to his lips and shook his head.

"I didn't mean...." Kristie looked over her shoulder, then faced him again. She took the cup from him and said, "Come with me."

If she'd have just walked away, Mission could've simply picked up another cup, made another Arnold Palmer, and gone back to the party. No, he wouldn't be able to ever talk to Kristie again, but if she wanted to talk about his parents, that would be fine.

But she took his hand—a gesture that sent another wave of electricity through him—and led him away from the drink counter, the party, and toward the front barn doors. She slipped inside and he followed, the cool air conditioning a welcome relief after the warmer outdoors.

Mission hadn't been this nervous since Deacon had offered him the foreman job. But being in the small lobby of the barn with Kristie? His first instinct was to kiss her. Then she wouldn't be able to ask him anything about his parents. At the same time, he hadn't kissed anyone in a long time, and he really wanted a chance with this woman.

So he couldn't kiss her, because when he crashed doing that, he'd never get a real first date with her.

He stood there, his hand in hers and his heart flopping around inside his chest, anchorless. *Wait*, he told himself. *Wait for her to say something before you blurt out too much.*

two

Kristie Higgins had hallucinated. Straight-up gone into fantasy-land. Otherwise, how else would she be standing inside the lobby of the administration barn, holding hands with Mission Redbay?

The warmth of his skin against hers sent a shiver through her body, and she quickly released his hand, suddenly aware of how forward she'd been. No fantasy-land. Just her asserting herself in probably an unwelcome way.

She reminded herself that Mission had picked her up off the floor of the barn and carried her across the farm to his house, fed her, and then insisted he drive her back to her van.

Months ago, she told herself. They'd been friendly

enough since then, but Kristie didn't truly know Mission. He made it very difficult for someone to get to know him.

She cleared her throat. "I'm sorry," she said, taking a step back. "I shouldn't—you don't have to tell me anything." She watched his eyes, noting how he didn't look away from her. He didn't flush or duck his head. "I thought maybe you needed a moment."

Mission's dark eyes fired with emotion, which Kristie actually liked. He'd been such an enigma, this mystery cowboy that had spent so much time camped out in her head. Seeing him show emotions made him so much more human, more relatable, and she settled her weight on her back leg to put a bit more distance between them.

"It's okay," he said so softly it almost sounded like a hum. "I'm okay."

Kristie nodded, unsure of what to say next. She'd acted on impulse, wanting to comfort this man she barely knew but felt inexplicably drawn to. Now, standing alone with him, a flutter of nervousness assaulted her stomach. "Okay, well, it's your party."

"My parents—it's complicated."

"Most families are."

"Can I tell you another time?"

"Of course. I didn't mean to put you on the spot." She'd simply wondered if his parents would be joining the party when his grandfather had.

"It's fine," he said, but it didn't feel like it was. He turned and looked over his shoulder and then faced her again. Everything about him, from his neatly trimmed beard to the energy in his eyes to that sexy navy jacket, called to her, which surprised her so much. She hadn't liked him much in the past, and now she found herself hoping he'd ask her to dinner.

"I should get back," he said. "I think Deac's gonna make an announcement and everything, as if everyone here doesn't already know tomorrow is my first day as the foreman."

Kristie nodded, a twinge of disappointment winging its way through her guts. "Right, of course. Let's go back." She wasn't sure what people would think if they saw her and Mission sneaking out of this barn. Part of her wanted to go down the long hallway and out the back, where she could rejoin the party without all the eyes on her. She didn't normally mind having people look her way, but she knew Mission did, and she didn't want to cause him any issues.

"I'm just going to head to the restroom really quick." She hooked her thumb over her shoulder. "I'll see you out there, okay?"

Mission met her gaze again, and he saw right through her, she knew. "Okay," he said.

Kristie held her head high as she walked in the opposite direction, trying not to feel like she was scampering away from the gorgeous cowboy.

Once she made it back outside, Kristie stood in the shade of the tent, out of the way but still part of the party.

She wasn't a Hammond, but she knew all of them. She'd been coming to Pony Power and the farm for a few years now, and she'd been to Travis and Poppy's farm as well as Mike and Gerty's.

"You okay over here?" a man asked, and Kristie turned toward Keith Whettstein. He smiled at her and added, "You won't drive all the way to Blackhorse Bay, will you?"

She grinned at him and leaned in for a hug. "I'm not sure where that is." She glanced over to the woman at his side, and she knew they'd gotten married a couple of years ago, but Kristie couldn't remember her name.

"Have you met my wife, Lindsay?" Keith asked.

"I'm not sure." Kristie shook her hand, her smile as wide as possible. "So tell me where Blackhorse Bay is."

"It's a big boarding stable about an hour north of here."

"Not as far as Tuck's place," Kristie said. "I'd come if you needed me." She glanced back out to the party and then focused on Keith again. "You're telling me a 'big boarding stable' doesn't have a vet on-staff?"

"We have two," Lindsay said. "But one of them is having a baby next month, so we're looking for someone else."

"A full-time position?" Kristie met Lindsay's gaze. "I own a roaming veterinary office. I have appointments at various ranches and farms every day, with emergency appointments available same-day."

"My dad says you're great."

"His mom too."

"She is great."

Kristie got whipped over to the third voice in the conversation, and now Mission stood there. He gave her a smile and stepped into Keith and Lindsay at the same time. "I sure miss you around here, brother."

Keith laughed, and Kristie even heard Mission issue a chuckle. "Maybe I'll come back if I can work for you."

"Nah." Mission shook his head. "You've got such a great gig at Blackhorse." He nodded over to Kristie next. "She's a great vet, but you can't steal her from us forever."

The way he spoke about her sent warmth spreading through her chest. She didn't want to melt into the compliment, but she found herself smiling, ducking her head, and tucking her hair behind her ear.

"Maybe just in a pinch," Keith said. "Bart's been having a hard time finding a full-time vet."

"I can give you my number," Kristie said.

"Yeah, sure." Keith smiled at her, and then someone tapped on a live mic.

"Ladies and gentlemen," Deacon said. "Cowboys and cowgirls." He grinned, which Kristie didn't see him do often either. She felt nothing for the cowboy standing several yards away, but the moment she looked at Mission, every cell in her body rioted.

The crowd quieted, all eyes turning to Deacon. Hunter stood nearby, but he also held his wife's hand, both of them smiling at Deacon. Kristie glanced at Mission, noticing the way he straightened his posture, his jaw tightening slightly.

"We're here tonight to celebrate two very important things," Deacon continued. "First, the retirement of a man who has been the backbone of this ranch for so many years. Matt Whettstein, would you please c'mon over here?"

Applause erupted as Matt made his way to the center of the tent, his weathered face creased in a broad smile. Deacon clapped him on the back as he reached him, and the two of them spoke to each other, with the mic out to the side so it wasn't broadcasted to the crowd.

Matt stepped back and wiped his eyes, and Deac lifted the mic back to his mouth. "Matt has been more than just a foreman," Deacon said, his voice filled with emotion. "He's been a friend, a mentor, and a part of our family. Heck, he's been here longer than I have." He grinned at Matt as several people laughed and agreed.

Kristie didn't know the whole history of the Hammond Family Farm, but she knew Matt had come to the farm as the foreman every summer when Deacon's parents went north.

"Matt, we can't thank you enough for your years of dedication and hard work here at the Hammond Family Farm." Deacon handed him an envelope, which seemed way too small for Matt's big hands. He then passed Matt the mic, and he looked around the crowd for a moment.

"I can't find my wife."

"Right here," Gloria called from back by the front of the barn.

Matt nodded, his throat working as he swallowed several times. "It's been my honor to work for the Hammond family for so long. Some of them know this, and my kids definitely know this, but this job saved me. It saved my kids' lives, and it provided a new start for Gloria and I that we needed so badly."

He glanced around and nodded to various people, including Travis Thatcher, Cord Behr, Hunter, Deacon, his own brother, Mike, Joseph, and finally, Mission.

He said nothing, and yet the air carried an emotional charge that had Kristie tearing up. Why, she had no idea. Perhaps seeing such camaraderie and loyalty and love simply reminded her that the world still had good people living in it.

"The Hammond family has become my family, and I can't wait to spend more free time with some of you." He grinned then, and extended his arm toward Mission. "And I know I'm leaving the ranch in extremely good hands."

Mission marched over to Matt, his legs barely bending as he did. He looked like he might start yelling at any moment, and then he stepped into Matt and hugged him. He softened then, and again, the two men talked without anyone else being able to hear them.

Deacon took the mic back, and Matt stood next to Mission, his arm around the man's shoulders. "Which brings me to our second celebration," Deacon said. "As one chapter ends, another begins. I'm thrilled to be the Hammond who gets to announce that Mission Redbay is the new foreman here at the farm, and we're all really excited to keep working with him."

He extended the mic to Mission, who looked at it like it had turned into a rattlesnake. Kristie ducked her head to hide her smile, because the thought of Mission making a speech was laughable.

Mission simply leaned over and said, "Thanks, everyone. I'm going to do my best." Then he straightened and looked straight at her. She grinned and grinned, and she started to clap along with everyone else.

The applause swelled up and up, a few cowboys adding whoops and hollers to the noise, and Mission's face turned an adorable shade of red Kristie would like to see again.

His words had been sincere, if simple, and Kristie whooped as the applause started to die down.

"Please, everyone, eat as much as you can," Deacon said. "We have so much food."

Mission got surrounded by friends and the cowboys he worked with, and since Kristie wasn't on the staff here at the farm, she felt slightly removed from everyone. Thankfully, one of the counselors at Pony Power, a woman named Hannah, looped her arm through Kristie's and said, "Come get something to eat with me."

"Yes, I'm starving," Kristie said, grateful to have a friend to go with.

"How are things at the office?" Hannah asked.

"Good." Kristie worked out of a home office to schedule her appointments at the farms and ranches where she worked. "I'm taking tomorrow off, in fact. I'm going to go through the files in my office and get everything put away."

"You'll be happy about that." Hannah grinned and picked up a plate.

"Yeah." Kristie kept her smile on her face as she moved down the table behind her friend, but she seriously wondered if her life's happiness had come to her cleaning up her client files in the spare bedroom of her house.

Holy cow, she thought. Because it had.

As she sat at one of the checkered-cloth covered tables, she couldn't help but keep glancing at Mission. He seemed more at ease now, laughing with some of the other ranch hands and accepting handshakes from what seemed like the same people as before.

"Mind if I join you?"

Kristie looked up to see Mission's grandfather standing beside her table, a plate of food shaking in his hands.

She jumped to her feet and took his plate. "Of course not," she said, pulling out the chair in front of him. "Please, sit with us."

"Mission can have that spot," the older man said as he went around the chair and sat. Kristie put his plate in front of him and glanced over to Mission. She found he'd moved to the buffet, and he'd have his food in only a few minutes. Surely he'd know to come sit with his grandfather, and Kristie's pulse rioted at the thought of eating with him.

"I'm Ted," he said, extending a hand. "Mission's grandfather."

"Kristie." She shook his hand. "It's nice to meet you, Ted."

"Kristie," Ted repeated thoughtfully. "Are you a veterinarian?"

"Yes, sir." She smiled at him. "How did you know that?"

"My grandson's mentioned you," Ted said without revealing much else.

Kristie blinked, not sure what to make of that. "Oh, I didn't realize he talked about me."

Ted chuckled and picked up his fork. "Don't worry, it's all good things. Though between me and you, I think—"

"Grandad," Mission said as he sank into the chair between Kristie and Ted. "I hope you're not tellin' stories you shouldn't." He turned away from Kristie to look at his grandfather, then cut her a look out of the corner of his eye.

Kristie's heartbeat skipped over beats as she thought about what Ted would've said. Or maybe that was the scent of Mission's cologne—a mix of cedar wood, something spicy, and a touch of delicious male. Or that mighty fine jacket.

"I was just telling Kristie here that I think you're sweet on her."

Kristie sucked in a breath, and Hannah coughed once, then started to laugh. Mission sat there, his face absolutely stoic. He seemed to have frozen; his chest didn't even rise and fall.

After a few seconds, where both she and Hannah stared at Mission and his grandfather simply ate a few bites of his cole slaw, Mission turned toward Ted. "You know what? I kind of am."

Kristie pulled in another breath, surprised she still had room in her lungs for more air. She and Mission had texted plenty of times in the past six months, but always about work. And moving forward, she expected to keep dealing with Gloria, but she'd have to copy him on the important things, because that was what she'd done with Matt.

He turned toward her, glancing over to Hannah before clearing his throat and meeting her eye. "I've been thinkin' about asking you to dinner."

"You've been thinking about it?" she asked, surprised her voice worked at all. "Or you're doing it?"

The heat in his eyes turned into a glare. "I'm hoping you'll be free for dinner soon," he said. "With me. Dinner with me." He looked over to his granddad. "See what you made me do?"

Kristie smiled, especially when Ted bickered back with him. Her curiosity about their relationship soared, and her pulse roared at her. She'd hoped he'd ask her out in the barn, and now he'd finally done it.

But she'd been hurt before, and getting involved with someone she worked with had never turned out well for her. Suddenly, everything felt exactly as Mission had said in the barn—complicated.

Mission turned back to her, his expression now a mix of hope, nerves, and irritation, and Kristie knew her next words could change everything between them. She cast a look over to Hannah, who nodded encouragingly.

Then she opened her mouth and prayed the right thing would come out.

three

Mission's heart had been replaced with a sack of flour. His chest constricted against it, and he struggled to find a way to keep breathing. He managed to look over to Hannah too, beyond irritated that Kristie had looked to her for—what? Permission?

The seconds of silence stretched into an eternity, each one feeling like a dagger to his pride. This was why he hadn't asked Kristie out before.

Panic surged through him, and he wished his granddad had just kept his mouth closed. He couldn't stand to get rejected in front of his grandfather, Hannah, and everyone else at this party.

His party—this was supposed to be *his* party.

He whipped his hand into his pocket, where his very still and silent phone sat. "Oh, Deacon's calling me." He rose to his feet and turned his back on the table, the need to get away from her before she told him no like an impossible-to-reach itch.

Before he could take a step, he spun back to the table. He took a deep breath, and his courage returned. He deliberately looked past Kristie to Hannah. "And hey, I was thinkin' me and you could go to dinner together too, Hannah. If you'd like to."

Her eyes widened, but she said, "Sure," easily and without hesitation, which salvaged his pride. Her gaze flicked over to Kristie, who still sat there like he'd flicked icy lemon juice in her face, and back to him.

He nodded, glared at his granddad, and wouldn't let himself look at Kristie before he turned again. This time, he stumbled over his own blasted boots, but somehow managed to stay upright.

Curses flew through his mind, but Mission made it around the corner. His chest heaved as he pressed his back to the warmed wood there and let his eyes drift closed.

He could only imagine Kristie's expression right now. Or the way she may have huddled together with Hannah, the two of them whispering about him.

Him.

His worst nightmare—being talked about.

Mission couldn't stay here, and he couldn't simply abandon the party. He opened his eyes, his gaze landing on the medical barn. He pushed away from the wall, his destination singular now.

Once inside the barn, Mission leaned against the wall, the cool, familiar scent of hay and leather surrounding him, offering a small comfort.

"Seriously," he chastised himself. "What were you thinking?" He shrugged out of that too-tight coat and removed his cowboy hat. He ran his hand through his hair, trying to settle down enough to find the nerve to return to the party.

The weight of his insecurities pressed down on him, pancaking him into the ground. Something about Kristie had made his mouth dry for months now. Made him eat more turkey sandwiches, his thoughts stuck on the time— the only time—he'd done so with her. Made him talk about her with Granddad—and look where that had gotten him.

The sound of the door to the medical barn opening put Mission on high alert. Not that he could do anything about it; he couldn't hide anywhere in the small barn. He straightened up, composing his features into what he hoped made a neutral expression. The last thing he needed was for someone to see him wallowing.

To his surprise, Kristie poked her head into the barn. "Mission, there you are."

Could that be relief in her voice?

Don't be stupid, he told himself.

She seemed to be trying to catch her breath as she

pressed one hand almost to her throat, her chest rising and falling quickly. "I should've known."

"You should've known I'd be in the medical barn?" Mission's heart rate picked up again at the saltiness in his own voice, and he raised his chin slightly. At the same time, he let his gaze draw down over her pretty purple sweater, the hip-swell of her jeans, to those cowgirl boots.

"I like your boots," he said, his eyes darting all around now.

"Thank you," she said, her voice crisp but kind, and that alone made Mission look at her again.

He swallowed even as the corners of her mouth tipped up. He had no idea what to do with a smile from her pointed in his direction.

"These are my favorite boots," she said. "I—"

Nope, not happening. "Look, Kristie, you don't have to explain anything. Really. I understand if you're not interested."

Did he, though?

Mission wasn't sure he did.

Still, he said, "I shouldn't have put you on the spot like that."

"That's not it at all, Mission." She ducked her head and tucked that gloriously golden hair behind her ear. And all this time, Mission thought he wasn't into blondes. How wrong he'd been.

"I'd like to go to dinner with you," she said. "I was just

caught off guard is all." She scuffed the toe of one boot against the floor. "I haven't dated in a while."

Mission blinked, sure he had misheard. "You...what?"

She looked up at him, but she was quite a tall woman, and he only had a few inches on her. "Do you really want to go out with Hannah?"

"No," he said flatly.

She took a step toward him. "But you do want to go out with me."

"I already said I did, didn't I?"

Her smile widened. "You don't have to sound so mad about it."

He stood there, just looking at her, the air between them charged with possibility. Mission found himself thinking about how easy it would be to lean in and kiss her, to finally know what her lips felt like against his.

Clearing his throat and hoping his thoughts would go too, Mission realized he was still holding his phone with the phantom call from Deacon. He quickly shoved the device away. "So, uh, maybe Friday night for dinner?"

Kristie pulled her phone out. "Friday...."

Mission hated this silence, because she'd just said she hadn't dated in a while. Did she really need to check her phone?

He tamped down his impatience, and raised his eyebrows as Kristie looked up from her device. "You're not going to believe this."

"You have dinner at your parents' house."

Kristie didn't crack a smile. "No," she said. "My parents don't live in Colorado."

Mission blinked, his curiosity about her doubling. "So...one of your cats needs a tooth pulled, and you've scheduled it for Friday night?"

That got her to lift the corner of her lips. "Not quite," she said. "I do have plans with some friends, though." She tucked her phone in her back pocket. "But I'm free on Saturday night."

"Great," Mission said. "I should be too." Farms and ranches and animals needed to be cared for twenty-four-seven, but Mission had worked at the Hammond Family Farm for years, and they always had lighter schedules on the weekends.

He planned to continue that tradition, and he could make sure he got back to his cabin for a shower by five o'clock for a dinner date. "Where do you live?"

"I could just meet you somewhere," she said.

Mission took a step toward her, then another one, his irritation lifting with every breath he took. "Like...what? We're just friends getting together for coffee? Or a plate of spaghetti?" He shook his head as she fell back against the door of the medical barn.

He pressed in closer, something firing through him he didn't quite understand. He reached up and tucked that loose lock of hair behind her ear. "I'm too old for meeting women places. If you don't want to go out with me, I'd rather you just said so. If you don't want me to come to your house to pick you up, just say so."

Kristie pulled in a breath, her eyes locked on his. "How old are you?"

"Forty-two," he said smoothly. "And just because I was raised by my grandparents doesn't mean I don't have manners." He managed a half-smile as he dropped his hand back to his side. "I won't ask you how old you are."

He really wasn't sure, but she had to be at least thirty. Women in their twenties put off a different vibe, and it wasn't anything like what Mission had seen from Kristie.

"My birthday is comin' up in October."

"My birthday is in October too," Kristie whispered, and he wondered if she just couldn't make a noise louder than that.

He backed up a step, his own chest unnaturally tight. "If you want to go to dinner on Saturday at seven, you can text me your address when you get a minute." He cleared his throat and reached for the doorknob at her hip. "I have to get back to my own party. Excuse me."

Mission twisted the knob, glad when Kristie moved to the side so he could leave. If he had to keep breathing in her tangerine-scented perfume and be tempted by those curves, he had no idea what he'd say or do.

"You've already proven you'll say and do anything," he muttered to himself as he left the medical barn. He'd only taken a few steps toward the party when another set of footsteps joined his.

Kristie.

She didn't touch him, and Mission sternly told himself not to reach for her. Everyone he knew and loved had come to this party, and he couldn't be seen walking in hand-in-hand with a woman who still barely seemed to like him.

Wouldn't let him come pick her up. They could meet somewhere.

He scoffed out of the side of his mouth as he rejoined the party, immediately deviating from Kristie's side as he went back to the buffet line and picked up a new paper plate. Mission kept his head down as he loaded a second plate with food, and he returned to the table, where Granddad was now surrounded by Hammonds.

Tucker, Deacon, Hunter, Gray. The five of them laughed about something, and they all looked to Mission as he pulled out a chair and sat down.

"I'm so glad you're going to be at the reins," Gray said, his heart of gold shining for all to see.

"I'll do my best, sir," Mission said, and the words sounded like a growl to his own ears.

"Hey, brother." Tarr Olson sat down beside Mission, a blue-wrapped present nearly landing in his potato salad. "I got you something."

Mission scooped a bite of mayo-mustardy potato salad into his mouth and set down his fork. He chewed quickly and swallowed. "You didn't need to get me anything."

"There's a whole table of gifts," Hunter said.

Horror moved through Mission, and he didn't dare pick up the long, rectangular gift Tarr had brought. He swung his attention to Hunt. "You're kidding."

"I'm so not." He nodded with his cowboy hat back over toward the corner of the administration building. "Tarr must've missed it on his way in."

"Tarr misses a lot of things lately," Tuck teased, and that earned him a glare from the former rodeo star. "You should ask him why."

"Why's that?" Deacon asked without missing a beat. He barely looked up from his plate of food as he spoke, and he didn't look at Tarr.

Everyone else had focused on him, though, Mission included. Tarr glared at Tuck, who continued to eat, his grin as wide as ever.

"You don't have to say," Mission said, shooting a look over to Tuck. "Not everyone likes to spill everything. Some of us like to keep things a little closer to the vest."

Deacon looked up then. "You have things you need to keep close to the vest?"

"No," Mission said at the same time Tarr said, "Leave the man alone. It's his first day on the job."

"Then divert the attention back to you," Tuck said. "Oh, he's not gonna say anything, so I will." He picked up a chocolate chip cookie, giving Tarr a place to cut him off.

He didn't. In fact, Tarr picked up a potato chip and

33

popped it into his mouth. He chewed slowly as Tuck dragged out the silence.

Finally, he said, "He's dating a woman named Casey."

"He's dating?" Deacon asked, no inflection in his voice. "That's what you're worked up about?" He rolled his eyes and reached for his napkin. He wiped his mouth and beard and added, "Tarr dates a lot. This is not a national event."

"It would be if you started dating someone," Hunter said.

Deacon's eyes flew to his oldest brother's. His shoulders deflated as he huffed out his breath. "Hunt. I expect such a statement from Tuck, but you? You wound me."

"Why don't you date someone?" Tucker asked.

"Because I haven't met anyone I care to spend more than fifteen minutes with," Deacon said dryly. "Present company included." He got to his feet, threw Hunter a glare, and tossed his napkin on his now-empty plate.

"Deac, don't go," Hunter said. "I'm sorry."

Deacon grunted as he turned and walked away, and Hunter frowned at his back, and then over to Tucker. "He's right; Tarr dates a lot. I thought you were going to have real news."

"Boys," Gray said, his voice powerful and quiet, the way he'd always been.

Mission looked at the four of them still there. "I could use some advice," he said, immediately clearing his throat. He'd only made it through half of his food yet again, but he sat back again.

"I have a date this weekend with someone I've liked for a while—and I'm pretty nervous about it." He cleared his throat and looked at Gray first. He'd gotten married close to Mission's age, and his and Elise's love story was one of the main reasons Mission hadn't given up hope that he'd find someone quite yet.

"I'd take some advice," Mission said, glancing over to Tuck and then Tarr. "You guys never seemed to have a problem getting a date."

"Neither have you," Hunter said. "So the real question is—why is this woman different?"

four

Kristie's doorbell rang, but the sound didn't send her pulse skittering through her body. She'd save that for tomorrow night.

Tonight, she tossed her pot holders on her kitchen counter and headed for the front door, her cat brigade in tow. All three of them followed her everywhere when she was home, with her orange tabby cat, Bob, yowling with every step she took.

"It's just Lennie," she said, glancing down at Bob as he darted ahead of the other cats. "Or Jocelyn." It wouldn't be Harper, because out of the four of them, Harper always arrived last.

She opened the door, and Lennie stood there in all her brunette glory—complete with dark, shining eyes and hugging an old-fashioned ice cream maker.

Kristie stepped back, grinning. "Wow, come in."

"It won't take long, I swear." Lennie stepped past Kristie, who hastened to close the door behind her to keep out the summer evening heat.

"I'm sure you'll get it done before Harper arrives anyway," Kristie said as she turned to follow her friend. Lennie had pulled her hair back into a ponytail, but it still hung all the way to her waist as she slid the ice cream maker onto the counter.

"I have the base done," Harper said as she lifted the plastic bag she'd brought to the countertop too. "I just need that ice I left here a few months ago." She exhaled, grinned at Kristie, and in all her enthusiasm, headed out to Kristie's single-car garage.

She kept a small chest freezer there, and when the cowboys she worked for paid her in beef or venison, she kept it out there. "Should be there," she called after Lennie. "Might be a solid block, but it should be there."

She'd never brought ice cream to their dessert night before, but Lennie always seemed to push the boundaries. Her doorbell rang again, and Kristie turned toward the door as it opened.

Jocelyn toed her way in, stumbling slightly as she stepped up into the house and tried not to drop her immaculately decorated cake. Her dream was to be on a baking competition show one day, and she'd made it her life's goal to know about and bake every kind of cake known to mankind.

Thus, Kristie and Lennie got to try a new cake recipe

every single month at their first-Friday dessert night. "What kind of cake is that?" It bore a beautiful, bright green exterior over a perfectly shaped dome. A precise, pink rose sat on the top, and Kristie couldn't help smiling at the beauty of it.

"It's a princess cake," Jocelyn said. "It's got a great vanilla cake, some raspberry jam, stabilized whipped cream, covered in marzipan. It's delicious—and beautiful when you cut into it."

She brushed her dirty blonde fringy bangs out of her eyes and smiled at Kristie. "Hey, how are you?" She stepped over to Kristie and hugged her as Lennie banged her way back into the house, this time toting a bag of ice. "Are we going to get to go over your date tomorrow night?"

Kristie hugged her friend back, and then moved to get out the rock salt for Lennie. "I don't know," she said. "How can we go over something that hasn't happened yet?"

"Because it's Mission," Jocelyn said. "And he finally asked you out."

"You could do a fashion show." Lennie popped the lid on her chocolate ice cream base. "I'm doing a trio of floats. Orange chocolate—like those sticks you get at Christmastime." She poured the base into the container of the ice cream maker.

"Then I'm doing a hot chocolate float—and I don't want to hear a word about how it's summer and we can't eat hot things." She pierced Kristie with a fierce look, and Kristie held up both hands.

"Hey, I haven't said a word."

"I also don't see your dessert, which means it's in the fridge," Lennie said without missing a beat.

"It's hot outside," Kristie said in her defense.

"And the last one is a bit odd, but it'll be fine."

"Define it," Jocelyn said as Lennie poured ice cubes around the container, plugged in the ice cream maker and got it started.

She reached for the rock salt and started sprinkling it over the ice. "The last one is a virgin mojito float. It's less lime and more mint, so it's almost a peppermint chocolate float."

Kristie met Jocelyn's eyes, and she shrugged one shoulder. "At least it'll be cold."

"Do you have a mortar and pestle?" Lennie asked.

"You've asked me that question before," Kristie said with a grin. "The answer is the same as last time—no."

"Ugh, fine." Lennie started opening cupboards, and Kristie simply watched the woman in all her whirlwind glory as she whipped through Kristie's kitchen, looking for what she wanted to put together her trio of floats.

The ice cream maker churned away, and Kristie moved over to her fridge and opened it. She took out her passionfruit cheesecakes, the bright yellow-orange domes with the coconut macaroon crust bringing an instant smile to her face.

"Those look like summer on a plate," Jocelyn said. She hip-bumped Kristie as she slid the tray next to her princess cake. "Did you end up using your grandmother's cheesecake recipe?"

Kristie shook her head. "It was too wet. I had to put it all into a single pie tin, and I took it down the street to Kenneth."

Jocelyn grinned at her. "I bet he didn't mind."

"Slurped it right up." Kristie giggled with her friends while Lennie set out a two-liter bottle of orange soda, a box of hot chocolate packets, and an expensive-looking glass bottle of sparkling lime water.

She started chopping mint, and the scent of it filtered throughout the kitchen. Kristie opened her silverware drawer and took out the small dessert spoons she'd bought specifically for tonight's tiny cheesecakes. She loved small things, and she peeled back the flap on the spoons, and then put one in each corner of the tray.

She'd made a dozen perfect cheesecakes, but she'd had to taste-test one of them, and she'd taken one to Kenneth Jorgenson down the block. That left her with two, and she hadn't stopped thinking about presenting them to Mission for their post-first-date dessert tomorrow night.

The other eight sat on the tray for her girlfriends' dessert night.

"What time is it?" Lennie asked, twisting to look at the clock on the microwave. "Where the devil is Harper?"

"Was she down in Littleton today?" Jocelyn asked.

"She has a lot of cases right now," Kristie said. "But I don't know."

Harper worked as a children's advocate, and she put a lot of miles on her car as she visited homes, conducted interviews with parents and children, and dealt with family issues in half the counties that made up the greater Denver metropolitan area.

Her phone chimed only half a second before Lennie's did. Kristie picked up her device as Jocelyn's did. "I bet this is her."

Sure enough.

I got stuck in an after-hours meeting. I'm on the way! Don't you dare have a bite without me!

Kristie smiled at the text, because it exuded Harper's sunny personality. "You can put the ice cream in the freezer in the garage if you need to. I bet she's still twenty minutes out."

"Twenty minutes is generous." Jocelyn turned away from the counter and headed around the end of the couch. She sank onto it with a groan, and Kristie left Lennie to finish up her dessert prep to join Jocelyn in the living room.

"So for real," Jocelyn said. "What are you going to wear tomorrow night?"

Kristie sighed as she sat in her favorite recliner—a wide-seated dark blue chair with splashy red, yellow, and orange flowers. "I think I'm going to go with what makes me the most comfortable."

"So blue," Lennie said from the kitchen. "And your hair half-braided back. Right?"

Kristie met her eyes and could admit that she'd just described all the things that made Kristie feel beautiful. She reached up and pushed her hair behind her left ear, exactly the move Mission had done while they stood in the medical barn.

Her stomach swooped at the mere memory of the man's feather-light touch. "I was thinking I'd curl my hair and leave it down, actually."

"Leggings?" Jocelyn asked.

Kristine wrinkled her nose and shook her head. "Too hot. I'm going to wear a white pair of shorts and my flower Crocs that match that blue-and-white-striped blouse I got from the Amalfi Coast."

She smiled just thinking about that trip. She'd taken it with Jocelyn, Harper, and Lennie, and it was a miracle Harper hadn't been left at the cruise ship port in Madrid, to be perfectly honest.

"Oh, that blouse is my favorite," Jocelyn said. "It's the perfect first-date outfit."

"White shorts?" Lennie asked as she came into the living room, wiping her hands on a towel. "Do you know what you're doing on the date?"

Kristie looked up at her, her mind going blank. "Uh, dinner, I think."

"Dinner takes an hour or two," Lennie said as she perched on the arm of the couch. "It won't even be dark when you finish up." She watched Kristie. "Surely Mission will have something else planned."

Kristie leaned back into the recliner. "He didn't say anything but dinner." And besides, she owned bleach. "I'm sure it'll be fine."

"Does he think you're outdoorsy?" Jocelyn asked.

"I am outdoorsy," Kristie said.

"So maybe it's not a white-shorts and Crocs date," Lennie said. Behind her, the ice cream maker started to chug along, the sound changing to a lower pitch. She jumped to her feet and hurried over to it, pulled the plug, and took the whole thing out into the garage.

Kristie looked at Jocelyn. "No white shorts and Crocs?"

"I think you should text him and find out if there's more to this date than dinner."

"Yeah," Kristie agreed, but she didn't want to do that. Thankfully, the front door opened, and Harper yelled for help.

Kristie jumped to her feet and went to greet the last part of their quartet. "Let me take that." She took the heavy earthen-ware dish from Harper, who still wore her pencil skirt and blouse combo. She really had come straight from work.

"I just need to change," she said, panting slightly. "I'm so sorry I'm late."

"It's fine," Kristie said, gazing down into the pan. "Are these cowboy brownies?"

"Yes, ma'am." Harper grinned at her and leaned in to press her cheek to Kristie's. "I can't wait to hear about your date. I hope you haven't talked about it without me."

"I haven't been on the date yet," Kristie said.

"Fashion show," Lennie called as she returned from the garage, where she'd stowed the ice cream.

"I'm not doing a fashion show," Kristie said. She gave Lennie a brief glare as she slid Harper's cowboy brownies on the counter. She loved the chocolatey, coconutty, butterscotchy treats, and Kristie's whole heart filled with love for her friends.

They'd met a few years ago in a community baking class they'd each signed up for. Kristie could admit she'd taken the class to learn how to bake something for her boyfriend at the time. Turned out, sugar and cream couldn't change a toxic personality, and the relationship had ended only a month later.

But her friendships with Harper, Jocelyn, and Lennie had just begun. When the class had ended, they'd started getting together for lunches, and eventually their dessert night on the first Friday of the month had been born.

It helped that they were all single, though they'd all had a man in their life at one point or another in the past. Sometimes they brought dinner and ate before they feasted on desserts, but tonight, Kristie had eaten before her friends had come over.

"Let's dessert up," she said as Harper returned to the room. She too sported dark hair, and she scrubbed her fingers through her locks now that she'd released them from her tight ponytail.

"I am so tired." She sank into the recliner where Kristie had been sitting. "I can't even get my own desserts tonight."

"Let's do floats first," Lennie said. "I'll serve everyone." She smiled at Kristie. "Go sit, Kris. Tell Harper about your first-date outfit, and then I have a story to tell over our float trio."

"A story?" Jocelyn asked. "About what?"

Lennie grinned as she pulled tall, skinny glasses out of the bin she'd brought in at some point. "About this potbellied piglet I saw online."

"No," Kristie said. "Lennie, just no."

"I have that pasture."

Kristie shook her head, because Lennie had tried to raise animals before—and it had not gone well. Kristie had ended up taking the calf out to a farmer she knew, and he'd raised it to maturity. "No, Lennie. Sorry, but no. I'm not coming over every day to teach you how to feed a pig."

"It's summer. I could—"

"But it won't be summer forever," Jocelyn said. "Once the school year starts, you won't even remember to feed yourself." She usually sided with Kristie on things, thankfully. She worked as a pediatric nurse and had only dated doctors in the past decade.

With that not working out, she'd branched over to an online dating app. She was the only one who'd tried that, and she hadn't had much luck there either.

No wonder they were all so excited about her date with Mission.

And honestly, Kristie was too.

Maybe even more than bingeing on a quartet of the most delicious desserts she'd ever seen. Yes, an evening with the handsome, quiet cowboy would surely be better than dessert night with her friends.

Right?

A quaking in Kristie's stomach told her that equal parts anxiety and excitement bubbled inside her, and she decided to quickly text Mission about the finer details of tomorrow night's date, just to quell some of her nerves.

I was thinking we could get dinner and do the Summer Stroll. Is that doable?

She looked up from her phone just as Lennie said, "Okay, up first, we have a chocolate hot chocolate float."

Kristie took hers, and once everyone had their knobbly mug of hot chocolate with a big scoop of chocolate ice cream in it, she said, "Mission is taking me to the Summer Stroll tomorrow night."

A beat of silence filled the house, and then all four of them squealed.

"Did you tell him that's your favorite thing ever?" Lennie demanded, her second float forgotten.

"I can't wait to see a plethora of pictures," Harper said.

"You can totally do that in white shorts and Crocs," Jocelyn said.

Kristie simply couldn't stop smiling, even though the orange soda-chocolate ice cream combo made her cringe, and the mint wasn't enough to cover the lime in the virgin mocktail chocolate float.

The Summer Stroll.

How had Mission known?

He listens to you, she thought, something tiny and true ringing through her. But she couldn't remember a single instance where she'd told him she absolutely loved the Summer Stroll in Ivory Peaks.

five

Mission blew out his breath and somehow got his lungs to inflate again. He picked up his cowboy hat and positioned it just-so on his head. He certainly looked ready for a date, the don't-meet-me-down-a-dark-alley frown on his face notwithstanding.

He tried on a smile, but it didn't feel natural, and he let his mouth settle back to normal. Turning away from his reflection, he left the bigger second bedroom at the end of the hall in the foreman's cabin.

He could admit he enjoyed living on his own, as quietness had never bothered him. He liked that everything in his cabin sat where he'd left it, and that he didn't have to worry about having a roommate who ate all of his peanut butter granola bars.

Cleaning didn't bother him, and he swiped his wallet

and keys from the corner of the countertop, his stomach growling at him for something to eat. Mission ate every couple of hours while working the farm, but he hadn't had anything since lunchtime.

Kristie had sent him her address a few days ago, and Mission had enjoyed texting her more personal things this week while he waited for this in-person date. At this point, he could only hope she'd smiled when he'd sent her veterinary memes, pictures of a couple of horses here, and general texts about himself.

"She's been responding," he muttered to himself as he left the air conditioning in the cabin and got hit with a wall of early summer heat. He started to sweat instantly, and he jogged down the steps to the front sidewalk.

He barely felt like he belonged at the foreman's cabin, what with its emerald-green grass, pristine front porch, and an actual carport. Matt had lived here for a long time, through many winters, and Mission liked that he could pull up to the side of the house instead of out front, and that he wouldn't have to scrape his truck before he went somewhere when it got cold.

That reality sat several months in the future, and Mission seriously needed to focus on the here-and-now. He couldn't afford to have his mind wandering into the past or down darker roads filled with self-doubt.

Not tonight.

Kristie possessed some serious intelligence, and Mission would need all of his wits about him to keep up with her. How did he tell her he'd never gone to college? She was a doctor of veterinary medicine.

Oh, yes, he was way out of his league.

Still, he continued on, and it only took him about twenty minutes to drive from the farm to Kristie's front door. She lived in a house that screamed her personality, with blooming rose bushes lining the front of the house, and he smiled at how she'd told him she'd planted them there as an intruder deterrent.

A single-car garage sat attached to the house, and she had three big trees in her front yard, all on the west side of the grass and providing shade for the house in the evenings. The front sidewalk curved from the small front porch to where he'd parked in the driveway, and Mission turned off the truck to force himself out of the vehicle.

His gait felt good and normal, but Mission wondered if an outdoor date was a good idea. The Summer Stroll took place in the downtown park every first couple weeks of June, and it included a quarter-mile of shops on the first leg of the stroll, and a quarter-mile of food booths, all culminating in a huge stage where bands and other musical artists performed throughout the fourteen-day event.

Tonight's concert was Foxtrot, a great bluegrass band that Mission had heard before. Kristie had told him she liked classical music best, as it helped her focus on something complex, and she'd claimed to have used it to calm and relax her mind during vet school, when she had something she needed to riddle through and couldn't find the way.

Mission leaned in to ring the doorbell, then fell back a step. He cleared his throat as he waited, and mentally coached himself that he'd been out with a lot of women in his lifetime. He'd had probably twelve or fifteen girl-friends over the years, and Kristie Higgins wasn't special.

Then she opened the door.

Every personal coaching statement Mission had just told himself flew out the window.

Because Kristie Higgins was absolutely special.

She wore a pair of white shorts that landed halfway down her thigh, showing her bare leg all the way down to a light blue pair of shoes with flowers punched out all over them. Not just shoes—Crocs.

Mission lifted his eyes back to hers, his smile abso-lutely genuine as he looked at her. The matching-blue blouse bore white stripes and every cell in his body tingled. "Hey, there," he drawled out. "My, don't you look amazing?"

Without thinking—and all of the advice the Hammond men had given him at last weekend's party completely gone—he stepped forward and slid his hand along her hip as he leaned in.

His lips brushed along her cheek, and then he pulled back as quickly as he'd moved in. "You ready?"

"Mm hm," she said, a glorious pink shining in her

cheeks now. At her feet, a cat yowled, and Mission looked down at the orange tabby.

He dropped into a crouch and held his hand out to the feline, expecting to be rebuffed with the swish of a tail. Instead, the cat meowed forlornly again and moved into his palm, rubbing his whole body all the way up to Mission's elbow.

He chuckled and glanced up to Kristie. "What's his name?"

"Bob," she said.

His laugh took a deeper form as he straightened. "You named your cat Bob?"

"He's a rescue," Kristie said, moving her Croc-ed foot out of the way. "They all are. I got Bob at a farm where the owner found a box of abandoned kittens in his barn."

"That's not a rescue," Mission said, reaching out as she came down the one step from the house to the porch. She'd looped a white purse over her forearm, and she gently toed Bob back toward the house.

"Go on, Bobby. I'll be back later." She reached back to pull the door closed, waiting until Bob hopped back inside. Mission caught sight of two other cats on the rug just inside the door, and Kristie had told him about her felines via text this week.

Mission followed her down the steps to the sidewalk, his need to hold her hand making him feel a little crazy. "I thought we'd go to Meltology," he said. "Have you been there?"

Kristie's blonde curls bobbed as she looked over to him and kept walking. Light shone in her eyes. "Yeah, it's great."

Relief rushed through Mission. "Yeah, Hunter's kids love the grilled cheese sandwiches, and they have a fondue pot I really like."

She beamed at him. "Really, Mission? You like fondue?"

He couldn't help smiling back at her. "Love it. And on the weekends, they have a dinner-date option, which is three courses. Cheese, main dish, and dessert." He reached the passenger door and opened it. "Do you like fondue?"

She paused close to him. "Yes," she said. "I do." She gave him an interested, almost appraising look, and it only set every piece of Mission's life on fire. "I'm just surprised you like it."

He lost his mind for a moment, just as he had at her front door, and he kneaded her closer. "Well, I was hoping you would, because I want tonight to be all things I like."

Including her.

She blushed again, ducked her head, and inched past him to get in the truck. Mission watched her, completely mesmerized for a reason he couldn't name. He snapped to attention just as she looked over to him, and he quickly moved to close the door behind her.

As he walked around the front of the truck to get behind the wheel, he glanced up to Kristie's front windows. All three cats perched in the windowsill watching him, and he tipped his hat to the felines with a smile.

He got behind the wheel, and had just turned the key in the ignition when Kristie asked, "Did you just salute my cats?"

He glanced over to her. "Uh, of course not." He grinned at her. "Who would do that?"

She laughed, and oh, Mission needed to hear that sound every day for the rest of his life. He backed out of her driveway and aimed the truck in the direction of the fondue restaurant.

"I was thinking we'd have dessert at the Summer Stroll," he said, glancing over to her again. "Do you have something in mind you want?"

"If the Greek mini doughnuts are there, I'll lose my mind."

Mission reached for the magazine that had come in last week's mail. "This lists all the booths. You could check."

She took it from him and started to leaf through it. Mission wondered what Kristie "losing her mind" would look like, and he secretly hoped the Greek mini doughnut booth would be there.

Seemed like a strange thing for a festival, as doughnuts had to be fried at a certain temperature, and while Mission had never worked on a food truck, he knew that not all foods translated well to going mobile.

Doughnuts definitely fell into that category. But hey, he'd try them if Kristie vouched for them.

"Ooh," she said. "They'll have fried ice cream."

"I'm sensing a type of dessert with you," he said.

"I love all desserts," Kristie said, closing the magazine. "The reason we couldn't go out last night was because I had dessert night at my house."

Mission expected her to look over to him, but she didn't. She also didn't go on. "You have dessert nights at your house?"

"Yes, sir."

"Who's invited to those?"

That got her to look over to him. He met her eye, his smile kicking up on one side. "I'm taking it not me."

"I saved you some of my cheesecakes from last night."

"Did you now?"

She nodded and looked back out the windshield. "They're passionfruit with a coconut macaroon crust."

"I didn't know you baked," he said.

"I took a cooking class a few years ago," she said. "Now I do the dessert nights on the first Friday of every month with a few women from the class."

"That's fun," he said, and he genuinely meant it.

"Lennie left you some ice cream, and Harper made me keep half the pan of cowboy brownies."

"Lennie and Harper," he said. "They sound like my kind of people."

"Jocelyn made a princess cake, but she took the other half of it to her niece today."

"I suppose I'll allow it," Mission teased. Talking to Kristie came easier than he'd anticipated, and he waited for her to name another friend. She didn't, and he put on his blinker to turn onto Main Street.

"Just the four of you?" he asked. "Or were some people missing?"

"Just the four of us," she said.

He nodded, continued down the block a bit, and then pulled into the parking lot at Meltology. "Doesn't look too busy," he said, wondering if he'd start commenting on the weather next.

Dear Lord, he prayed. *I hope not. Surely we have more to talk about than dessert.*

He found a parking spot and pulled in, still praying with all he had. Thankfully, Kristie waited for him to drop to the ground and hurry through the heat to open her door for her.

Did he dare hold her hand on the way into the restaurant? In the end, he simply put his hand on the small of her back as he guided her around the tailgate. He moved to her side, but a large group approached them, and he fell back behind Kristie as they flowed by.

She reached the door and opened it, and she moved through the foyer to the second set of doors. Someone else opened them, and Kristie ducked inside. Mission followed just as another man said, "Kristie?"

Both she and Mission turned toward him, and oh, Mission did not like the way he smiled so suggestively at Kristie.

"Bradford." She edged back into him as well, and Mission rested his hand on her waist in a show of solidarity.

"You never did text me back," Bradford said, and Mission knew him. Most cowboys around Ivory Peaks at least knew of one another, and Mission had been in town for years now.

But Bradford didn't even look at Mission, and he'd never felt so invisible. He took a micro-step in front of Kristie, gently guiding her to the left. "Hey, Bradford." He turned his shoulder toward the man, effectively boxing him out.

"Let's go, kitten," he said in a softer voice, the term of endearment sending a shockwave through him. "We have a reservation we don't want to miss."

His message conveyed, he kept Kristie pressed against his side as they moved away from Bradford and toward the hostess station. "Mission Redbay," he said. "I had a reservation at seven-fifteen."

"Howdy, Mission," the woman there said. She looked over to Kristie and back to him, and while Mission hadn't gone out with her, he had dated a friend of hers.

"Hey there, Heidi." He crowded in closer. "Is Bradford coming or going?"

She looked past him, but Mission didn't do the same.

"I think he just got here." She met Mission's eyes and then flicked her gaze over to Kristie. "I'll make sure you're not near him."

"I'd appreciate that," Mission said, the whole right side of his body surely smoking for how hot it was, touching Kristie's the way he did.

He settled back and did what all serious, protective boyfriends would do when their girlfriend encountered another man they clearly weren't interested in—he leaned over and pressed his lips to her forehead.

"You're really playing this up," she murmured.

"Am I?" He pulled back and looked at her, the brim of his cowboy hat creating a private bubble for just the two of them. "I don't even want him looking at you, and if he does, I want him to know you're not available."

"Mish, this way."

He looked up at Heidi, then guided Kristie in front of him, keeping himself as a barrier between her and Bradford. He didn't care if he'd acted a little overprotective, especially since he got to touch Kristie, and whisper with Kristie, and show Kristie a little bit of how he felt about her.

You're really playing this up.

Hopefully, he hadn't pressed his luck too far, too early. Then he remembered what he'd said, and Mission cursed his runaway tongue as he sat down opposite of Kristie and waited for Heidi to give them their menus and walk away.

six

Kristie enjoyed the stillness and silence of the summer night as she dropped out of Mission's truck for a second time that evening. "Dinner was great," she said. "I've only done a dessert fondue; I didn't know you could do all those meats in different broths."

He reached over and secured her hand in his. "I'm glad you liked it."

The conversation had been easy during dinner, and they'd talked about her cats, the food, her favorite desserts to eat, the ones she liked to bake, and how long they'd each been in Ivory Peaks.

She'd skirted questions about where she'd moved from, and she'd noticed Mission hadn't spent any time on his childhood either. She had asked him about his grandfather, and Mission didn't seem to have a problem talking about him—but nothing about any siblings, his parents, or even his grandmother.

Kristie hadn't pushed the issue, because she didn't feel like opening that can of worms for herself, at least on the first date.

"So," she said as he led her through the dirt parking area and toward the Summer Stroll. Twilight had started to blanket the town, and Kristie felt twenty years younger, reverting to her teenage self who'd gone to the fair to meet boys and ride the Ferris wheel with the cutest one.

She already had the most handsome man holding her hand, the lights of the food trucks on the parallel line to the booths, and the cooling evening air. All of it combined brought pure happiness to her heart.

"So...what?" Mission asked.

"That woman at the restaurant," she said. "She called you Mish."

"Yeah," he said. "A lot of people do."

"Do they?"

"Sure," he said. "My friends; people who know me."

She bumped him with her hip. "I guess it's better than 'kitten'."

Mission made a choking sound, his hand tightening in hers. "That just came out," he said. "I don't...." He trailed off, a somewhat frustrated sigh seeping from between his lips a moment later.

"Well, I'd say I don't have to call you that, but I kind of liked it."

"What made you think of the word kitten?" She slowed as they approached the first booth, which had wood-burned crafts.

"The cats acting as sentinels in your front window," Mission said. "And maybe a touch of panic."

She smiled over to him and moved to the next booth. "That magazine said the music starts at nine-thirty."

"Yeah," he said. "If you don't want to stay that long, it's fine."

"Will there be dancing?" She reached out and touched one of the dog bandanas in the next booth—everything for pets, including bedazzled collars and leashes, as well as treats for cats, dogs, and horses.

"I'm not sure," Mission said just as casually as she'd asked. "Would you dance with me if there was?"

Her mind fractured for a moment, part of it flying back to the one and only time he'd asked her to dance at Opal Hammond's wedding.

"Yes, I would," she said.

"Then I hope there's a dance floor," he said. "You never really gave me a chance to show you my dance skills."

"Oh, you have dance skills?"

He leaned closer, and the nearness of him made her shiver. "I have so many skills you don't know about." He straightened, gave her a sexy smile, and stopped in front of the next booth.

"Maybe my granddad would like a new wallet." He picked up one such item, then set it down a moment later. "Who am I kidding? He likes to pick out his own things, and he's very picky."

Kristie nudged him with her hip again. "He reminds me of you."

"You think so?" He looked over to her. "You think I'm stubborn?"

"I think you like things done a certain way."

"On the job, sure," he said. "There is a right way—and a procedure—for how things are done on the farm." He shot her another grin and sauntered toward the next booth, gently tugging her along with him. "But I'm not nearly so rigid in my personal life."

"If you say so," she said, very aware of the teasing, flirtatious tone of her voice. Jocelyn would be so proud, and she'd never be able to tell Lennie about this shame-less behavior. Harper would tell her to lay it on even thicker, and she focused on the next booth down, looking away from Mission to hopefully hide her smile.

"At the risk of me bringing up your shoes again," he said. "You're the one wearing...questionable footwear for dancing."

Kristie looked down at her flowery Crocs. "I love these shoes. I can do anything in them."

"Making a mental note of that," Mission said, his Flirt set on high too. Kristie realized she hadn't truly allowed herself to see any other side of him, other than the stoic, observant, quiet cowboy who'd once insulted her boots.

"Tell me what you like to do when you're not on the farm."

"Ah, let's see." Mission exhaled out and looked up into the sky. "I like to go horseback riding. Play the guitar. Find new restaurants and try them out." He glanced over to her. "You?"

"Have you ever done the Dancing Wolves Trail—it's horseback only, and absolutely incredible."

Mission stopped right in the middle of the walkway, with plenty of people streaming past them on both sides. "I've done it a few times with Deacon. It is beautiful up there." He tilted his head at her, curiosity burning in those dark, dreamy eyes. "Do you have a horse that can handle that trail?"

Kristie swallowed, sudden nerves bumping in the pulse in her neck. "I go with friends," she said.

"The baking friends?"

She shook her head and couldn't quite hold his gaze for much longer. She started walking again, and he easily fell to her side. "No, some friends of...my brother."

"I see."

No, he didn't, but Kristie didn't explain further. She'd have to tell him eventually, but the first strains of music came from the parallel stroll, and she turned that way, thinking, *No, you won't have to tell him unless you keep dating.*

But one look over to him, and she wanted him to ask her out again. So she slid her hand up his arm and then reached over with her right one, clasping his arm in both of hers. "We can cut through up here and go listen to the band."

"I thought you liked the shops in the Stroll," he said.

She smiled at him, because this cowboy had planned the perfect date. "Yeah, I do," she said. "But they'll be here for another week, and I just like looking." She pressed in close to him as more people started cutting through on the marked path between the shops and the food booths. "I'd love to see the entertainment."

"Yes, ma'am," Mission said, and they joined the flow of the crowd over to the parallel Stroll. Kristie didn't normally love crowds, and she noted Mission seemed more tense now as well. She wasn't sure why, but a thrill replaced all of her worries when she spotted the dance floor laid out in front of the stage.

Musicians moved about on stage, setting up various stringed instruments, and she nodded toward them. "What are all of those?"

"That guy in the blue shirt has a banjo," he said. "There are two fiddles on top of the piano. An upright bass—that's the big one over on the right."

"Acoustic guitar," she said. "I know that one."

"And the woman in the red has a mandolin," he said. "They probably have a resonator guitar too, but I don't see it right now...."

"All right, folks," a man called into the microphone. "Find a seat or find a partner, because we've got Foxtrot on the stage, ready to turn even the shyest cowboys into amazing dance partners!"

Kristie grinned, because she couldn't wait to stand within the circle of Mission's arms, feel the weight of his pulse against hers, breathe in the scent of his clothes, his cologne.

A man started plucking the upright bass, the deep thrum of it filling the space with energy, lighting up the sky with sound.

The acoustic guitar joined the bass, and a fiddle came in, and Kristie absolutely sank into the vibe of the music streaming from the stage. People flooded the dance floor, setting themselves up in long lines to go with the upbeat rhythm provided by the band.

There didn't seem to be room for even two more, and Mission nodded to a couple of seats on the end of a row. Kristie went first, and he quickly followed to sit beside her. He put his arm around her, and she easily snuggled into his side the way she'd seen other couples do in this exact situation.

She hadn't had a boyfriend in a while, and she felt warm and cared for at Mission's side. She told herself she might feel like this in another man's arms, but the thought didn't sit well in her mind.

No, she wouldn't. Mission Redbay possessed some magical charm that she really liked, even if he had insulted her boots the first time they'd met. She didn't have to hold it against him forever, and she smiled up to the stage, clapping along to the beat of the poppy-blue-grassy music.

The fast-paced song ended, and the crowd whooped and hollered. The band easily slid into their next tune—a slower ballad—and Mission got to his feet. He offered her his hand, and she watched his eyebrows go up, a silent invitation for a dance.

She put her hand in his and let him help her to her feet. He led her onto the dance floor as others left it. The band settled into the slower song, and all of Kristie's fantasies about slow-dancing with Mission came true.

He moved effortlessly for one of his height, and he held her with just the right amount of pressure against her back. He rubbed one thumb in a slow circle and kept his head bent low toward hers.

Her phone vibrated in her back pocket, but Kristie ignored it. Whoever was calling her at nearly ten p.m. on a Saturday night could wait. The only people she'd pick up for knew she had a date with Mission tonight, and Lennie, Jocelyn, and Harper wouldn't be calling right now.

That fact made her heart squeeze a bit too tight, and Mission murmured, "You okay?"

"Yes," she whispered back.

"You tensed up."

She tilted her head back. "I'm okay."

He searched her face, then blinked, his expression softening. "All right, kitten." The hint of a smile tugged at the corners of his mouth before he pressed his cheek to hers and kept her swaying back and forth on the hard tiles which had been laid over the grass here in the downtown park.

She appreciated that he simply accepted her declaration that she was okay...and then held her closer, which only made her feel more protected, more cherished, and like what he'd said back at the fondue restaurant could be true.

He didn't want another man looking at her, and if they did, he wanted them to know she wasn't available.

Because she was with him.

The song ended, and another began. This one had a faster tempo, and Mission stepped back, a sly grin on his face. "Can you really dance in those Crocs?"

She put her hands in his, ready for the swing dance several other couples had already begun. "I told you, these are my dancing shoes."

"Let's see then." Mission pulled her toward him, whooping like the pure country cowboy he was. Kristie laughed, the noise flowing out of her mouth in a steady stream that honestly barely sounded like her.

She hadn't danced like this in a long time, as she thought she'd gone past the age where she could let loose in a public park and do so. But dance she did, grinning as Mission spun her effortlessly and always, always brought her right back to him. Even if she'd stumbled, Mission wouldn't have let her fall.

Her phone rang again just as the song ended, and she ignored it once more as she fell into Mission's arms, trying to catch her breath.

"Well, those shoes passed the test, kitten." He swept his lips along her temple. "Answer your phone, okay? It's making me anxious, and I don't believe it's not bothering you too."

"It's probably nothing," she said, as several minutes had passed between calls. The moment she stopped speaking, her phone buzzed again.

"I'm going to take it out of your pocket," he said, and it sounded like a warning.

She gaped at him. "You wouldn't dare."

"I don't care if you answer it."

The new song that had started was a piano solo, and Kristie tugged her phone out of her pocket and edged off the dance floor. She frowned at the name on the screen— Johnny Clovis—and she tilted it toward Mission, who'd come with her.

"What could he want?"

"Another man you never answered?" Mission teased, though he had to know Johnny was ten years older than him and happily married. "Answer him." He pointed to the screen. "He's called three times."

Kristie swiped on the call, her heartbeat suddenly flinging itself against her ribcage. "Johnny?" she asked. "What's going on?"

"Praise the Lord you answered," he breathed out. "I've got a mare in labor, and the placenta appeared before the foal."

Kristie turned and started walking away immediately. "How long ago?" He'd called three times, and regret lanced through her like a hot knife. "We knew she was going into labor about fifteen minutes ago, but Alan just now saw the placenta."

"I'm in downtown Ivory Peaks," she said, glancing over when Mission caught up to her. "I can be there in ten minutes, and I'll stay on the phone with you and Alan to direct you."

Mission jogged ahead of her to get the truck door's unlocked and himself in the driver's seat. "Put gloves on," she said as she ran to catch up. She didn't want to leave the lights and music behind, but she couldn't stay on a date when a mare and her foal could possibly pass away.

"You need to sterilize a pair of scissors, and—"

"I know what to do," Johnny said. "I still want you here as fast as possible, but we'll try to get the foal out as quick as we can."

"I'll get there as fast as I can," she promised, and she launched herself into Mission's truck and slammed the door. "Tell me everything you're doing; everything you see." She nodded to Mission, who wasted no time in getting them away from the Summer Stroll.

Kristie hated that their first date had to end this way, but she hoped she could still somehow get another dinner and dancing invitation from Mission once she delivered this foal and made sure the mama mare was okay.

seven

Opal Crow stood in her kitchen, a small smile on her face as she stirred the potato salad one final time. She'd been up since five that morning baking, chopping, and preparing the perfect Sabbath Day feast. The smell of slow-roasted beef filled the farmhouse kitchen, mingling with the scent of fresh-baked rolls and the apple pie cooling in the windowsill—just the way her grandma Hammond had done.

"Steele just texted to say they've left," Tag said, his Alabama drawl wrapping around her like a warm blanket as he came up behind her and slid one hand along her waist.

"Great," she said, abandoning the potato salad as it didn't need to be stirred anyway. "Deacon's bringing Mission, and Tuck and Bobbie Jo have Tarr with them."

"Sounds like your idea of a great time." Tag grinned at her as she faced him. "You feelin' okay, honeybee?"

She nodded, though the scent of the mixed mayo and mustard had made her stomach turn that morning. And eggs? Forget about it. Opal would never eat another egg again.

His hand drifted down to rest lightly on her tiny baby bump, the one she'd kept covered with loose T-shirts and blouses in the past couple of weeks. "Are you going to wait until we're done eating to tell everyone?"

"I don't think I can keep it in much longer," she said. Jane and Cord couldn't come to lunch today, and Opal had told them about her pregnancy already. The more people she told, the easier it was to simply say things as if everyone already knew.

But they didn't, not yet.

"At least wait until they're all here," Tag said just as the back door opened.

"Just us," Mike called, the sound of little feet running into the house.

Little feet. Opal loved—absolutely *loved*—the sound of little feet coming her way.

"Ope," West yelled. He'd turned three at the beginning of the year, and he could say her name properly now. He just never did. "Daddy says there be slithers out there." He pointed back the way he'd come.

"Snakes," Mike said as he followed his son toward Opal.

She bent down and picked up her favorite three-year-old. "Slithers? Were they hissing?"

"Hisssss," West said, grinning at her.

"You've got a couple in your pumpkin patch," Mike said. "Nothing dangerous." He hugged Tag, then took West from Opal and hugged her too. Their parents lived hundreds of miles away, in another state, and Opal gripped her brother, inhaling deeply, as if she'd be able to feel or smell her father on him.

"You okay?" Mike asked. He held her tight for another moment and then stepped back.

"Everyone should be here soon," Tag said loudly, and Opal got the hint. They'd already called her parents and told them about the baby too; Opal didn't have to make the announcement several times.

Tears pricked at the corners of her eyes. "Yeah, I'm fine," she said as she stepped out of her brother's arms. "Where's Gerty?"

"She was in the barn with Steele. They're coming." Mike snagged a black olive out of the pasta salad and popped it into his mouth. "Two salads?"

Opal swatted his hand away from swooping in for a second olive. "Gerty doesn't like the potato salad, Mister. So I made the pasta."

Mike grinned at her, something sparking in his eyes. Thankfully, the doorbell rang, which diverted his attention. Deacon entered the house, followed by Mission. Neither of them said a word—not shocking—though they both lifted their hand in a wave before they hung their cowboy hats on the rack near the door.

"Howdy," Tag said, going to greet their guests. He loved the cowboys at Opal's cousin's farm, and she smiled as they man-hugged and shook hands. Steele and Gerty arrived next, the two of them going back and forth about one of the horses on the farm.

"He needs his own stall," Steele said. "There's the stable out by me, and we should move him there." He gave Gerty a blue-gray stare, and then moved over to Tag, Deacon, and Mission.

Gerty watched him with fiery blue eyes, her bluster falling when she turned toward Mike and Opal.

"Momma," West said, rushing over to her. The boy never walked anywhere, that was for sure. He started rambling off a string of words, and Opal caught "Frog... hisses...pummins..." and not much more.

Gerty grinned at him as she lifted him into her arms. "Auntie Opal has snakes and frogs in her pumpkins?" She looked over to Opal, now all joy and sapphires. "Maybe we do too."

"I look," West said.

"We'll look tomorrow, buddy," Gerty said. "We're having a party this afternoon, and then it'll be time for bed."

"No, Momma," he said, his eyebrows drawing down into the cutest frown ever. "I look...slithers...pummins."

"We didn't even plant pumpkins, bud," Mike said.

Opal's stomach growled, and her pregnancy had definitely brought with it cravings and an increased appetite.

Gerty set West on his feet without arguing further with him, and Opal distracted him with his toy chest. Since she babysat him a few days each week, she had everything the little boy needed right here at her house, including a bright red race car bed in the spare bedroom.

Laughter came from the direction of the front porch, and Opal's nerves vibrated at her. Tucker, Tarr, and Bobbie Jo had arrived. Her cousin had a very bright personality, and she'd recognize his laugh anywhere.

Sure enough, they came through the door a moment later, all three of them wearing smiles. Tuck and Bobbie Jo had been engaged for about three months now, with their wedding coming up in September.

She was as cowgirl as they came, and she took care of over one hundred goats on Tucker's farm, though she didn't live there yet. He and Tarr trained rodeo animals, as well as humans, on a beautiful piece of property north of the city—and about an hour from Tuck's family farm and what had become Gerty's rescue ranch.

"Hey, guys." Opal moved around to hug everyone hello, and then all eyes came to her. Her mouth suddenly felt like she'd been snacking on cotton all day.

"We have the food in here," Tag started, and his voice thawed the freeze that had come over Opal. His hand landed on her hip, giving her a steadying warmth, and she managed to draw a breath.

"But I've set the table out on the back deck," she added. "It's completely shaded, and we've got overhead fans too."

She loved her covered back deck, and it was such a beautiful time of year. The summer hadn't gotten too hot yet, and the view of the rolling farmland stretching out behind their little house was too perfect not to share.

"Thanks for cookin' for us, Opal." Tucker grinned at her, and she took a quick step to block him from being the first to pick up his plate. He blinked at her, and Opal had no idea what showed on her face, but Tucker fell back to Bobbie Jo's side.

"We have an announcement before we eat," Opal said. She looked over to Tag, knowing he wouldn't tell their loved ones unless she made him.

She didn't want him to anyway.

Her soul filled with love as she gazed at her husband, and she transferred that out to everyone who'd come for this Sabbath Day luncheon. "Tag and I are going to have a baby."

After a single beat of silence, Gerty squealed, and Mike whistled shrilly through his teeth. Bobbie Jo started to whoop and clap, as did everyone else.

"Daddy, too loud," West complained, pulling on the hem of Mike's shirt. He didn't look down at him at all, and Opal stepped away from Tag to receive Gerty's hug.

"When are you due?" she asked.

Opal sniffled, her tears seemingly so close to the

surface all the time lately. She pulled back and wiped her eyes. "December," she said.

"Right after Christmas," she heard Tag tell Mike and Steele.

She turned to face her brother, and Mike had nothing but joy in his expression. "Congratulations, sissy," he said as he engulfed her in a bear hug. "I guess you've told Momma and Daddy."

"Yes." Opal once again clung to him, so many of her dreams coming true with this one thing. She'd tried not to attach all of her happiness on being a mother, but it had happened all the same.

She moved back, and Bobbie Jo took Mike's place, beaming as she hugged Opal. "I'm so happy for you both."

Deacon offered a rare, full smile. "Congratulations," he said simply, but the warmth in his eyes spoke volumes. Mission and Tarr added their congratulations, both looking genuinely pleased despite not being as close to Opal as the others.

Steele hung back, but when Opal caught his eye, he gave her a shy smile and a thumbs up that made her laugh through her tears.

"Westy," Mike said, turning to his son. "Did you hear? Auntie Opal is going to have a baby. You're going to have a little cousin to play with."

West looked up, his big brown eyes curious. "Baby?" he repeated.

"That's right, sweetheart," Opal said, sinking into the

couch near where he played. She got right back to her feet, because she had no time to rest right now. "Let's eat." She scurried into the kitchen, ready to move on with the day now that the news didn't live inside her anymore.

In the kitchen, Gerty cornered her with a knowing look. "How have you really been feeling? And don't give me that 'I'm fine' business."

Opal sighed, allowing herself to be honest now that the announcement was made. "Exhausted. Nauseous. Terrified." She smiled weakly. "But also happier than I've ever been."

Gerty nodded, understanding in her eyes. "The first trimester is the worst," she said. "It gets better, I promise. We're just down the road for anything you need."

"I was hoping you'd say that," Opal said. "I have about a million questions."

"Ask away," Gerty said, stacking plates in the sink. "Though I'm no expert."

"You're here, though," Opal said, missing her mother powerfully in that moment. She told herself women all over the world went through pregnancies and had babies without their mothers living next door. She could too.

"Molly's not far away," Gerty said. "Are your parents going to come down?"

"At Thanksgiving," Opal said. "They'll stay until the baby is born."

"And then some," Tag said, sidling up to them. "Babybee, I'm gonna pray, okay? Tucker's already eating his second roll."

"Sure." She looked over to Mike, and she didn't even have to ask her brother to whistle through his teeth. He did, and into the resulting silence, she said, "Tag is going to pray, and then we can eat."

Tucker shoved half a roll in his mouth and froze, his eyes falsely widening in innocence. Tag chuckled and ducked his head. Her brother and cousins and the other cowboys had removed their hats and hung them on hooks when they'd arrived, and a sense of peace and serenity fell over the farmhouse.

Opal truly felt the hand of God in her life in that moment, and while she didn't hear all the words of her husband's prayer, she certainly felt the spirit of it.

After the resounding, "Amen," people swarmed the island, picking up plates and piling them with food. Opal stayed out of the way until everyone had what they needed, and then she followed everyone out onto the back deck.

Tag had gotten her lunch for her, and she slid onto the end of the bench, with West in his highchair on the end and Tag on her right.

"Have you thought about names yet?" Bobbie Jo asked, sliding into the spot opposite her.

"A few," Opal said. "But we're keeping those to ourselves for now." She and Tag had spent countless nights whispering possibilities for both boys and girls to each other in the dark, but those felt too precious to share just yet.

"Smart," Bobbie Jo said with a nod. "Once you tell people, everyone has an opinion."

Tucker leaned over, a mischievous glint in his eye. "Just remember, Tucker works for a boy or a girl."

"We are not naming our child Tucker," Opal said firmly, but she couldn't help laughing with everyone else.

Thank You, she thought, because God had blessed her with a very good family, and she couldn't wait to expand it with a precious son or daughter of her own.

eight

Mission hadn't expected to be at a baby announcement today. He'd gone to church with Deacon that morning, as usual, and his boss and best friend had asked, "Do you want to go to lunch at Opal's this afternoon?"

Mission rarely said no to a meal he didn't have to make, and that had been that.

The news that Opal was pregnant had brought a smile to his face, though, and Mission was absolutely happy for her and Tag. Something tugged in his own soul, and he could admit he'd like to be in Tag's position.

Not with Opal, of course, but the idea of being a father appealed to Mission. He'd lived a lot of years alone, and honestly, he was ready for a change.

He thought of Kristie, instantly frustrated all over again at how their date had ended last night.

He currently sat at the end of the long picnic table, with Deacon at the head of it on his left and Steele on the bench at his right. The Hammonds always made everyone feel welcome, so it wasn't that he didn't belong there.

He simply wanted to be somewhere else—with someone else.

Glancing over to Steele, he found the younger man grinning at his phone, his thumbs flying across the screen. "Who are you talkin' to?" he asked.

Steele looked up, his eyes wide and suddenly wary. "Uh...." He shot a look down the table to where Tag sat with Opal.

"Must be a woman," Deacon said in that slow, casual, country-boy way he had.

"Yeah, all right," Steele said. "It's a woman. I guess you could call her my girlfriend. I don't know." His face turned a ruddy shade of red as he flipped his phone over and left it face-down on the table. It chimed as he did, but he didn't pick it up again.

"Haven't defined it yet?" Mission asked, his heart pumping hard right now for a reason he couldn't name. Perhaps because Steele had never really dated anyone that Mission knew of, and it felt like if he'd started seeing someone, Mission definitely needed to up his game.

"We've been out a few times," Steele said. "I really like her, but no. We haven't talked about the superficial labels."

"I hate that conversation anyway," Deacon said. "It's so dumb. If we're goin' out, then she's my girlfriend. Why do we have to define it?" His grouchiness shone through, though Mission happened to agree.

"Amen, brother," Steele grumbled.

Mission looked between the two of them, deciding a topic change was in order. "How's it goin' out here?"

Steele shrugged, his demeanor not changing much. So maybe not a great topic to switch to. "Good. Busy. Got a new horse yesterday that's giving us some trouble."

"Yeah?" Mission dropped his napkin on his mostly empty plate, grateful for the distraction of farm talk. "What kind of trouble?"

"He's skittish. Won't let anyone near him except me—not even Tag—and even then...." Steele trailed off, his eyes drifting down the table to Gerty.

Mission nodded, understanding all too well how it felt to have strong opinions about animal care that others might not share. His mind went straight to Kristie and how she'd handled that emergency call last night. He'd been impressed by her calm professionalism, even as she'd raced to help a mare in distress.

"Even then?" he asked when Steele didn't go on.

"He needs to be isolated until he's healed up and properly socialized, and I think it's the first time me and Gerty don't agree about something." Steele crossed his arms, then sighed as he relaxed again. "He's causing problems with all the other horses, but she doesn't want to move him."

He glared down the table to her, but softened when he looked at Mission and then Deacon. "She's just stubborn, and I'm still learning how to talk to my boss like an equal."

Boy, Mission understood that, and he flicked a glance over to Deacon.

"She wants your opinion," Deacon said. "I'm sure of that." He finished the last of his pasta salad and wiped his mouth, his eyes zeroing in on Mission. "How'd your date go with Kristie?"

Great. Another topic change—this time straight to what Mission didn't want to talk about.

"You went out with Kristie?" Steele asked, keen interest in his voice. "Kristie Higgins?"

Mission ducked his head. "Yeah, sure did." He grinned over to Deacon and then Steele. "It went pretty well, I think." He could still feel the shape of her in his arms, smell the fruity scent of her perfume as he stood close to her, see the way she smiled as they twirled and danced.

"I'm sensing a *but*," Deacon said.

"But we got interrupted by an emergency veterinary call." Mission glanced over to Steele and shrugged one shoulder. "It wasn't how I'd have liked to have ended the date. That's all."

"That's rough."

"She's a mobile vet," Mission said as if Steele didn't

know. Of course he did; Kristie had come out to Gerty's farm to work plenty of times. "Had to go deliver a foal."

Steele's phone chimed and chimed, and Deacon chuckled. "Go talk to her," he said.

"Hazel's fine to wait," Steele said, but he still swiped up his phone as he stood. He picked up his plate, then stacked Mission's and Deacon's on it before he headed back into the farmhouse.

"We have apple pie for dessert," Opal called down the table. "I'll go start the coffee." She went inside too, and Mike and Tag got up and started taking in dishes too.

Mission's thoughts went right back to Kristie and stuck. She hadn't texted him at all that day, and since he'd left her at the Clovis farm last night, he could totally ask her for an update without seeming clingy.

It only took a few taps to get a message sent. *How did everything go last night? I never heard from you.*

He set his phone on his thigh, screen up, and looked over to Tarr as he started telling a story about one of the calves he and Tucker were training for a roping event in the rodeo.

"And how's Rosie settling into life in Colorado?" Deacon asked, and now Tuck and Tarr had plenty to say.

Fine by Mission. He looked down at his phone and found Kristie had messaged him back.

Both doing well! Mama had some complications, but I got her stitched up, and the little guy is nursing like a champ. Got home around 3 AM.

Mission smiled, imagining Kristie's tired but satisfied expression after successfully delivering the foal.

Glad to hear it. Sorry our night got cut short.

He hesitated, then added: *I had a really good time.*

He wanted to ask her out again. Had he been able to see the date through to completion, with him walking her to her door, he'd have asked her out again.

I guess I did too, she said.

You guess? He sent the message with plenty of irritation firing through him, because what kind of response was that?

She *guessed* she'd had a good time? What wasn't to like?

He worked to calm his temper, even going so far as to press his eyes closed. He drew a long breath in through his nose and did what the pastor had talked about at church today: He went still.

The sermon hadn't been about anger management, but the pastor had spoken about taking time to be silent and still, so he could hear and feel God in his life.

But the tactic worked to calm Mission's ire too, and he added a prayer for good measure. *Lord, I like this woman, probably too much. Help me to be patient and not jump to conclusions.*

He opened his eyes and looked at his accusatory text.

Oh, and if I could control my tongue better, that would be nice too.

His phone buzzed—he was smart enough to turn off

the sound, so everyone else wouldn't know when he got a message—and he looked down at Kristie's text.

I'm super disappointed about missing out on the mini doughnuts, she said. *But the dancing made up for it, and the handsome cowboy I was with didn't hurt either.*

Mission's heart rate sped, his annoyance completely gone. He glanced up to make sure no one was paying attention to him, but everyone seemed engrossed in Tucker's stories about Rosie down in Texas. Normally, he would be too—anything that kept the spotlight off him.

How's your Sunday going? He sent the text and reached for his nearly empty glass of lemonade and finished it.

Quiet. Just catching up on sleep and paperwork. You?

At a lunch at Opal and Tag's. They just announced they're having a baby.

Oh, that's great. Tell them congratulations from me.

Mission's thumbs hovered over the keyboard. *Just ask her,* he told himself. The worst she could say was no. And based on last night and this conversation, he didn't think she would.

Would you like to go out again sometime? I bet they sell mini doughnuts other places besides the Summer Stroll.

He sent the message before he could overthink it, then set his phone down and forced himself to his feet. He didn't want to be on this deck, with these people.

He wanted to head over to Kristie's.

Yeah, I'd like that, she said. *And you know, I still have your cheesecake. We never did make it to dessert last night.*

Relief and excitement washed through him in equal measure. *Maybe I could come by for dessert tonight.*

I'm home and not planning on going anywhere.

Mission grinned, and he looked up to find Deacon watching him with a raised eyebrow. "Important business?"

Mission burst out laughing. "I look like Steele, don't I?" Moony eyed and grinning at his phone.

Deacon grinned too. "You really do."

"Coffee's almost done," Opal called from the back doorway. "And we have vanilla ice cream to go with the pie."

Panic built beneath Mission's breastbone. He sank back onto the bench and met his best friend's eye. "Could you catch a ride with someone else?"

Deacon's eyebrows went up. "You're turning down Opal's apple pie?"

"I know, it's practically a sin," Mission said with a small smile. "But I've got some things I need to take care of tonight."

"*Things*, sure." Deacon grinned at him. "I'm sure I can get a ride back to the farm. Go."

Mission wasted no time in getting to his feet again and striding into the house. He moved right over to Opal and hugged her. "Lunch was delicious. Thank you for having me. And congratulations again on the baby."

Opal's eyes flickered with surprised, but she smiled.

"It was good to see you, Mish. You've got something to do on the farm?"

"Yeah," he said. "Deacon said he could get a ride back with someone."

"I'm sure Tag or Mike can take him," Opal said.

Mission did his best not to run out, and he shook Tag's hand and thanked him too, denied taking any apple pie with him, and finally managed to exit calmly through the front door.

The drive back to his cabin took about twenty minutes, giving Mission plenty of time to think about what he was doing.

"Two dates in two days," he muttered. It had been a long time since he'd been this eager to spend time with a woman.

There was something about Kristie that drew him in— her intelligence, her confidence, the way she lit up when she smiled. And last night, dancing with her under the stars, he'd felt something he hadn't experienced in years.

Connection. Real connection.

Inside, Mission changed into fresh clothes—dark jeans and a navy button-down that his grandfather had once told him brought out his eyes. He debated wearing his good boots or more casual ones, finally settling on the nicer pair. This might be a casual dessert-only event at her place, but it was still a date.

At least in Mission's mind.

He'd been home for ten minutes, but he couldn't sit idle—and alone. So he headed back out to his truck, aiming it toward the town of Ivory Peaks—and Kristie's house—this time.

Now, he simply had to hope he didn't come across as too eager when he showed up less than an hour after texting her.

nine

Kristie pushed the vacuum cleaner across the flat, burgundy carpet, the familiar hum filling the empty chapel. Late afternoon sunlight streamed through the stained glass windows, casting colorful patterns across the pews and floor.

Pure peace filled her, and she loved being in the church when everyone else had gone home.

She hadn't actually gone to church that morning, due to her late night at the Clovis farm. Thus, she'd completely forgotten it was her Sunday to clean the church after Sabbath services. When the pastor's wife had called twenty minutes ago, that familiar wave of guilt had washed over her.

Doesn't matter, she told herself. *You're here now*—and vacuuming was her favorite chore. There was simply something about the white noise and the vibration of the machine in her hand—and the way she could put perfectly even lines in the carpet.

Well, hers at home, anyway. The church's carpet was too flat and thin to see many lines.

Once she finished vacuuming and tidying up the chapel, she'd empty the trashcans in the classrooms, shine the glass in the front doors, and clean the bathrooms. With any luck, and with her working at a steady clip, she'd be back home in ninety minutes.

Mission had been at lunch with the Hammonds; surely he wouldn't be at her house for another couple of hours anyway. The thought made her stomach flutter with anticipation all the same.

She'd really enjoyed their date last night, and she'd hoped her flirtatious teasing had come through in her texts. Mission was a pretty literal cowboy, though, so she'd decided to simply spell it out in exact words and letters that he couldn't misinterpret.

But the dancing made up for it, and the handsome cowboy I was with didn't hurt either.

Yes, she'd sent that text, because he hadn't seemed to get her teasing. It was hard to do via text, and Kristie wasn't a great flirt anyway.

She finished with the vacuuming and moved onto the bathrooms. She'd just finished in the women's when her phone buzzed in her back pocket. She pulled it out and wiped her hair back out of her face at the same time.

Mission: *I'm at your house but you're not answering the door.*

Her heartbeat fell to the soles of her sneakers. She'd told him she wasn't planning on going anywhere, and then the call to clean the church had come in.

She tapped to call him, only imagining his displeasure at the change of plans. His phone rang a couple of times, and then he said, "Hey, there."

"I'm so sorry," she said in a rush of words. "I forgot it was my turn to clean the church, and the pastor's wife called after I told you I'd be home for the rest of the day."

"So you're at the church?"

She couldn't tell if he was upset or not. "Yes," she said, quickly calculating how much longer she'd be there. "I'm probably going to be another thirty or forty-five minutes."

"I'll come over," he said. "See you in a sec." He ended the call, and Kristie stared at her phone for a moment. She swallowed, because she knew Mission went to church. She'd seen him sitting in these very pews with various cowboys over the years.

She simply hadn't anticipated telling him about her service in the church quite yet. Not that she had a plan for when that came up, but usually not on the first date.

"Or the second," she muttered, wondering if sharing three-day-old cheesecake could be considered a date.

She hurried into the men's room and started cleaning. Then she and Mission could go through the chapel to reset the hymnals, collect the trash, and wipe windows together.

"Kristie?" Mission's voice came before she'd finished in the bathroom, and she wasn't sure why she was so nervous.

"In the bathroom," she called. Several moments later, the sound of his footsteps clacked on the tile.

She exited the final stall, that work done. Her hands bore bright yellow gloves that went to her elbow, but Mission didn't seem to notice. He didn't look anywhere but straight into her eyes.

"Hey." She'd never been in the men's restroom with a man before, but Mission grinned at her like this was nothing to him.

"Hey, kitten."

Her smile sprang to her face unbidden. Him and that *kitten* endearment. She'd almost forgotten about it.

He looked over to the dual sinks and mirror. "Have you done this?"

"Not yet," she said.

"I saw the trash bag in the hall."

"Yeah," she said. "We have to get them out of all the classrooms too."

Mission bent and plucked the sponge out of the bucket. "I didn't know you cleaned the church," he said as he got to work wiping down counters.

"Yeah," she said, reaching for the glass cleaner. "I've been doing it since I moved to town."

He looked over to her, pure curiosity in his expression. So much so, that he didn't have to ask anything more.

"It...It makes me feel connected to something bigger than myself," she said. "And I really needed that when I came to Ivory Peaks."

"And that was what? Five years ago?"

"Five in January, yes," she said. "Helping out at the church gives me—I don't know. It helps me feel like I belong here." She swallowed and focused on going round and round to clean the glass.

"I think there's more to this story," he said quietly.

"You'd be right."

He gave her a slow, gorgeous smile. "So you'll tell me when you're ready."

"Yeah," she said fondly. "Like you'll tell me about your parents and what brought you to Ivory Peaks when you're ready."

A swallow moved down his neck too, and he nodded without saying anything. They finished in the men's room, and Kristie picked up the bucket. "We still need to dust the altar and pulpit, collect the hymnals, and take out the trash."

"I'll get the trash from the classrooms and meet you in the chapel." He leaned closer and brushed his lips along her cheek. "It's great to see you, Kris." With that, he left her standing in the men's room, pure heat stinging in her skin where he'd touched her.

And how did he speak in that tender, husky voice that made all the cells in her body tingle?

Kristie pulled herself together and went to the altar to begin dusting. She ran her cloth carefully over the wooden cross, the podium where the pastor stood to speak, and the table where the sacrament got administered.

This part of her cleaning routine always felt more like worship than chore. There was something sacred about caring for these symbols of faith, making sure they were ready to serve their purpose for the next service.

"You come here every Sunday?" Mission's voice startled her from her thoughts. He'd returned with a roll of trash bags and currently emptied a small bin near the entrance.

She shook her head. "I only clean once a month."

"I didn't know patrons did it," he said, clearly asking for more information.

"I talked to the pastor and his wife when I first came to town," she said. "I think they ask others to do it for... various reasons." She tucked the dusting supplies back into her bucket and started up the first aisle. She knew the others who cleaned the church, and it was usually as part of their repentance process, or because they were getting financial help. She didn't need to know, and she didn't care. She simply liked the way it made her feel more connected to her church community.

"We just need to check for left-behind toys and trash

in the pews," she said. "And collect the hymnals and put them in the shelves at the back."

"All right," Mission said, moving to go up the aisle with her. "Where'd you move from?"

The question was casual, but Kristie tensed slightly. "Arizona," she said after a moment. "The Phoenix area."

Mission seemed to sense her hesitation and didn't press further. "I came from New Mexico," he said. "When I found the job at the Hammond Family Farm, and I told my granddad I wanted to stay here, he moved here too."

Kristie bent to pick up a snack-size bag of Cheerios that had been left behind. "He's Native American, right?"

"Yes, half Navajo," Mission said. "Thus, the last name of Redbay."

"That makes you...what? An eighth Navajo?"

"Yes," Mission said. They worked their way down both sides of the chapel, from front to back, and then back to front again.

Kristie sighed, pleased with her work that afternoon. "Cleaning the church is my way of giving back. When I first came here, I was in a rough place. This church became my family when I needed one."

Mission had stopped collecting trash and was watching her, his dark eyes attentive. "I get that," he said softly.

The sincerity in his voice made her look up. There was understanding in his gaze, not judgment or pity. It made her want to tell him more.

"I've always struggled with feeling...worthy," she admitted. "Like I need to earn my place. Cleaning the church started as a way to feel useful, but it's become more than that."

Mission nodded, still wearing his ultra-serious mask. She'd seen it so many times, but never laced with this undercurrent of concern and compassion. "Sometimes the simplest acts of service mean the most."

"Exactly." She smiled, grateful he understood. "And then I met my friends in my cooking class, and my mobile vet office took off." She sighed, pleased and proud at how far she'd come in only a few years.

"But I still love coming to the church when it's still and quiet like this." She looked around, drinking in the peaceful spirit of the building.

He gazed up at the two-story roof high above them too. "It has a different feel." He picked up the bag of trash and asked, "I'll follow you back to your place?"

She nodded and went to put the bucket of supplies in the janitorial closet while he took the trash out. Outside, he waited in his truck, which he'd parked next to her SUV, and she led the way back to her house.

The drive home gave Kristie time to think through the conversation with Mission. She hadn't expected to share as much as she had with him, but something about him made her feel safe enough to lower her guard, if only a little.

When they arrived at her house, all three cats waited

in the window again. Kristie laughed as she parked in the garage and waited for Mission to drop from his truck.

"Your fan club is eager to see you," she told Mission as she pushed into the house and the cats immediately swarmed around their feet. Bob practically bellowed his meows, simply starved for attention, the greedy feline.

"Oh, heya, Bob." Mission crouched right down and started stroking the cat. Bob pressed into his palm, his purr like a lawn mower engine.

Kristie refrained from rolling her eyes, and instead, got out the cheesecakes she'd saved for herself and Mission.

"You've got a way with animals," she said.

"You hum while you clean." He straightened and grinned at her. "I never had the patience for school, but if I had, I probably would've been a vet like you."

Kristie had not realized she hummed while she cleaned, but she now acknowledged that she did.

Her house felt different with Mission in it—warmer somehow, less empty. She arranged the individual passionfruit cheesecakes on small plates, adding a sprinkle of toasted coconut on top to hopefully freshen them up.

When she turned toward the living room, Mission had settled on her couch, with Bob already curled up beside him.

"I see Bob has claimed you," she said, handing him a plate of cheesecake.

"I'm honored." Mission accepted the dessert, his smile absolutely devastating. "This cheesecake looks amazing."

"Thank you." Kristie sat in her favorite flowered chair, tucking her feet underneath her. "I hope they taste as good as they look."

Mission took a bite and closed his eyes as he moaned. "Even better," he said after swallowing. "The passionfruit is perfect—it's like the tart answer to the sweet cheesecake."

He took another bite—a big one—and pride bloomed in Kristie's chest at his genuine enjoyment. "I'm glad you like it."

They ate in comfortable silence for a few moments, the only sounds the occasional purr from one of the cats and the clink of forks against plates.

Kristie finished after Mission, and she stood to take his dessert plate back into the kitchen. She didn't care about the dishes, and when she returned to the living room, she didn't want to sit all alone in the recliner, even if it was her favorite chair.

Instead, she sank onto the couch next to Mission, who lifted his arm and settled it around her shoulders. She leaned into him, a happy little sigh escaping her mouth. It felt natural for her to lay her arm across his stomach, so she did, and Kristie settled into his side like she belonged there.

They still had plenty to talk about, but Kristie was

really enjoying the silence, and it seemed like Mission was too.

She didn't want to destroy this peace, and she told herself she'd have plenty of time to tell him all the things he needed to know to truly know her as they continued to date. Assuming he asked her out again, of course.

"When can I see you again?" Mission whispered as if he could see right into Kristie's mind.

She let a smile inch across her face. "Barring any more emergency calls, I'm almost always free in the evenings."

"So I could order pizza tomorrow night, and we could find a good place to watch the sunset," he said.

"Yeah," Kristie said, surprised at how perfect Mission's dates were. In fact, everything about him surprised her, and everything about him reminded her that she couldn't make lasting judgments about someone from a single encounter.

"A pizza-sunset night sounds heavenly."

"Mm, okay." Mission pressed his lips to the top of her head. "Do you want to just come out to my cabin when you're done tomorrow?"

"Maybe about six-thirty?" she asked.

"Six-thirty is just fine, kitten." He really drawled out *just fine*, reminding Kristie how much she liked cowboys.

Kristie smiled, knowing she'd have to wait hours until sunset if she showed up at Mission's house at six-thirty.

And since she'd get to spend all that time with Mission, that was *just fine* with her.

ten

Mission didn't normally mind working from sunup to sundown. It made for long hours in the summer, to be certain, but he enjoyed being outside, spending his time with animals, breathing in the fresh air, and enjoying all of God's creations.

He'd been at the Hammond family farm so long that he had plenty of friends, and thankfully, none of them had started treating him differently now that he was the foreman. Of course, it had only been a week, and nothing major had happened on the farm yet. He hadn't had to reprimand anyone, do any interviews, try to settle any disagreements, or otherwise be the boss.

In fact, in many ways, Mission acted the exact same way he had when he hadn't been foreman. He normally had no problem staying after the horseback riding lessons to help put all the equines away, answer questions, and wait with kids whose parents were late coming to get them.

Today, he walked with a couple of ten-year-olds down the side of the red barn toward the parking lot, his eye on the clock on his phone. Kristie would be at his house in only ten more minutes, and it would take Mission that long to walk home if he left right now.

He hadn't ordered pizza yet, because he wanted to ask her for her favorite kind, and they had plenty of time before the sun would go behind the Rocky Mountains in the west.

Part of him worried that there was *too* much time— how could he possibly find anything for the two of them to talk about for hours?

He told himself that Kristie knew at least a little bit about him, and if she hadn't worked out that he wasn't the most talkative cowboy in the state yet, that said more about her than him.

"My momma said she just pulled up," Trevor, one of the boys, said.

"Oh, great." Mission smiled over to the child. "You got your certificate from Molly?"

The boy lifted it up, pride beaming from his face. "I can't believe I'm moving up to the next level so fast."

Trevor had been riding at Pony Power for a few years now, so Mission wasn't that surprised. The other boy, Zach, had not moved up to the next class, but he'd only been at Pony Power for a year.

They reached the corner of the barn, and Trevor ran off to climb into his mother's minivan.

Zach paused and looked around. "I don't see my dad."

To Mission's relief, he spotted Cosette Whettstein standing several feet down near the front doors of the administration building. She ran the behind-the-scenes at Pony Power with utmost precision. As Mission had been drawing paychecks from both the farm and the equine therapy unit for years—two separate entities housed on the same land—Cosette kept everything straight, proper, and running according to tax laws.

"I'm gonna have you go wait with Cosette," Mission said to Zach. "Is that all right?"

He nodded down toward the front doors, and Zach started moving that way. "Yeah, it's fine."

"See you next week," he called to the boy, who turned around and walked backward for a couple of steps as he waved good-bye.

Mission smiled and waved back, and the moment he could, he spun on his heel and headed for his cabin. He usually only drove to town for groceries or church, and he'd never minded the walk to and from work. Today, though, it felt like a constant thorn in his side as he hurried down the lane, past the farmhouse, and through the Hammond's backyard.

Even then, he still had to walk the long road to the very back of Cowboy Row, where the foreman's cabin stood two stories tall while all the other cabins were only one.

And Kristie's car already sat in his driveway.

"Great," he muttered.

He wiped the sweat from his face and told himself everything would be fine. It was pizza and a sunset, and she wouldn't care if he took ten minutes to shower. They'd have to wait for the pizza anyway.

As he drew closer to the cabin, he realized Kristie sat on his front steps. She wore a pair of cutoff jean shorts and a sleeveless blouse in lavender. She seemed haloed above with light from heaven—or maybe that was just how Mission perceived her.

Her focus stayed down on her phone, but Mission couldn't look anywhere but at her.

She glanced up, finally, and Mission raised his hand in a wave, though he still had half the distance to go to reach her.

She got to her feet and pushed her phone into her back pocket as she came down the steps. From several yards away, she called, "Your truck was here, so I thought you'd be home."

"Just finishing up the horseback riding lessons," he said, his stride long and eating up the distance between them quickly.

When he reached her, he slid one hand along her waist to her back and leaned in as if he might kiss her on the mouth, right there for anyone to see.

Mission had kissed plenty of women, and the movement felt natural to him. But his brain screamed at him that he had *not* kissed this woman yet—and he certainly didn't want the first time to happen in broad daylight where any number of cowboys could see and then tease him about it.

"Hey, kitten," he said, slowing his forward motion. He lifted his chin too, and that got his lips closer to her temple. He swept a kiss there and then stepped back easily, curling her fingers between his.

"How was your day?" It felt like such a mundane question to ask, but Kristie smiled and tilted her head back so that she faced the sky.

"It was a great day," she said. "I helped a cocker spaniel deliver some puppies, and then I did some cattle immunizations out at Southby's."

"The puppies sound nice," he said.

"They are the cutest things *ever*." Kristie smiled over at him. "What about you? You seem busy around here."

"No busier than any other day."

They went back up his front steps to the porch. When Matt had lived here, Gloria always had something welcoming anyone who came to the house—a seasonal sign in red, white, and blue for the Fourth of July, pumpkins at Halloween, and scarecrows and Santa Clauses at appropriate times throughout the year.

"I just had to finish up with the kids," he said. "And I

figured it would be okay if I grabbed a shower while you figured out what kind of pizza you want."

"Yeah, sure," Kristie said. "Where are you going to order from?"

"I was thinking San Diego's," Mission said. "They have a pan-style pizza that's been calling my name for a couple of days."

She laughed, the sound glorious and wonderful. "Ah, now I know why you suggested pizza."

"If you'd rather we got something else—"

"No," Kristie said. "I love pizza, though I can't say that I've ever had the pan pizza from San Diego's."

"Have you been to San Diego's before?" he asked.

"Yeah," she said. "But my girlfriends and I got the thin crust. And you would *die,* but Lennie likes veggie pizza." She tacked a giggle onto the end, and Mission grinned at her.

He opened his front door and stepped back to let Kristie go in first. Blessed air conditioning came out to greet them, and she took three steps into his cabin and stopped.

He entered after her, squeezing in close so that he could swing the door closed behind him. "It's not much," he said, moving to her side. "The foreman's cabin is the biggest, though, and Matt lived here with his family for quite a while. Then they wanted more land, and he moved to town, and he and Gloria just came out here to work."

"Gloria is still around, right?" Kristie asked.

"Yep." Mission moved past her. "Feel free to snoop around." He grinned and turned back toward her as he reached the corner. "And look at the menu at San Diego's. We can get more than one pizza, so if you want a thin crust, it's no problem."

Her eyes roamed through his living room, the dining room with a table and four chairs, and the kitchen before they settled on him.

"I'll look at the menu," she said. "I'm not going to snoop through your stuff."

He grinned and reached up to tip his hat at her, then took it off and hung it on the hook on the other side of the corner as he headed down the hall toward the master suite.

The foreman's cabin had a second bedroom, two bathrooms, and a loft. Mission knew Matt had once put Keith in the loft—only because he and his sister weren't the same gender and were too old to share the bedroom. Mission wouldn't have that problem for a while...if he ever did.

"Hey, don't think like that," he muttered to himself. Things were going great with Kristie—and they were. But as he quickly stepped into the shower to scrub the day's dirt, horses, and sweat off his skin, he also reminded himself that this was only their third date. They wouldn't be getting married and starting a family anytime soon.

As he toweled his hair dry, he realized how long it had

gotten. He grabbed his phone and headed back down the hall to the living room.

Kristie sat at the bar—not at the table or on the couch—and she looked up as he entered.

"I actually think your place is bigger than mine," she said.

He chuckled and shook his head. "I doubt that."

"My place is only two bedrooms, and you have a loft," she said.

"You have a basement."

"It's not finished, so your living space might be more than mine."

"Okay," he said, because he saw no point in arguing about it; he didn't really care anyway.

"I'm just gonna text Molly real quick," he said.

"Oh, yeah? About what?"

He glanced at her as he tapped on Molly's name. "Just gonna ask her to cut my hair," he said. "I realized it's getting a little too long."

Kristie got to her feet. "I can cut your hair."

Their eyes met, and time slowed into small, thin strands connecting the two of them.

"You can?" The words came out of his mouth, though his lips didn't move.

"Sure." Kristie reached up and swept her fingers through it, pushing the long fringe to the side. She swallowed and dropped her hand as her eyes widened—like she'd just realized what she'd done.

And what she'd done was electrocute Mission from the skull down. He couldn't move or think, and the only reason he kept breathing was because his lungs did so of their own volition.

"I used to cut my brother's hair."

She fell back a step, and Mission felt like she'd blown open the conversation.

He wanted her to know more about him, and the only way that would happen was if he talked to her. He'd lost a little bit of sleep last night just thinking about such a thing. But now, he tucked his phone away and said, "I won't ask Molly then. Do you have a hair-cutting kit?"

"I used to," she said. "I can get another one."

He nodded and took both of her hands in his. "Did you decide on what kind of pizza you want?"

"I want to try the pan-style Hawaiian," she said. "But with Alfredo sauce, not red sauce. Will they let you do that substitution?"

He looked down at her fingers with her manicured nails, though she wore no polish. "They let you do whatever you're willing to pay for, kitten."

He lifted his eyes just enough to look at her face and catch a smile.

"Great," she said. "Then that's what I want."

"You want a salad or anything?"

"Yeah, a garden salad would be great."

"Let me order, and then we can talk about where we want to go to eat and watch the sunset."

She nodded, and Mission pulled his hands back to send in the order. He did it via text, and with the message sent, he looked up again.

"You can text San Diego's?"

"Yep," he said.

"And they deliver out here?"

"It's an extra charge," he said. "But totally worth it."

He took her hand again, and this time, led her into the living room. He sat on the couch first, hoping she'd choose to cuddle in next to him the way she had at her house last night. She did, and Mission traced a slow circle on her shoulder.

His nerves tightened his vocal cords and rendered him silent, but he knew he needed to tell her more about his past. He hoped and prayed that would allow her to open up about hers as well.

"I was raised by my grandparents," he said. "In this tiny town called Steel Blade, in New Mexico."

"Is that right?" Kristie asked, her voice barely more than a murmur.

"Yes," Mission said. "From about the time I was two or three. That's always what Granddad says." He gave a light chuckle that didn't really hold any happiness.

"See, my mom and dad weren't married. And my momma wasn't ready to be a momma, so she ran off and left me with my dad when I was a baby. My dad tried, but Granddad says he just didn't have it in him, and he dropped me off at their place and left town too."

"Wow," Kristie said. "I'm so sorry."

"My grandparents were good people," Mission said. "But quiet. Steeped in Navajo tradition though my grandmother was White. I wasn't great at reading, or math, or writing—or any of it—and to stay out of trouble, I got a job at a farm on the outskirts of town."

Kristie rested her hand on his knee, and Mission dang near jumped out of his skin. He settled down and said, "I was only twenty when Paul Bluefeather made me foreman."

Kristie turned her head and looked at him then. Mission simply gazed down at the denim where her hand sat.

"I did my best, but I think I was a lot like my dad—I didn't have it in me."

"That's just not true," Kristie said. "You're the foreman now."

"Twenty-three years later," he said.

"Only twenty-two," she whispered.

Mission finally looked at her, but he couldn't muster up the courage to smile. He didn't mind their back-and-forth, and he actually liked that Kristie felt comfortable enough to speak her thoughts.

"I was there for a couple of years," he said. "Then we had a real bad accident...and it was my fault."

She pulled in a breath and held it.

"Everyone told me it wasn't. And maybe it wasn't. But I sure felt like it was."

"What happened?" she asked.

"It was a horse ranch, and we trained wild horses that we rescued from various parts of Arizona, New Mexico, and Texas," he said. "One evening, one of the horses wasn't secured right, and that's part of my job as foreman, you know? To make sure everyone knows how to take care of the horses the way they should."

He paused. "Anyway, that didn't happen, and we had a big stampede. Three men were hurt real bad, and one of them ended up dying a few weeks later."

"Oh, my goodness," Kristie said, with just the right amount of concern and disbelief, the words also laced with compassion.

"I couldn't stay," Mission said. "I left the ranch, packed up my stuff, and came to Colorado. I bounced around from farm to farm until Matt hired me. And I've been here ever since."

"I'm sure it wasn't your fault," Kristie said.

Mission shook his head, his jaw tight, but at least the words were out. "Doesn't matter if it was or not," he said. "I *felt* like it was, and it haunted me for a long time."

She curled her hand around the inside of his knee and squeezed. "Thank you for telling me."

"I might seem insecure sometimes," he said. "Or indecisive about what I'm doing on the farm, and it comes from that. I'm trying not to be, and Granddad's told me a million times how good of a horseman I am. But sometimes my brain doesn't believe him."

He sighed, glad to have the story out. "My grandma died only a year after that. When I went back for the funeral, I told Granddad I really liked Ivory Peaks and the Hammond family farm, and I wouldn't be coming back, so that's when he moved here."

"And what does he do?" she asked.

Mission grinned, because he loved his grandfather with his whole heart. "He makes Native American drums," he said. "And he's real good at it."

"Wow," Kristie said with a smile. "Where does he sell those?"

"To people he knows back home," Mission said. "A lot up in Canada. He's got himself a little online business. Does pretty well."

"That's great," Kristie said.

Mission's phone beeped with a notification. He looked and flipped it over in his hand. "Oh—pizza's on the way." He turned toward her and found pure energy vibrating in her gaze. He leaned toward her and pressed his lips right against her cheek.

"Thanks for letting me talk," he said. "I promise I won't clutter up the sunset with chatter tonight."

She leaned into his kiss. "I don't care if you do."

"I'm sure that's true, kitten. But I'm all talked out."

She nodded. "All right then. Where are you going to take me for this amazing Rocky Mountain sunset?"

eleven

"This is for sure the best pizza I've ever had," Kristie said.

Mission smiled over to her as he chewed his deep dish pepperoni pizza—with extra cheese and extra pepperoni. He had gotten himself a small Caesar salad to go with her garden salad, but they'd eaten those first at the dining room table in his cabin.

Then he'd taken the two pizza boxes in one hand and her hand in the other and led her out his back door. She hadn't questioned him, because she trusted Mission— and Kristie couldn't remember the last man she'd liked or trusted as much as him.

He'd taken her along the edge of the woods at the back of his property and past acres of fields that angled away from the part of the farm where Kristie was used to working. She could see the stables and walking circles in the distance. Eventually, Mission had taken her to a cabin that clearly didn't get used very often.

The walk had taken maybe thirty minutes, and he'd ended it with, "We sometimes stay out here when we're hunting or have to work on the fields and fences on the south end of the farm."

Nothing but fields existed beyond the cabin, and instead of going inside or sitting on the steps—or even getting out lawn chairs and positioning them to face west —Mission had taken her to the west side of the cabin and nodded his cowboy hat at a ladder.

"You want me to climb up there?" she'd asked.

"Yes."

And Kristie had done it.

He'd followed, using only one hand to climb that ladder, and joined her on the roof of the single-story cabin. It had a gently sloping roof that probably only rose up ten feet at the very pinnacle. Someone—she was guessing Mission himself—had put a loveseat there, facing west.

Kristie now sat on the dark brown microfiber, her stomach full, her soul rejoicing, and her heart happier than it had been in a long time.

They still had at least an hour until it would be full dark, but the towering, majestic Rocky Mountains in the west did cause the sun to officially set earlier than it would otherwise.

Mission had told her a lot of heavy things about his

past, and that had only spurred Kristie to want to tell him about the reasons she'd left Anthem—a suburb in the Phoenix area—and never gone back. At the same time, he'd said he was all talked out, and Kristie didn't want to lay more at his feet than either of them wanted tonight.

He'd kept the conversation easy and light, talking about how he'd like to adopt a dog that could keep him company on the walk to and from work every day.

They'd talked about his favorite holidays—Christmas and Easter—and she'd learned that both were because of the food. He didn't care about decorations or dressing up. He liked having ham and potatoes, or turkey, mashed potatoes, and gravy. She'd teased him about how almost all of his good memories had revolved around food.

"Including this one," he'd said and taken another bite of his pizza. He sure knew what to say to make Kristie's insides turn to goo, and she didn't mind that one bit.

She tossed her crust into her box at her feet and toed it further away from her. "I am so full," she said.

She'd only eaten three pieces of pizza, but Mission had gotten larges for both of them, so she'd have plenty of leftovers for lunch tomorrow and the next day.

"Same," he said, though he'd eaten half his pie before even slowing down. "I'm just gonna have one more piece," he added as he separated it from the rest. "Do you know much about the mountains?"

"I mean, a little bit," she said. "While I was starting up my veterinary practice here, I worked as a school aide. We did some field trips where we had to take the kids on hikes and read all the signs on the trails."

He smiled over at her. "That sounds so like you."

"Does it?" she asked.

"I mean, I think so," he said. "I can see kids liking you."

"Why would they like me?"

"You're pretty, and smart, and patient."

"Pretty, and smart, and patient." She grinned at him, not sure she'd use all of those words to describe herself. But from him, they sounded like the truth. "Thank you, Mission."

He stuffed his mouth full of pizza, and while the sun had definitely turned more golden since they'd been on the rooftop, she could still easily see the flush that colored his cheeks.

"I'm going to order a haircutting kit right now," she said, retrieving her phone from where she'd stuck it under her leg.

"You won't be able to get service out here," he said.

Sure enough, she had no bars. "Huh. I bet I can get one in town," she said. "I was just going to order online."

Mission hummed and dusted his hands together, closing his pizza box. Then he leaned toward her as he opened the armrest on the side of the loveseat. "You want a bottle of water, kitten?"

"You have water in that thing?" she asked.

Mission chuckled as he lifted an ice-cold, dripping

bottle of water out of the armrest. "This thing has a cooler in it," he said. "I was hoping it would last all day, because I came this morning and put ice and drinks in it. And it looks like it did."

He'd come this morning and put ice and drinks in the couch on the roof. Kristie wasn't sure why, but that simple gesture of preparing in advance for their date made her fall a little bit in love with him.

"What else you got in there?" she asked.

"Diet Coke," he said. "Diet Dr. Pepper—that's for me. A Sprite. And this is...."

She heard the clunking of ice against the side of the cooler.

"Apple juice, looks like," he said. "I just took whatever Cosette had in the front of the barn, and I had to promise her that I would replace it all. So whatever you want is fine."

"I'll take the Sprite," Kristie said.

He handed her the bright green can. The satisfying pop-hiss of carbonation met her ears when she opened it, and she took a drink while he opened his can of Diet Dr. Pepper.

"This is an incredible setup you've got out here," she said.

"Sure is," he murmured.

"Did you do this?"

"All the boys have been doing lots of stuff out here for as long as I can remember," he said. "Matt put picnic tables down by the river too, because it's nice to have a quiet place to sit and eat."

"But the couch was your idea, right?" she pressed.

"Boone was getting rid of the couch," Mission said. "It needed to go somewhere."

Kristie giggled, surprised that such a sound could come out of her mouth—especially in Mission Redbay's presence.

She'd been wrong about him for so long, and that made something inside her coil and curdle as she sobered. She liked being asked out by a man, but it wasn't a necessity. Mission had asked her out three times now. So she said, "I just want the record to show that we still have not gotten any mini donuts."

Mission threaded his fingers through hers and turned toward her. "I suppose we haven't," he said.

"What do you think about going back to the Summer Stroll tomorrow?" she asked, trying to make her voice casual and light.

Boy, asking someone out sure was hard, and she suddenly had more sympathy for every man who'd ever invited someone on a date.

"They'll be there," she said. "I won't take your whole evening. Just dessert."

"I don't mind dedicating my whole evening to you, kitten."

"Well, I don't want you to be in a rush," she said, remembering the way Mission had practically jogged down the lane to her—clearly irritated that she'd been at his house before him.

"So I won't rush," he said. "Dessert's after dinner, right?"

"Yeah."

"So I'll come by and get you at, say, eight?"

"I don't want to keep you out too late either," she said. "You texted me last week that you're always one of the first on the farm."

He nodded and brought her knuckles to his lips. "It'll be fine, Kris."

When he used her name instead of "kitten," she decided to let this go. He was a grown man, and he could turn her down if he wanted to.

"Eight o'clock then," she said, wondering when they'd simply move into seeing each other every day without the need to make plans. She liked that stage of dating, though she sure did like this getting-to-know-Mission part as well.

The sun sank lower and lower, the sky turning various colors of gold, orange, lavender, and navy. The mountains started to swallow it, the bottom edge of the sun now mirroring the jagged peaks.

It always seemed to take so long for the sun to disappear completely—and then, one moment, it was simply gone.

"There it goes," Mission said quietly.

Seemingly, the top third of the sun disappeared in the next few seconds, plunging them into inky twilight.

Kristie suddenly didn't want this evening to end. She felt her time with Mission slipping away, just like the sun had disappeared behind the mountains.

"We shouldn't linger," he said. "We have to get down to the ground, and we'll want to be back closer to civilization before too long. There are coyotes out here."

"Okay," Kristie said, but panic paraded through her when Mission released her hand and leaned forward to pick up his pizza box.

"Just answer one more thing for me," she said.

He leaned back and looked at her, curiosity raging through his expression.

"What's one thing in your life you really want? Something you dream about doing?"

Mission blinked, clearly not expecting such a question. He cleared his throat and ducked his head, using that sexy cowboy hat to hide his face. "My granddad taught me not to worry about things I don't have," Mission said.

"But you must have dreams," Kristie said.

He sighed and looked back toward the mountains, as if she were being difficult on purpose. "Tell me one of yours then," he said.

"I want to win a blue ribbon at the Colorado State Fair for my baking," she said.

That brought a smile to Mission's face. He nodded and said, "I think you'll be able to do that, kitten."

"All right, your turn," she said. "It doesn't have to be a big thing."

He turned to face her. "What if all I've got is a big thing?"

"That's fine too."

His eyes drifted down to her mouth, and every cell in Kristie's body rioted. Would he kiss her on this rooftop in the afterglow of the summer sunset? She suddenly wanted nothing more than that.

"A wife," he said. "And a family. Been thinking about those things a lot the last couple of years. I've been out with several women, trying to find the right one for me."

Kristie reached up and trailed her fingertips down the side of his face, feeling the softness in his beard. "And you haven't found her yet?"

"Jury's still out on you, kitten," he whispered.

He lifted his hand to cradle her face too, his dark eyes buzzing with such intensity. He hesitated for one breath of time—which was so classically Mission that it made Kristie smile—before he leaned down and touched his lips to hers.

She slid her hand to the back of his head, threading her fingers through his hair and pulling him closer.

She kissed him back, realizing that she should have been dreaming of something different since the moment she'd met Mission.

She should have been dreaming of this very moment, where he kissed her like she was royalty, perfectly worthy of his love, and absolutely desirable by a good-looking, hardworking cowboy.

She'd never been kissed like this before. And once again, she found herself praying that this night would never end.

twelve

olly Hammond watched as Poppy Thatcher braided the seven strands of cinnamon raisin bread together. She looked over to Opal, who wore a wide-eyed, semi-horrified look on her face. Honestly, Molly felt the same, and seeing Opal's reaction so blatantly made her start to laugh.

Poppy looked up, but her hands didn't stop braiding. Seriously, the woman was a genius in the kitchen, and Molly had no idea how she would ever make this cinnamon twist braid at all.

"What?" Opal asked, the hand that had been holding her small notebook dropping to her side.

Molly never took notes at the neighborhood cooking demonstrations, but Opal always did. "Your face," she said, giggling around the words. "It was just funny. It was showing exactly how I feel inside."

She looked over to Poppy, who hadn't quite gotten the joke. "There's just no way I can do this."

"Yes, you can," Poppy said. "You just always take the outside braid into the middle." She stretched over a piece of dough. "See, now this one's on the outside. We'll do that one after we do this side."

Poppy looked up at Opal and Molly. Jane stood in the kitchen as well, and she scratched something into her miniature notebook. Thankfully, Britt never made any notes either, and nothing seemed to ruffle her—even braiding bread.

A couple of other counselors from Pony Power came to these midday demonstrations, and Molly looked over to them. Gemma, Hope, and Judy didn't seem overwhelmed at all.

"I've seen someone do this on TikTok," Judy said.

"Oh, my word," Molly groaned. "Now I know I'm never going to be able to do it. I'm too old for TikTok."

"You are not," Poppy said. "I'm older than you." She scoffed and went back to braiding. "Now, when you get to the bottom, we're just going to sort of squish it all together so that it makes a rectangle."

She kept moving and demonstrating. "I know you can braid, Molly. I've seen Charlotte's hair."

"I really hope I have a boy," Opal said. "Then I won't have to do hair."

Molly snorted as she looked over to her cousin-in-law.

"Are you kidding? Ryder spends more time in the bathroom than any of my kids."

Opal blinked at her, that semi-horrified look back on her face. "Really? What's he doing in there?"

Molly rolled her eyes toward the heavens. "Lord only knows."

That caused everyone to giggle. Then Jane asked, "How are the driving lessons going?"

"Good," Molly said. "I mean, he's been driving around the farm for a while now, so it's really just a matter of trying to get him to pay attention when there's a lot more happening on the road."

"Sure," Jane said.

She'd brought her little boy, Clint, who was about ten months old now. He babbled happily in the living room behind them, and Jane would only go check on him if he started to cry or shriek. He had a stubborn personality already, but Molly supposed that both of his parents did too, and being headstrong wasn't the worst thing a person could be.

Molly had grown up with her daddy as the pastor. She'd learned to cook from a young age, and she actually loved making bread. She'd made it for Hunter early in their relationship, in fact.

As the owner of Pony Power and the matron at Hunter's family farm, Molly had coordinated and hosted plenty of meals, parties, and luncheons, but Poppy existed in a different league.

Molly could make bread and rolls, but she'd never braided it. She'd never studded it with golden raisins and cinnamon or currants and rosemary. But Poppy did all of those things and more. Now that Molly's kids were fairly grown up and would start leaving the house soon, she wanted to start learning some new things too.

Ryder had one more year of high school left, and then he would graduate and be gone. Pinning him down to what he wanted to do after he earned his diploma was like pulling teeth, and Molly had stopped asking. Her oldest talked more about those kinds of things with his father anyway, and Molly had been letting Hunter handle such things for years.

Her girls talked with her. Lisa was only a year behind Ryder in school. She spent almost every afternoon at either Molly's mother's house or her sister's, helping with something. She was definitely more of an indoor person than an outdoor person, despite Hunter and Molly's attempts to get their kids away from screens and out of the house as much as possible.

Charlotte, their third child, and Clay, their youngest son, had taken to Pony Power—probably because they'd grown up the most at the farm. They both worked in the stables before and after school and had been helping with horseback lessons in the summer for a couple of years now, though Clay was only twelve.

Molly loved her family and her farm life and Pony Power with her whole heart and soul.

As Poppy continued with instructions about how to bake the bread and when to put tin foil over it if the cinnamon and butter started to sizzle too soon, Molly zoned out a little bit. She would probably never make this bread, and even if she did, it would absolutely come out burnt on the bottom—just as Poppy was warning them against.

She enjoyed last month's lesson, where Jane had taught them how to make her grandmother's hamburger stew. Molly had had it before, of course, at family functions, but she hadn't seen the recipe until then.

Jane said she'd found it in an old journal of her grandmother's, and that she'd share anything else that she found.

Molly came from a core family steeped in tradition as well, and such things made her feel like she stood on solid ground and always had somewhere to go should she have a question or need help.

"And that's it," Poppy said, dusting her hands on her apron as she turned from the oven, where she'd just slid the braided bread. "Any questions?"

Everyone gathered in her kitchen simply stood there, and then they all started to laugh at the same time, Molly included.

A few days later, Molly rode atop her beautiful pinto horse named Lady. She'd had Lady, with all her soft browns and whites, for several years now, and she loved riding the gentle creature.

She'd gone out with the youngest horseback riding students this morning—the eight-year-olds. Some of them looked like they were still five or six, and though it was only the third week of summer riding lessons, they faced their equines with courage and determination.

Pony Power did a weekly riding lesson, as well as twice a week for beginners, so they could get a handle on the skills faster. She employed over twenty cowboys and cowgirls to help with the riding lessons, and she'd instructed them to always have two people up front and two in the back.

She never wanted anyone to feel alone or afraid if something happened and they got left behind. At Pony Power, it was impossible to be left behind. That could be a scary thing when riding a horse for one of the first times.

Carver and Samantha, a couple of young adults in their twenties, led this group, and Molly rode with Mission in the back. As the foreman of the family farm, Mission really didn't have time to assist with horseback riding lessons anymore—and yet he'd thrown a pretty royal fit when Molly had tried to take him off the schedule.

"I can do it," he'd insisted. "It's one of my favorite

things about being on this farm. Please, at least let me have one lesson a week."

She'd agreed, as long as he didn't have to teach it.

"Fine," he'd said. "I can be a back rider."

And a back rider he had become.

She glanced over to him, though he rode about fifty yards away, over on the other corner of the group, where a couple of girls were slowly plodding along. Molly suspected they were doing a lot more chatting than riding, but on this slow summer day, no one seemed to care.

Molly had spread further south to keep her eye on a trio of boys who certainly didn't have the skills to command the huge horses they rode. But Molly's horses were calm and used to children, and for the most part, they would obey the commands they were given, no matter who gave them.

Something rustled in the long grass to her right, and Molly looked that way, suddenly on high alert. After all, they had snakes on the farm, and horses didn't seem to care if they were harmless or not.

Lady lifted her head and tossed it, then she started to prance sideways.

"Whoa, whoa," Molly said.

Then she heard the rattling.

Lady heard it too, and while she was normally calm and submissive, now she reared up, a whinny coming from her mouth.

The rattling got louder somehow, which made no sense, and then her horse screamed.

And bolted.

Molly had tightened her grip on the reins when she'd first heard the rustling in the grass, and though she was an experienced rider, she could not stay on a spooked, terrified, *bolting* horse.

She slipped from the saddle, panic and fear striking at her as if they were the rattlesnakes sinking their venomous fangs into her heart.

She hit the ground *hard*, a sound she'd never heard before echoing through her head and reverberating through all non-hearing parts of her body. As pain roared through her back and legs, she couldn't get a breath. Her head felt like it had just been split in half.

She heard commotion around her, but she couldn't separate the individual noises enough to make sense of them.

She heard a man call—and she vaguely recognized the voice—but couldn't put a name to it.

More rattling. Louder than before.

Molly groaned, the sound full of desperation mixed with pain, but she still couldn't move. Everything had gone dark, but she wasn't sure she'd closed her eyes.

Help me, sounded inside her head, but she was pretty sure she didn't say it out loud.

"Molly!" Mission yelled, and then he touched her shoulder. "Molly, wake up."

She hadn't realized that she'd gone to sleep, but Mission sounded pretty adamant that she had.

The rattling continued, and she wanted to shout a warning to Mission. *There's a rattlesnake. Don't come too close.*

"Molly, look at me," he demanded again, but the last thing she heard was, "She's not waking up, Boone. Call Nine-One-One."

thirteen

Something spooked that horse, boy.

Mission heard the words in his head in his grandfather's voice, but they could have just as easily come from God.

He currently knelt in the grass next to Molly, and he quickly got to his feet and looked around. One moment she'd been riding along, the horse moving perfectly fluid and gentle as normal. He'd worked plenty with Lady, and the horse never had a problem.

They'd thankfully almost been back to the stables, and Boone had heard Lady scream and come running outside.

Mission had been the closest to Molly, and he'd barked at the girls in front of him to join their group quickly. Then he'd galloped to where she'd been lying on the grass after being thrown from Lady's back.

"Dear Lord," he prayed right out loud. "I cannot have this happen again."

It's not a stampede. The words sounded like Granddad. *This is not your fault. But something spooked that horse, boy.*

He held up one hand as a couple more cowboys came running.

"Lady totally spooked!" he yelled, his eyes roaming the grass in front of him. "There's something here."

Then he heard the rattling.

"Snakes." Panic gripped him right behind the throat, and he forced himself to take a breath—to reason through the fear, to think rationally.

Frantic, he scanned the area in front of Molly, then near her head, where her honey blonde hair splayed out across her shoulders as well as the ground. How in the world could he tell Hunter that something had happened to his wife while on Mission's watch?

He wouldn't have to. This was an accident, and Molly had been in them before.

He looked beyond her, and there—probably eight feet away—sat the coiled rattlesnake.

"It's just past her," he called. "I think there's some over in this long grass too."

"No, she's not waking up," Boone said into his phone as he approached.

Mission moved around Molly and stood between her and the snake while Boone knelt down to check on her.

"She has a pulse. She's just been knocked out. She got thrown off the back of her horse."

"There's definitely rattlesnakes over here too," Zeke called. "Whoo-ee, there's *three* of them over here!"

"All right," Mission said calmly. "I've got my eye on this one. You keep your eye on those."

"Yes, boss," Zeke said.

"Eli."

"Right here," Eli said from Mission's left shoulder.

"Come stand next to me and get your eyes on this snake."

He did.

"You see it right there?"

"I see it, boss."

"I'm gonna send out a farm-wide text. The moment you see it move, you tell me."

"Yes, sir."

Mission's thumbs flew over his phone. *At least four rattlesnakes on the south side of the stables and barn. Keep everyone away.*

He sent that text and immediately started another one.

Lady bolted with Molly on her back. She got thrown and is currently passed out. Boone's called 911 and the paramedics will be coming. Anyone who sees Lady, please secure her and get her back to the stable for an assessment as soon as possible.

I don't think we need more men over here right now, so

please just hold where you are, especially if you have kids with you.

He looked up. The clear blue sky was suddenly the wrong color. How could this happen on such a perfect day? Why did it have to happen here, in only his third week of being foreman?

There have been snakes on this farm before. This time, the voice belonged to him, and it was calm and rational.

Mission turned to Eli. "Hunter is going to come out."

"I'd come out if it was my wife too," Eli said.

"Paramedics will be here in seven minutes," Boone said.

Mission nodded. "She still hasn't woken up, even a little bit?"

Boone shook his head. "Did she hit her head?"

Since Mission didn't have to watch the snake anymore, he pressed his eyes closed and rewound time to when he'd heard Lady scream. Of course, he'd immediately looked over. Molly was already falling from the saddle as the horse beneath her bolted away.

"She hit the ground *hard*," Mission said. "Couldn't catch herself at all."

"I bet she hit her head then. Might have a concussion," Boone said. "She's breathing real good right now."

Mission's phone rang, and Deacon's name sat there. Deacon had grown up with Molly as Hunter's wife, and Mission knew they were close. He took a steadying breath and swiped on the call.

"Paramedics are six minutes out," he said. "Molly is still passed out. She hit the ground pretty hard, sir. I've got the boys bringing out poles to collect the snakes."

"Right here!" Zeke called. "They're here. Mish, they're here right now with the poles."

He nodded over to Zeke and tried to focus on the phone call. "We'll try to clear them before the paramedics get here, so they don't have to worry about the snakes while they're trying to take care of Molly."

"Good," Deacon said. "Hunter is on his way over."

"Of course," Mission said.

"I'm in the north quadrant. I can come if you need me," Deacon offered.

Mission hesitated because he wanted to be strong enough to handle this situation on his own. But Deacon knew every sort of detail of Mission's past, and his offer was really a question: *Do you need me? I will be there if you need me.*

"I got it, boss," Mission said. "Boone's here too, and Hunter will be here soon enough."

"All right then," Deacon drawled. "We'll catch up when I get back to center."

"Yes, sir," Mission said.

For the longest time, Deacon had told everyone that they didn't need to call him *sir*. While he was fifteen years younger than Mission, he owned the farm. He ran it. He was the ultimate boss, and of course, everyone was going to call him *sir*—including Mission.

"These three are cleared," Zeke said.

Mission turned away from his thoughts and the phone call to find Eli reaching for one of their snake hooks and Zeke pushing a big blue trash barrel over the ground toward them.

"They're in here," he said. "We can take them out and let them go somewhere else."

"All right," Mission said. "We don't hear or see any others. I want everyone to fan out and look. We don't need paramedics getting bitten."

They didn't need *anyone* getting bit—but that went without saying.

His phone buzzed, and he glanced down to see a text from Clyde. *I've got Lady and she's hurt. It doesn't look good, boss.*

His heartbeat didn't feel normal in his chest, and he wasn't sure how to get it to stop throbbing so violently against the vein in his neck.

I'll call Kristie, he said, and the moment that text went through, he tapped to do just that.

She didn't pick up on the first ring or the second, and Mission turned his back on the cowboys who were scooping up the last rattler and putting it in the bin.

"Come on, Kris," he muttered under his breath.

Then her bright, "Hey, baby," came through the line.

They'd been dating for almost three weeks now, and Mission sure liked her a whole lot. She'd settled into calling him "baby" and "cowboy" while he still called her "kitten" and nothing else. But now was no time for flirting.

"I need you at the farm immediately," he said in his no-nonsense, super-serious cowboy tone. "Molly's horse got spooked by a snake, and she got thrown—and the horse is injured."

"Oh, no," Kristie said. "I'll be there as soon as I can."

With that promise, Mission softened. "Thank you, kitten. I haven't seen the horse yet, but the report from one of my boys is that it's not good. I'm gonna stay with Molly until Hunter or the paramedics get here. Then I'll be with Lady."

"All right," Kristie said. "I'm just finishing up with a momma pig, but I'm about twenty minutes away."

Mission gritted his teeth, as there wasn't much else he could do. "Okay," he said. "See you soon." He ended the call just as Hunter rounded the corner at a jog. Mission waved his hand above his head, as if Hunter couldn't see them standing there.

"Lady got spooked by rattlesnakes," he said as Hunter approached. "She couldn't stay on. She hit the ground pretty hard."

Hunter nodded, and he hurried past Mission to his wife. Torn between staying with Molly and going to find Lady, Mission took a few steps back toward the people who'd given him a place to belong and a second chance at everything.

"Mols," Hunter said. "Hey, Mols, you gotta wake up, baby, okay?"

She groaned, and Hunter immediately added, "Don't move, baby. Just wake up for me. Just look at me. Let me see your eyes."

Boone took a couple of steps away and said, "She's waking up."

"Well, that's good, right?" Mission asked.

"It's not bad," Boone said. "Other than now she's going to be able to feel whatever hurts."

Mission nodded. "Clyde's got Lady. He says it's not great. I'm going to go see what's going on with that."

"You called Kristie?"

"She's on the way."

"All right. I'll stay here with Hunt," Boone said.

"You boys," Mission called out. "Carver and Samantha are gonna need your help finishing up the riding lesson. Can you get over there and do that? Molly and I were the back riders."

"You got it, boss," Zeke and Eli said.

Mission then turned to find his own horse standing several paces away, as if nothing at all had happened. He strode over to Templeton and swung onto his back.

"Come on, boy," he said. "Let's go find Lady."

He moved away from the chaos—though it still existed in his soul. When he felt certain no one would overhear him, he gripped the reins a little tighter and prayed. "Dear God, please bless Molly to make it through this with the mildest of injuries. Bless Lady that she won't be so injured that we can't save her. And please, *please* bless Kristie to get here fast, fast, fast."

fourteen

Kristie rounded the bend, and the big red administration barn came into view. An ambulance had been backed in, lights still flashing, and the seriousness of the situation descended upon her. People and cars seemed to be *every*where, and she couldn't find anywhere to park until she had gone halfway down the fence toward the house.

She pulled in and jumped out, the busyness of Pony Power and the farm making the air tight and hard to breathe. One hundred yards away, the ambulance went *whoop, whoop* and pulled out—siren silent, but lights still rotating. The tension snapped, but Kristie's emotions still wobbled within her.

Everyone here loved Molly—from her family to the cowboys and cowgirls, to the counselors, to all the kids who came here for horseback riding lessons. Heck, Kristie herself loved Molly, and all she could do now was pray the woman would be okay. She did that and forced herself to be calm and rational as she moved with purposeful yet measured steps to the back of her SUV.

She'd been in emergency situations before, and she didn't need to panic. It never helped anyone. She lifted the gate and shouldered her heavy backpack of medical supplies. She had two cases with more equipment and medicine. She dragged those out, closed the gate, and headed down the fence.

Mission had texted ten minutes ago that they had gotten Lady safely into the last stall in the back stable. That meant Kristie had to walk down the length of the fence and then turn right and walk the entire length of the administration barn, the first stable, and then the second.

She put her eyes on the ground and focused on putting one foot in front of the other. As she walked, she passed the pasture and the two walking circles on her right. All of the buildings were connected by roofs to keep snow and muck off the dirt ground.

Under the roof between the barn and the first stable, she found a second group of horseback riders getting ready to go out for their lesson. The teenagers parted for her, and she gave them a tight smile as she moved through their midst and kept going.

The first stable had pastures beyond it, with the counselor cabins for the kids' therapy sessions on the other side of them.

Kristie kept walking, the afternoon heat beating down on her and causing sweat to run down the side of her face and the back of her neck. She couldn't brush it away, so she simply kept going.

She finally ducked into the shade of the second stable and entered the door there, her muscles quivering.

"Hello?" she called, hoping Mission would hear her and come relieve her of one of these cases.

No one answered, and no one came, so Kristie kept going. The scent of hay and wood filled the stable, and she told herself that was better than blood. No one had texted an update on Lady's condition, and Kristie had no idea what she'd find in the last stable.

Her steps became shorter and more stilted as her body started to protest more violently that she could not continue like this. Exhaling, she paused and set down the cases. She had passed another several stalls, so she tried again with, "Hello?"

"Yep, I'm coming," Mission called, and his footsteps came jogging toward her.

Relief filled her from head to toe, and she managed to smile at him.

"Hey," he said, and the absence of his usual grin told her how anxious and serious he'd become.

"Hey." She shook her hands out to relieve the tightness from gripping the case handles.

"You should've texted me you were here."

Kristie glared at him, because while they'd been dating for almost a month now, she hadn't told him she absolutely loathed it when someone started a sentence with, *You should've.*

She was the professional, and she wouldn't have texted other farm owners or foremen to come help her with her heavy equipment.

"It's crazy out there," she said instead.

Mission looked beyond her for just a moment. "Yeah. That's why we've got her back here," he said. "Everyone's been told not to come into this stable, so it should stay quiet."

Kristie nodded as he bent to pick up her cases. "She's back here." He moved that way, and Kristie went behind him.

"How many people are back here?" she asked.

"Just me and Gloria," he said.

Kristie nodded. That was good.

"Has Lady eaten or had anything to drink?" she asked.

"No."

Also good, and Kristie shouldn't have been surprised. Gloria Whettstein was a master horsewoman and the barn manager here at the farm and for Pony Power. She ran a meticulous stable and knew a great deal about horses. She'd probably already diagnosed the injury, and if she couldn't take care of it, that told Kristie it would be something serious.

"It's her front right leg," Mission said over his shoulder. "We've got her in a stall, but she won't put any weight on it."

"She's tied?"

"Yep. She shouldn't give you a problem."

Gloria came forward to meet them, giving Kristie a quick hug. "Thank you so much for coming so fast."

"Of course," Kristie said.

As Gloria faded back, Mission set her cases down, and Kristie looked at the horse in the stall. "Can we open these doors?"

Mission moved to do that, and Kristie took a breath to calm herself even further. Horses could *feel* energy, and she wanted Lady to read nothing but a calm, powerful, caring presence from her.

The horse stood in the center of the stall, trembling. Her eyes were too wide and rimmed with a little bit of white. That didn't settle Kristie's worry. Lady was one of the most beautiful horses Kristie had ever laid eyes on, and it felt like a punch to the chest to see her like this—hurting and afraid and unable to stand on her own.

Gloria and Mission had put her front leg in a sling, with the knee resting there and the hoof pointed toward the back. Other than that, she didn't look injured, and Kristie stepped over to her with her palm forward.

Lady's nostrils flared and her ears twitched, but she didn't move, as she'd been tied in cross ties.

"Hey, Lady," Kristie said in a calm, even voice. "Remember me? We're friends."

She placed her hand on the long bridge of the horse's nose, glad when Lady pressed into it. She ran that hand up and over Lady's head, down both sides of her neck and over the left shoulder, simply feeling and connecting to the animal.

"I put a blanket on her," Gloria said. "Just to keep her warm."

Kristie nodded. "It's okay," she said, though she really would rather analyze a horse's injuries without any interference. "Heard you got spooked by some snakes," she said, smiling at Lady.

The horse blinked, but her eyes didn't soften; her anxiety remained.

Kristie turned and gathered all of her equipment closer to the right front side of the horse. Since she didn't have to work behind Lady, she wasn't worried about getting kicked or hurt.

She met Mission's eyes, and she didn't ask before he moved to Lady's left shoulder and put one quiet, firm hand against her neck. His expression had been carved from stone, drawn in that way that Kristie had learned meant he was trying not to feel too much.

Gloria simply stayed out of the way and said nothing.

"All right, Lady," Kristie said. "Let's see what we've got."

She knelt down on the right side and looked at her injured leg. Sweat, dirt, and blood streaked the horse's rich brown and white coat, starting at about the knee and moving down and over the hoof.

Kristie reached to unzip her backpack, which she did slowly, so as to not startle anyone with the noise. She pulled out the spotlight and set it up so she could see better. She opened her case and pulled out her cleaning supplies.

"I'm going to clean and flush this to see what I've got."

"Okay," Gloria said, while Mission grunted.

Kristie pulled on a pair of gloves and worked quickly and efficiently from there, noting that Lady's shoe was completely gone. She didn't look up as she asked, "Did either of you take her shoe off?"

"No," Mission and Gloria said together.

"She got into something, then," Kristie said.

"She has one tiny scratch along her chest," Gloria said. "Clyde found her by the wood pile."

Kristie immediately thought of anything sharp that could be near a wood pile, and an ax or a hatchet came to mind. Lady would have had to step on that exactly right —or exactly wrong—and perhaps she had.

With everything clean, Kristie could easily see the wound, and it wasn't good. She reached for a syringe and rattled through her medications to find the numbing agent.

"I'm going to numb this," she said. "I can't stitch it. There's too much movement and risk of trapping bacteria inside."

"What do you see?" Gloria asked.

"She's got a deep laceration," Kristie said, keeping her voice low, even, matter-of-fact. "It went into the laminae."

She glanced over at Gloria, who exhaled a slow breath, her eyes narrowing slightly. Mission didn't move at all.

Kristie focused back on the hoof. "The laminae connect the hoof wall to the internal structures. They're too delicate to stitch, and the risk of infection is huge. When they're injured like this, it can go south really fast."

"How fast?" Mission asked.

Kristie hesitated—not because she didn't know the answer to his question, but because this horse mattered. To the farm, sure, but also to Molly. To Hunter. To Mission. And likely to a whole tangle of kids who came through Pony Power and found their courage from seeing Molly sitting on Lady's back.

"We'll have to watch this closely for infection," she said. "And we need to get the inflammation down. If we can't control both of those, we're looking at laminitis. It's painful. Very hard to recover from."

She paused and looked at Mission, then Gloria.

"Some horses don't." She had to be honest; it wouldn't be fair to give Molly and Hunter false hope. Silence settled over the three of them like a wet blanket on a dark night.

"But we're not there yet," Kristie said as brightly as she could. "Right now, she's doing great. She's letting me treat her. She's scared and hurting, but I'm going to numb this and clean it more thoroughly."

Hooves were so dirty—really the worst part of a horse that could be injured—but Kristie kept that to herself.

"I'll text Hunter and Deacon," Gloria said, and she moved away to do that.

Kristie kept working, and Mission kept Lady right at his shoulder, holding her and shushing her when she snuffled or moved. Kristie administered the shots to numb the wound and gave Lady the pain medication that would make her more comfortable.

She also administered an antibiotic and flushed and cleaned the wound three times to make sure she'd gotten everything. The scent of metal, antiseptic, and medicine filled the air, and Kristie found it oddly comforting.

She started to wrap the hoof. "We want to check this and make sure it's not bleeding several times a day."

With the hoof partially bandaged, Kristie got out her portable X-ray machine and set it up. "I'm just going to make sure there's nothing broken," she said. "I don't think there is—I think we'd see a lot more damage to the leg if there was."

"All right," Mission said, as if she needed his permission to do her job.

She took the images and examined them. "I don't see any broken bones," she told Mission.

"That's good news," he said.

She clipped the image to the clipboard on the wall, not knowing what it was for but assuming Gloria—and perhaps Molly—would want to see it.

"I'm going to finish this bandage and put her in ice boots," she said. "I have those and some hoof support pads back at my house. I'll have to go get them."

"What've we got?" Deacon asked as he returned with Gloria.

Kristie quickly went through everything again for him, and then asked, "How's Molly?"

"We just heard," Deacon said. "She's awake and doing well."

"They're going to keep her overnight, though," Gloria said, shooting Deacon a look that said so much. "She's got a moderate concussion."

"She lost consciousness for a long time," Kristie said. "I'm surprised they didn't say it was severe."

"Oh, it's severe," Deacon said. "But she can remember before and after the fall. She hasn't thrown up. She does have some trouble answering questions, and she's got a headache. They've put her in a dark room."

"She'll need several days of rest," Kristie said. "Have they done a CT scan?"

"Yeah. Everything came back okay," Gloria said. "She doesn't have any broken bones."

Relief rushed through Kristie. "Oh, that's great news," she said. "Lady doesn't have any broken bones either." She indicated the X-ray on the clipboard. "But it could take months for the laminae to heal. And Lady will need around-the-clock attention for the next few days."

Deacon moved over to the X-ray but didn't touch it.

"I'm not sure what my schedule is," she continued. "But I told Mission I needed to run home and get a few more things for her. Then, when I get back, I can clear tomorrow to stay with her."

"We'd appreciate that," Deacon said. "Is this stall gonna be okay?" He nodded to where Lady stood comfortably, her leg back in the sling.

Kristie turned and surveyed it, noting that Lady's eyes had softened, and she only held them halfway open at the moment. She moved over to the gentle creature and stroked both hands down her neck.

"She has a scratch here?" she asked.

"Right there," Mission murmured, moving lower than Kristie had. It was superficial—barely any blood.

"I'll clean it anyway," Kristie said, collecting an anti-septic wipe from her backpack. "I think this stall is too big. I don't want her to feel trapped in a small stall, but I don't want her to be able to move too much."

She turned toward Mission, Deacon, and Gloria and tossed her cleaning towelette in the garbage can. "The medical barn would be better," she said. "I know you guys air condition and heat that, and we don't want Lady to be too hot or too cold. We'll have to monitor her temperature, keep track of when she gets medications and antibiotics, make sure she's eating and drinking, and check her bandages every few hours."

She met Deacon's eye. "Have you got a whiteboard where I can set all that up, so everyone knows where she is in her care?"

"Yeah, sure," Deacon said.

"I can bring one from my house."

"We've got 'em," Deacon said.

She nodded and turned to Gloria. "Can one of you continue to administer her medications after the first couple of days?" Kristie asked. "I won't be able to stay here indefinitely."

The three of them looked at one another, with all eyes finally settling on Gloria.

"I can do it," she said. "I can have Gerty come out too. She's really good with that kind of stuff."

Kristie nodded. Gerty Hammond *was* exceptional with horses as well, from training them to nursing them back to health.

"All right," she said. "The whiteboard will help keep track of all of that." She turned to pack up her backpack and put her equipment and supplies back in the cases.

"I'll just run back to my house and get the hoof

support pads and the ice boots. We'll keep this wound iced tonight to keep the inflammation down."

"Thank you, Kristie," Gloria said.

"Yes, thank you," Deacon added.

Kristie put on her backpack, and Mission picked up her two cases. "I'll walk you out," he said.

"Can you guys get her in the medical barn while I'm gone?" she asked.

"Sure thing," Deacon said, like it would just be a walk in the park.

Kristie nodded, glad the injury wasn't worse, and hopeful that she would be able to nurse Lady back to full health.

She just had to, because she couldn't imagine how devastating the loss of Lady would be to everyone here at this farm.

* * *

The sun had slipped behind the mountains hours ago, but the heat and exhaustion of the day still lingered in Kristie's clothes and beneath her skin. Tension buzzed under her ribs like static, and she walked away from the medical barn and into the darkness to release it.

She took a deep breath and pushed the noise out, relieved when it streamed away.

Lady had been moved to the smaller stall with rubber

pads and plenty of straw for comfort. The temperature was being perfectly regulated, and Kristie had just administered the second dose of medication, checked the bandages, replaced them, and put on the ice boots for the second time. The horse was as comfortable as she could possibly be, and the wound looked as good as Kristie could've hoped for.

She stretched her back and did a few knee lifts to work out the stiffness from being down on the ground so much tonight.

"When's the last time you ate?" Mission's soft voice came out of the darkness.

She turned toward him as he approached and let out a tired breath that was almost a laugh. "Lunch?" she guessed.

He reached up and pushed her hair back, leaned down and kissed her chastely for only a moment, then threaded his fingers through hers and took her back toward the medical barn.

"Gerty came to sit with her for tonight," he said. "To give us all a break."

Kristie almost started to cry in relief, though part of her wanted to stay with Lady herself. The barn lights cast long shadows into the night, but Mission avoided them, and the scent of bandages and blood got replaced by the sweeter smells of hay and sweat and summer.

As he led her along the fence of the back pasture, he stayed close—but quiet—and she didn't need words to feel what settled between them.

Exhaustion, absolutely, but she felt strong with him at her side.

He made the uncertain steadier, and she...trusted him. With every step he took up toward his cabin, Kristie fell a little bit more in love with him.

The slide usually scared her, but after tonight—seeing his calm steadiness in the face of emergency and fear and injury—Kristie trusted that he wouldn't let anything bad happen to her either.

fifteen

Mission really appreciated that Kristie did not argue with him about leaving Lady with Gerty—or going with him back to his cabin. In fact, she stayed silent all the way back to his house. The front steps creaked as he walked up them and opened his front door.

"Do you want to shower?" he asked quietly, making his voice match the night around them.

She looked at him with a measure of hope in her eyes. "Could I?"

He smiled and nodded. "I have two bathrooms, so you won't even have to use mine." He took off his hat and hung it on the hook, then gestured down the hall. "I already got some extra clothes from Judy, and she gave me some...more feminine toiletries as well, so you won't smell like a cowboy."

He cleared his throat and moved into the kitchen, so Kristie could go past him and down the hall. "I put it all in the bathroom for you."

She blinked at him, her eyes wide. "Thank you, Mission," she said, the level of sincerity in her voice unlike anything he'd heard from her before.

She looked absolutely haggard, and Mission didn't blame her. The workday had almost been finished when he'd called her, and she'd worked on Lady, gone back to her house, then returned and done more with the horse.

Mission hadn't had time to go to town for groceries, but he had made all other arrangements so Kristie could be comfortable, get cleaned up, and sleep in his guest room—should she choose to.

"How do you feel about breakfast for a late-night dinner?" he asked. He, too, felt as if he had been run over by a thresher, but he opened the fridge to get out the eggs.

"Breakfast sounds amazing," she said, and then she rushed at him.

"Hey, okay." He set the eggs on the counter quickly and received her into his arms. She clung to him, and Mission wished he could erase time and get those rattlesnakes somewhere else before Molly and Lady happened by.

"I'm going to shower for a while," she finally said. "Just to calm down. So don't make anything until I'm done, okay?"

"All right," he murmured.

She pulled away and looked at him, reaching up to brush his hair off his forehead. "I still haven't cut your hair."

Before he could respond, she tipped up and pressed her lips to his, kissing him in a new and needful way. She didn't carry on too long, quickly settling back onto her feet and clearing her throat.

She let her hair fall between them and then tucked it away. "I'll go shower." She turned abruptly and hurried out of the kitchen and down the hall. Mission stared after her until he heard the click of the bathroom door, which jolted him back to himself.

He wouldn't start Kristie's sandwich until she came out of the bathroom, but he needed other elements to put everything together.

He pulled out the package of bacon and put several slices in a frying pan. He sliced a tomato and then several pieces of Colby Jack cheese. He tended to the bacon until it was crisp, then tonged it out of the pan onto a plate with a paper towel and set that aside. Then he whisked a couple of eggs together with a tiny bit of milk, salt, and pepper.

That went next to the stove, ready to be poured in the pan. The shower still ran in the bathroom, which sat right on the other side of the wall. He didn't know what "a long time" meant for Kristie, but she did stay in the shower for a while.

Mission sometimes didn't like being at-one with his

thoughts in the silence, but tonight, he opted for that instead of turning on the radio or the TV. He settled on his couch and looked at his phone, hoping to find a dog well-suited to farm life. He'd been looking for a couple of weeks and hadn't felt good about any of the canines that came up for rehoming.

He pushed his hand through his hair as it kept falling over his eyes, and he really did need to get it cut. He really wanted Kristie to do it, but summer was a very busy time on farms and ranches, and while he saw her almost every day, he hadn't been able to schedule a haircut yet.

He lifted his head when the water turned off in the bathroom. He got to his feet and went into the kitchen, lit the stove again, and set the pan that had fried the bacon over the flame. He used a paper towel to soak up some of the fat and tossed that in the trash. Then he poured the eggs in, the satisfying sizzle making him sink into the comforts of home.

He laid two pieces of cheese at the top of the pan and two at the bottom, the egg making the round shape inside it.

Kristie joined him just as he picked up the two slices of bread. "You like egg sandwiches, right?" he asked, though he knew she did.

She pressed right into his left side, looping her arm through it and holding it with both of her hands. "What are you doing here?" she asked as he laid the top piece of bread over the cheese, with the curved top near the curved edge of the pan.

He did the same with the second piece of bread, matching up the curves, and tilted his head to look at her. She gazed into the pan as if he was completing some sort of magic spell.

"The egg is going to cook," he said. "Then I'll flip the whole thing over to toast the bread. I'll add more cheese on the other side, so you'll have cheese, egg, cheese. Then we fold the round parts of the egg in on the sides, and I add a little tomato and a little bacon, and then fold the whole thing together."

"So that's why you put the two bottoms of the bread together." She pointed to where they met in the middle.

"Yep," he said.

She turned her head and beamed up at him. "This is genius, Mission."

He smiled on a day when he didn't feel like smiling, because Kristie made everything warmer and brighter. "It's an egg sandwich, kitten."

"I've never seen anyone make an egg sandwich like this."

He looked back into the pan. "It's how my grandmother made them. It's great if you don't want a runny egg."

He slipped a spatula under the whole thing and flipped it over.

"Now the bread will start to toast," he said, reaching for more cheese.

"Genius," Kristie said.

He finished putting on more cheese, then folded up the sides of the scrambled egg patty, and laid bacon on the top half, and a slice of tomato on the bottom. Sometimes he didn't wait long enough for the bread to get toasty, and he forced himself to wait.

With a hot pan and bacon grease, it didn't take long, and then Mission folded the top piece of bread over the bottom one and pulled the whole sandwich out and put it on a plate.

"It's pretty toasty," he said, pleased with the crisp brown outside of the bread. "And you got it fried in bacon fat, so it'll be doubly delicious."

She didn't move away from his side, and he looked at her with the plated sandwich in his hand. "Do you want to sit on the couch or at the bar?"

"Couch," she said.

She finally moved that way, and even in someone else's clothes, the sight of her struck lightning through Mission's heart.

"There's pajamas in the bedroom," he said, glancing at the clock on the microwave. Ten-thirty already. He should've been in bed an hour ago, as tomorrow would dawn at the same time as always—and it would be another day on the farm as usual.

The sun and stars and rotational gravity of the earth

didn't seem to care when someone got thrown from a horse and had to stay in the hospital. Or that a beloved equine now had to be monitored around the clock to ensure her survival.

Life marched on. Mission had learned that from his granddad.

"Oh, I don't think I'll sleep here," she said.

Mission handed her the plate and cocked his eyebrows. "No?"

"Someone will have to go check on Lady at...." She peered around him. "Two-thirty."

"Gerty can do it," Mission said.

"Gerty has a three-year-old." Kristie picked up her sandwich and took a bite.

Mission turned his back on her and went into the kitchen. He'd managed to eat a protein bar about seven o'clock. Having Matt come out to help pick up the slack Gloria had left when she'd stuck by Lady's side for the past several hours had been a real help.

He scrambled together a couple more eggs and poured them into the pan. "I think they already have a schedule for tonight."

"Well, no one told me about that," Kristie said. "I'm the vet."

"And you've got Lady exactly where she needs to be." He didn't want to argue with her, but his frustration started to foam within him. Why couldn't Kristie just accept that she didn't have to do everything?

"Gerty came over, and she's going to be here until five, when Deacon is going to go out and sit with Lady. They both know how to check bandages, and Gerty can administer the meds. Gloria will be here by six-thirty to do the next round of antibiotics and medicine. You said nine-thirty, two-thirty, and six-thirty, right?"

Mission knew he was right. He had paid close attention to what Kristie had said. He, Deacon, and Gloria had put together the whiteboard she'd asked for, and she'd filled it out with the columns she wanted to keep track of —antibiotics, pain meds, bandage checking, what Lady ate and drank, and her temperature.

Everyone was perfectly dedicated to making sure Lady made a full recovery.

"Yes," Kristie said. "But—"

"There's no 'but.'" He slapped down the cheese and put the bread over it, then turned toward her. "Kris, you don't have to personally be there."

She'd taken a few bites of her sandwich, and now she set it back on her plate. "She's *my* responsibility."

"Is she?" Mission asked. "You're the vet, like you said. You came and did your job. Do you sit at a horse's bedside for days on end every time there's an injury on a farm?"

Her expression stormed. Her jaw tightened, and Mission had the answer to his question. Exactly. She didn't at other farms, and she didn't need to here.

"There are plenty of capable people here," he said to drive his point home. He probably shouldn't even be having this conversation right now. Not when they were both exhausted, hungry, and worried.

But he couldn't help adding, "You don't have to be the one sitting outside the stall."

"Who else is going to do it?" she barked at him. She picked up her sandwich and took another bite. When she looked at him this time, her expression held plenty of challenge.

"You don't trust us here, is that it?"

Her eyes fired lasers at him as she chewed and swallowed. "That horse has a very serious condition, and—"

"We know that," Mission said, almost over the top of her. "A lot of us have a lot of experience with horses. And I don't know all the technical terms, and I don't have a portable X-ray machine in the back of my car, but I understood you when you told me what was wrong with Lady, and what we needed to do to make sure there was no infection. Those we've put on the schedule know how to check that, and they all have your number. We don't expect you to rearrange your whole schedule to sit with Lady."

He turned back to the pan and flipped his bread and eggs. He added the rest of his sandwich ingredients and folded his bread together.

Realizing he'd rushed the toasting out of frustration, he put it back in the pan and turned to the fridge.

"I've got milk or orange juice," he said. "Or water."

"Orange juice, please," Kristie said, her voice made of meekness.

Mission pulled out the carton and poured her a glass. He took it over to her and crouched down in front of her. "It's okay to rely on someone besides yourself."

Her face turned red. She looked like she might spit some harsh words at him, but she took a shallow breath and puffed it out. Then another one. The third time it became longer, and the color in her face drained away.

"I'm trying," she said. "It's hard for me to trust people." Open vulnerability sat in her expression then, and Mission nodded because he understood.

"Do you trust me?" he asked.

It took her a moment while she glanced down at her sandwich before she looked at him again—and nodded.

"All right, then, kitten." He smiled at her. "So let's just take this night to rest and recover. Okay? You can sit with Lady all day tomorrow, if you want."

He expected her to throw some of her sass back at him, but instead she nodded and said, "Okay, Mish. Thank you."

He dropped to his knees and took her face in his hands. He wanted to tell her that he admired her strength and resilience. That he'd loved watching her work with such a cool and calm demeanor that evening. That he would stand between her and *anyone* who dared to hurt her, and that his heart ached knowing she'd been living in a place where she didn't trust anyone around her.

He didn't know how to put all of those feelings into words, so he simply leaned forward and kissed her.

They'd shared many kisses over the past couple of weeks, but again, this one felt different, even from the quick one she'd given him before going to shower.

Mission felt like he needed to have his mouth on hers to keep breathing. He needed her presence in his life for it to have any meaning at all, and he kissed her with all of those powerful things flowing through him, hoping she would feel and understand them as if he had spoken them out loud.

The best part about kissing Kristie was that she kissed him back with the same level of passion and power and, yes, trust.

As he kept kissing her, Mission hoped and prayed that he could lose his heart to this woman...while keeping it intact.

sixteen

Kristie lay down on the couch while Mission finished up with the dishes in the kitchen. She wasn't surprised that he couldn't leave them until morning, but she was surprised that she didn't fall asleep instantly.

He'd said he'd set out pajamas in the spare bedroom and that she could stay there until morning if she wanted to. And she wanted to, because she'd parked back over at the red barn and would either need to walk back to her car or get a ride and then drive home.

The noise in the kitchen dulled as Mission finished cleaning up. He turned off the lights, leaving only one pale yellow one shining above the stove. His footsteps came closer, and his fingertips whispered across her forehead.

"You asleep, kitten?"

"Almost," she whispered.

He knelt down in front of her. "Do you want to sleep here or in the bedroom?"

"I don't know where my phone is," she said. "I need it to set an alarm."

"It's on the counter," he said. "Here or the bedroom?"

She opened her eyes and found him close. The world narrowed to just the two of them in this small living room. Nothing could get to her here, and if anything tried, Mission would stand between her and it—protecting her, feeding her, and making sure she had every comfort life could offer.

She reached out and curled her hand around his ear, this connection between them so real and vibrant.

"I really think you'd be more comfortable in the bedroom," he murmured.

"All right," she whispered.

The next thing she knew, Mission had stood and was lifting her into his arms. She gasped and then grabbed onto his shoulders. He swiped her phone from the counter as he passed by, and he turned left into the first room.

"There's a fan in here if you get hot," he said before he carefully laid her down on the soft bed with the downy pillows. She tucked her feet under the blanket that had already been pulled back, and he started to pull the comforter up.

She stopped him with her hand on his and asked, "Will you hold me until I fall asleep?"

The faint light that shone in from the kitchen barely illuminated his face, and Kristie didn't need to see it anyway. He sat down on the edge of the bed and removed his cowboy boots, then rolled onto the bed, taking her in his arms with great ease.

She sighed fully, relaxing into his embrace as she twined her fingers through his. He pulled the blanket up over both of them and exhaled over her shoulder.

"You didn't change into the pajamas," he whispered.

"If I get called in the middle of the night," she whispered back. "I want to be ready to go."

"Wake me up if that happens," he said.

Kristie had no doubt he'd probably just sleep on the couch, so she couldn't try to sneak out without telling him. Warmth spread through her with her back pressed against his chest, and everything inside her stilled and calmed.

"My dad owns a big animal and farm supply company in Phoenix," she whispered. Everything was so much easier to say when she didn't have to see Mission's face. "Everyone knows the Higgins."

The words came out bitter, and as Kristie let them go, she realized they didn't have to live and fester inside her anymore once they'd been spoken.

"We were a picture-perfect family," she said. "We went to church every week. My mother hosted book club.

Our lawn won Garden of the Year three times when I was a teenager."

"Wow. Three times?" Mission whispered.

A small smile came to Kristie's face. "I'm six years younger than my older brother, and Dean didn't go to college. He worked with my dad."

"Mm." Mission traced a slow circle on the back of her hand with his thumb, further calming her.

"They were thrilled when I got into veterinary school, and there was a place waiting for me to open my clinic in the back of the commercial store that my dad and brother ran when I graduated."

"Sounds like a nice setup," Mission said.

"It *was* a nice setup," Kristie said. "Dad had a regular stream of customers coming in who owned farms and ranches, even if they were small or hobby-like. I had a lot of business."

She stilled there, memories of her old life streaming through her like someone flipping pages in a book. Mission didn't need to ask why she left, and she simply breathed into the space he gave her by remaining silent.

"One day, about a year after I finished school and everything was going well, Dad brought me a stack of prescriptions. Things used with livestock—steroids. Sedatives. Tranquilizers. Definitely things I had written prescriptions for in the past. They weren't illegal, but they also weren't for clients."

"I asked him what they were for, and he said he sold

them to his friends on the side. That veterinary clinics could definitely do that. A vet doesn't always have to administer every shot, you know."

She heard the bitterness in her own tone, and how it had lowered to mimic something her father had said to her.

Mission's arms around hers tightened, and Kristie realized that she had tensed as well. She breathed in and then out, trying to release her muscles. It only sort of worked.

"My name went on all the prescriptions. On all the orders. But I had no idea how the medications were being used. Then one of my dad's family friends—that I had known my whole life; who we'd gone to church with for decades—came into the clinic, and he wanted more controlled substances—not for animals. I was a doctor; I could do it.

"I didn't want to do it, and when I talked to my father about it, he said, 'We're helping people. That's what you do as a doctor.'"

"I'm sorry, Kris," Mission murmured.

"And of *course*, I want to help people—and animals. I still didn't fill the prescriptions, and the next day, my dad *and* his friend came in together to confront me. I heard things like, 'Don't be so rigid, Kristie. You want your practice to survive, don't you? We can go somewhere else.'

"Dean texted me all day long and told me this type of

thing was normal. That everyone in the farming industry did it.... So I filled the prescriptions."

She let out a shuddering breath, the story almost done. "And I've hated myself for it ever since."

"Oh, I'm sorry, kitten," Mission said, pressing his lips against her earlobe.

"I didn't feel right about it—whether it was legal or not—and I wouldn't do it again. When my dad confronted me, I told him he'd have to find someone else to write the prescriptions. Dean tried to convince me, and I told him the same thing. They came together, and I told them I would shut down my clinic and leave town. And you know what he said?"

"I don't know, kitten," Mission said.

"'Then go. Good luck starting over somewhere else.'" Kristie could still hear the words as if they'd just been spoken to her.

"They told me I'd have to leave the state. That I wouldn't be able to set up a practice *anywhere* in Arizona, and since my clinic was part of their family business and tied to their supply store, I lost everything."

"Really?" Mission asked.

"I packed up my apartment with my dad and my brother standing outside the door, checking every box that went out. It was humiliating and horrifying. I was angry and hurt, and I thought, if I couldn't trust my own father and brother, then I could never trust anyone ever again."

"Kitten, that's just not true."

"I know that now," she said. "But it's still very hard for me to trust others. I learned that love and loyalty was conditional. If I did what Dad said, everything was great. If I didn't—good luck out there."

"Oh, I'm so sorry." He moved his hand to her hip and traced slow circles there. "Love and loyalty from family should not be conditional."

"I clean the church, because my faith in God was shaken by what happened. How my mom and dad and brother were these pillars of our church, and yet doing questionable things in the dark." She took a breath, not quite done yet.

"I clean, because it's how I make peace with what I don't understand. And it's how I show God that I'm not perfect, but I'm also *not* broken by what happened."

"I don't think you're broken, Kris," Mission said. "I think you're the strongest woman I've ever met."

She turned to face him, burying her face in his chest and breathing in the powerful, woodsy scent of his clothing.

"I know I could bend more than I do," she said. "I try to do everything the right way, no exceptions, even when it's hard, and even when it hurts. And I know God doesn't expect that of me. But it's still hard for me to let go of it."

"You've built an amazing clinic here," Mission reminded her. "And you've got your baking friends, and *so* many people who love and admire and respect you."

She nodded against his chest. "Lennie and Harper and Jocelyn were sent from God. They've taught me that friendship doesn't have to come with strings. They don't make me talk about my family. They just pass the brownies and make me laugh."

Mission moved his hand slowly up and down her back. "I'm glad you have them."

"For a while, I was convinced that there was something wrong with me," she said. "That I wasn't trustworthy or lovable or worth protecting."

She pulled away slightly and looked up at him. Since she'd been in the dark for a while, her eyes had adjusted, and she could see him quite clearly.

"And it's weird," she said. "Because *you* seem to trust me. And *you* seem to like me. And *you* have done so many things to take care of me and protect me."

Tears filled her eyes, and Kristie couldn't go on, lest her voice would come out squeaky.

"I'm falling in love with you, kitten," he whispered. "I like the fiery side of you that questions me and everyone else. Sometimes rigidity is a good quality."

She nodded as he pressed his lips to her forehead. Kristie settled into his embrace again, her story out. Because it didn't infect her anymore and the story didn't have to run from one side of her mind to the other until she was simply too tired to stay awake, Kristie was able to close her eyes, exhale, and fall asleep in a single breath.

seventeen

Tarr Olson wiped the sweat from his brow with the back of his forearm, stepping back to survey his handiwork. The new goat enclosure was coming along nicely. The tallest, sturdy cedar post was firmly planted in the ground, ready for the fencing to be attached. The "Goatel" that Bobbie Jo had commissioned him to make stood proudly behind that, and Tarr needed to finish the fencing and the gate, and then her kids could move in.

The summer sun beat down mercilessly, but Tarr didn't mind. He'd always preferred physical labor outdoors over being cooped up inside. When he'd gotten too sweaty, he'd draped his shirt on a nail on the side of the barn and kept working. But now, he moved into the sliver of shade there to pick up his water bottle.

"Looking good," Tuck said.

Tarr turned to see him standing at the corner of the barn. He held two water bottles and added, "I guess you don't need this."

"I'll take it," Tarr said, reaching for what would surely be colder water than he had.

Tucker was Tarr's best friend—and technically his boss, but he never acted like it. When Tarr had worked at the Hammond family farm, he'd learned that all the Hammonds treated their employees more like extended family than hired hands.

He downed another couple of swallows of ice water, his throat aching, but the rest of him grateful that he'd stopped to take a drink. "I should have the fencing up by tomorrow. Then Bobbie Jo's goats can have their new playground."

Tuck chuckled and joined Tarr in the few inches of shade that the roof of the barn gave off at this time of day. "She'll be thrilled."

Tuck surveyed the goat hotel and grinned. "She's really happy that your construction skills will be able to save her goats from the coyotes."

"I'm surprised there weren't stronger fortifications here already," Tarr said, grinning back at his best friend.

Bobbie Jo was definitely a goat whisperer, and her enthusiasm for the animals was infectious—even if Tarr didn't quite understand the appeal of the cockeyed creatures himself.

"When did you guys get back?" Tarr asked.

"Oh, about half an hour ago," Tuck said.

"How was the food?"

"It was good." Tuck reached up and wiped his hand along his forehead—his tell for things he had no real opinion about. "I think she's going to hire that company for the wedding."

Tarr nudged his friend. "It's because of the paninis, isn't it?"

Tuck full-on belly laughed and leaned one shoulder into the side of the barn. "I can't tell a lie—I love a good sandwich."

"Yeah, and Bobbie Jo doesn't really care what she serves at the wedding."

With July fast approaching, Tuck and Bobbie Jo would be married in only another couple of months. And Tarr, once again, worried and wondered about what would happen with him.

"You got that look on your face again," Tuck said.

"I just don't want to be your roommate when you're newly married. I'm going to get my own place."

"You don't need to do that," Tuck said. "The house is enormous. You practically have your own apartment as it is."

"*Practically* and *actually* are two different things, Tuck."

Tarr was only a couple of years older than Tucker, and he knew his friend genuinely didn't mind sharing the mansion that had come with this new farm he'd bought.

Bobbie Jo claimed she didn't either, but they weren't married yet, weren't living together yet, and didn't really have to deal with Tarr as a married couple.

Yet.

Something inside him told him it *would* be bothersome to Bobbie Jo once she and Tucker said *I do*. Maybe Tucker too.

And Tarr was definitely bothered by it.

"All right." Tuck sighed the way he did every time Tarr brought this up. "Well, I don't want you to go far."

"Yeah, because you need me here to take care of everything when you're gone."

"Exactly," Tuck said, not denying it. He could wear fire in his eyes if he had to—and right now, he did.

Tarr glanced down the fence that separated the pastures from the barns. "Maybe I could just build a small cabin out here."

"That's not gonna work," Tuck said.

"Why not?" Tarr asked, genuinely surprised. Tucker usually went along with most things, but he wasn't mindlessly scratching his forehead now. "It's not like you need the land."

"You're gonna build what—a rudimentary cabin and live in it? No power, no plumbing?"

"I'd put power and plumbing in it," Tarr said.

Tucker laughed and shook his head. "You're good at building strong, sturdy, straight enclosures for chickens and goats, but you ain't never built a house, Tarr."

"They have classes at the hardware store," he said.

"You better build it big enough for you and the rest of your life...else you'll just be movin' out soon enough."

"Will I?" Tarr challenged. "Last time I checked, I wasn't dating anyone. Do you know about a girlfriend of mine that I don't?"

Tuck rolled his eyes. "Come on, you know what I mean."

Do I? Tarr silently challenged, but bit the words back —because now Tuck had him thinking about Briar Prescott and her pretty, curly hair and dangerous-to-his-health hazel eyes. They'd been out once, though their first encounter before that had not been great. Tarr had really enjoyed the date and would go out with her again.

In fact, the woman followed him into his dreams and sometimes accompanied him around the farm as he worked with the rodeo animals and the rodeo stars they trained.

Briar lived in a corner of the property, as her animal care services came with the farm. She got to remain in her house and her job for a full year—at which point she and Tuck would have to figure out whether she would continue on, or move along with her life.

"Anyway," Tuck said, "Bobbie Jo said she texted you and hadn't heard back."

"My phone's around here somewhere," Tarr said. He looked down to the small backpack he brought outside with him whenever he worked away from shelves and power outlets. He had snacks and water in it, as he'd lived in the wild—or close to the wild—for long enough to know he should always be prepared.

He fished his phone out of the front pocket and found Bobbie Jo's message.

Briar is bringing by those signs I asked her to make. Will you see if they fit on the Goatel and the Lambulance?

His heart did weird things in his body—twisting and spinning and leaping—and he wasn't sure if he was excited to see Briar or irritated.

No matter what, his chest felt too tight as he sent back a quick *Yep, you got it* text, then shoved his phone in his back pocket.

He turned away from his best friend to hide the flush creeping up his neck at the mere thought of seeing Briar in the flesh, but Tucker said, "I think she's on her way now."

"All right. Great," Tarr said, trying to make his voice as even as possible.

"Just thought you might want to, I don't know, put on a shirt or something."

Tarr glanced down at his bare chest, then over to the dirty T-shirt he'd shed an hour ago as he'd become soaked with sweat.

Anyway, it seemed ridiculous to cover up just because Briar was coming by. It wasn't like she cared what he looked like. They had each other's numbers, and yet, they barely spoke.

He hadn't even known that Briar made signs until Bobbie Jo had told him about it—and then he'd been jealous of their friendship, which in and of itself was absolutely ridiculous.

He could talk to Briar anytime he wanted; he'd never had a problem talking to women.

Tuck's phone rang. "This is my brother," he said. "He said he'd call about Molly." He swiped on the call as he walked away. "Hey, Hunt."

Tarr looked back over to the goat enclosure, which still had plenty of work that needed to be completed. So he got back to work.

A few minutes later, he heard the clicking of dog claws on gravel, and he lifted his head from the bottom rung of the fence he was currently attaching to find Wiggins running toward him. Pure joy seeped onto Tarr's face in the form of a smile, and he crouched down and opened his arms for the dog. "Heya, buddy."

Wiggins ran straight at him, and Tarr scrubbed the dog up and down his back and along his sides. "How are you, bud? What've you been doing? You been chasing rabbits again? I bet you've been chasing rabbits."

The arrival of Wiggins meant Briar couldn't be far behind, and Tarr looked to the same corner of the barn while he showered love on the canine. She didn't appear, but Tarr heard the shifting of gravel, and he stayed down scrubbing the dog as Briar came around the corner of the barn—this time lugging a sign that had to be a two-by-twelve plank at least ten feet long.

He instantly got to his feet and started toward her. "Let me," he said.

She froze as if his voice had that effect on her and did nothing but stare as he approached.

He'd never felt more naked as he took the sign from her. The tall, blocky letters in bright blue read *Lambulance* just the way they'd have looked on the side of the emergency vehicle.

"I'm not sure where Bobbie Jo wants this one," he said.

"She said she was going to put it on the side of a wagon," Briar said.

Tarr backed up several steps so he could turn around without hitting her with the board. Then he walked away, expecting her to join him.

She didn't.

Wiggins followed him, and he leaned the sign up against the side of the barn. "Oh, right. The wagon. I'm building the box for that, but it's coming after the enclosure."

"You mean the Goatel?" Briar asked with a smile.

She still had not moved, and it seemed as though her feet had planted themselves in the ground and grown roots.

Tarr grinned in her direction. "Oh, yes. Excuse me. The *Goatel*."

He indicated the enclosure. "I've got it done, and she wanted me to see how the sign looked on it and send her a picture. I guess she's doing a video call with her mom about the catering for the wedding."

Briar nodded. "Yeah, that's what she told me."

She did an about-face and started walking away. "I've got the sign in the back of my truck."

Tarr wasn't sure if he could follow her or not, but the Southern gentleman inside him got him to move. Briar had parked at the opposite corner of the barn, and he caught up to her easily due to his height and longer legs.

"How you been?" he said. "I haven't seen you much this summer."

"I see you every day, Tarr," she said.

"Yeah, maybe. I guess I meant we hadn't talked."

She'd already lowered the tailgate on her truck, and he jogged ahead a couple of steps so he could reach the sign first. He pulled it out, creating a grating sound against the bed of her truck. She hissed out a small sound while he watched her shoulders box up before she released them. She pressed her eyes closed and exhaled.

"Sorry," he said. "But look how pretty this is." He lifted it as if she hadn't seen the lettering and golden wood grain.

This sign had also been done completely out of wood. The word *Goatel* had been done in a scripty font and arranged in an arch along the top of the sign, which also belled up. A wooden goat had been cut out and painted white with brown spots and placed beneath the words.

Tarr grinned at it, so much appreciation moving through him. "You're really talented, Briar."

She blinked at him and then looked at the sign. "Thank you?"

"Why'd you phrase that like a question?" he asked, throwing her a minor glare. "How'd you do this? You got a machine?"

"A little jigsaw," she said. "And templates for the letters. I can make almost anything if I sketch out a template first."

Tarr gazed at the sign, still amazed by it. "And you sell these online?"

"I have a little online shop, yes," she said. "I don't get tons of orders, though. It's a very specific clientele."

"My momma would love something like this." He turned. "Let's go see how it looks on the actual Goatel."

Talking to Briar was easy, and Tarr wished he could kick down the walls she kept firmly erected between the two of them. Everything about her still made his skin sizzle, sent his heart leaping, and coaxed the feelings he kept carefully repressed pressing against the box where he'd put them.

Could she seriously not feel any of that?

What are you going to do about it anyway? he asked himself.

She never came back to his side, but Tarr continued to

the peaked roof he'd already put on the enclosure. She walked a few paces behind him and stopped as he moved onto the stepladder in front of the enclosure and held up the sign.

"Yeah, I think it's gonna look real nice here," he said. "Do you want to help me get it even, and we'll attach it?" He looked over his shoulder and found her with her arms folded and a glare on her face.

"What's wrong?" he asked. "It fits great." So great, in fact, it was like he'd been given the exact measurements for this sign and told to make room for it on the front of the enclosure. Perhaps Bobbie Jo had come out and measured while he'd been working with the cattle and horses.

"Could you put a shirt on?" she asked.

Tarr turned to face the sign only a couple of inches away from him—his nose almost meeting the painted wooden goat.

Oh, she feels it, he told himself as he started to chuckle.

"Yeah, okay. It's on the nail there on the side of the barn. Will you grab it for me?"

She muttered something he couldn't quite catch, but he heard her marching through the gravel.

He got down off the stepladder and carefully leaned the sign against one of the fence pillars. He stayed right where he was and made Briar come all the way to him with that shirt. She thrust it at him from a couple of feet away.

"Am I too distracting for you, sweetheart?" he asked.

"And too arrogant," she shot back.

Tarr only chuckled, because he knew he wasn't arrogant. "You know, we could go out again," he said. "I didn't think our first date was that bad."

Briar looked away instead of saying no, and Tarr was actually surprised the invitation had come out of his mouth. He'd thought about asking Briar out again, of course, but he'd never done it.

"I don't know, Tarr," she said. "We just feel so different."

"That's because you don't know me very well," he said. "You've made all kinds of assumptions about me that may or may not be true."

She didn't argue with him. so Tarr knew he was right.

"I did want to ask you something," Briar said. Her voice was hesitant, like every word had to be pulled out of her mouth by the wind.

"Go on then," he said. "And Bobbie Jo really does want pictures of this sign."

"I know," Briar said. "Can you just let me ask this?"

"Go ahead and ask it."

She remained silent.

Tarr swore their entire conversation on their first and only date had been recorded in his mind so it could torture him whenever possible. She'd literally told him she didn't like the rodeo or any of the athletes in it. She found it too dangerous.

And yet, she'd been at the ranch working with Tuck and Tarr as they trained rodeo athletes and animals.

She'd only been here a few years, and he couldn't understand why she didn't just go find another job. She had the veterinary degree. Surely, there were dozens of places that would take her knowledge and experience.

She'd flat-out told him she only wanted to be *friends* and *neighbors* with him. But then, why did she want him to put on his shirt?

"I have to go out of town," she finally said, swallowing. "It's not until next week, but I need someone to take care of Wiggins."

"Yes," Tarr said automatically. "I'll do it."

He wasn't sure if jumping straight to the acceptance made him a fool or pathetic. Probably both, but right now, he didn't care.

"Do you want to bring him over to the house, or do you want me to stay at your place?"

Her eyes finally landed on his, pure horror filling them. "You can't stay at my place."

"Okay," he said easily despite the bite in her voice. "I mean, you're not going to be there. I just wasn't sure if that would be easier...." He trailed off as her hazel-eyed gaze continued to sharpen.

"I'll bring you everything you need for him," she said.

"How long are you going to be gone?" Tarr asked, though it didn't really matter.

"I'm leaving on Thursday afternoon," she said. "I'll be home around the same time on Monday."

"So just a quick weekend thing," he said.

"Yeah," she said, but her tone came out haunted. "Just a quick weekend thing." She looked down at their feet, something very vulnerable streaming from her.

Tarr knew she had a past—everyone had one, after all. He knew hers had the rodeo in it, whether she liked it or not. The very male, very protective side of him wanted to take her hand in his and whisper things about how he would never, ever hurt her, and that he would protect her from whatever ghosts in the past still plagued her.

Instead, he backed up a step, knowing that space—for Briar—was like oxygen. And that moving on when things got uncomfortable was her love language.

"So...do you want to help me with the sign?" he asked.

She looked up and nodded.

"Great." He pointed to a spot a couple of feet over. "Stand right in front of it and tell me if I need to lift it higher or lower on whichever side."

He pulled the shirt over his head, then walked back over to the sign and picked it up. He bent down, grabbed his nail gun, and climbed back onto the stepladder.

As Briar bossed him around—*lift it a titch higher on the left, now a bit lower on the right*—Tarr thanked the good Lord above for softening her heart enough to ask him to dog-sit Wiggins.

If this is a door being opened, he thought. *Help me to walk through it the right way.*

eighteen

Deacon Hammond entered the farmhouse where he'd grown up and moved past the formal living room and down the hall to where the house opened up into a massive kitchen, dining room, and living room. A front office sat around the corner, and Deacon had visited his father there many, many times.

Cosette had texted him that she'd put his monthly paperwork there and that it needed to be signed by five o'clock tonight. When he'd become the owner of the farm, he hadn't realized how much *paperwork* his father and brother had done.

He knew he was lucky to have Cosette, and he had no idea what he'd do when the woman decided to retire. She probably still had a good ten years in her, and Deacon pushed away the worry.

"Hey, Jane," he said to his sister, moving over to give her a side squeeze at the island. "How's Molly today?" He glanced into the living room, where he often found his sister-in-law sleeping in the afternoons.

"Hunter just took her out for a walk," Jane said, and Deacon nodded.

"I just saw her parents leaving."

"Yeah, they're going to town to get a few things," Jane said. "I know her mom's coming back tonight."

Molly had been out of the hospital for a week, but she still struggled with all the classic symptoms of a concussion. Hunter had sent horrifying photos of deep blue and purple bruising down the left side of her ribcage and toward her hip.

She'd been to the doctor almost every day since the accident, and she had not been back out to the barns or stables at all.

Well, that part wasn't entirely true. She'd visited Lady a couple of times on the three short walks that Hunter made her take every day. She got visually and auditorily overstimulated easily, and she had to retreat to a dark room and be alone—or at least, the person who sat with her had to be silent.

And one of Deacon's superpowers was being quiet.

He often came to sit with Molly in the afternoons so that Hunter could deal with his restless teenagers, as well as anything out on the farm that needed to be done. Jane ran her husband's mechanic shop, but she'd been bringing food and company whenever she could.

"I have to go," Jane said. "You guys are all okay here? Her parents said they wouldn't be back until after dinner."

"We're fine here," Deacon said. "I just have some paperwork to sign in the office, and then I need my afternoon downtime." He smiled at his sister, and she hugged him again before she left.

Deacon followed her out and sat in the swing his brother had installed on the front porch.

I'm just sitting in the swing, he texted. *Text me when you get back and I'll come sit with Molly while she naps.*

It's not a good day, Hunter said. *Our walk won't be very long.*

No problem, Deacon replied as his heart ached for both Hunter and Molly. He should probably get up and get that paperwork signed while he had the chance. Just like Lady, he didn't like leaving Molly alone once she was in his care.

A car came around the curve a couple hundred yards away, and Deacon watched as it slowly trundled toward the barn. He recognized the SUV as Kristie's, and she turned and technically went off-road on the south side of the barn.

She was here to check on Lady.

Deacon admired her tenacity and dedication to the horse's care. And if there was a man who spoke less than Deacon, it was Mission Redbay. He had not brought up his relationship with Kristie since their Sabbath Day lunch at Opal's—that had been three weeks ago now—and as far as Deacon knew, they were still together.

Deacon had turned twenty-six a few months ago, and he certainly wasn't old by any means. Hunter had returned to town when he was twenty-six, and he and Molly had been married soon after that. Deacon had been almost seven at that time, and he'd grown up with Molly on the farm and in his life—as Hunter's wife and through all his most important memories.

She was practically a second mother to him, and she'd always treated him with love and kindness. Like he was the smartest person in the room.

Deacon knew he wasn't, and most days, he could barely believe that he owned this farm. He and Hunter ran it together right now. Tuck hadn't wanted it, and neither had Jane. The farm felt like it lived in Deacon's blood, fused into his DNA, and he'd never wanted anything but to work the land, raise the cattle, and ride the horses right here where he'd grown up.

He thought of his parents, who now lived in Coral Canyon, Wyoming, and a powerful wave of missing rolled through him.

Everyone in his immediate family now had a significant other except for him, and he had never felt so lost and alone and afraid as he did in that moment.

You could do something and change that, he said to

himself as he toed the swing gently back and forth. *You could ask a woman out.*

He met plenty of women at church and around the farm. They had cowgirls who worked here, and female counselors, and a dozen suppliers who came and went. The fact was, no one had ever really caught Deacon's eye or intrigued him very much.

And with those thoughts stuck in his mind and a huff coming out of his mouth, he pushed himself to his feet and went inside to get his paperwork done.

* * *

A couple of hours later, Deacon sat in the dark bedroom with Molly several feet away, asleep in the bed.

He liked the recliner in the corner best, as it faced her. He could instantly look up from his phone—or open his eyes, if he'd been resting—and see her.

But the noise he just heard had not come from her.

He also liked this spot because once Molly fell asleep with her weighted blanket and her eye mask over her face, he could twitch the curtain back a little bit and let the daylight in. He'd done that and cracked the window at the same time, so he could listen to the Colorado breeze as it rustled through the trees.

Another sound came. A small cry. Almost like the tiny meow of a newborn kitten. An extra rustle followed, and

Deacon realized he was not listening to Molly have a fitful dream—or the cries of a cat.

The rustling had been a sniffle, and the sound was very much human.

His heart beat a little faster. Deacon wasn't the most emotional man on the planet, and he would rather avoid conflict than run headlong into it.

His muscles tensed.

He waited.

When he didn't hear the sound again for several long moments, he turned his head a couple of inches and looked out the narrow two-inch strip of the window he could see.

Nothing seemed amiss.

So he went back to reading about sprinkler systems and pest management.

He'd never gone to college, but he'd grown up in the era of the Internet and currently lived in the Information Age, where anything he didn't know probably had a dozen videos online to explain it.

His brothers had joked with him more than once about how he should start a video channel with his dry humor and grumpy attitude about everything on the farm. He could come up with the funniest, wittiest captions and get millions of views.

Deacon had less than zero interest in that, and, in general, found social media to be a waste of time. He appreciated the information videos that taught him how to change a filter on a fifty-year-old tractor or de-ice a fuel pump during a sudden freeze, though.

The cry sounded again.

Deacon whipped his head up. This time, he got to his feet and pulled the curtain back a little further. He searched the backyard, still seeing absolutely nothing that would cause such a cry. Perhaps Molly was nightmaring.

Then, a dark-haired woman came around the corner of the house and into one of the most intimately shaded parts of the yard. Deacon himself had probably never set foot there, as this corner of the house nearly butted up with the back corner of the generational house, where he lived, and tall aspens and pines filled the space all between and along this side of the houses.

Judy Foster had her eyes on the ground as she walked in a very straight line, and Deacon realized there were railroad ties there, creating raised beds around the basement window wells. She was most likely walking on one of those.

She sniffled.

The previous sounds aligned with the one Deacon now saw her make as he heard it at the same time.

Deacon didn't know her—not really. She worked at Pony Power as a children's therapist, and Deacon had nothing to do with that.

He quickly cut his eyes over to Molly, who ruled the roost at the juvenile equine therapy unit. He could barely see her now, as his eyes were not adjusted to the dark.

Then—another startled cry. Much louder than before.

A gasp filled his ears and stole his attention back out the window.

Judy now stood maybe a foot from him, the wall of the house and the window the only thing separating them.

Her eyes widened. Deacon could very clearly see that she had been crying.

He had no idea what to say, and Judy froze like a deer caught in headlights.

Finally, the cowboy side of Deacon caught up to the situation, and he asked, "Do you need help?"

Judy dissolved right in front of him, her face falling and tears flowing down both cheeks. But she shook her head, squeaked out a strangled, "No," and turned her back on him before she ran away.

Go after her, Deacon thought, but the words hadn't come from himself.

He pulled the curtain closed again and looked over to Molly. A quick glance at the digital alarm clock on the nightstand told him that Judy had just gotten off work about fifteen minutes ago, and that he could probably get Charlotte or Lisa to come sit with their mother for a few minutes.

Deacon crossed the room quickly and eased out of the bedroom.

He found Lisa in the formal front room, playing the

piano, and he said, "I have to run out for a minute. Can you sit with your mom?"

"Sure, Uncle Deac," she said, abandoning her song mid-note and going down the hall.

Deacon faced the back of the house, once again hesitating. Unsure.

He hated feeling like this, but pure Hammond stubbornness drove him forward and out the back door, in search of the lovely Judy Foster, who'd said she didn't need help, but had clearly been lying.

nineteen

"I will be *livid* if you cancel," Molly said.

Hunter Hammond sighed and turned away from his wife. "Everyone will understand."

"You don't seem to understand that *I* need the bonfire to happen." Hunter knew Molly hated being sidelined, but the truth of the matter was, she couldn't do even one-tenth of the things she'd done three weeks ago.

She relied on Hunter and the kids, her brothers and sisters-in-law, her siblings, and her parents to bring her every morsel of food she ate. The doctor told her she still couldn't be trusted with a knife, as her vision blurred sometimes. She absolutely couldn't ride her horse, couldn't go out to the lessons, and couldn't watch TV for long periods either.

Molly's life had become a set of *couldn't's*.

She thrived in the darkness, and while he suspected

the jumping, blazing, blitzing flames would cause her problems, he'd already told her she could go for ten minutes. The doctor had not strictly forbidden bonfires.

He wouldn't let her stay outside for the fireworks, though. On that one, Hunter would be the bad guy if he had to be.

Hunter didn't mind helping his wife at all. He had no other job, and it was summertime. Their kids were always around, and due to the nature of running a very busy farm and a children's equine therapy program, there were literally dozens of people to help at any time.

Of course, Hunter knew Molly hated that as well.

"I won't cancel," he said. "But you have to promise me that you will monitor your own health. I know you'll want to be out there, and you can't overexert yourself."

"I promise, baby." She got up from the couch and came over to where he stood in the kitchen putting together sandwiches for lunch.

Yes, it would be difficult to cancel that evening's Independence Day bonfire, but it could be done with a simple text. People would be disappointed, but they'd find somewhere else to watch their fireworks.

The Fourth wasn't until tomorrow anyway, but Hunter never liked doing the bonfire on the actual day, as there were so many town celebrations that people enjoyed attending—himself included.

"Go over the food again with me," Molly said.

Hunter gave her a withering look and a long sigh.

"Your mother and Lara are bringing the hamburgers and hot dogs and all of the toppings for those. Jane has organized all of the desserts with various people from the farm and Pony Power. They're bringing a few people from their neighborhood as well."

She nodded and picked up a slice of Muenster cheese.

"The cowboys have been out at the fire pit, raking out the new gravel and setting up stumps and chairs in rows for a couple of hours already." He gestured toward the glass sliding doors that led out onto the back deck. They had vertical blinds that Hunter and Molly had never closed before, but now they kept steadfastly shut. "You could go look. Oh, but it will probably hurt your eyes."

Molly gave him a withering look. "Your sarcasm is not appreciated."

Hunter sighed and took his wife into his arms. "I'm sorry, sweetheart. It's frustrating to me that you think taking care of yourself is a burden."

"I just don't want to be a burden to you," she whispered.

"You are not, and have never been, a burden to me," he murmured. "I love you. You're my wife, and I will do anything to help you get back to full health as fast as possible. If that means I have to chain you in the bedroom when you overexert yourself, then that's what it means."

He pulled back and grinned at her.

She managed a soft smile too, and Hunter was

grateful for that. "Good thing we don't own any chains," she said.

Hunter laughed, realizing a moment too late that his voice was too loud. Molly flinched slightly, and he quieted. "Sorry, baby."

"Will you please let me make one pan of Rice Krispie treats?" Her voice stayed strong, but she wiped quickly at her eyes. "It will make me feel normal, and I need to feel like that now more than ever."

Hunter considered the ingredients—marshmallows, butter, and cereal. He could supervise the use of the microwave, as he'd done for their four-year-old when Lisa had wanted to start making desserts at Molly's side.

"All right," he said. "The counting of the marshmallows might be good for your brain."

"Yeah, or utterly exhaust me," she said.

Still, she turned to the cupboard and got out the cereal and the marshmallows, while he pulled one cube of butter from the fridge. He got down a big plastic bowl from the cupboard above the fridge and unwrapped the butter into it.

She started dropping full-size marshmallows into the bowl, and when she got to forty, she stopped.

He grinned at her. "No slurring, no skipping."

She shone like a new penny, and Hunter chuckled softly and swept his arm around her waist as he pressed a kiss to her cheek. "You're gonna get better really fast, okay, Mols?"

"I'm trying," she said.

"It's only been a couple of weeks," he said. "We just barely moved out of the first stage, and you can start to drive and do a few things around the house this week."

"I know," Molly said. "I just can't believe I have to live like this for eight weeks."

"It's okay to be served," Hunter said. "You don't always have to be the one providing the service."

Molly pressed her lips together and nodded. She picked up the bowl and put it in the microwave while Hunter wondered if he'd irritated her with his mini lecture.

"I better tell you something before tonight," he said.

She turned to face him, a wary look in her eyes that he could barely see in the limited light they allowed in the house during the day.

"I collected a list of people who are willing to come sit inside with you," he said. "So that you don't have to be alone. Not everyone loves a huge party with a lot of noise."

Molly folded her arms and cocked one hip out. "Who's on the list?"

"Lisa," Hunter said with a smile. "Opal. She says she can barely do anything after five p.m. these days."

That got Molly to smile too.

"Lindsay," Hunter said. "Apparently, she and Keith are going to have a baby in October, and they've only told the people they work with."

"October?" Molly said. "Wow, she must be showing then."

"I think that's going to be a surprise tonight," he said.

"Go on," Molly said.

"Jane." Hunter held up one finger and ticked it off. "Deacon—you know he loves sitting with you. Kristie—she said she loves getting away from all the noise after a little while, and she always has something to do on her phone. You know she's been sitting by Lady pretty much constantly these past two weeks."

Molly started to weep, and Hunter hated that she was in any distress at all. He moved over to her and gathered her into his chest, glad when she clung to him as if *he* were the anchor in the turbulent world that *she* needed.

"Your momma and daddy," he continued in a whisper. "Lara and her husband. Every counselor at Pony Power who will be here. Cosette. Gloria. Matt. Boone."

"All right," Molly said in a tinny tone. "Stop."

"The fact is, Mols, they all love you and want you to heal fast. And if that means you have to sit inside and have someone bring you a hot dog and one of the indoor s'mores, then that's that."

"I know," she said. "Just don't cancel it."

"I'm not going to cancel it," Hunter assured her.

The microwave beeped, and he released her to go stir her marshmallows. She did, then set the bowl in the microwave for another sixty seconds.

"Will you grease the pan?" she asked.

Hunter set about doing that while she measured out twelve cups of crispy rice cereal. He hated stirring it all together, but he loved how his wife put in extra marshmallows to make extra-gooey treats.

When she finished pressing down the cereal, he said, "Come lay down for an hour while I feed the kids. I'll send them in one at a time to talk to you."

"Okay," Molly said.

The fact that she didn't argue told Hunter how tired she had become by simply making a five-minute dessert where the microwave did most of the work.

He'd just gotten Molly settled when he heard Clay and Charlotte's voices. He quickly moved down the hall to feed them, remembering that Ryder had been put on a fencing rotation that week and wouldn't be able to come to the farmhouse for lunch.

His non-outdoorsy Lisa had a job at the fabric store in town, and Hunter had to check the calendar for her schedule. They lived and died by the Google calendar in their family, and he saw she wouldn't be done with her shift until two.

He wrapped up the extra sandwiches and put them in the fridge, because Ryder seemed to have four stomachs and always wanted something to eat at the most inopportune times. Honestly, Hunter could relate.

Before he knew it, he'd completed the evening animal feeding on their personal farm and started pulling tables out of the shed to set up in the backyard. The bonfire officially started at eight, but they roasted hamburgers and hot dogs for a couple of hours before that. Then they would put on the big pieces of wood and build the fire up into the towering twelve-foot monster that had become a tradition here at the Hammond family farm.

"Howdy, Hunt."

He turned toward the most familiar voice in the world —besides his father's. "Hey, Matt." He laughed and shook the man's hand before pulling him into a hug. "How's everything in your neck of the woods?"

"Going great," Matt said.

"I know we've been keeping Gloria out here a lot," Hunter said. "What with Lady and Molly being down and all."

"No more than usual," Gloria said, sliding her bowl of frog-eye salad onto the table.

"Did you bring the girls?" Hunter asked, looking around for Alma and Roxanne.

"Just Alma tonight," Gloria said. "Roxy's still in the city."

"Oh, right," Hunter said. "She's doing the summer semester."

Matt nodded, and Hunter couldn't tell if he was pleased or not about that news. Others started arriving, including Matt's brother, Boone, and his wife, Cosette. Both of their kids were still at home, with Amy being the same age as Lisa.

Poppy and Travis approached from the north, as

they'd obviously walked over from their farm, which sat across the street and bordered Hunter's.

Relief paraded through him when Molly did not come out. But Hunter realized then that he needed to bring the food out, so he excused himself from welcoming everyone as they continued to arrive and headed across the back lawn to do that.

Inside, he found Molly's mother and Jane making final preparations on the trays of toppings, buns, and meat that they would soon take outside.

"Hey, ladies." He hugged them both and did the same with Lara as she came down the hall from the bathroom. "Did you see Molly?"

"I just checked on her," she said. "She's still asleep. Is that normal?"

Hunter nodded. "Yeah. Deacon's in there with her, right?"

"Yeah, he was," she said.

"We'll wake her up soon," Hunter said.

The four of them got all the food outside, and more people had arrived in his absence, bringing bowls and trays and plates of deviled eggs, brownies, baked beans, pasta salad, potato salad, creamed corn, and bags of chips. *So* many bags of chips, in so many flavors.

Hunter snapped pictures of the people standing around chatting, so he could show Molly who had come. He also wanted to send a text to his parents in Coral Canyon, who had decided to stay up there for the Fourth of July festivities. Hunter himself had attended them many times over the years, as Daddy and Elise had taken their family to Coral Canyon every summer before finally moving there themselves.

Getting ready for the big bonfire, he said, before he texted both Dad and Elise the tables laden with food and the candid snapshots of those they knew—Matt and Gloria, Boone and Cosette, Travis and Poppy, Keith and Lindsay.

He'd just sent the photos when someone said, "Holy cow, Linds, are you pregnant?"

An uproar started from there as Jane put her hand on Lindsay's obviously pregnant belly, her expression one of stunned shock.

"We didn't want to make it a big deal," Lindsay said.

"Sending a text would have been not making it a big deal," Jane said. "Showing up wearing maternity clothes makes it a very big deal."

"I knew," Britt said, and she moved in to hug Lindsay. "Isn't it great?" She stepped back and smiled at Jane. "They're going to have a boy—like you did."

Jane softened then, because sometimes she could be a little bit harsh without realizing it. "Yes, it's absolutely wonderful." She drew Lindsay into a hug, and a line of women moved to do the same.

"I don't know if I want a boy or a girl," Britt said.

"Well, it's going to be one of those," Keith said.

Hunter paused completely. Britt was pregnant too?

Jane had obviously heard the same thing he had, for she spun toward the white-blonde woman who had been a huge part of the farm and Pony Power for such a long time. Britt currently worked in the counseling department here at Pony Power, and she was exceptionally skilled with children, dogs, and horses.

"Are you going to have a baby too, Britt?" Jane asked, her voice somewhat softer and less demanding.

Britt shone like the noonday sun as she said, "Yes." She reached for her husband's hand. "Lars and I are going to have a baby next year."

"Oh, my goodness," Jane exclaimed. "That is such great news, Britt. Congratulations."

Hunter glanced toward the house, because Molly would hate missing both of these announcements—but there wasn't much he could do about it.

The sliding glass door opened, and Mike came out, carrying West in his arms. Gerty followed with a tray of something, and Opal and Tag came after them.

"Howdy, brother," Mike said.

"Hey," Hunter said, as he met Mike halfway across the lawn. "Is Molly in the living room? Did you see her?"

"I didn't see her," Mike said, looking to the commotion happening back over near the fire pit "What's going on out here?"

Hunter turned to see what his cousin did and found all the women congregated together, chit-chatting like chickens.

LIZ ISAACSON

"Holy cow, Lindsay is pregnant," Gerty said.

"How do you know?" Mike asked.

"Look at her baby bump."

Gerty hurried away while Opal said, "I swear, men are so unobservant."

Tag stopped with Hunter and Mike, and Hunter said, "PS, Britt is pregnant too."

"Ah, that's why I see so many tears," Tag said. "Opal will be thrilled."

"Did you bring Steele with you?" Hunter asked.

"Yeah," Tag said. "And he's got his girlfriend with him as well."

"Oh, yeah, I heard he'd started dating someone," Hunter said.

"She's great," Tag said. "But he noticed one of his tires was low, and he's looking at it out front. So they'll probably be around in a minute."

"All right," Hunter said. His phone chimed a few times, but he ignored it as he hurried away from the crowd. He'd coordinated the bonfire with Cord and Mission, two longtime friends who'd worked here at the farm for many years. He didn't need to be out there to direct traffic, or get the flames going, or give any directions.

He'd just entered the house when Deacon came down the hall. "Oh, hey," he said. "Molly's up."

"Great," Hunter said. "I was just coming to check on her."

"Everyone's out back?"

Well, almost everyone, Hunter thought. Not his parents, and he suddenly wished that he'd been more insistent that they make the drive down for tonight's bonfire.

But he hadn't, and he couldn't change that now.

He clapped Deacon on the shoulder as he moved by and waited for his brother to exit the house and cross the deck before Hunter followed him.

He stood on the edge of the deck above the activity happening twenty yards from him. He took several pictures in the evening sunlight, marveling that this many people knew and cared enough about him and Molly to attend this bonfire.

As he stood there and watched, another truck pulled up, and Tucker, Bobbie Jo, and Tarr spilled out of it. Tarr turned back and got down a dog that Hunter had never seen before, but he figured, *What's one more mouth to feed?*

Steele and his girlfriend had joined the party, and Mission currently had his arm around Kristie and was saying something with his mouth close to her ear. She laughed, and Mission smiled.

Hunter's heart continued to fill, and fill, and fill with love and joy and gratitude for these people who came to his farm and were part of his life.

He noticed Deacon moving over next to a brunette—one of the counselors whose name Hunter couldn't remember in that moment. He said something to her, and she looked like a scared rabbit about to bolt, but she nodded. He did too, and then moved through the crowd, very much the politician, going around to say hello to everyone.

As he should, Hunter said to himself. *After all, he owns this farm.*

With that, he went back inside and hurried down the hall to show Molly all the people who'd come to celebrate the Fourth of July with them that year.

She gushed over the pregnant pictures of Lindsay and the news of Britt and Lars's forthcoming baby as well. She knew exactly who Steele was dating—a woman named Hazel Monson—and when Hunter pointed to who Deacon was standing next to, she said, "That's Judy Foster."

Molly sighed and pushed her hair back. She hadn't gotten out of bed yet, and Hunter would keep her there as long as he could. "He told me she's having a hard time right now, and that he would keep an eye on her and report anything to me."

"Oh," Hunter said. "I didn't know that."

"Yeah. And your daddy just texted."

Hunter took his phone back and looked at the message from his father. *We wish we could be there so much. But remember, we're always under the same sky, being watched over by the same God.*

Hunter didn't know why, but tears pricked his eyes. When he'd first gone away to college in Massachusetts, he'd been so lonely. His daddy had always told him, *We're*

*under the same sky, in the care of the same God. You'll be all
right.*

He hadn't said that in many years, but tonight, it was
exactly the reminder Hunter needed. So he sent a text
back to his daddy, telling him just that.

Then he helped Molly out of bed, carefully checking
her back and ribs and tailbone the way he did every day
when he got her up from her nap. "It's actually looking
really good, sweetheart," he said. "That deep bruising is
gone on your ribs."

"You know, I feel a lot better," she said. "Than even I
did earlier today."

"We're still going to take it slow," he said, as he let her
exit the bedroom first.

"Right," she said. "But if you can get me into a chair in
the back row, I bet I can sit out there for a half-hour."

That was twenty minutes longer than Hunter thought
she should, but he would keep an eye on her and watch
for any signs of exhaustion or distress.

Oh, and he'd set a timer, because he wanted his wife
to get better as fast as possible, and he believed God
would bless both of their efforts in her recovery.

So ten minutes went on the timer, and then Hunter
would enlist the help of his sister or cousin to get Molly
back in the house.

twenty

"But you're going to submit the application this week, right?" Mission raised his bottle of Dr. Pepper to his lips and took a casual sip so Kristie wouldn't think he was pressuring her.

But he was totally pressuring her to turn in the paperwork so she could enter the King Arthur Baking Company contest that was part of the Colorado State Fair.

He wouldn't even know about it if she hadn't told him, and the application window had been open for two or three weeks now.

"I just need to finalize which dessert I'm going to make," Kristie said. She scooped up another bite of sweet pea salad and popped it into her mouth. "You never told me which one you thought I should do."

No, Mission hadn't. The only thing he knew about baking and desserts was that he liked them. Fruit pie, chocolate pie, cookies, brownies, tarts, ice cream—Mission liked it all.

So whether Kristie made a cake with a fancy name like *torte* with a bunch of other modifying flavor words, or if she made an apple crisp, he didn't care.

"I don't know," he said. "That's why I didn't answer that particular text."

She got to her feet, leaving the space next to him empty. He'd taken a spot on a long wooden bench in the second row back from the fire. "I need another indoor s'more. Do you want anything?"

"I'm good," he said. "There's room at the fire for hamburgers now. You want me to make you one of those?"

Kristie beamed down at him. "Yes, please, baby." She leaned over and touched her lips to his in a quick peck. "I'll be right back."

He watched her walk away, everything about her so captivating to him on this slow, easy, hot summer night, with the sun gone behind the Rocky Mountains and the fire blazing on the farm.

Mission didn't particularly love a larger crowd of people, but he knew everyone here, and he'd always loved the gatherings Molly and Hunter did here. And before them, Gray and Elise.

Mission had always felt so welcome by the Hammonds, and that extended to those important to him.

He switched his attention from where Kristie perused

the dessert table to his granddad. He sat on the end of the bench only a few feet away, and he met Mission's gaze. "You want something to eat, Granddad? I'm going to make hamburgers for me and Kris."

"Yeah, I'll take a hamburger."

Mission grunted as he got to his feet. He knew the toppings and sides his grandfather liked, and he moved over to the table to get the burgers and buns he needed.

He took a spot at the griddle and laid down the trio of hamburgers. They immediately started to sizzle, and Cord turned to him and handed him a spatula.

"I'm done with that," he said with a smile.

"Thank you." Mission grinned back at Cord.

"I didn't know you were seein' Kris," Cord said.

"Yeah," Mission said with a nod. He picked up the salt and pepper shakers that had been stowed in the gravel nearby. "For about a month now." He seasoned the meat and put the shakers back.

"That's great," Cord said. "She's really pretty."

"I've never been out with a blonde, is what you mean." Mission grinned at him.

Cord chuckled and glanced over his shoulder. "I don't think I've ever paid attention to the type of woman you date."

"I'm more naturally drawn to a brunette," Mission said. "But there's something about Kristie I really like."

"I'm glad," Cord said. "Good for you, brother."

Mission slipped the spatula under the first burger and flipped it. "I miss you here, Cord."

"I was just going to say, everyone's said how awesome you are as foreman." Cord passed the plate with hamburgers on it to Jane and turned back to Mission. "I knew you'd be great."

"Glad one of us did."

"New job, new girlfriend," Cord said. "Anything else new I should know about?"

Mission shook his head. "I still don't like living alone, so nothing new there."

"And your granddad didn't want to come stay with you?"

"He's got his drum studio," Mission said, casting a glance across the flames to his granddad. "He's definitely getting older. I'm worried about him."

If he lost his grandfather, Mission would have no one. Literally. He tried not to dwell on the idea of a world where he was the only person in his family, but the truth was, the thoughts came more and more often.

Every time he saw his granddad, he was reminded that the man was almost eighty-six years old, and he wouldn't be around forever.

"You need cheese for those," Cord said, and he took the few steps to the toppings and got the slices for Mission. Cord laid the cheese over the burgers, and Mission pulled the top from the bottom on the first bun and placed it on the griddle over the fire too.

Things moved quickly then, and Mission placed the finished burgers on paper plates Cord held for him only a few seconds later.

"Thanks, brother," he said. "You should go eat. I think your wife is waiting for you."

"Probably." Cord handed the plates to Mission and nodded. "Good to see you, Mission."

"You too." He turned to the toppings table and added condiments to his and Granddad's burgers, then lettuce, tomato, and bacon to his, with those same things, plus onions, to his grandfather's.

He put avocadoes on his burger, and set the bun on top, looking up to find Kristie.

She stood with Gemma, Samantha, and Karly—a counselor, a horseback riding instructor, and one of Mission's cowhands—easily chatting with them. Her hair glinted in the firelight like spun gold, and she tipped her head back and laughed.

He filled his granddad's plate with sides of barbecue potato chips, baked beans, and a cob of fire-roasted corn and took it over to him.

"Something to drink, Granddad?"

"I've got something." He nudged the travel mug at his feet, and Mission suspected he had coffee in that.

He returned to the throng, stepping into Kristie and leaning his hand on her waist as he asked, "What do you want on your burger?"

She faced him. "I'll come do it."

231

He stepped back as Kris said something to her friends and then came with him. He observed as she put on ketchup and mustard but no mayo, then added tomato and lettuce, but nothing else.

"Spying?" she asked as she joined him at the table with all the sides—some of which they'd already tried.

"Observing," he clarified. "Then, next time, I'll know how to make your burger without interrupting you."

"You didn't interrupt anything important."

Still, Mission thought. Now he knew.

With their plates full, they retook their places on the bench and ate. Mission finished and looked over to his granddad and knew immediately he was done for the night.

"Finished?" he took his grandfather's empty plate and got up to put it in the flames with his.

He loved an outdoor fire, with food cooked over it. The breeze shifted, and a wave of complaints moved through the group as the smoke did too.

Mission didn't love smoke in his face, but he did love the scent of it. He took a long breath and sent a prayer up to heaven for his granddad's health.

Then he faced him and Kris again. "I'll drive you home," he told his grandfather, though the real bonfire hadn't even been built up yet.

Granddad would argue if he didn't want to go—if he wasn't truly tired—but he didn't. He groaned as he got to his feet, and he said, "Let me go say good-bye to Matt and Boone and say thank you to Hunt."

"All right," Mission said, and he watched his grandfather shuffle off through the gravel.

He sat down next to Kristie again. "I'll only be gone for about forty-five minutes," he said. "Did you want to come?"

"Do you want me to come?"

Irritation fired through Mission, but he bit it back. "I want you to do what you want."

"You'll be back for the bonfire and fireworks, right?"

Mission glanced at his phone and found that the bonfire would begin in about ten minutes. "Plenty of time to enjoy the bonfire—and the desserts—before the fireworks," he said.

She looped her arm through his and leaned into his shoulder. "Then I'll stay here. I'll have to ride in the back, and that's weird."

Mission chuckled. "People ride in the backseat, Kris. You won't have to stay in the back on the way home."

"You take him," she said. "I need more of that sweet pea salad, and I have to figure out how Molly made those Rice Krispie treats, because they're magical."

Mission hadn't seen Molly at all tonight, and he wasn't surprised. He'd seen Hunt run into the house several times, and Jane and Opal seemed to be going back and forth regularly as well.

"All right." He turned toward Kristie and kissed her. "I'll be back soon, then."

He got to his feet and went over to his granddad, because walking over grass—especially in low lighting—was hard for him.

Granddad finished shaking Hunter's hand, and Mission steadied him with a hand to his elbow as they started across the lawn toward the house.

Mission waited until they'd both gotten in the truck and he'd driven off the farm before he asked, "You feelin' okay, Granddad?"

"Yep."

Mission's heart squeezed, but what could he do?

Pray.

That was about it.

So Mission did that as he drove his grandfather home, helped him inside his modest house, and made sure he had everything he needed for the evening.

Mission checked his grandfather's medications—all seemed good there—and the food in his fridge. Also good.

"You don't need to mother me," Granddad said as he shuffled over to his recliner and sank into it.

"Someone's got to." Mission turned away from the inspection of his grandfather's living conditions.

He moved into the living room and sat down on the couch near Granddad. "I'm just worried about you."

"You're worried about yourself," Granddad said.

"Both can be true," Mission said.

"You've got the whole farm, boy," Granddad said as he flipped on the TV. "A good life, full of people." He looked at Mission. "You'll be okay after I'm gone, and that's all I've ever wanted."

Mission nodded, his heart suddenly so full. The way Granddad spoke, he'd been thinking about his time on Earth too.

"Things goin' okay with Kristie?"

"Yeah," Mission said. "Good enough." He looked over to Granddad. "She'll need someone to walk her down the aisle if we get married."

Granddad sighed and let his eyes drift closed, though he'd just turned on the TV. "Something to hold onto, then."

"I'm something to hold onto too," Mission murmured.

"Both can be true," Granddad said.

Mission chuckled and stood up. "I love you." He leaned over and hugged his grandfather, wishing he could keep him with him forever. He knew he couldn't, but that didn't mean it didn't hurt.

Mission squared his shoulders as he straightened and held his head high as he headed for the front door.

"I love you too, boy," Granddad called after him, and Mission grinned his way out of the house. Being loved by a good man meant a great deal to Mission, and he sat in the silence with that feeling as he drove back to the farm.

He loved the Fourth of July, and he let himself get swept up in the festivities around the fire pit, eating s'mores made of peanut butter cups and Oreos, singing campfire songs, and watching the kids draw words with sparklers.

Eventually, he settled onto a blanket with Kristie in his arms. The two of them looked up into the dark, country sky, and Mission felt nothing but content and comfortable with her—and with his life.

The first firework screamed through the sky, exploding into red sparks, and the crowd cheered.

Mission included.

twenty-one

Kristie stood right at Lady's right side and clicked her tongue. "Come on, sweet girl. You can come out."

She hadn't put anything on the horse. No saddle. No rope. She just wanted to get Lady out of the medical stall where she'd been for a month now, with limited and supervised visits to a closed, small pasture without any other equines.

Today, though, Kristie wanted to see how Lady's month of stall rest and medical care had helped her heal. Her wound had looked good all week, and Kristie had some news for the horse she wanted Lady to know.

Finally, Lady moved forward slowly, her big head making it out of the stall ahead of her strong shoulders and body.

"Lookin' good, Lady," Mission said, and Kristie moved

her attention to her boyfriend for a moment. "Hardly a limp at all."

Lady still limped plenty, but Kristie had her in a padded support boot, and as long as they moved slowly and kept her calm, she should be fine. Lady shook her head and huffed at Mission, but she veered toward him all the same. He chuckled as he ran his hands down both sides of her face. "Yeah, you're out, girl. Lookin' so good too."

Kristie wanted to observe Lady from various positions, so she nodded at Mission, who started along their predetermined path. Apparently, a bunkhouse sat a couple hundred yards away from the back of these buildings, and Mission had suggested they could walk Lady there and come back.

Good grass back there too, he'd said. *She'll be so spoiled, she won't eat anything we give her again.*

Kristie trailed behind, watching Lady find her gait and stay at Mission's shoulder. He didn't talk to her, and Kristie dictated some notes on Lady's progress, then tucked her phone away and moved to join Mission.

She caught his hand as she matched her step to his, and he glanced at her. "Satisfied?"

"She's doing really well," Kristie said. "I'm a little surprised, actually. I thought the wound was far worse than it seems to be."

"Maybe she just has a really great vet." He kicked her a grin, and Kristie shook her head.

She believed any vet would do for Lady what she'd done, but she accepted the compliment. "I turned in my application today."

"I was just going to ask."

She bumped him with her hip. "You were not."

Mission laughed, something he didn't let loose and do very often. "The deadline is tomorrow, though, and I would've definitely asked before the day ended."

"Well, now you won't have to," Kristie said. "I wanted you—and Lady—to know."

"What did you decide to bake?"

"The apple crumble."

"But it's not called a crumble."

"Of course it is," she said. "It's a spiced apple chai *crumble tart* with maple glaze."

"Oh, holy horses," Mission said between chortles.

"I'm going to practice tonight, and you should come try it."

"Yes, ma'am."

Satisfaction drove through Kristie, because she'd love to have Mission taste-test her desserts. "Lennie, Jocelyn, and Harper all confirmed they entered, and there's no way I can beat them. But it's okay. They give out a lot of blue ribbons."

"I'll make you a blue ribbon any day you want, kitten."

Warmth and love tugged through Kristie, because

Mission didn't say idle words. "I might take you up on that if I don't get anything."

"You'll get the biggest, most ribboniest ribbon at the fair." He grinned over to her, and Kristie wished she had his confidence. "Whose recipe are you using?"

Kristie had told him once—*once*—that she loved looking through old recipe books and using family recipes. They didn't have to be *her* family recipes either. She just liked thinking she was using a well-loved, well-tested recipe that another human being had once labored over. She really liked thinking of these faceless, nameless people as she baked. Then it wasn't just an apple crumble tart, but so much more.

"This one came from my aunt's husband's mother."

"That's quite the branch in the family tree," he said.

Kristie smiled into the sky, though big, puffy clouds filled it from side to side. She wasn't one who checked the weather before she left the house. She figured she'd find out if she needed a jacket or an umbrella when she stepped out onto the front porch.

So she didn't know if those clouds were supposed to turn gray and dump rain, as they sometimes did in the summer, especially later in the day.

Right now, it didn't matter, because right now, she'd turned in her application to compete in the King Arthur Baking Company contest, Lady was walking decently well, and Mission held her hand.

After fifteen or twenty minutes of slow, plodding

walking, the bunk house came into view. Tall trees towered over it, casting the area in shade.

"This is beautiful," she said. "And not the same house where we watched the sunset."

"I guess they do some summer camps here," Mission said. "Or did once-upon-a-time. It's not used for much anymore."

"What a shame," Kristie said. "This is a great place." She moved Lady into the shade, where the horse started to snack on the cool grass there, and Mission took her hand again and they settled against the trunk of a nearby tree.

"I love summertime," he said.

"But you live in Colorado."

"I don't mind all four seasons," he said. "It's different than where I grew up."

"It can get cold in the high desert," she said.

"It can," he agreed, saying nothing more.

Sometimes, Kristie would like him to continue to debate with her, and sometimes it didn't bother her. This time, she simply wanted more of an explanation as to why he liked summer...so she asked.

"It feels like nothing can go wrong, I guess," he said. "It's warm, so I know even if my truck breaks down, I won't be stranded on the side of the road in conditions I won't survive."

Kristie snuggled further into his side. "Mm, I don't

know about that. I've seen you when you're hungry, and it's not pretty."

Another round of laughter burst from his mouth, and pure happiness filled Kristie. She'd never imagined she'd be in this moment when she'd left Arizona a few years ago.

She'd dated here and there while in Ivory Peaks, but nothing felt as sparkly and wonderful as getting a text from him, or seeing his handsome face, or being fed by him.

Mission simply possessed something that spoke to Kristie's soul, as he *saw* her and *heard* her, and seemed to *want* to go out of his way to make sure she had what *she* wanted. Her eyelids felt heavy, and her mind drifted, and Kristie let herself float with the warmth around her.

Sometime later, she wasn't sure when, Mission's voice said, "Kitten, we should get back."

Her eyelids fluttered open as she woke up, her awareness coming back in a jolt. "I fell asleep." She looked over to find Lady laying down in the grass several yards away.

"Yep." Mission pressed a kiss to her cheek.

"How long?"

"Forty-five minutes or so."

Kristie frantically tried to piece together what else she needed to do that day—shopping for crumble ingredients, baking...and this. Her adrenaline started to calm just as the wind kicked up.

Mission tipped his head back and looked up, though

they couldn't see the sky through the branches and leaves. "It's going to rain."

"It is?"

"Feels like it to me." He groaned as he got to his feet. He turned back to her and offered her his hand. She took it and let him help her up.

"The clouds were white earlier," she said.

"Well, they're not anymore," he said. "And Lady doesn't move very fast."

Kristie's pulse rebounded from the front of her body to the back. No, she didn't want to rush or push Lady. That would undo all the hard work and care they'd put into her treatment.

"Let's go, then," she said, and she let Mission go get Lady to her feet. The horse lumbered, and Kristie regretted not bringing a rope to help the horse gain her hooves. But she managed, and she moved with Mission easily.

Kristie shook off the last dregs of sleep as she reentered the sunshine that wasn't really sunshine anymore. One glance up confirmed what Mission had said—it was going to rain. Really, really soon.

"Fun fact about me," she said as she caught up to Mission. "I don't like having water on my skin."

He looked over to her. "Really? How do you shower?"

"That's different."

He chuckled. "It's summer rain. It'll be warm."

The wind blew across them, moving from west to

east, and it didn't feel that warm. "Lady's clean-up will be murder," she said. "I really don't want her to get wet."

"I should've woken you sooner," he said as thunder cracked through the sky.

Kristie didn't dare tell Mission to hurry, though she really wanted him to hurry. But he kept on at the same slow pace they'd used to come out to the bunkhouse. She turned and looked behind her, and it didn't seem like they'd put any space between them and her afternoon napping spot.

Nothing can be done, she told herself, but she hated feeling this powerless, this out of control of a situation.

"We'll be okay," Mission said as Lady tossed her head. "All right, Kris? I'll help with whatever Lady needs, but I don't dare push her faster than this."

She grabbed onto his hand as the light changed above them, the clouds shifting and moving in a new pattern that only made Kristie's nerves swirl too. Mission looked over to her as a gust of wind tried to steal his cowboy hat.

"It's a summer thunderstorm," he said. "Not a tornado."

She nodded, and she trained her eyes on the structures in the distance. Thunder growled again, and she watched the sky for lightning but didn't see any. Wind whistled past her ears, tugging on her hair and forcing Mission to remove his cowboy hat completely.

With her head bent, Kristie simply put one foot in

front of the other, feeling very much like she and Mission and Lady were the last living creatures on the planet.

When the first raindrops touched her forearm, she flinched.

"Almost there," Mission said. "Come on, Lady, it's just right there."

Kristie looked up, and sure enough, the open stall doors of the medical barn only another fifty yards away. But fifty yards in a summer downpour could be hazardous to her health, as well as Lady's well-being.

The wind seemed to whisk the raindrops away, and Kristie finally hurried ahead to get Lady's stall cleaned quickly and a few blankets out. She'd barely had time to do the fastest clean-up job possible before it sounded like bullets pelting the roof.

She looked up and groaned, because Lady and Mission weren't inside yet. The rain sounded like a tsunami, with everything being so loud, and Kristie hurried to the open door as it got grabbed and slammed into the outside of the shed.

She yelped as a clap of thunder bellowed its voice into the shed too, and then a moment later Mission walked slowly into the stall.

"Praise the Lord," she breathed out, quickly striding past him so she could secure the door. Lady huffed at her as she entered the barn, as if it was Kristie's fault that it had started to rain.

Her shoulders strained as she pulled against the door,

the wind, the very elements themselves. She groaned and cried out as she finally got the door to move.

And, boy, did it *move*.

She yelped as it suddenly blew inward, and she got thrown into the stall with a dripping Lady, the scent of wet horseflesh, and all of her adrenaline shouting at her.

Thankfully, the stall was still padded with foam and straw, but pain still shot through her tailbone and up her back.

"Whoa," Mission said, and he left Lady to come to Kristie's aid. "Are you okay?" He put both hands on her, stilling her and holding her steady. "Look at me, Kris."

She blinked and managed to move her eyes to meet his. He nodded and leaned closer. "Are you okay?"

"I got the door closed."

"You sure did, kitten." He cut a look over to Lady as the horse shuffled. "I'm going to get Lady cleaned up and secured for the night." He helped Kristie to her feet and led her toward the inside door. "You're going to sit right out here and sip on a bottle of water."

"I'm okay, Mish," she said.

"Yeah, you are," he agreed, which sent frustration through her. He set her on the bench outside of Lady's stall, where so many people had sat with the horse over the past month. He handed her a water bottle and turned back to deal with Lady.

Kristie wanted to help, but it was a small stall, so she twisted the lid on her water bottle instead. The cool liquid slid down her throat nicely, and she took a deep breath, only a slight sting in her back and tailbone now.

Mission's low voice rumbled from the stall as he worked with Lady and got her cleaned up and after a few minutes, Kristie felt more like herself. She pushed to her feet and poked her head into the stall.

"Can I help?"

"I'm almost done," Mission said, and Lady's coat gleamed from his care. "Thanks for getting the stall ready."

"Is the straw wet?"

"I piled it over there." He nodded to a pile near the door. Kristie could scoop it into the bin, and she turned to go get the green bucket to do that. Working together, with the bullet-like rain overhead as a background, when she scooped the last bit of wet straw into the bin, Mission stepped out and closed the lower half of the stall door.

"She'll be good for the night," he said. His phone went off, and Mission sucked in a breath, frowned mightily, and pulled his phone from his pocket. "That's not good."

"What's that?" she asked.

"Farm-wide alert—sent by Deacon. It has a special sound." He tapped and swiped and read. When he lifted his head, his eyes turned wide and he searched hers. "The road is washed out."

Kristie felt like she was still asleep; her mind couldn't seem to comprehend those words in that order. "What?"

"Ivory Peaks called—" His words got drowned out by

both of their phones as they *screamed* warning alert noises into the small space.

Kristie's attention jerked to her own device, and she saw the flash flood warning. All the dots lined up, and she knew—she wouldn't be leaving the farm that evening.

She silenced her alert, and Mission did too. The resulting silence seemed to deafen her, but Kristie managed to put her phone away. "Sounds like the rain is letting up," she said.

"Maybe we should use the break to get to my cabin." He inched closer to her as the pelleting started up again. He didn't look away from her, and he'd put his cowboy hat somewhere else. "Or maybe we can find something to pass the time while we're hunkered down here."

Kristie grinned at him. "I guess I won't be making my apple crumble tart tonight."

"I think I have a boxed brownie mix in my pantry." Mission's big, warm hand curled around her and came to rest on her lower back.

Horror ran through Kristie. "Mission, you have got to be kidding."

"Kiss me, kitten," he whispered, and he leaned in and left a couple of inches for her to close herself. "And I'll throw the boxed brownie mix out."

His eyes held nothing but teasing and pure flirtation. Kristie's chest vibrated with a whole new type of adrenaline—and she wanted to kiss Mission in the medical barn while the rain pelted the roof above, and washed out roads leading off the farm, and soaked the world outside.

But in here...she was safe and dry and with Mission.

So she tipped up an inch or two, which eliminated the distance between them, and pressed her lips to his. He growled somewhere deep inside him and swept his other arm around her.

She pulled away slightly. "Will you make me dinner tonight?"

"So I have to cook for you *and* throw out the brownie mix?" He seemed genuinely grumpy about both things.

But Kristie simply smiled and said, "Yep."

"Deal," Mission said, and then he pressed her into the wall behind her and kissed her again.

twenty-two

The scent of chicken broth surprised Mission as he opened his bedroom door and headed down the hall. He and Kristie had been in the medical barn for about twenty minutes while the storm lashed rain over the farm. It had still been drizzling as they'd made their way back to his house, and he'd analyzed the food in his fridge and freezer while she showered. Then he'd jumped in to get clean, dry, and warm.

"You're cooking?" he asked, coming to a complete stop next to the fridge.

Kristie stood in his small kitchen, taking up nearly the whole alleyway between the sink and the island. As she turned from the sink with a mug in her hand, she said, "I saw you had chicken broth, and I thought it would be okay if I made some."

"Of course it's okay." He smiled at her. "But this from a woman who won't eat hot desserts in the summer?"

She'd told him she was a seasonal eater and baker, and that her friends often teased her about it.

"It feels really cold and dark outside," she said, turning back to the window.

"It's July," he reminded her. "And we've been really busy on the farm lately, so I don't have much in the way of gourmet groceries."

"Anything is fine," Kristie said, as he pulled open the fridge to once again consider his options.

He did have a roll of breakfast sausage that he could fry up—after he thawed it. It had come from his freezer and one of the pigs that Travis and Poppy had raised last year. But he'd made breakfast sandwiches for Kristie before, and he didn't want to be pigeonholed.

Ridiculous, maybe, but how Mission felt nonetheless.

"I have a few frozen meals," he said. "Spaghetti and meatballs, meatloaf, a lasagna. And I've got bread, so I could toast up some garlic bread."

Sometimes work on the farm simply wiped Mission out, and he didn't feel like cooking when he got home. To be honest, Mission felt like that most days. But since he'd started dating Kristie, he'd been eating less out of his freezer and more at restaurants—or whatever she brought him when she came over in the evenings.

"Let's just do that," Kristie said. "It doesn't have to be a big thing."

Mission got out four or five freezer meals and set them on the island in front of her. "Pick the one you want, and I'll get the broiler going."

He turned back to the stove to do that, then pulled out his Texas toast and a stick of butter. He grabbed his jarlic, garlic salt, and garlic powder. Kristie picked up a couple of the boxes and actually turned them over to read the back, but in the end, she still picked the spaghetti and meatballs.

"What have you got going on there?" she asked as Mission used the back of a spoon to mash the pre-chopped garlic, a little bit of juice from the jar, garlic salt, and garlic powder all together into buttery deliciousness that he would spread onto the toast.

"Garlic butter," he said.

She picked up the jarred garlic—jarlic—and looked from it to him, raising her eyebrows. "I'm surprised you use such a convenience item."

"Oh, you are?" he teased. "Well, I haven't been to culinary school, Miss Higgins, so you'll pardon me if I use jarred garlic. It saves a lot of time, and it's always good when you pull it out of the fridge."

"I didn't go to culinary school either," she said, giving him a pointed look as she turned around.

Mission used the spoon to spread copious amounts of garlic butter on each piece of toast, then slid the tray into the oven. He ripped open her spaghetti and meatballs and stuck it in the microwave.

"What's everyone else entering into the baking contest?" he asked.

Kristie sighed as she sank onto a barstool and lifted her chicken broth to her lips. "I don't know...Lennie will do something eccentric—she likes to experiment in the kitchen."

"Jocelyn's will be a cake, I'm assuming," Mission said. Kristie had told him that Jocelyn wanted to learn about and bake every type of cake there was and then enter a televised baking competition.

"Of course," Kristie said, wrapping her fingers around her mug as if to warm them. "Harper sometimes surprises us," she added. "But she's busy and her desserts are definitely on the scaled up end of normal."

She settled into silence, then got up and turned her back on him. "I'm just hoping I can keep up with them," she said as she strolled over to the front window and looked out.

Mission sensed the vulnerability in her and heard the insecurity in her tone. "Let's say you don't," he said, causing Kristie to whip back to him. "Just go with me."

He prayed she would, for long enough to understand where he was coming from. "Let's just say you don't win anything. Let's say we show up at the State Fair, and we're wandering around the baked goods section..."

A small smile came to Kristie's mouth, and Mission tilted his head. "Oh, is it not the baking section?"

"The Pantry has all kinds of things," Kristie said.

"Canned goods, jams, honeys, even homemade soaps and ointments. But the King Arthur Baking Company competition is in their own building."

"Okay, great," Mission said. "And let's say we're in that building, walking around, looking at all the desserts with ten words to describe them, and we get to yours...." He raised his eyebrows, just to check to make sure she'd come on this mental journey with him.

She folded her arms and cocked her hip, clearly with him.

"And let's say there's nothing there," he said. "No blue ribbon. No yellow ribbon. No red ribbon. No ribbons of any color at all." He smiled, because Mission had no idea what color the good ribbons would be. "What will happen?"

"You want me to imagine the worst thing possible?" she asked.

"Sometimes I like thinking of what the worst thing could be," he said. "Then I'm prepared if it happens, and I'm pleasantly surprised if it doesn't."

"Maybe then you're just worried about something you shouldn't be," she said.

"Maybe," he said, and he turned back to the microwave as it beeped. "Maybe you could tell me how I'm supposed to act if the no-ribbon thing happens."

"If I have to tell you," she said. "That defeats the whole reaction."

"Does it?" he asked. "Maybe it won't bother you, and

so if I go overboard, it'll just be ridiculous. But if I don't give you enough support, then you think I'm a total tool. So will you be disappointed?"

"I don't know," she said.

"Maybe I need to know for me," he said. "So, will you be disappointed?" He stirred her spaghetti, her noodles and sauce, and put the tray back into the microwave.

"Yes, I'll be disappointed," Kristie said, a definite bite in her voice. "Is that what you want to hear?"

"Of course I don't want you to be disappointed," he said, turning to face her.

"I don't want you faking anything either," she said.

"I won't *fake* anything," Mission said. "Have I ever done that for you?"

"No," she said grumpily. "And the overall winner gets a *purple* ribbon, Mish." She turned her back on him again and walked away, something slow yet strained in her step. No matter what, Mission didn't like it, but he didn't know how to make it go away.

Mission suddenly smelled garlic and quickly pulled open the oven, a curse riding the back of his tongue. He wasn't great with the broiler and had burned more things than he cared to admit. Thankfully, the back pieces had just started to sizzle and brown. He quickly flipped the baking sheet around to put the front pieces in the hot spot of the oven. He closed it and remembered to set a timer on the stove.

Then he opened the Salisbury steak meatballs and

mashed potatoes, and got the tray ready to put in the microwave. After Kristie's spaghetti came out, steaming and hot, he arranged it into a perfect Italian pile on a plate, took out the garlic bread, wedged a piece on the side, and said, "Dinner's ready, kitten."

She came toward him then, and Mission put his own frozen meal into the microwave. He pulled out the last little bit of parmesan cheese he had and sprinkled it over the top of her spaghetti as she sat down at the bar.

"Thank you, Mish," she said. "This looks great." Their eyes met. "Should we pray?" she asked.

Mission had never prayed with Kristie before, but he quickly folded his arms and said, "Sure, would you like me to do it?"

"Yes, please." She'd softened, and Mission truly hoped that he hadn't upset her with his talk about what she would do if she didn't win the baking competition—or even get a ribbon.

"Dear Lord, we're really grateful for this summer day, especially for the rain, as it's been real dry lately, and our fields and animals need the moisture. We're grateful that we got Lady back in time, and that she seems to be doing well."

He took a breath, his mind stretching in too many directions. "We're grateful that we have warm shelters in the winter and cool ones in the summer, and we're grateful for the bounty of food that we enjoy. Please bless what's been prepared tonight, that it will serve us in a way that will allow us to serve Thee. Amen."

Mission wanted to stuff his cowboy hat back on his head. Normally when he prayed over a meal, it was in a large group—at Hunter's house or in the backyard at the farmhouse. He wasn't sure why, but his face heated as embarrassment squirreled through him.

"That was nice," Kristie said. "Thank you."

"Was it?" Mission asked.

She twirled up a bite of noodles as he turned to get a piece of garlic toast from the tray. "Yeah," she said. "Simple. I liked it."

Simple ran through his mind. Yes, Mission was a simple man in so many ways.

He frowned as he bit into his bread and watched her take her first bite of noodles and sauce. Her eyes sparkled as brightly as ever—until she noticed him glowering at her.

She swallowed quickly and wiped her mouth with a paper towel. "What's wrong?" she asked. "What did I say?"

"I am simple." The words scraped his throat on the way out. "It's probably best that you know that now. This is my life. This is all there is."

Kristie looked like he'd flung ice water in her face. "I know who you are, Mission."

"Do you?" he asked. "And you're willing to live on this farm with me if we get married?"

Her eyes widened, and she stared at him, her food forgotten.

"I run this farm now," he said, feeling combative for a reason he couldn't name. "And I've worked here for eighteen years. I've never been on an airplane, and I have no desire to visit fancy places and see the world. I do want to get a dog, but that's about as exciting as my life gets."

The microwave beeped and he turned away from her to stir his freezer meal. "I can eat a sandwich for any meal," he said, the words like poison as they streamed over his tongue. "And I eat out of the freezer sometimes, and I work a lot. Yes, my life is simple—because *I'm* simple."

"That's not what I meant," Kristie said.

Mission slammed the microwave shut and put his meal back in for its final two minutes. He kept his back turned to her, even ignoring her when he heard the barstool scrape and her footsteps come closer to him.

She joined him in front of the stove and reached for another piece of garlic toast. "This is the most complicated garlic bread I've ever had," she said.

Mission huffed and grunted, very much like a horse who was being asked to do something he didn't want to do. He cut a look at Kristie out of the corner of his eye, and she offered him a bright smile.

"I didn't mean anything by it," she said, her smile fading as her sincerity shone through. "It was a nice prayer, *because* it was simple. Sometimes people have a tendency to overcomplicate things, don't you think?"

"Like the names of their apple crumble," he said. For one horrifying moment, Mission thought he may have pressed his luck too far and said something he thought was witty, but was actually hurtful.

Then Kristie sent peals of laughter streaming through his cabin, and he knew his life would never be the same without that sound in his ears—and this woman in his life.

"Yeah," she said, giggling as she went back to her plate. "Like the overcomplicated names of their apple crumble." She pointed her fork at him. "But just for that, Mister, you won't get to taste it until after the State Fair."

"Oh, come on," he said. "That's not fair."

But Kristie wouldn't budge. Mission didn't really mind, because if he couldn't taste her apple crumble until after the State Fair...that meant they'd still be together in September.

twenty-three

Kristie checked her plastic tote to make sure she had all the ingredients she needed for her spiced chai apple crumble tart with maple glaze.

She was doing a pâte sucrée crust with a very delicate blend of spices on the apples—which couldn't be cooked for too long, but definitely had to be cooked for long enough. The maple glaze took everything to a new level and then toned it all down at the same time.

Some of the spices in this recipe she had found scrawled in the margin of an old church cookbook during one of her first cleaning Sabbath days definitely had a medicinal quality—like tea—but the apples, sweet pastry crust, and maple glaze made this a beautifully balanced dessert.

"All right, guys," she said to her cat army. "I left the

back door open; you can go out, and there's plenty of food and water. Bob, don't be greedy." She pointed at the orange tabby. Bob simply yowled at her as if she were leaving him for a month instead of just the afternoon and evening.

She, Lennie, Jocelyn, and Harper had agreed to meet at Lennie's house to practice their bakes and have dessert night. Since everything took hours, they'd moved it from the first Friday of the month to the next day—Saturday.

Kristie had been in a farrowing pen that morning, but now she had everything she needed to work in Lennie's oversized kitchen for the rest of the day. She wasn't sure how she felt about it—Lennie was like a whirlwind in the kitchen, whereas Kristie preferred a more careful and calm approach.

There would be so many different flavors and smells in the room, and her nose wrinkled. Still, an excitement built beneath Kristie's breastbone as she loaded her big plastic bin into the back of her SUV and headed toward her friend's house.

Jocelyn had already arrived, but Kristie wasn't surprised to see she'd beat Harper. She was probably at the grocery store right now, buying what she needed for her peach bourbon layer cake with brown butter frosting. Kristie could admit she loved brown butter on almost anything, and mixing it with cream cheese and powdered sugar to make a frosting simply added up to heaven for her.

Jocelyn had been extremely tight-lipped about her dessert, but Lennie had been talking about her chocolate espresso pavlova for days now.

Thankfully, Lennie stood at the screen door and held it open for Kristie as she lumbered under the weight of her tote and climbed the front steps.

"Hey, girl," she said, the scent of coffee drifting onto the front porch.

"Hey," Kristie said brightly as she entered the house.

Lennie's kitchen sat in the back corner, with an enormous peninsula that allowed them to work on either side. Kristie took the station next to the wall, as Lennie and Jocelyn had already taken the other two spots in the kitchen. Lennie had double wall ovens—as they all had to bake something that day—and she had three stand mixers lined up down the middle of the countertop.

"I've got your apron right here," Jocelyn chirped as she held up a blue apron with an apple on the front and Kristie's name embroidered beneath it.

"Jocelyn, this is amazing," Kristie said. "Where did you get this?"

"This lady in my neighborhood makes them. She said she'll embroider anything you want onto anything." She glanced over to Lennie. "And Lennie got the aprons from her school."

"Well, thank you," Kristie said, looping the apron over her head and tying it around her waist. "Yours has a lemon on it." She raised her eyebrows, but Jocelyn only shook her head. She probably wouldn't work from a recipe either, so Kristie couldn't even steal a peek at that.

"It's Mission who wants to know what you're making," she said as she started removing her ingredients from her tote.

"It's Mission who wants to know what I'm making?" Jocelyn repeated, her eyebrows sky-high now.

Kristie cut a glance toward Lennie, whose pink apron featured a bar of chocolate on the chest. The last remaining apron lay on the counter—and of course, it had a peach in the center of it.

"Yes," Kristie said, holding her head high. "Okay, so, I told him I would try to get samples of all your desserts today so he could taste-test them tomorrow."

"Why wait until tomorrow?" Lennie asked. "He should come over tonight and do dessert night with us."

Jocelyn sucked in a gasp as if this was the greatest news she'd ever heard. "That's an *amazing* idea, Lennie. Text him right now, Kristie, and invite him over tonight."

She froze, not quite sure she wanted to unleash all of Lennie, Jocelyn, and Harper—and their complicated desserts for the State Fair—on Mission in one go.

"Well, he might be busy," she said, her voice too light.

"Oh, she's deflecting," Lennie said. "Why don't you want us to meet your boyfriend?"

"You talk about him all the time," Jocelyn added. "We practically know him already."

"I do not talk—"

"Help!" Harper yelped from the front door, interrupting her.

"Oh, cocoa beans," Lennie cried, running to get the screen door. "I'm so sorry. I thought I'd hear your car."

"I had to get a ride," Harper said darkly, entering with her arms laden with grocery bags. "The driver was in one of those electric things, and you know—they're totally silent."

Kristie had been totally right that Harper had just come from the grocery store, and she helped get all the loops off her friend's arms as she put the bags of ingredients on the counter in the last baking station spot.

"So where's your car?" Lennie asked.

"It's in the parking lot at Farmer's," she said. "I'm gonna have to figure out how to get it started later." A long sigh escaped her lips, and she started unbagging her ingredients and looking at them like she didn't know what they were for.

"I could call Cord," Kristie said. "He might be able to go look at it."

"Who's Cord?" Jocelyn asked, glancing up from where she'd already started to sift her flour.

"He used to work at the Hammond family farm," Kristie said matter-of-factly. "But he left a couple of years ago, and now he owns that mechanic shop over in Cherry Creek."

"Could you?" Harper asked, wiping her bangs off her face. "I already feel like I can't take on one more thing."

"I'll text him right now," Kristie said.

"Then she's going to text Mission," Lennie said, giving Kristie a knowing look.

"No, I'm not." Kristie threw her a sharp look right back.

"Why are we texting Mission?" Harper asked, glancing around at the three of them.

"She promised him she'd bring some samples of all our desserts," Jocelyn said. "And we told her she should invite him over for tonight's tasting."

"Oh, that's a great idea," Harper said, instantly brightening. "You know what? He could be a blind judge! We won't tell him who made what, and he'll come taste them all, and then he'll declare a winner."

She looked around at everyone like she'd just come up with the best idea in the world—and to Kristie's horror, Jocelyn was nodding, and Lennie looked like someone had plugged her in.

"This is a very bad idea, you guys," Kristie said. She set her phone face-down on the counter. "I texted Cord."

"Why is it a bad idea?" Lennie asked.

"Number one," Kristie said. "He already knows what I'm making, so it won't really be a blind taste test."

"You could tell him you changed your mind," Harper said.

"And then still serve an apple crumble?" Kristie gave her a death glare, then turned it on Jocelyn. "He won't like being put on the spot."

"Just ask him," Lennie said. "If he doesn't want to, he'll say no, right?"

"You've said he's opinionated," Jocelyn added. "That he just tells you what he thinks."

"I didn't say he was *opinionated*," Kristie said. "You make that sound like a terrible quality."

"I did *not* make it sound like a terrible quality," Jocelyn said, glancing at Lennie. "Did I make it sound like a terrible quality—being opinionated?"

"It'll help with my presentation," Jocelyn added.

Kristie almost rolled her eyes, but she managed to refrain. "You can't present your own dessert to him—then he'll know it's yours." She looked at Harper—who was usually the level-headed one in the group—before she remembered that she was the one who had brought it up.

"I'd like to meet him," Harper said. "You talk about him all the time, and you said he has a sweet tooth. Maybe he'll be able to help us refine our recipes."

"That's why *we're* tasting them for each other," Kristie said.

"Let me just be clear," Lennie started. "You don't want to invite him, because you don't want to put him on the spot? Or...you don't want us to meet him?"

"Of course I want you to meet him," Kristie said.

"Will you be embarrassed of us?"

"Of course not."

"Are you worried you'll be embarrassed of him?"

"No," Kristie said more emphatically.

"I really don't see why you can't invite him, then," Jocelyn said. "He doesn't have to stay for all of dessert night. He can come see the finished products right when they're done. We can present them to him as if we were on a baking competition."

Her eyes lit up then, because she so wanted to be food chef and critic on TV. "We'll serve him, and he can taste each dessert. Then he can tell us what he likes about them and what he doesn't—and we'll send him home."

Kristie cleared the last of her spices from the tote and pulled it off the counter. She really didn't have a good reason for why she didn't want to invite Mission, other than it would be stepping onto new ground she'd never walked on.

"Would you like one of us to do it?" Lennie asked, pinning her sunny smile in place. "Because I bet Harper can get him here in no time flat."

"We don't want him here in no time flat," Jocelyn said. "We need a few hours for our desserts, right?"

Lennie twisted and looked at the clock. "Should we say six-thirty? It's three o'clock right now. Does anyone need more than three and a half hours?"

Kristie did not need that long, and she shook her head.

Harper slowly started to reach for her phone, and Kristie made no move to stop her. She collected Harper's plastic grocery bags and put them in her tote, then moved to set it over the back of the couch.

When she turned around, she found all three of her friends gathered around her phone, with Harper's thumbs flying across the screen.

"No, don't say that," Lennie said.

"Which part?" Harper asked while Lennie pointed.

Kristie's heartbeat flooded through her chest. She couldn't *believe* she was allowing her friends to do this. At the same time, she'd like Mission to meet her friends—and she'd like to see their reaction to him, too.

"Yeah, that's perfect," Jocelyn said. "Don't make it more complicated than it needs to be."

"All right," Harper said. She looked up at Jocelyn, then Lennie, and finally Kristie.

They all looked at her.

Kristie swallowed, unable to speak, so she nodded instead.

Harper's thumb dropped onto her phone. "Sent," she said.

That seemed to break the tension in the room. Lennie clapped her hands together. "All right! We each get to pick a song, and you only get one skip. Jocelyn, you go first."

"I want something by Fleetwood Mac," she said, and Lennie started fiddling around with the playlist on her phone.

Kristie took her device from Harper and moved down to her station, looking at her recipe. She'd made this apple crumble three times since she'd turned in her entry form for the King Arthur Baking Company Championship. One of the rules was that they had to use the King Arthur brand flour in their recipe, and Kristie planned to put hers in the apple pie filling, the crust, and the crumble topping.

Her phone whinnied, and everyone pulled in a breath at the same time—herself included.

"What did he say?" Lennie asked.

Kristie reached over and picked up her phone, glad when she only had to read five words.

"Sure, I can do that."

Lennie shrieked in delight, which startled Kristie enough to drop her phone to the counter. Jocelyn whooped, and Harper clapped, and then Lennie said, "All right, ladies! Let's get serious. We have a real-life judge coming in only three and a half hours."

And Kristie didn't even scoff at *real-life judge*; she simply started measuring her sugar and salt into the nearest stand mixer.

twenty-four

"All right, Granddad," Mission said. "I'm gonna head out."

"All right," his grandfather said. "Thanks for coming and keeping me company today."

"Anytime," Mission said, and he leaned over to hug his grandfather, who sat on a low stool, working a piece of hide that he would use for one of his drums.

"What are you nervous about, boy?" Granddad asked.

Mission sat right back down. They hadn't talked much that afternoon, but Mission didn't need constant chatter to enjoy himself or feel close to someone.

"Kristie invited me over to her friend's house tonight," he said. "They usually do dessert night on the first Friday of the month, but they're practicing for the State Fair, so they moved it to today—and they want me to judge their desserts."

Granddad didn't slow in his scraping of the hide. "That sounds fun," he said.

"Does it?" Mission asked. "Because it sounds like a great way for me to get myself in trouble with my girlfriend."

Granddad chuckled. "I thought you said you already knew what she was making."

"Yeah, I do," Mission said. "So how do I not pick hers?"

"I don't think they're expecting you to pick hers, son." Granddad looked up and met his gaze. "It's not about what you pick anyway."

"It's not?" Mission asked. He'd gotten a text from Kristie, but it had started with *This is Harper, one of Kristie's best baking buddies.*

"These friends mean a lot to Kris, Granddad. What if they don't like me?"

"Sounds like a them-problem," Granddad said without missing a beat. "They don't have to like you."

"But they kind of do," Mission argued.

They wanted him to blind-taste all the desserts and pick a "purple ribbon winner." But now that Granddad had said they probably didn't expect him to pick Kristie's, some of the pressure eased from his chest.

"Just be yourself," Granddad said. "You've been out with lots of women, and the reason it didn't work out wasn't because they didn't like you. You're a real likable guy, Mish."

Mission thought back to the conversation he and Kristie had had a couple of weeks ago—the night the rain had washed out the road. Was *likable* synonymous with *simple?*

He wasn't sure, but most of the time, he barely felt like he could handle Kristie. And now he would have to be in the room with four women and their fancy desserts—all of their eyes on him.

His stomach slithered as if he'd swallowed snakes, and he got back to his feet, because he didn't want to be late. "I have to go," he said. "If you don't hear from me by morning, maybe send out a search party for my body."

Granddad chuckled again. "You're going to be fine, son. Try to enjoy the desserts."

With that advice in his mind, Mission left and made the drive to Lennie's house, which sat in a newer suburb on the northeast side of Ivory Peaks.

He recognized Kristie's SUV as he pulled up to the curb. He gripped the steering wheel and looked out into the bright summer evening. "Lord," he said.

But then he didn't know how to pray for a dessert taste-testing with Kristie and her friends. He should have said no. Made up something on the farm that would keep him there that night and sent his condolences.

I'm so sorry, I wish I could, but I've got this...thing going on at the farm tonight.

He pressed his eyes closed, his mind suddenly full of the words he needed to send to God's ears.

Just don't let me make a fool of myself. Don't let me embarrass Kristie in front of her friends. Help me to be kind and constructive with my feedback. And most of all, Lord, please bless these desserts to be delicious.

The passenger door opened, and Mission's heartbeat rattled like a tambourine. He yelped and squished himself into the driver's side door, startled by the sudden intrusion.

"Whoa, whoa—it's just me," Kristie said as she climbed into the passenger seat. "What are you doing out here?"

"Trying to decide if I should come in or not," he admitted as his adrenaline clouded his mind.

She smiled at him. "Are you nervous?"

"Absolutely."

She nodded and ducked her head. "I told them you would be."

"Were you watching for me?"

"Yeah," she said. "My dessert's been done for a while, and when you didn't come in...." She trailed off, looking over at him.

She wore a blue apron with an embroidered apple and her name on the front, a gray t-shirt under that, and a pair of shorts short enough that the apron covered them, with just her bare knees poking out the bottom.

"I didn't think I'd see you today," he said with a smile. "And I'm sure glad I am." He leaned toward her, glad when she met him halfway and kissed him.

"It's just desserts," she said.

"It's meeting your friends," he whispered against her lips. "That's a lot more than desserts, kitten."

"They're really nice," she offered.

Mission nodded, sure they were. "Let's not keep 'em waiting, then."

He got out of the truck and joined her on the sidewalk. She took his hand and squeezed it, and that meant more to Mission than she knew. She led him up the sidewalk and then the steps, straight into the house—which smelled like every bottle of extract, every tin of spice, and every fruit in existence had been opened, used, and squeezed.

"Smells good in here," he said, not able to distinguish any one flavor above the others.

He could only see one woman as they walked into the kitchen area—someone with dark hair and dark eyes, with her name stitched across her pink apron.

"This is obviously Lennie," Mission said.

"Yes," Kristie said. "Lennie, this is Mission. Mission; Lennie."

"It's so great to meet you," Lennie said, gushing and rushing toward them.

"Lennie teaches elementary school," Kristie added.

"It's a pleasure, ma'am," Mission said, stepping forward to shake her hand as he tipped his hat at her.

He noticed the glance Lennie exchanged with Kristie,

but he was too busy trying to figure out how to swallow properly to interpret it.

"Oh, he's here," another woman said.

Mission turned toward her. She wore a green apron with a bright yellow lemon on it and had long, dirty blonde hair with thick bangs

"This is Jocelyn," Kristie said. "Jocelyn, this is my boyfriend, Mission Redbay." She linked her arm through his, claiming him.

"It's great to meet you," he said, leaving off the *ma'am* this time.

"Well, you are *very* handsome." Jocelyn grinned and grinned at him, as if she knew a great secret he didn't.

Mission looked over to Kristie, who just rolled her eyes. "You've been talking about me, kitten?" he asked.

"Kitten?" a trio of voices said in unison—including one that belonged to a woman he hadn't met yet.

He turned toward her. She didn't wear an apron, but Mission knew this must be Harper.

"I'm Mission," he said. "It's nice to meet you, Harper."

"And you," she said, then all three of her friends zeroed in on Kristie again.

"He calls you *kitten*?"

Kristie's cheeks blazed with color, but Mission didn't feel bad. In fact, his own smile formed on his face and would not fall away. "It's just because of her cats," he said. "She said they were real grumpy and didn't like anyone, but they took to me real quick."

"I bet they did," Lennie said.

Kristie gave her a severe look that had Lennie zipping her lips.

"Who wants to go first?" Harper asked.

"Weren't we going to draw numbers?" Lennie asked.

"Oh, yes—let's do that."

The two brunettes put their heads together and quickly came up with some numbers.

"We want you to sit right here," Kristie said, showing Mission to the head of the table. "In baking competitions, they judge on appearance, too."

"You're kidding." A new bolt of fear struck through him, but Mission swallowed it down.

"Nope, not kidding. Twenty-five percent on appearance, twenty-five percent on creativity, and only fifty percent on taste."

"Ah." He took his seat and removed his cowboy hat. "Now I know why you go with all the different flavors. The creativity."

Kristie smiled. "Now you know."

"But we want you to look at the dessert as a whole," she continued. "And then look at it as it's served, because a *piece* of the dessert is not the same as the *whole* dessert."

"All right," he said, just going with it. "And then taste, of course."

Jocelyn put a notebook down next to him. "We got you this in case you want to take notes."

He looked at her blankly but managed a nod.

"Harper's going to go first," she added. "And just so you know, this is a *blind* taste test. We're presenting each other's desserts, so Harper is presenting someone else's dessert, not hers."

"Got it," Mission said. He wondered if he could ask for a glass of water because his throat was just *so* dry. He refrained as Harper stepped forward and lifted one of the cakes.

It was a double layer with cream bulging out of the middle and artfully draped over the top, but the sides were still naked. The top only had cream on one side with an assortment of perfectly curled lemons and lemon rinds to make a beautiful decoration.

"This is a lemon basil olive oil torte with a mascarpone whip," Harper said. "It should be just the right amount of sweet and savory and tart, and all of those flavors should be delicately balanced in every bite. The mascarpone whip is somewhat heavy and tangy, and every item on the cake is edible."

With every word she spoke, she moved closer and then set down the cake right in front of him. Mission could now see the flecks of basil in the yellow, spongy cake, and he desperately wanted to swipe his finger through the white cream and lick it.

"There's a lemon curd in the middle," Harper added as she cut delicately into the cake to make a triangle. When she pulled it out, one of the women gasped.

"Oh, that's beautiful."

Mission knew now—this was a *big* deal. And just like Kristie had confessed she would be disappointed if she didn't get anything in the baking competition, so would all of these women. He needed to take this taste test seriously.

Harper placed the slice of cake on a plate, while Jocelyn pulled the rest of the cake away. Harper handed him a fork and pushed the slice in front of him.

"You should be able to smell the lemon and basil as well," she said.

Mission leaned in and drew a deep breath. He definitely got lemon and something creamy, and he honestly couldn't say what basil smelled like.

He put his fork in the tip of the cake, making sure he got a bit of the curd, the cream, and the sponge. Then he plucked one of the candied lemon peels from the top and placed it on his bite. He lifted the fork to eye level, turned it left and right, and said, "This cake has a good crumb."

Then he took a bite.

The entire house seemed to hold its breath.

Flavor exploded across his tongue. Tart lemon, tangy cream to tone it down, the sweetness of the cake—and right at the end, the herby, earthy quality of basil.

"This is fantastic," he said around a mouthful of cake. "From the smooth curd to the thicker cream to the crumb —this dessert has texture and flavor going for it."

He took another bite, moaned this time, and said, "If

this doesn't win, it doesn't matter. This is the *best* cake I've ever put in my mouth."

He looked toward the four women at the far end of the table. They all seemed to be glowing.

"He's a keeper," Jocelyn said. "He knows how to taste a dessert."

"He sure does," Lennie added.

Kristie looked at him with pure adoration. "Because now you have that to live up to," she teased.

He grinned and took another bite, just because he could.

"Kristie, you're up," Lennie said. "Go take that away from him before he fills up on it."

"Oh, right," Kristie said.

Mission managed to get one more forkful of cake before she swooped in and whipped the plate away. She gave him a look, like he'd done something wrong by taking more than one bite, but he didn't feel bad. That cake was *delicious*.

She set the plate on the counter, then picked up another dessert. "This is a chocolate espresso pavlova with salted caramel cream." She walked toward him, and Mission had no idea what a pavlova was but stayed quiet.

"If you haven't heard of a pavlova," she explained. "It's a whipped egg white, similar to a meringue, that's been flavored and then baked. It should have a crisp outer crust and a soft, marshmallowy interior. The two textures together are luxurious—just like the chocolate and coffee flavors. The salted caramel cream should be *just* sweet enough to cut through the bitterness of the coffee and chocolate, creating a bite that is both rich and intense."

She set the pavlova in front of him, and Mission had never seen a more beautiful dessert.

"This is stunning," he said. "I've never seen a pavlova before, but if someone gave me this, I'd want to eat every bite of it."

"It's a very technical dessert," Kristie said. She brought the knife down over the pavlova, which had been done in a ring mold with pretty ridges along the top, each one perfectly browned and unbroken.

"Ooh, did you hear that crack?" she asked with a grin. "That's the perfect sign of a good bake on a pavlova."

She pulled out a slice—it was almost like eating a bundt cake. He could see the softer interior, but it held its weight just fine. She dolloped the salted caramel cream on top and handed him a new fork.

Mission gazed at the dessert in wonder. Though Kristie had just described the flavors, he wasn't quite prepared for them when they hit his tongue. He loved the toasted crunch of the exterior, the creamy interior, and the way the salted caramel brought it all together.

As he went in for a second bite, he said, "I have no other words but *utterly fantastic*."

This time, when Jocelyn came to take the plate, he pulled it closer and managed to get another big bite before she took it.

"That was absolutely amazing," he said. "If whoever made that doesn't get a purple ribbon, the judges must not have taste buds."

The women all tittered at the end of the table. Jocelyn stepped forward with Kristie's apple crumble. "This is a spiced apple chai crumble tart with maple glaze. Kristie told us she told you what she was going to make, and though I don't see how you can top your last two reactions...I'm thinking you better do your darnedest for this one."

She smiled teasingly as she set the tart in front of him, then turned back to the counter for a clean knife.

"This tart is steeped in cozy, nostalgic flavors that say *home*," she said. "There's apple, chai spices, and a crumble made with oatmeal, butter, and wait for it...fried quinoa —something a little different blended with tradition. It's got a pâte sucrée crust, and the spices should be balanced between the sweet apples and even sweeter maple glaze."

She cut a triangle out of the tart. Not a single drop oozed out, though it still looked juicy and delicious. She handed him a spoon this time to go with his apple crumble.

Mission held Kristie's gaze for one...two...three searing seconds before he took a bite.

The moment the spiced apples and sweet glaze touched his tongue, he let out the loudest groan he'd ever made in his life.

"Oh, my word," Kristie muttered, rolling her eyes.

Her three friends burst out laughing.

"This is apples like I've never had apples before," Mission said, really playing it up. He took another bite. "I really like the spice in there, though I'd never be able to tell you what it is. The sort of...medicinal quality of it is perfectly balanced with the apples, which have the most amazing chew I've ever had. And this quinoa—"

He put his fork down and started to clap, his smile huge as he prayed this was the right reaction for Kristie and her friends.

His girlfriend's face turned crimson, but Mission couldn't stop smiling.

Then Jocelyn moved toward him. He held up his fork and pointed. "You're not taking this one. I want to savor the *whole thing.*"

She paused, eyes wide. He held her gaze. The message came across loud and clear—he would let them take the other desserts because they weren't as good as Kristie's.

Jocelyn finally held up both hands in surrender. "All right." She turned back to the others. "Lennie, you're up."

"Our last, but not least, dessert," Lennie said. "Is a peach bourbon layer cake with brown butter frosting."

She picked up the cake, which had been completely iced this time, with pristine swirls in the frosting. Beautiful, ripe peaches sat on top with a few scattered raspberries that looked like they'd been artfully placed.

"Everything is better with butter," Lennie added. "This is a showstopper of a cake that feels like a big warm hug. The brown butter really sinks into your soul and reminds you of the South and its traditions. The cake is layered with peach-infused bourbon, more frosting, and a peach compote in between each layer."

She placed the towering cake in front of him. "You're not just getting sweetness. You're getting *depth*."

Mission could only stare at such a beautiful cake. This had to be Jocelyn.

Lennie cut a tall triangle and placed the slice in front of him. She handed him another fork.

Mission salivated over the moist-looking cake with the frosting and peaches. He forked off just the top layer —there was no way he could lift all three layers in his mouth—and examined it the same way he had the lemon olive oil cake.

"This crumb is a little bit tighter," he said. He took a deep breath, his taste buds yearning for those peaches. "But it smells like heaven."

Kristie linked arms with Jocelyn and Harper as he took a bite.

"Man, I love peaches," he said. "This really does remind me of the South." He chewed and swallowed. "The alcohol is just right—not too much. And that frosting...."

He reached out and swiped his finger through it, just like he'd wanted to do when the first dessert was presented. "I could eat a *bucket* of this."

He took one more bite of the peach bourbon cake before Lennie swept it away.

"How much time do you think you need to declare a winner?" she asked. "You didn't write down any notes."

He looked at the notebook. Then at the four hopeful faces watching him. Mission casually took another bite of the apple crumble.

"If I can't pick this one...." He trailed off, dragging the moment out. "I think the purple ribbon would go to that pavlova. I've never seen anything like it, and it had a range of textures—it just seemed so unique."

"Second place?" Jocelyn asked.

"I'm gonna go with the lemon basil cake," he said. "There was so much there—I'm sure I didn't even taste it all. Every piece was fantastic."

"Which means the peach was last," Harper said, immediately turning to her friends. "It's fine. I know my cake is more basic."

"It wasn't basic at all," Mission said, even as the other women rushed to comfort her. "It was amazing, Harper. You clearly can bake. It really was like a big warm hug. I'd eat more of all of them. I'd eat so much of that peach cake, I'd be sick."

Harper beamed at him.

"Jocelyn baked the lemon cake," Kristie said. "And Lennie was the chocolate pavlova."

All the dots connected in Mission's head, and he said, "Oh...now your aprons make sense."

Lennie looked down at her chest—as did everyone else.

"I told you to take those off," Harper said, the only one without an apron.

Lennie looked up wide-eyed. "We're not very good at this blind taste test thing, are we?"

"I was great at it," Harper said.

"I wasn't even in the competition." Kristie just shrugged.

Jocelyn and Lennie blinked at one another—and Mission simply chuckled.

Then he got up and gathered all four plates of desserts. While the women chattered over one another about his feedback, he moved from plate to plate, because tonight—getting to taste all these amazing desserts, baked by these amazing women—made him the real winner.

And he could only hope Kristie's friends liked him enough to gush about him to her once he left.

twenty-five

Kristie crouched beside the nesting boxes, brushing aside a tuft of straw as a disgruntled Rhode Island Red puffed herself up like a feathered balloon. The morning sun filtered through the slats of the coop, highlighting the fine layer of dust already clinging to her jeans. She pulled off a glove to gently lift one of the hens and gave her a slow, practiced once-over.

"No signs of mites," she murmured to herself. "Feathers look good, no discharge, comb's healthy."

From behind her, a woman in her fifties hovered nervously at the edge of the coop. "They've just all stopped laying," Alice said, wringing her hands. "And poor Beatrice there, she's been waddling like she's got a bowling ball stuck somewhere it shouldn't be."

Kristie bit back a smile. "Honestly? That might not be far off."

She cradled the hen in question—Beatrice, apparently —and gave her a gentle abdominal palpation. The bird clucked softly, clearly uncomfortable.

"I think she's egg-bound," Kristie said. "It happens sometimes, especially with diet or stress changes. We can help her pass it."

The woman looked horrified. "Pass...it?"

"It's not too hard," Kristie said with a reassuring grin. "We'll try a warm soak, some calcium, and gentle massage. Worst case, I can come back tonight and inter-vene more directly if she's still straining."

As she walked the hen toward the chicken coop, she continued her assessment. "And the laying issue? Most likely some nutritional imbalance. What are you feeding them?"

"Well...mostly scraps," Alice admitted. "Old pasta, some rice, the ends of salad mix."

Kristie nodded, already pulling a laminated page from her clipboard. "Here's a little cheat sheet I give to all my new chicken owners. Hens need balanced layer feed. Scraps are okay in moderation, but you want them getting the right protein and calcium levels consistently. Like us, they lay better when they're not living off takeout."

She offered a smile, trying not to let the ticking clock in her head show. She still had to shop for her dessert ingredients tonight, and at this rate, Mission would be at her house before her. Worse, she'd miss the window to drop off her apple crumble tart if she didn't get started soon.

Her friends would surely be halfway done with their prep by now. But she couldn't leave until Beatrice was comfortable and Alice had a handle on things here. Kristie's conscience wouldn't allow it.

They got the hen soaking in a warm Epsom salt bath —Kristie holding her with steady hands while Alice cooed words of encouragement and wiped away a few tears with the sleeve of her flannel.

Finally Beatrice passed her egg, and Kristie managed to smile her way into her SUV.

Then, it was all business as she drove to the grocery store to get fresh apples for her tart. She had to have it in the Creative Arts Building by two o'clock.

As she waited for the woman to scan her grocery items, she texted Mission. *Can you start preheating my oven? Three-fifty, please.*

You got stuck at the Kyler's, didn't you?

New chicken owners are clucking needy.

Twenty minutes later, she pulled into her driveway. Thankfully, Mission's truck took up the other half of the driveway, and he came down her front steps to help her with her groceries.

"You got everything?" he asked.

She nodded, suddenly so nervous.

"Hey, kitten." Mission swept a kiss along her cheek. "Don't be nervous. You've got this. Let me help, okay?"

Kristie blinked at him. "You bake now?"

"Nope. But I can carry in groceries and stand around very supportively." He took all the bags into the house, leaving Kristie with the only job of following him. He started unbagging them, and she joined him, taking a deep breath and then another.

She dropped her keys on the counter and gave him a grateful look. "Thank you, Mish." She glanced over to his freakishly long hair. "While the crumble bakes, I can cut your hair."

Mission didn't respond right away. He watched as she pulled out her stand mixer, the carefully labeled jars of spice, and the handwritten recipe.

"Whenever is fine with me, kitten."

Kristie had told him multiple times she'd cut it...and he'd been waiting for her to do it. Her emotions wavered, but she strengthened them. She needed all her focus on the crumble for right now. She could catalog all the ways Mission showed how much he cared about her after she'd dropped off the dessert.

As she creamed the butter, sugar, and salt together, she asked, "We're still going to lunch after I drop off the tart, right?"

"Mm hm." Mission sat at her bar, his focus on his phone. He didn't have to talk to keep her company, and he seemed to sense that she didn't want the distraction of his voice.

She kneaded and refrigerated. She blind baked and sliced apples. She spiced and stirred and squeezed a bit of lemon into her filling.

She measured and tasted and adjusted. Finally, the tart was assembled, and she slid it into the oven. "I have about twenty-five minutes before I need to make the glaze."

Kristie stepped over to the sink and washed her hands while Mission finally looked up from his phone.

"It's fine, kitten. Just come sit down."

"No, I want to do it," she said even as he joined her at the sink and took her into his arms. She sank into his strength, his warmth, stealing it for her own.

"Smells really good," he murmured.

"I want you to have a fresh haircut for our lunch date." She stepped out of his arms and smiled. "I'm going to go get the scissors, so you just have a seat back on the barstool, okay?"

"Kris."

"It's fine," she insisted. "I want to." When she returned, she carried a drape and her hair cutting kit, as well as a bottle each of shampoo and conditioner. The kitchen remained quiet, save for the occasional ticking from the oven and the low hum of her air conditioner.

Mission's eyes held hers for a beat too long. Then he

set his phone aside, and Kristie wetted her lips. "When I used to cut my brother's hair, he'd take off his shirt."

Mission reached up and pulled his tee over his head, and wow, Kristie wasn't prepared for the definition in his muscles. She quickly swept the drape around his neck and snapped it into place. She settled slightly as she combed her fingers through his too-long hair.

He shivered, which caused a slow smile to curve Kristie's lips in a secret smile he couldn't see.

"Come over to the sink," she murmured, and Mission dutifully got to his feet and looked at her like he'd follow her anywhere. She dragged one of her dining room chairs over to the sink and indicated it.

He sat, his dark eyes devouring her openly.

"You'll have to lean back a little," she said as she turned on the water and moved it to warm. "Tell me if it's too hot." She pushed a button that turned the regular stream into a spray, and Mission leaned back.

She pulled the faucet out, using the hose to get closer to Mission's head. She combed her fingers through his hair as it got wet, and then filled her palm with shampoo and started massaging it into his hair.

Her heart pounded at this intimate moment, at the way he said nothing but also wouldn't close his eyes. One of her favorite parts of getting her hair done was the scalp massage during the hair-washing, and she took her time as she slowly and rhythmically stroked her fingers and thumb along his head.

He finally rewarded her with a moan and a murmured, "Feels good, kitten."

That sound and those words did something to her. *He* moved her.

The intimacy of it, the vulnerability of this cowboy—usually so steady, so unreadable—sitting at her mercy, while she cradled his head in her hands. She felt his breath deepen, his body relax under her touch, and the kitchen, warm and fragrant and golden, shrank down to just the two of them.

She rinsed the suds away, running her hand once more over his scalp, and continued with the conditioner. With his hair clean, she gently dried it with a hand towel, and then said, "Let's go back to the barstool, please."

Mission went back to the chair and he sat with the towel still draped around his shoulders. Kristie combed through his damp hair, parting it with gentle care, and then lifted her scissors. The first snip echoed softly in the quiet room.

She worked slowly, methodically—her hand steady, her body so close to his. The back of her knuckles brushed the nape of his neck as she trimmed the ends. She felt the warmth of his skin even through the drape that kept the tiny hairs from sliding down his back

He didn't move. Just let her sculpt and shape and work in silence.

She moved in front of him, and for a second, their eyes met. She was close now, between his knees, angled toward his face as she trimmed the front of his hair. Her breath hitched as her fingers brushed his temple, and he didn't look away.

Neither did she.

She finished the last snip, set the scissors down, and stepped back just a bit—but not far. Not far at all.

"There," she whispered. "Done."

Mission didn't move. His eyes were still on her, unreadable, but *very* aware.

Kristie swallowed. Her hands were still half-lifted, like she didn't know whether to step away or cup his face.

"You smell like apples and maple sugar," he said softly.

"You smell like peaches and cream shampoo," she teased, but her voice had gone breathless.

His smile undid her completely as he encircled her in his arms and brought her to sit in his lap. "You are my favorite person."

"I thought you tried not to tell lies." She swept her fingers through his shorter, still-sexy hair. "Because we both know your grandfather is your favorite person."

"Both can be true," he whispered as he cupped her face and guided her mouth to his.

twenty-six

B riar Prescott enjoyed the easy gait of her horse beneath her. Sagebrush performed every movement with grace and power, and she didn't make Briar ask twice.

Once Briar had put her through her exercises for the day, she moved her into a walk and adjusted her cowgirl hat so that it covered her face, ears, and neck. In the open pasture, she closed her eyes and tipped her head back, memories of a life that belonged to a different woman from a different time crowding into her mind. They'd been doing that a lot more since Tucker Hammond had bought the farm and facilities and turned it into rodeo training grounds.

The very thing Briar had retreated from had caught up to her.

The movement of Sagebrush beneath her was as

familiar as breathing, and Briar knew the exact moves it would take to go from sitting in the saddle to standing in it. She'd had extraordinary balance her whole life—even after that fateful day that had changed everything for her.

"You're a fool if you think you can outrun the rodeo," she told herself.

Her eyes opened as Sagebrush lifted her head, and Briar reached for the reins to hold the horse exactly where she wanted her. If she hadn't wanted anything to do with rodeo, or cowboys, or country living. Briar could've chosen a city to settle in. Veterinary assistants were needed everywhere.

A slip of guilt moved through her that not everyone who worked at Tucker's place knew she wasn't a full-fledged vet. In fact, Briar suspected he was the *only* one who knew—and he hadn't even told Tarr, his best friend.

Oh, Tarr Olson was going to be the death of Briar. She'd known it from the moment she'd laid eyes on him several months ago, framed in the doorway of the mansion Tucker had bought. Tarr had been staying there and getting it ready for him while Tuck was off training one of his newest stars. And Wiggins, the dog with a wandering heart of gold, had immediately sniffed out the weakest link on the ranch.

Tarr.

He was as dark as midnight on the outside and as bright as noon in his personality. Even now, a small curve lifted her lips, and Briar scoffed out a sound of disgust as she straightened her mouth back to flat.

But Tarr *was* personable and funny, extremely good-looking, and talented with every animal he encountered.

She shelved him in her mind, the way she'd been doing since she met him. It would do no good to dwell on things she couldn't have—just like she tried not to let her thoughts linger on a life that had come and gone.

"This is your life now," she said out loud, her voice firm, almost demanding that she recognize it and admit how good it had become.

She had virtually no bills, and the responsibilities around her small cabin and parcel of land were things she actually enjoyed doing. She got to spend the rest of her time with cattle and horses and goats.

Oh, the goats. She'd found she quite enjoyed them— and she'd met an unexpected friend in Bobbie Jo Hanks. The woman reminded her of the friends Briar had once had, but with far less makeup and hairspray.

Bobbie Jo was tough, strong-willed, and smart. She also knew when to let others lead, and she'd allowed Tucker to rope her heart completely, both things Briar had never been good at.

Bobbie Jo and Tuck would be married in only another couple of weeks, and since Bobbie Jo had been hanging out here at the farm for eight months now, she'd asked Briar to walk in the wedding party as a bridesmaid. By some miracle, Briar had agreed.

"Let's go back, girl," Briar said to Sagebrush, and she gently guided her with her heels to turn and head back to the epicenter of the farm, where Tucker had been gracious enough to allow Briar to stable her horse.

She'd lost sight of Wiggins at some point, and now she reached up, put her fingers in her mouth, and whistled. That usually got the mutt to come if he was anywhere within hearing distance.

She'd found the dog on her solo trek from Calgary to Colorado, and she'd bonded with the stray instantly. They'd both been cast out, left behind, and forced to find their own way in the world.

But they approached things very differently these days.

Wiggins thought every human or other living creature he met had come just to see him. He loved them all and had enough room in his heart to take them as they were.

Briar, on the other hand, had closed every door around her. Built walls as high as she could. She actually did manifestation exercises where she told herself she didn't need anyone else. The only person she could trust was herself—and she shouldn't even try with others.

The previous owner of the facility had been kind, yet distant, and allowed Briar to participate on the ranch as she saw fit. But Tuck and Tarr were humans cut from a separate cloth—one where they wanted the people around them to be like family instead of acquaintances.

She and Tucker had actually had one quite heated

conversation about exactly that, and it had been Bobbie Jo who'd finally laid her hand on Tucker's forearm, looked at him, and said, "Not everyone is like you. Let her be who she is."

That was only another reason Briar liked Bobbie Jo so much. To be honest, Tucker's status had lifted significantly as he'd acquiesced to his fiancée, looked at Briar with that blazing fire still burning in his eyes, and said, "All right, Briar. As long as you keep showing up to work and doing a good job, I'll leave you alone about this."

And he had.

He'd stopped insisting she come for Sabbath day meals, or to their rodeo parties and send-offs. She attended staff meetings every Thursday morning, and she did her job as requested.

As she neared the new goat enclosure that Tarr had just finished building for Bobbie Jo, she heard the pathetic bleating of several kids. Her ears perked up at the same time her pulse did.

"That's not right," she said, swinging Sagebrush in the direction of the enclosure.

The older goats had an enormous pasture that they also grazed in, and when Briar looked over to the fence, she found dozens of them pressed up against the barrier keeping them away from the babies that Bobbie Jo had separated.

They shifted and bleated too. Something was definitely wrong.

Briar slid from her horse as easily as taking another step and quickly lashed the reins over the top of the fence post, all while still moving toward the enclosure.

Another round of panicked bleating filled the air, and Briar's eyes searched right, left, right, left, looking for the source of commotion and turmoil.

She opened the gate and entered the enclosure, careful to close the latch behind her. Just because they were only a half-hour from Denver didn't mean there weren't wild animals out here. There were. Thus, the reason for the enclosure to keep the kids safe from predators who'd like to eat them for lunch.

The kids came running down the side of the Goatel that Tarr had built—all of them in a herd, their high-pitched voices screaming into the sky.

They crowded into the corner only a few feet from Briar, and she came to a complete standstill when she saw the coyote crouched low to the ground, in hunting mode.

When she'd worked in the wilds of Calgary, she'd had to carry a whistle with her, not only to scare off predators but to alert others of problems. Briar had no whistle now, but she quickly put her fingers in her mouth and fired off the shrillest sound she could manage.

The coyote froze, but only its eyes moved to her. Its tall ears stayed forward, and it remained hunched low to the ground.

She held up both hands, trying to make herself seem bigger, and she yelped as loudly as she could, the way she'd been taught by some First Nations people in Canada.

"How'd you get in here?" she asked the coyote, as if it might answer. She took a step back, wondering if, when she opened the gate, it would simply run past her. The animal didn't seem to have any blood around its mouth, but he'd frozen and wasn't giving her any ground.

Briar whistled again, and this time, the coyote backed up one low step.

"I need help here!" she yelled as loud as she could, hoping someone would be leaving the stable or the barn and would come her way. She didn't know what time it was or what Tuck had scheduled at the facility that day. She only knew it was her day off, and that she needed to work with Sagebrush to keep the horse healthy and exercised.

She'd done that. This afternoon, she'd planned to go to the grocery store, then pick up the bridesmaid's dress she'd ordered and had to have altered.

The coyote growled—and then it laughed at her. Chilling, high-pitched yips that made Briar clap her hands over her ears.

The goats in the other pasture bleated and cried. The babies did too.

Briar needed to get out of the enclosure. She needed to take the babies with her. Or should she stay? Get them into the Goatel and then try to deal with the coyote?

Why are you trying to deal with a coyote at all? she asked herself. Wasn't *her* life more important than a goat?

Indecision ran through her, along with her warring thoughts, until she felt confused and clouded. She backed up slowly, reached the gate, and opened it.

She stood behind it to protect herself from the coyote when she heard another growl—this time, on her right.

She watched in horror as a second wild animal pushed itself under the fence on the south side, where they had clearly dug a hole. Panic streamed through her. She whistled again. And again. "Help!" she yelled.

Then she remembered her phone. She gripped the gate with her left hand, her fingers tight around the wire, and reached into her back pocket with the other.

The horrible calls of the coyotes—yipping, laughing, chattering—filled the air as Briar typed in her passcode and saw that someone had texted her.

Tarr.

She didn't bother to read the message. She tapped his name, then tapped the phone icon, looking up to find where the coyotes were.

One of them now stood five feet from her—clearly unafraid.

Briar yelled, "Help!" and kicked the gate, trying to scare the coyote and get it to back up. It did, but it didn't go far.

Tarr finally answered on the third ring. "Hey, Briar, did you get my message? I need—"

"Tarr," she said, cutting him off. "There are coyotes in the Goatel. I need help."

Tarr said nothing. More animal sounds filled the sky —one horrible scream from a kid that could only mean it had been caught.

Briar didn't dare look.

She yelled into the phone, "I'm in the enclosure, and there are coyotes here! Help me!"

Then she screamed too, unleashing all of her fear and panic into one horrible, primal sound—and then she ran at the wild canine only a few feet from her.

twenty-seven

"I'm going to get as close as I can," Tuck said as they raced down the side of the barn, past where they would normally park to get to the goat enclosure. Tarr hadn't bothered to buckle his seatbelt, and he already had both hands on the door handle as Tuck gained the corner of the barn.

"Let me out here," he said, and he opened the door while Tuck was still moving. Tuck slammed on the brakes, and that sent Tarr catapulting out of the truck. A hard jolt moved through his ankle, but Tarr didn't care. He kept running.

"Briar! Where you at?" he yelled as he fumbled with the latch on the front of the Goatel.

Behind him, he heard the slam of a door and the cock of a gun, but he barreled into the enclosure in a much more irrational way. Briar hadn't said where she was, but a scream rent the air on the other side of the building.

"Briar!" he called, already running again.

So many things streamed through his mind. Snatches of movement. Sounds. But the moment he rounded the front corner of the building, he could see all the way to the back fence.

Briar was currently wrestling with a full-grown coyote. She kicked and scratched and screamed at it again.

Tarr's heart fell right out of his chest. He was a country boy from the South, but he hadn't had to deal with wild animals in a while.

"Hey! Hey!" he yelled, clapping as he ran forward.

The back gate stood open, and Tarr watched as another coyote—this one with a limp lamb in its jaws—ran out of the enclosure.

Briar gave the coyote one final kick. It yelped, fell back, and followed its companion.

Tarr skidded on his knees at her side, hands hovering above her, unsure of where to put them.

"Hey, hey, I'm here," he said. "Briar, look at me. Look at me."

She panted hard, tears streaming down her face. A smudge of blood marred her chin, but her eyes finally came to his.

"Hey, hey, you're all right," he said. "You're all right."

"It bit me." She fell back limply to the ground. "Somewhere on my leg." Her voice shook, and her eyes closed.

"No," Tarr said. "Stay awake. Briar, look at me. Talk to me. Tell me all the things, sweetheart." He spoke in a commanding voice, hoping to keep her awake and with him.

"The baby goats were crying," she said, the words barely a whisper. "All the other goats were upset, so I came in here, and there was a coyote...."

His eyes scanned down over her chest and torso. She had one hand pressed to her left side, and Tarr carefully placed his fingers over hers.

"Does it hurt right here, sweetheart?"

"It bit me," she said again, her chest and stomach rising and falling in rapid breaths.

"Tarr," Tucker called. "The ambulance is four minutes out."

"We're back here." Tarr didn't dare look away from Briar. "There were two of them," he said. "Did you see more?"

She shook her head slightly. "He caught my right leg," she said. "Then on my side. Right here. On the left."

Right, left, right.

"I'm gonna look," Tarr said. "Okay? But you're all right. The ambulance is almost here. You're all right. Look at my shirt and tell me what color it is."

Her right leg was actively bleeding, and Tarr swallowed hard and looked away from the wound. On second thought, he didn't want to move her hand. Instead, he knocked his cowboy hat off, then pulled his T-shirt over his head.

"I'm just going to put some additional pressure on here. Can you lift your hand?"

She did, and through the blood and dirt, in that split second of time before Tarr folded his shirt and pressed it to her side, he saw that she had an old wound there.

Scars. Lots of little but prominent scars.

He pushed back her shirt to reveal more of her stomach and wiped the blood carefully with the corner of the fabric—but he did not find a wound.

"I think it's just down on the side," he said.

"Two minutes." Tucker arrived. "They're gone." A pause filled the air, and then he added, "Oh, this is bad."

"Tucker," Tarr chastised. "Be quiet."

Briar whimpered, and Tarr's eyes drifted over the trail of scars that started about an inch from her belly button and ran down her left side. They disappeared under the waistband of her jeans and beneath the shirt he now used to stop the bleeding.

"Hey, look at me, baby," he said gently. "It's fine. Everything's fine. It's not that bad."

She closed her eyes, and panic reared inside Tarr. "Hey, Briar, honey. Come on," he said. "You never told me what color my shirt was."

"Not wearing a shirt," she whispered, her voice faint and fading fast.

"Briar, stay awake now, sweetheart. What's your full name? First, last, middle."

"Briar...Heather...Prescott," she said, a long pause between each word. "I represent the County of Winnipeg," she added suddenly. "And I'm here to show you around to all the rodeo facilities."

Tarr frowned, utterly confused. "All right," he said carefully. "What are you going to show me first?"

A small smile tugged at the corner of her mouth, despite everything.

Tuck had knelt on her right side and was currently cutting back her jeans, using the discarded piece as a wrap. She didn't seem to feel it as she didn't flinch at all.

"You kids will really like the sheep," she said dreamily. "How many of you are going to do Mutton Busting?"

Tarr looked over at Tuck, who met his gaze with the same worry and wonder. Briar was speaking like a rodeo ambassador. And Tarr, once again, let his eyes drift across the scars on her side even as the sound of a siren pierced the air.

"I'll go get them," Tuck said, hurrying away.

Tarr stayed right at Briar's side, these new pieces of her not making sense to him yet.

"I'm going to do the Mutton Busting," he said, keeping his voice as calm and even as possible.

"Great," Briar whispered. "And make sure your parents get your tickets to the Stampede when we're done with the tour." She took one big, shuddering breath, and her head fell to the side as she passed out. Her chest rose nice and even after that.

Tarr only moved out of the way when forced to by the paramedics. He stayed right at her side while they checked her vitals and loaded her onto a stretcher.

"Where are you taking her?" he asked.

"Deerfield General," one of the medics replied. "You can ask about her in the emergency room."

Tarr nodded and watched as they took Briar away, one of them still pressing his T-shirt to her wounded side.

"Come on," he barked at Tuck. "Let's go."

Tucker followed him silently back to the truck, and they tailed the ambulance down the side of the barn. But when it came time to turn right toward the highway, Tucker turned left toward the house.

"Where are you going?" Tarr growled.

"You don't have a shirt on, brother," Tucker said. "And you're covered in blood. Let's take five minutes and get you cleaned up before we go. It's not going to make a difference."

Something snapped back into place inside Tarr. He looked over at his best friend, everything in the world now different.

"You're right," he said, suddenly relaxing. He looked down at his hands and closed his eyes against the dried blood there. "Did you see all those scars on Briar's side?"

"No," Tucker said. "Did she have a lot of scars?"

"Almost looked like she'd been burned." Tarr tried to

picture them again. "But not quite. Burn scars are almost wavy. This was more like...single, straight slashes."

"Healed, though, right?" Tuck asked, looking over. "Not coyote claw marks?"

"No." Tarr shook his head, wondering how a person could get scars like that. He looked out the windshield as Tuck came to a stop in front of the mansion. "These were old wounds," he said quietly, the realization hitting hard.

Briar carried many more wounds than Tarr had even imagined, and he wanted to know the story behind all of them. Physical. Mental. Emotional.

Everything. He wanted to know everything about her.

He vowed to himself, right then and there, that he would be at Briar's side for every step of her recovery.

After all, *she* had called *him*.

And Tarr, once again, felt like God had kicked down one of Briar's walls and allowed Tarr into her life... whether she liked it or not.

twenty-eight

Kristie paused outside the Community Arts Building and put a hand against Mission's chest, gently pushing him aside so other fair-goers could enter and exit through the double doors.

"What's going on?" he asked, genuine surprise in his tone and expression.

Her heartbeat thrashed against the cage of her ribs. "What if I don't have a ribbon?" she whispered.

"Don't worry, kitten." Mission took her face in both of his hands. "You're going to have one."

"But what if I don't?" she asked again. She felt wholly unprepared for this moment, despite their earlier conversation on the topic.

"Kris, it would be impossible for you not to," Mission said. "But let's say you don't. That's fine. We'll leave, and we'll go to lunch. We'll enjoy the rest of our day off together. Because a ribbon doesn't make you a good chef, and a ribbon doesn't make you a good person. Having a ribbon or not having a ribbon isn't going to change how I feel about you."

Kristie nodded, glancing over her shoulder toward the glass door. "It doesn't change anything."

"It doesn't change anything," Mission echoed. "You're still going to make that chocolate cake for my birthday, and we're still going to have a great day together."

He slid one hand over her shoulder and down her back, pulling her closer. "In fact," he murmured. "I'm kind of praying you *won't* have a ribbon, so then you'll be upset, and maybe I'll get to hold you in my spare bedroom again."

She whipped her gaze back to his and searched his face—only to find teasing in his expression. "You're not helping," she said.

He grinned and leaned closer. "Yes, I am."

She tried to slip out of his arms, but he dropped the second one and kept her close. "Seriously, Kris. Take a minute, and just think about what I said."

She closed her eyes and drew a breath.

Having a ribbon doesn't make you a good chef. You won't be a better person if you have one. And it won't change how I feel about you.

Her eyes popped open. "How do you feel about me?"

"You extracted that bit, did you?" he asked, his voice low as he leaned in, his mouth just a breath from hers.

"I'm *crazy* about you, kitten. And it doesn't matter what color your ribbon is—or if you don't have one at all. I'm still going to be absolutely crazy about you."

With that, he released her, took her hand solidly in his, and opened the door to the Community Arts Center. He led her inside the air-conditioned building, where the first thing they saw was an enormous purple ribbon. The head of it was at least a foot across that read *Best in Show*, with several frilly arms hanging down. A honey lavender opera cake sat beneath it, accompanied by photographs of the cake whole and a slice showing all twelve delicate layers with a beautiful, deep purple mirror glaze dripping down the sides.

Kristie stopped in front of it, complete awe running through her. "Wow," she managed to say, though her lips barely moved.

"Lavender tastes like soap," Mission said. "But it's a pretty cake." He cut a glance at her out of the corner of his eye. "I don't want my chocolate birthday cake to have lavender in it."

She smiled, pure appreciation blooming in her chest for the way he could acknowledge something impressive while still being honest.

"Jocelyn is going to be obsessed with opera cakes now," Kristie said.

"Have you ever made one?" He guided her gently to the right, as the baking competition required everyone to move in the same direction to view the entries.

"No," Kristie said. "They're very finicky. Lots can go wrong."

"And you bake for fun, right?" he asked, though it wasn't really a question.

Kristie hadn't really thought about it lately. She'd set a goal to earn a ribbon at the State Fair—and she realized now that goal had stolen some of the joy from her baking.

"Yes," she said softly. "I bake for fun."

She wasn't trying to start a business or get on a baking competition show. She'd just wanted to improve something about herself. She'd signed up for a community course and enjoyed baking—until these past couple of months.

And then she saw it—Jocelyn's lemon basil cake. A white, first-place ribbon gleamed beside it, only a few feet away from the purple-ribbon winner.

Kristie squealed. "Look, it's Jocelyn's cake!" Pure happiness streamed through her. She snapped a picture and quickly texted her friend.

I know what you got in the baking competition. Do you want me to tell you?

No, we're almost there. Don't you dare tell me, Jocelyn sent back.

"They're almost here," Kristie said. "Should we wait for them?"

Mission had taken a few steps ahead, but now he turned back to her, his eyes wide, something tense flowing off him.

Kristie stepped toward him. "What is it?"

He nodded his cowboy hat toward his left shoulder. Down the aisle, a few desserts over, Kristie saw her apple crumble tart.

She gasped. Air rushed out of her lungs as she hurried over.

There it was. Another white ribbon. First Place.

"Turn around, kitten," Mission said.

She did, and he snapped her picture. "Now scoot in a little tighter, baby." He took several photos, and she crowded next to him to look.

"I got first place," she breathed.

"You got the same as Jocelyn, baby. I'm so proud of you."

He kissed her, but only for a moment as someone catcalled, and Mission stepped back with a growl just as they were swarmed by familiar faces.

Tucker Hammond and Tarr Olson approached with wide grins.

"Hey, guys," Mission said with a chuckle. "What are you doing here?"

"Oh, we needed an afternoon away from the farm," Tucker said.

He fell back beside Bobbie Jo, who moved forward and hugged Mission before shaking Kristie's hand. "Hey, how are you guys?"

"Good," Kristie said with a smile.

"She just won first place," Mission said proudly.

"You're kidding," Bobbie Jo said, stepping down to inspect the apple crumble tart. "You made this?"

Kristie nodded, a bit of heat rising in her cheeks.

"That's incredible," Tucker said.

Tarr turned and reached for a blonde-haired woman walking with a crutch. She didn't have much color in her cheeks, and Kristie's concern immediately spiked.

"Hey, are you okay?" she asked, moving over to them.

"This is Briar Prescott," Tarr said. "She's regretting letting me get her out of the house, but the doctor said it would be good for her to walk around a little."

Briar managed a tight smile. "Being upright is harder than I thought."

"I told you I'd get you a chair," Tarr said.

"And then you'd be pushing me around in a chair," Briar shot back. "Absolutely not."

"There's a bench right over here," Bobbie Jo said. She moved to Briar's non-crutch side and linked arms with her. "Come sit for a minute. It was a long walk from the parking lot."

Kristie watched them go, then turned back to Tarr and Tucker. She'd met them before, and she knew Bobbie Jo, but she hadn't met Briar.

"What happened to her?" she asked.

Tuck and Tarr exchanged a glance, but it was Mission who answered. "She's the one who got attacked by the coyote, right?"

Kristie sucked in a breath. "*She's* the one who got

attacked by that coyote?" She turned to look at Briar again, catching her just as she eased onto the bench. "Tarr, she should not be out."

"Oh, here we go," Tuck said, immediately walking off.

Tarr glared at Kristie. "The doctor said she needs to get up and move. You should see her at home. She doesn't even get off the couch, and she hasn't left the house in a week."

"It only happened about a week ago, right?" Kristie asked.

"About nine days now," Tarr said.

"The ride here probably wore her out," Kristie said. "Promise me you'll take her home soon."

"Trust me, she doesn't hold back with me," Tarr muttered. "I'm lucky if I make it out of her house alive every night. You should be praying for *me*." He tipped his hat at Mission and strode over to the bench.

Kristie watched for a moment, then heard a very familiar squeal. She turned toward the voice and saw Jocelyn standing in front of her cake, with Lennie and Harper at her side. Kristie hurried over to her friends.

"First place," Jocelyn said. "I can't believe it."

"Have you seen all of ours too?" Lennie asked.

Kristie shook her head. "Nope. We stalled right here when we ran into some cowboys from the farm."

"Take my picture," Jocelyn said, handing over her phone. Kristie snapped several shots as Jocelyn struck pose after pose.

"Do you want one with all of you?" Mission asked.

"Oh, it's not the purple ribbon," Jocelyn said. "We don't need a group shot with my cake."

"Well, I want all of us by *mine*," Kristie said brightly. She waved dramatically at her apple crumble tart like a game show hostess, and her friends squealed in delight as they crowded around for a picture.

Only a few stalls down, in the very corner, sat Lennie's pavlova. It had been placed on a higher shelf at eye level —and it had *two* first place ribbons.

"What does that mean?" Lennie asked, gaping. "Two ribbons?"

"Look," Harper said, reading the card. "It means there were multiple judges who wanted to give this the purple ribbon. In the end, it wasn't chosen as the overall winner, but the judges wanted to recognize its excellence for creativity, appearance, and taste."

She turned wide-eyed to Lennie. "One judge even wrote, I've never had a pavlova this delicious. This should absolutely be the purple ribbon winner."

Kristie gripped Lennie's hands and bounced on her toes. "You *almost* won it, Len."

"Congratulations," Jocelyn said, giving Lennie a side squeeze. "What are you guys doing after this? Do you have a lunch date we can crash?"

Kristie looked to Mission, who chuckled and nodded. "Yeah, but we're going to that sushi place," he said.

"Ew." Harper wrinkled her nose. "Are you *serious*?"

"I'm dead serious," Mission said. "I like sushi."

"Yeah, but you shouldn't eat it in a landlocked state," Harper muttered, turning down the aisle and passing the bench where Briar still sat with Tarr.

Tension radiated from both of them. Tarr sat with his arms folded, making his biceps and shoulders look even bigger. He stared past Kristie while Briar stared in the opposite direction. Kristie had no idea what their history was, but they didn't exactly look like they were on good terms.

"Oh, mine is right here," Harper said. "I barely made it into first."

The dessert next to hers had a second place ribbon, but Harper's had the white first place tag. She wanted pictures too, and the five of them wandered the rest of the building, commenting about the desserts and pastries in the competition.

Mission marveled at all the chocolate chip cookie entries at the end. "Who knew there were that many different ways to make cookies?" he said. "And how in the world do you decide which one tastes better?"

"Oh, you can tell," Lennie said, very seriously.

"There are all kinds of different chocolates too," Jocelyn said. "Semi-sweet, milk, bittersweet, white...."

"Some people put butterscotch chips in," Kristie said.

"That's *not* chocolate," Jocelyn said as they reached the same doors they'd entered.

Kristie let her three friends walk ahead of her and

Mission and took his hand, letting it swing gently between them.

"They don't have to come to lunch with us," she said softly as they exited the building.

"It's fine, kitten," he said. "I don't mind sharing you. At least a little bit." He pulled her closer and pressed a kiss to her temple. "But tonight," he said. "You're all mine."

She grinned up at him and then scoffed. "Right. All yours—and your grandfather's. Aren't we going over to his place tonight?"

Mission grinned and reached up to press his cowboy hat firmly onto his head. "Oh, yeah, I forgot about that. You don't mind sharing me with him, do you?"

"No," Kristie said playfully. "As long as I get to have you alone for at least a few minutes today. We need to celebrate my white ribbon."

"Mm, that's a promise I can keep," he said.

Jocelyn turned around and walked backward. "Hurry up, you guys. We don't even know where the sushi place is."

twenty-nine

Tucker Hammond paced in the big kitchen of the farmhouse where he'd grown up.

It was his wedding day.

A day he simultaneously thought would never come and yet had arrived all too soon. Because there he was, turning in a pair of black shiny cowboy boots, wearing a tuxedo, and fretting over everything.

"I'm so nervous," he said, shaking his hands as he approached his father. "Were you nervous like this when you married Momma?"

Daddy chuckled. "Yes, son. How you feel is pretty normal. Come sit down."

Tucker absolutely could not sit down. Even on a good day, when he knew exactly what to expect, Tuck had a hard time sitting still. He certainly couldn't do it on a gorgeous autumn day like today—when he'd been told to stay in the farmhouse and not come out until Hunter came to get him.

"Shouldn't he be here by now?" Tuck paused behind the chair kitty-corner from Daddy and leaned both hands on the back of it. "Doesn't the wedding start at ten?"

"Sure does," Daddy said, completely unconcerned that the clock read nine fifty-eight and no one had come to get him.

Bobbie Jo had planned the wedding with her momma and his—both of them helping long distance. Molly, Jane, and Opal had gone with Bobbie Jo for her dress fittings, the catering appointments, and to rent all the physical facilities they needed.

She'd wanted to get married on his family farm, since it was the central hub for all Hammonds and where they'd met.

Tuck hadn't complained about the venue. He loved his family farm in autumn, and Mother Nature had played nicely this year. The trees still had their gloriously golden leaves, the bright reds, the oranges, and the burnt rusts.

They'd staged the wedding over in the family picnic area, which had a wide lawn, a couple of pavilions, and two grills. Tuck hadn't helped with any setup; Bobbie Jo had hired someone for that.

He looked toward the front door, then the back. He had no idea which way Hunter would enter. He just wanted him to come. Now.

Right now!

The words screamed in Tucker's head, and he pushed away from the chair and resumed his pacing when Hunter didn't come through either door.

Deacon sat at the table with Daddy, as did Cord and Mike. Tarr sat over on the couch with Keith and Mission. Along with Tag, they comprised Tucker's groomsmen, and he sighed as he looked over to Opal's husband in the kitchen. He held a can of Diet Coke, finished it, and tossed it in the recycling bin.

"Hunt's coming across the back deck now," he said.

Tucker straightened, every nerve in his body suddenly on fire.

Sure enough, Hunter pulled open the sliding back door and poked his head in. "We're ready for you guys." He stepped inside and closed the door behind him— which was the wrong thing to do if they were ready.

"Do you want to do a prayer, son?" Daddy asked.

Tucker's gaze flew to his father. "Yes," he said, the word choked. Oh, how he hoped he wouldn't sound like that when he said *I do* to Bobbie Jo. He wanted the day to be nothing but magical for her. She cared a lot more about what their wedding looked like and felt like than he did, and he'd promised he'd be on his best behavior.

If it were up to him, he'd have married her on the side of the road with just the two of them. When he'd told her that a couple of weeks ago, she'd laughed, shaken her head, and said, "Silly cowboy, we can't do that."

And so, there he stood, watching as Tarr, Mission, and

Keith got to their feet. Everyone came over and gathered around the dining room table. Hunter stepped between Tucker and Tag and took Tuck's hand.

"Will you do it, Daddy?" Tuck asked, finding his father's hand and gripping it tightly.

"Absolutely," his father said.

Daddy had aged a lot in the past couple of years, and as Tuck pulled down his cowboy hat and bowed his head, he silently thanked God that his father was still alive.

"Dear Lord," Daddy said. "We gather before Thee as Thy sons on this sacred and hallowed day where Tucker and Bobbie Jo have chosen to get married."

Tucker's emotions wavered and flooded his body, pricking at him and testifying to him that this was indeed a sacred, holy moment.

"Lord, we ask Thee for patience—with each other, and with Thee. We ask Thee to bless Tuck, that he can be patient with Bobbie Jo, and that she will be patient with him. We ask Thee to bless them with an abundance of love and compassion, not only for each other, but for those around them. They are both good people doing a lot of good things, and we ask Thee to please use them as instruments in Thy hand to bless and serve Thy children wherever they are.

"We're grateful that we get to make commitments to each other and to Thee, and ask that all of us here at the wedding will be able to reflect on those sacred commitments and covenants we have individually made, set right any wrongs in our lives, and continue on the path of faith Thou hast chosen for us."

Someone at the table sniffed, and Tucker almost burst into tears.

Thankfully, Daddy kept going. "We love Thee, Lord, and ask for any other blessings Thou hast in store for us at this time. Amen."

"Amen," echoed around the kitchen in the deep rumble of male voices.

Tucker barely had time to put his cowboy hat back on before Hunter drew him into a hug. "This is the best day of your life, brother," Hunter said with pure joy in his voice.

Tuck clearly remembered Hunter's wedding. He'd been nine years old, and his father and uncles had danced down the aisle to rock music.

His older half-brother had always been his idol, so Tuck gripped him hard and said, "I love you."

"Love you too, Tuck," Hunter said.

He went around the circle, hugging everyone, and then they lined up in order. He expected Tag and Opal, Cord and Jane, Keith and Lindsay, and Mike and Gerty to walk together. Deacon was taking one of Bobbie Jo's roommates, Cara, down the aisle, and Mission would escort the other. He'd told him he could walk with Kristie, but Mission had said it was fine. Kristie didn't know Tuck and Bobbie Jo all that well, and it was a thirty-second walk down an aisle.

Momma and Daddy would already be seated for the ceremony. Tarr would have Briar on his arm. Tucker prayed for her every day, morning and night. If Tarr wasn't at her house taking care of her, then Bobbie Jo was. Tucker had been over a few times himself, and Briar had healed quite well in the past three weeks. She'd moved from walking with a crutch, to a cane, and today, Tuck expected to see her in a sturdy pair of boots and nothing more.

As he embraced Tarr, he had the distinct thought that *he* would be Briar's crutch that day. Honestly, Tucker thanked God every evening when Tarr returned to the house in one piece. Briar wasn't exactly easy to get along with, and Tarr refused to let her run him off.

Tucker knew the exact turmoil that lived inside Tarr. He'd experienced it himself when he'd watched Tarr get hit by a bull and lose consciousness before he even landed on the ground. That helplessness and pure fear—he wouldn't wish it on his worst enemy.

Tarr hadn't ridden in a rodeo in a while, but the man had been born with nerves of steel. He could come home at night, completely exhausted and sobbing...and four minutes later be ready to ride again.

The men left the house in a single file line, with Daddy slipping out the front since he wasn't part of the wedding party. Hunter led them, as he'd been doing for many years now, and joined up with Molly near the fire pit area.

"Where's Bobbie Jo?" he asked.

The family picnic area sat on the other side of a line of pine trees and down the road about one hundred yards. He had teased Bobbie Jo that they could get married on horseback and ride off into the sunset, but she'd planned a morning wedding without equines.

Or so he thought.

Everything shifted as he watched cowhands from the farm and Pony Power arrive with horses. Molly's fall had been almost three months ago now, but she still accepted help from Hunter and a cowboy named Rich to get into the saddle. Hunter swung onto his horse beside her, and Tucker started to laugh as the entire wedding party mounted up.

Finally, Matt Whettstein steadied Freckles for Tucker. The moment he landed in the saddle—tuxedoed and ready to be married—Hunt said, "Tuck, you're supposed to be up here."

He moved Freckles to the front of the line, the only solo rider in the group. "What am I supposed to do?"

"Head to the altar," Hunter said. "It won't be that hard, trust me."

Tucker swallowed and faced the road. He moved past the pine trees, the big tents immediately coming into view in front of him. As he got closer, he realized there were two tents for guests, with a wide aisle between them and open sky above. He knew right where to aim his horse, and he took Freckles down the aisle as the crowd stood and watched from both sides.

He would definitely be getting married on horseback, because the altar stood as tall as Freckles's chest, and Pastor Benson climbed several steps to stand behind it as Tuck arrived.

"Hello, Pastor Benson," he said as Bobbie Jo had asked Molly's father to marry them.

"Good morning, Tucker," Pastor Benson said jovially. "That's a beautiful horse you've got."

"He's the best." Tuck turned to watch the rest of his wedding party clip-clop down the aisle toward him. They arrived, each of them dismounting and tethering their horse to poles set up in a semicircle behind the altar.

The only person missing was Bobbie Jo.

Tuck turned his horse to watch for her. He expected to see her from farther away, so surprise bolted through him when her father stepped out from the back of the tent on his right, and her horse, carrying her, emerged on the left.

Had he ridden right past her and not seen her? Impossible.

She rode a horse, her glorious white wedding dress cascading in a waterfall of fabric over the left side of the animal. She rode side saddle, with thick straps coming up over her shoulders and a beautiful pearly white cowgirl hat perched on her head.

She looked like royalty, and for Tucker, she was certainly his queen.

Her daddy led the horse toward Tuck. When they arrived at the altar, he handed the reins to Pastor Benson.

Tucker couldn't tear his eyes from Bobbie Jo. "You are so beautiful," he said aloud.

She smiled at him and leaned forward. "You gotta turn around, cowboy," she said in a much quieter voice.

A few people still laughed as Tucker quickly moved his horse into position.

Pastor Benson held out his hand. "Can I have your reins too, Tucker?"

Tucker leaned forward and passed them to him. Pastor Benson lifted both sets of reins into the air. That brought the horses closer together, their noses nearly meeting at the altar.

"Today," he called into the crowd. "We unite the hearts, minds, and lives of Tucker Hammond and Bobbie Jo Hanks."

He quickly looped the reins together. "We make this union symbolically with these ties, but their covenant and commitment are real and binding between them and God."

He looped the joined reins around a handle protruding from the front of the altar that Tuck hadn't even noticed until now.

He'd always been bored at weddings, but as Pastor Benson started in about what it meant to be married and to put another person's cares and needs above his own, Tucker tried to stay present.

After all, this was *his* wedding day—and he planned to only have the one.

Pastor Benson spoke about sacrifice and compromise, and Tuck questioned so many things. He was right in the middle of rodeo season, and the moment he and Bobbie Jo came home from their honeymoon, he'd be off again. Another place. Another event.

And for what?

He didn't need the money. He simply didn't like standing still.

He didn't know what the right answer was, but he'd lived the last year of his life asking God to show him the way. And Tucker felt like the Lord had; he didn't want to keep asking for an answer he'd already received.

So he basked in the warmth of the autumn day and the pastor's words.

When it was his turn to say *I do*, he did it.

"And do you, Bobbie Jo Hanks, take Tucker Allen Hammond to be your lawfully wedded husband? To love and to cherish, to serve and to build a life with?"

"I do," Bobbie Jo said.

Tuck finally let his nervous energy get the best of him. He reached up, grabbed his cowboy hat, and threw it into the air as he whooped.

Pastor Benson laughed, as did many in the crowd. "You may kiss your bride, Tucker."

Tuck quickly slipped from his saddle and climbed onto Bobbie Jo's horse with her, taking her into his arms and sealing their marriage with a kiss he hoped wouldn't be too embarrassing for her.

thirty

L indsay Whettstein opened the front door and reached up to take down the fall wreath she'd hung there last month. She wasn't a domestic goddess by any stretch of the imagination, but she'd signed up for an online kit to be delivered to the house—one that provided all the materials and instructions to make one home décor item each month.

Specifically, a wreath.

The company staged the kits so she could make the wreath for October in September, and today, just a couple of days into the month, she was finally getting it up. She took down the one filled with autumn leaves and scarecrows and balanced it on the back of the couch near the door. The wind slithered through the doorway, reminding Lindsay that fall had fully arrived in Colorado.

She was due with her first baby next week, in only eight days.

And while she'd insisted she could keep working at the horse boarding facility that her uncle owned—and her husband, Keith, ran as the agricultural manager—they'd both insisted she take it easy. So today, she'd finished her October wreath and was finally hanging it only a couple of days late.

This one bore jack-o'-lanterns, ghosts, and a bubbling cauldron of green goo. She'd painted the jack-o'-lantern faces and tied fabric around the foam circle to fill in between the die-cut wooden pieces that had come with the kit.

She'd then painted all three letters that spelled out *Boo* at the bottom, waited for them to dry, and attached them. The whole thing had taken her a couple of hours this morning, and she'd enjoyed the process.

Lindsay could admit she got tired faster than usual, and she was glad she wasn't still living on her hobby farm —that had been too much for her as a single woman. She and Keith had moved closer to Blackhorse Bay, where they both worked. They had ten acres now, enough for a few of their own horses and all of Lindsay's beloved chickens.

She needed to get out to the barn today and make sure everything was ready for winter. She used a mobile chicken coop in the colder months, so the hens could be wheeled outside in good weather and kept warm and safe when it snowed. October was a temperamental month, and Lindsay wanted to have the generators full and tested before the baby came.

She stepped out onto the front porch, pulled her door closed, then went down the steps, being careful to hold the handrail. She put one hand on her very pregnant belly and turned back to the door to admire the new wreath.

"Very festive," she said with a smile, and then she went around the house to the backyard.

They had a couple of barns and a big stable back here, as well as her outdoor chicken coop, a back lawn that had served them well through picnics and parties with both her family and Keith's. A pasture occupied the rest of the space, and Lindsay headed over to say hello to her horses before moving into the barn to deal with the generator and mobile chicken coop.

She loved being a hobby farmer, and she once again wondered if she should tell her uncle that she wouldn't be returning to Blackhorse Bay after the baby was born. Keith could support them on his salary, and Lindsay knew she could ask Uncle Jack for a favor any time she needed it.

She didn't move nearly as fast as she once had, and since she couldn't eat very much either, her stomach growled as she finished with the latch on the last nesting box. She took an extra moment to make sure it was right, and then she checked all of them again.

This six-by-six contraption would hold all of her hens,

and give her enough room to leave a few boxes down on one end for sick bays.

She unlocked the wheels and leaned her weight into the wire chicken coop. She needed to take it outside so she could scrub it down, rinse it clean with the hose, and then place wooden slats on the bottom and fill the boxes with straw.

But the mobile coop didn't budge.

It felt like she still had the brakes on, but she'd just released them. She stepped around the back wheel to check, and sure enough, the red pedal was lifted up into the unlocked position. She only had to glance down ten feet to see the other one, and it was also unlocked.

So why wouldn't the coop move?

Lindsay walked around the whole thing, didn't see a problem, and tried again. It moved a little bit and then stalled completely all over again.

"What in the world is going on?" she grumbled.

She moved behind it again and pushed it forward.

It moved in that direction, and Lindsay wondered if the wheels needed to be greased. She only used this coop in the winter, so it had endured several months of sitting against the back wall of the barn, neglected.

She moved it forward as much as she could, and then she definitely needed to push it sideways.

"Move," she told Hamlet, her blue heeler. Since she'd been pregnant, he had not gotten too far from her, and this trip out to the barn was no exception.

Hamlet moved, and she walked around to the end again, braced her palms against the upper half of the coop, and once again gave it a mighty shove.

This time, it *moved*.

In fact, it slid right out from under her, and Lindsay toppled forward, the weight of her baby belly dragging her down.

She cried out, knowing she was going to fall. She didn't want to break a wrist or an arm, and she tried to roll—and ended up landing on the outer ridge of her belly. She quickly rolled onto her hip and braced her head for impact. Thankfully, that never came, and she settled onto her back, which was the most uncomfortable position for her at nine months pregnant. She sucked in a lungful of air as the baby kicked and kicked.

Then a white-hot pain slashed through her lower abdomen.

She cried out again, the sound turning into a groan as she clutched the bottom of her baby belly. She rested her head on the cement, trying to take stock of all the different parts that had been hit, and unable to do so as she realized—

Her water had just broken.

She gasped, her mind flying through where she had put her phone.

She suddenly felt it pressing into her backside, and she managed to slide one hand around her hip to get it out.

She groaned as a dull, aching pain moved from her back along the bottom of her baby belly and up over the top, settling almost right between her breasts, and causing her to gasp over and over as she struggled to breathe.

She needed to call Keith. She needed to get to the hospital.

She lifted her phone and found the screen cracked.

"No," she whimpered, praying with everything she had that she hadn't broken her phone.

If she had, she would have to walk to the neighbor's house to get in touch with her husband, and right now, Lindsay couldn't even imagine getting up off the barn floor.

She pressed the button on the side, and praise all the stars in heaven and God above, the phone lit up.

She noted the time—eleven twenty-three—even as her first contraction abated. She and Keith had taken a birthing class, and she knew she needed to keep track of how far apart the contractions were, and when they had started.

Tears trickled out of her eyes as she continued to fight for breath and send a text at the same time. She wasn't sure where Keith would be at this very moment, and he worked about fifteen minutes away from the farm.

"You can make it that long," she told herself right out loud.

She watched as her text got delivered. When it didn't immediately change to *Read*, Lindsay tapped to call Keith.

The call connected in the middle of the second ring. "Hey, sweetheart," he said. "What's going on?"

"Keith, I f-f-fell," she said, stuttering over the words. Everything inside her shook, and Lindsay felt like she was going into shock.

"You fell? I'm leaving right now."

A sob wrenched its way out of her throat. "I'm in the barn," she said, sucking in a new breath. "I finished with the mobile chicken coop, and then I couldn't get it to move. Something was stuck, but I don't know what, and I pushed on it so hard. When it rolled away, I toppled after it."

"I'm on the way," Keith said.

"My water broke." Lindsay sniffled, hating that she was crying over this. She and Keith had been waiting for this baby for a while now, and she wanted this to be the happiest day of her life, not one where she turned into a blubbering mess on the barn floor.

"I had a contraction," she said.

"I'll be there in ten minutes. Stay on the line with me." He somehow knew that she couldn't talk, and he filled the space between them with words.

She continued to weep quietly, and she groaned when she had a contraction. By the time Keith's footsteps ran toward her in the barn, she'd had two more contractions and managed to get herself to a seated position.

"Let's go, sweetheart," he said.

He helped her up, but Lindsay paused and said, "Just give me a second. My head is swimming."

He gave her the time she needed and then helped her to the truck. He dashed back inside and emerged with the baby bag she'd packed earlier this week. Keith gripped the wheel hard as he drove them toward the hospital. He'd already mapped the route and driven it a couple of times.

As another contraction struck, she reached over and gripped his hand. He'd been her strength, her anchor through so much.

"Hold on, baby. We're almost there." He lifted her hand to his lips and kissed it as the contraction calmed.

"We have to decide," he said. "What do you want to name him?"

They'd thrown names back and forth for months now, especially once they'd learned she would be having a boy.

"I think Nash," she said. "It's a good, strong cowboy name. Nash Lewis Whettstein."

"It's perfect," Keith said.

Lindsay prayed that her baby would be perfect as well. "What if I hurt him?" she asked.

"He's coming right now," Keith said. "One fall isn't going to hurt him that much. He's been in there for nine months, and he's fine."

"He's early," Lindsay said next, feeling completely wild and irrational.

"We just get to love him on this side for longer," Keith said.

"Thank you for letting me use my maiden name," she said, as she had no brothers and no other way for her branch of the Lewis family to continue.

"Thank you for making me a daddy," Keith said. Only sixty seconds later, he pulled up to the emergency bay doors. "Stay here," he said, and jumped out.

He returned only a few seconds later with a wheel-chair, and he'd just gotten her settled when a nurse came outside with a clipboard and started asking him questions.

Lindsay relaxed then, because she wouldn't have to give birth on the barn floor. And now, all she had to focus on was praying that she hadn't hurt their son too badly when she'd fallen.

thirty-one

Mission jogged the last few steps to his front yard and kept hurrying across the now-dormant lawn to his front porch.

Rich had called to say he'd seen something dripping out of the back window of Mission's cabin as he'd walked by that morning.

The bathroom window, and Mission expected to find his whole cabin flooded when he opened the front door. He'd just finished their morning meeting on the harvest and everyone's role in it when he'd gotten Rich's text.

He really didn't have time for anything to go wrong right now. Harvest time on a farm was the busiest time of year, as everyone tried to get in everything they'd been carefully cultivating for months.

Travis had so much alfalfa this year, he'd hired extra hands just to get the job done. Mission had done the same, as summer had been so good to them and this final crop of hay couldn't be lost.

He also didn't want their squashes, corn, apples, or peaches to go to waste. Molly usually headed up the farm stand that sold their extra produce, but Hunter had asked her to pass the job to someone else.

Britt and Gemma had taken it on, and Mission needed to get them another trailer full of corn for the stand that day.

He so didn't have time for a leak or flooding his home, especially today, as he and Kristie had planned to sneak away from work an hour early to have chocolate cake for their birthdays.

Hers was actually today, and his would arrive in another four days.

"If her gifts got wet...." Mission shoved his way into his house, ready to take on the world so he could get back to work and wouldn't miss his date that evening.

He expected to smell something moldy or damp. Step into an inch or more of water. Something.

His cabin sat in stillness, the morning sunshine filtering through the open blinds and highlighting the dust motes in the air.

There was no flood. No smell of something gone wrong.

He came to a stop at the corner of the wall and looked down the hall. No evidence of water at all, and he growled as he scanned the kitchen.

His breath caught in his chest when he saw the chocolate cake on his dining room table.

"That's not a leak," he said as he moved along the island and bar to the table. Someone had been in his house all the same.

Not just someone.

Kristie.

This looked like a normal chocolate cake, though it stood three tiers tall, and Mission had never had such a large cake made just for him. Granddad usually bought an ice cream cake, and the two of them sat on his back deck and enjoyed the dessert together.

A note had been placed next to the cake, and Mission recognized Kristie's handwriting from her veterinary records and invoices.

Happy birthday, cowboy! I hope this chocolate cake meets your standards—its official name is Triple Chocolate Chip Cake with German Chocolate Coconut Filling.

She'd added a smiley face, and Mission chuckled at the ridiculously long name of the cake.

Cut into it, and you'll see all your favorites. I used the good, flaked coconut and semi-sweet chocolate chips, according to your preferences.

Can't wait to see you tonight, and don't eat all the cake, because I want to taste it too.

She'd drawn a heart and signed *Kris*, and Mission lowered her note, his heart expanding into a bigger version of itself with every breath he took.

As he stood there and gazed at the chocolate-frosted cake which concealed so many things—including the attention and care Kristie had paid to his likes and dislikes—he knew he'd fallen in love with her.

"You can't tell her on her birthday," he lectured himself as he turned to get a knife. The "flood" in his house had clearly been a lie, and Kristie had clearly staged things with Rich.

He pulled a knife from the block on the counter, grabbed a plate from the dish drainer, and opened the drawer to get out a fork.

Kristie knew he was in the middle of the harvest and didn't have much time. She'd been extraordinarily busy this autumn too, as she dealt with an outbreak of a cattle illness on several farms, something she claimed happened when the weather changed.

But there was always time for Triple Chocolate Chip Cake with German Chocolate Filling.

He cut into the cake and removed a triangle to the plate, delighted with the rich chocolate cake on the bottom layer, the checkerboard pattern of chocolate and white cake in the middle layer, and the white cake with chocolate chips on the top layer.

As promised, a rich, coconutty German Chocolate filling rode between each layer, and Mission grinned at the cake so hard his face hurt.

He quickly pulled out his phone and took a selfie with

the slice of cake, then pulled out a chair and sat down to take the first bite.

He snapped selfies of himself as he reacted to the perfectly moist cake, that nutty filling, and the rich, creamy, smooth frosting. He swiped his finger through it and took a picture of that.

He ate the whole slice of cake without wolfing it down, and then he took a few extra minutes to send Kristie every picture he'd taken, complete with captions.

I am so happy right now.

This is the best cake I've ever eaten.

This filling? I could bathe in it.

My new favorite frosting!

Thank you so much, kitten. I can't wait to see you tonight.

Then, the urgency to get back to work pressed down on him, and Mission quickly pressed a piece of plastic wrap to the exposed parts of the cake, left it on the kitchen table, and headed back out to the farm.

Worry accompanied him, because now his simple gifts and dinner plans for Kristie's birthday might not be good enough—and it was actually *her* birthday today, not his.

He'd already texted her that morning about it, and he told himself—not for the first time—that he couldn't be anyone but who he was. If a bracelet and a new set of mixing bowls wasn't good enough for her, he'd rather know now. She should break up with him and move on if dinner at her favorite restaurant didn't make the cut.

She could find someone else who could pull out all the stops, because all Mission had done was ask Jocelyn to make her a birthday cake and have it at her house, with candles, by eight p.m. that evening. He'd planned to surprise her with the treat after their birthday dinner celebration.

"If that's not good enough...." Mission let the words die there, but they continued to simmer and fester inside him as he made it back to the barn and pulled on a pair of gloves so he could get out to the corn fields and get the cobs coming in prettied up for their farm stand.

*If that's not good enough...*then Mission wasn't good enough.

Later that day, Mission stood on Kristie's front steps with her gifts, his hopes up in the clouds, and a leather jacket warding off the evening chill. She answered the door wearing a dark green dress that glittered in the light, and Mission's mouth went dry.

"Hey, cowboy." She stepped back to let him enter, and she toed a cat out of the way.

She had a runner, so Mission stepped into the house and cleared his throat. "We have time for presents, don't we?"

"You're the one who made the reservation." She

followed him into the kitchen, where Mission set down her gifts and then turned back to her.

"You are a gorgeous woman," he murmured as he found his voice. He drew her into his embrace and leaned down to kiss her. Yep, he totally loved this woman, and as he kissed her, he realized he'd never felt like this about anyone else, ever.

Still, he kept the kiss slow and simple before he pulled away and smiled at her. "We have time." He picked up the mixing bowls, the box bigger than the amazingness of the gift inside.

"Don't expect anything amazing," he said, practically thrusting the box toward her.

Kristie held his gaze as she took it. "They're wrapped amazing." She flicked a look over to the smaller box still sitting on the counter. It had been wrapped in silver, glittery paper very unlike the pink and white striped box in her hand. "And there are two."

"Does the number matter?" he asked.

She shook her head, her curls softly swinging back and forth as she did. "Not usually."

He swallowed and nodded to the gift in her hand. "I did my best."

"Mish." She sank into the nearest dining room chair and started ripping paper off the box. She pulled in a breath when she recognized the box, and her gaze flew back to his. "The mixing bowls."

He'd had to go to three different stores—and the city —to find them, but he kept that tidbit to himself.

"These are sold out everywhere," she said, finally clearing the paper and standing to open the box. "Are they really—?"

She squealed when she saw the box did indeed hold the bowls advertised on the outside.

"I must've gotten lucky, then," he said. Persistent was more like it. Unyielding. He'd made calls and sent Tucker to get these, because he couldn't get there on time.

"Thank you." She pressed into him and kissed him again. "You liked the cake?"

"It was incredible," he whispered. "Just like you are."

"I noticed you didn't have a cake with you." She gave him a playful smile.

He chuckled and shook his head. "The night is young, kitten." He picked up the second gift and handed it to her. "Again, I did my best."

She smiled as she plucked the wrapping off the box and lifted the lid of the black jewelry box inside. She inhaled sharply and didn't look away from the bracelet inside.

"Mission."

"It's just something simple," he said, suddenly embarrassed. "They're not even real diamonds."

He couldn't afford such things, and he suddenly wanted to blurt that out so she'd know. She had to know, didn't she? He worked someone else's farm, for crying out loud. Of course she knew.

"It's moissanite," Mission said, reaching to lift the bracelet from the cotton where it rested. "It is sterling silver, though, so it shouldn't turn your wrist green."

He undid the clasp so he could put the bracelet on for her. "I know you don't wear much like this, but I thought it would only add to your beauty when you go to church or meetings or...when we go out."

She dutifully held out her hand, and Mission draped the bracelet over her wrist and clasped it on.

She admired it, the real diamonds in her eyes. When she looked at him again, her smile sent shivers of love running through his whole body.

He was so going to fail at his personal promise not to tell her he loved her tonight. But he couldn't tell her right now, because she eased into his personal space, cupped his face in her hand, and kissed him again.

Mm, yep. Mission had fallen, and fallen hard, and he wouldn't be able to keep his feelings to himself for much longer.

thirty-two

"So he got *four* chocolate cakes for his birthday?" Gerty asked when Kristie had finished telling her and Mike about Mission's birthday.

"Not just chocolate cakes," Mission said while Kristie simply grinned and grinned.

"Jocelyn made me a Crispy cocoa opera cake with a constellation chocolate mirror glaze."

"Are those even English words?" Mike asked, and the four of them laughed together, Mission included.

Warmth filled Kristie, as she had delivered a surprise chocolate cake to Mission every day for the four days leading up to his birthday—which was today.

They'd planned to go to a livestock auction with Mike and Gerty, and they were meeting Keith and Lindsay there too.

Right now, Kristie reached over and took Mission's

hand while Mike drove and Gerty moved the conversation to Opal's pregnancy. She only had two months left, and while things had been going well, Gerty wanted to find someone else to watch West once the baby came.

"My friend Harper might have some ideas," Kristie said. "She works with a lot of kids."

Not really in the same capacity, but she had a lot of resources when it came to childcare.

"I'm thinking of asking Steele's girlfriend," Gerty said over her shoulder. "Have you met her? Hazel? She's out at the farm all the time anyway, and I don't think she works full-time."

"They're probably going to get married," Mike said.

Surprise ran through Kristie, though she didn't know Steele well. "Really?" she asked.

"Didn't they start dating this summer?" Mission asked.

Like us? hung in the air between the two of them in the back of Mike's truck, but Mission didn't look at her.

"Yeah," Gerty said. "They're so cute together, though, and Steele doesn't take long to make up his mind. It's one of his best qualities."

"Yeah, it's sure not arguing with you," Mike teased, and Gerty fixed him with a tight look.

"I admitted he was right about that horse."

Mike chuckled, and Gerty turned back to Kristie and Mission. "She's a Monson," she said. "I'm pretty sure you know her family farm."

"Oh, sure," Kristie said, putting the pieces together. "They have the petting zoo. I go out there a couple of times every month while they're operating."

"You've probably met her, then," Gerty said. "She runs their gift shop in the summer, which is why I think she'd be a good one to ask to help with West in the winter."

"You could probably have her help on the farm too," Mission said.

Gerty switched her gaze to him. "West loves to feed the chickens, and I'm worried Opal will slip and fall once the snow comes. Being pregnant is so awkward."

She faced the front again, adding, "I'm going to ask her, maybe today."

"Oh, are they going to be there?" Kristie asked.

"Yep."

The conversation moved on as Mission asked Mike about his job in the high-rise building downtown. Kristie looked out the window, ready to be out of the truck, where she didn't have to think about someone who'd been dating as long as she and Mission had been getting engaged and then married, about pregnancies, about anything.

She'd turned thirty-five a few days ago, and Mission was forty-three today. She wondered if he ever felt this coiling, tight jealousy in the center of his gut, and if so, how he dealt with it.

Thankfully, they arrived at the Belfast arena only a few minutes later, and Kristie was able to let the conversation out of the truck—and her ears—when she opened the door. She took a deep breath and calmed further when Mission rounded the back of the truck and took her hand.

"You okay, kitten?"

She put on a brave smile that made him cock his head as he saw right through it. She sighed and let her lips flatten again. "Do you want children, Mission?"

"Yes," he said simply. "Remember how one of my goals was a wife and family?"

"That was your *only* goal," she reminded him.

"And I'm doing great at it," he said, reaching to zip up his jacket. "The wind is harsh out here."

Kristie stumbled after him. "You're doing great at it?"

Mission kept his focus ahead, as if he needed to see where he was going in a dirt parking lot that led to an arena where the animals would be shown. "Yes, I think so," he said. "Do you want kids, Kris?"

When he used her name and not "kitten," Kristie knew things had turned serious. "Yes," she said, the word made mostly of air. "I've never admitted it out loud, but yes. Listening to Gerty talk about West and Opal being pregnant was a little hard for me for a minute."

He took her hand again. "I'm sorry," he said.

"It's fine," she said. "It's just life." She pressed her teeth and then her lips together and took a breath. She needed to shake off the damaging feelings and try to enjoy the afternoon at the auction. She and Mission then had plans to go to dinner for his birthday, and Kristie had his presents—two, just like he'd gotten for her—at her house she hoped to give him when he dropped her off later that night.

"Kristie Higgins?"

She turned toward the harsh voice growling her name, dread settling into her stomach at the very sound of it.

She recognized the tone before she saw his face, and she swallowed quickly as she lifted her head up. "Hello, Carl," she said. "How are—?"

"Hello?" he barked out. "How dare you try to pretend nothing has happened between us?" He puffed up his chest and took a demanding step forward.

"Hey, now," Mission said, moving to stand partially in front of her. "Back up."

"Mission," Kristie said quietly.

"She's a fraud," Carl said, his voice growing louder. "Came out to the ranch to work with my cattle—charged me a metric ton of money—and my cows are still sick."

"This is not the place for this," Mike said.

Carl took another step forward as pure humiliation streamed through Kristie.

"Back. Up." Mission's fingers curled into fists, and Kristie tugged on his arm.

"Let's go," she said.

"You said you couldn't come until Monday," Carl said,

glaring at her past Mission's shoulder. "And you're here? My cattle are sick."

"You're here too," Mission said. "If they were that sick, you'd be back home with them."

"Who are you?" Carl demanded.

"And if they were that sick," Mission said, his voice rising too. "Kris would be there too. I've seen her rush off to care for any number of animals, and I don't appreciate you insinuating that she's not a good vet."

"I can insinuate anything I want," Carl bellowed.

"Folks," a security officer said, and Kristie looked around, horrified when she saw a few people recording the exchange. "You're going to have to take this some-where else."

"I will!" Carl yelled as the security officer nudged him away from Mission. He backed up then, thankfully, but he still yelled, "I'm going to file a report against Kristie Higgins—and no one should ever use her as a vet! They have to learn they can't get away with just writing prescriptions and *abandoning* their clients."

"Let's go," Mission barked, and he grabbed Kristie's arm and hauled her away from the scene.

"I didn't," she stammered as her feet somehow moved with him. "I didn't do that, Mission."

"I know that," he growled, and she pulled her arm away as plenty of people kept staring at her—at both of them. "I wanted to hit that guy so bad."

Kristie shook from head to toe, and she made up an

excuse and ducked into the bathroom, where she locked herself in the privacy of a stall and pressed her back to it as if she could keep the world out that way.

She couldn't, and this time, she also couldn't just pack up and leave town.

How humiliating, she thought as tears spilled down her face. She had no idea how to go back out there and face Mission, face her friends, face anyone at all.

Her name had been screamed through the parking lot, and that couldn't be called back. She knew better than most that the truth didn't matter—what people believed was what mattered, and all of those people had heard Carl Levan call her dishonest.

She stayed in the stall until she heard Gerty say, "Kristie, you have to come out."

She did, and she kept her face averted and used a wet paper towel to wipe the evidence of her tears from her face. She slid her stone mask into place and went with a very concerned Gerty out to the auction.

She sat next to Mission, unfeeling, silent, and miserable. After a while, he tapped her leg and tilted his phone toward her.

Do you still want to go out tonight?

She did and she absolutely didn't. Tears pricked her eyes, and she shook her head. She took his phone and typed into the notes app where he had.

Maybe we could just go back to my house, and I could give you my gifts.

He took the phone. *That guy means nothing, Kris.*

She knew that intellectually, but her heart squirmed and pinched and cried, and she swiped angrily at the tears that spilled out of her right eye again.

"Let's go," Mission said quietly, and she stood up. "Hey, sorry, guys." He gave a tight smile to Mike and Gerty, Keith and Lindsay, and Steele and Hazel. Kristie hadn't even looked at or spoken to any of them.

"We have to go," Mission said. No further explanation. He looped his arm through Kristie's and gave her a small smile.

Everyone looked at her with wide, worried eyes, and it felt like the whole world knew of her inadequacies and indiscretions.

"It's fine," Gerty said. She jumped to her feet and hugged Kristie, who stood there unyielding before she realized how cold she was coming across. Gerty stepped back before Kristie could hug her back. "Go. I'll call you later to come look at Dusty." She tried to smile, but it didn't sit right on her face.

And why should it? Now Gerty knew Kristie wasn't a good vet. *Of course* she wouldn't really call for her to come look at Dusty. She'd only said that to be nice.

Mission led her out of the stands, where everyone seemed to be staring at the two of them. A few people even whispered. In the parking lot, Kristie caught up to the situation. "Where—? How are we going to get home?"

"I called my granddad," he said. "He's here, and he won't ask any questions."

Great, because Kristie was asking plenty.

Had she done something wrong on Carl's farm? His cattle had the same sickness that was sweeping through the area. She'd treated them, given him the medicine, and taught him how to administer it.

What else was she supposed to do?

Was her burden as a veterinarian more than that?

Should she have canceled her plans with her boyfriend, on his birthday, to go check on a non-life-threatening sickness in cattle she'd already treated?

She let Mission put her in the backseat of his grandfather's truck, and she leaned her forehead against the window as they left the auction.

None of it matters, she told herself. She'd ruined Mission's birthday all the same, and she just wanted to go home.

When she looked at Mission, he nodded, leaned forward and said, "We have to drop Kristie at her house, Granddad, okay? She lives just north of that park where you had the drum festival."

"Okay, son," his granddad said, and Kristie let herself weep silently on the rest of the ride to her house.

"Thank you," she said to Ted, and she got out of the truck on her own. But she was delusional if she thought Mission would let her escape into the house by herself.

Oh, no. He came with her, and Kristie paused near the end table where she'd set his gifts.

"I'm so sorry, Mission," she said.

"Don't be." He took her hand and led her down the hallway to her bedroom. "I can stay," he offered.

She shook her head, because while she appreciated what Mission was trying to do, she really just wanted to be alone.

She grabbed onto him and sobbed into his chest while he held her. "I'll be okay," she said. "I just need...."

"I'll call you tomorrow," he said, and he pulled back her blanket, and Kristie simply climbed into bed, let him tuck her in, and she managed to wait until she heard her front door snap closed before she started to cry again.

thirty-three

Mission kept his head down as he went back to his cabin for lunch, mostly to keep the wind from stinging his eyes.

But not really.

He kept his chin pointed at the ground lately, because he didn't want anyone to see him. He didn't want to talk about Kristie and the lack of her presence in his life.

No, he hadn't told her he loved her on her birthday—and he'd been proud of his self-restraint.

Now, it felt like a lost opportunity, and he kept going back to it. Perhaps if he had, she wouldn't have iced him out over something silly and untrue.

I just need some space, Mission.

That text haunted him, and it had only been two days. He'd gone over to her house on Sunday, the day after the auction, when she didn't show up for church. She hadn't answered the door and claimed to be in the city for a couple of days, at a veterinary training—which she hadn't told him about previously.

Mission hadn't believed her, and when he'd pressed her, she'd admitted that she'd decided to take a few days off, have a spa day in the city, and just escape for a minute.

He'd tried to set up dinner in the city. She'd said no. He'd asked her which hotel she was at, so he could send flowers.

That was when she'd sent him the horrible *I just need some space, Mission,* text.

But if Mission knew how to do one thing, it was give someone space. He hadn't texted or called Kristie again, though he felt part of himself dying with every moment that passed where he didn't know where she was, how she was, and when he'd hear from her again.

He'd just finished his lunch of leftover soup when his phone chimed with a non-farm notification. It wasn't Kristie's either, but his eyes shot to his device all the same. Then his heart dang near flopped up his throat.

Lennie's name sat there, and he practically stabbed at his screen to get the full message to show. *Hey, this is Lennie, Kristie's friend. None of us have heard from her for a couple of days, and we're starting to worry. Do you know where she is?*

Mission took some comfort in knowing that Kristie had slammed the door on everyone in her life, not just him. At the same time, he knew how it felt, and he didn't want Lennie, Jocelyn, or Harper to worry.

Instead of texting back, he tapped on the phone icon to call Lennie. She answered on the first ring with, "Hey, Mission."

"Howdy, Lennie." He sighed the biggest sigh he'd ever sighed. "Kristie...something happened at the auction on Saturday, and she's shut me out."

"Mm-hm, that tracks for her."

"She told me she went to the city for a spa day, some shopping, and an escape. She wouldn't tell me which hotel."

"What happened?" Lennie asked. "No, you go outside, Luke. Go on now; lunchtime is almost over, and it's not raining." She spoke the last bit in a softer voice as she'd probably moved her phone away from her mouth. "Sorry about that."

"It's fine." He didn't want to tell Lennie what happened, because he only knew it from his perspective. "A disgruntled client confronted Kristie in public," he said. That was right, and he didn't have to offer commentary on the situation. "She took it really hard."

"Oh, no," Lennie said. "She works so hard. Her job means everything to her."

Mission tried not to let that sting, but it did nonetheless. He sighed again. "I'm in love with her, Lennie, and I don't know what to do."

"You're in love with her?" She sighed too, a happy

sound that made Mission feel even worse that he'd said so to her before Kristie.

"I obviously haven't told her," he muttered. "Can you not say anything, please?"

"Of course I won't, Mission. But how sweet." She let out a long sigh too. "Let me text the other girls. I bet the three of us can figure out where she is."

"Okay," Mission said. *And then what?* he wanted to ask. Then he'd...drive into the city and show up at the hotel? Get loud and demand to know which room Kristie was staying in?

Him getting loud had been the problem. Kristie had gone silent, and Mission's overprotective nature with her had stormed right out. He'd only been matching his tone and energy to Carl's anyway.

He'd apologized a dozen times via text, and he'd say it out loud to her face as many times as she needed him to.

"Give me a few hours," Lennie said. "Lunch is almost over, and then I'll be doing science with fourth graders."

"Sure," Mission said. What was a few more hours? Less oxygen in his lungs? A couple hundred more dying breaths?

The call ended, and Mission struggled to focus enough to move on to the next thing. He wasn't sure if his lunchtime had ended, or where he needed to be next on the farm. The harvest was still in full swing, and Mission surely had somewhere to be.

He certainly couldn't stay here, in his too-quiet, empty cabin. No dog. No yowling cat. No chocolate cake.

Nothing in Mission's life felt right without Kristie in it, and as he jammed his hat back on his head and left his house, he muttered, "You can't let her end it like this."

But he didn't know what to do. None of his prayers on the matter had been answered, but Mission tipped his head back into the foaming October sky and sent God another plea that He would somehow, some way, soften Kristie's heart and provide Mission with a way back to her.

*   *   *

Later that evening, after he showered, he picked up his phone, hating how darkness had already started draping its dark claws over the farm. He'd worked a normal day and hadn't even eaten dinner yet.

"Tonight'll be a freezer meal," he grumbled as his phone vibrated in his hand. He lifted it to see who'd messaged, his pathetic heart sending a zing through him that it could be Kristie.

It wasn't, but Lennie.

We found her. She's at Stag Hollow Lodge, cabin 712.

His heart stopped. Just right there in his chest, stopped beating.

Good luck, Mission.

His pulse raced forward again, as did his thoughts. He

needed to look up where the Stag Hollow Lodge was immediately. He had to get there. But he couldn't show up empty-handed.

His mind spun then, with everything he could take to show Kristie how all-in he was with her. Good days. Bad. Accusations. Anything at all.

Of course he didn't believe Carl. Who would?

And could Kristie really blame him for stepping in and defending her? He hadn't thought he'd done anything wrong. In fact, he'd do exactly the same thing again if he had to. The only thing he regretted about the confrontation at the arena was that he hadn't gotten Kristie away from Carl before he'd said such terrible things.

He stood stock still on the edge of his kitchen, where he'd paused when he'd looked at Lennie's text. She'd given him no direction for what to do, and Mission suddenly felt like the rest of his life hinged on this moment.

He searched for Stag Hollow Lodge and found it on the northeast side of the city, out near the airport. It would take him ninety minutes to get there, and by the looks of the aerial shot, Mission most definitely couldn't show up with just him in a leather jacket and his cowboy hat.

"But you absolutely have to go," he told himself. He picked up his keys as someone knocked on his door. He was heading that way anyway, and he snagged his jacket from inside the closet on the way.

Whoever stood on his doorstep would simply have to go away; Mission had so much to do, a plan formulating in his head as he pulled open the door to find Deacon standing there.

"Deac," he said, surprised. The man hardly ever dropped by unannounced, and since Mission met with him often, Deacon rarely surprised him.

"Evening, Mission." He reached up and touched the brim of his cowboy hat. "Do you have a minute?" He glanced down to where Mission clutched his keys and his jacket.

"I was just leaving, actually," Mission said.

"I thought you and Kris had...."

Mission's eyebrows went up. "We'd what? Broken up?"

"There have been rumors," Deacon said evenly. His dark eyes blazed. "I was actually hoping you could help me know what to do with Judy."

Mission stalled completely for the second time that night. "Judy?" He asked like he didn't know who Judy Foster was, but he did. "What about her?"

"She's...well, I helped her out a bit a couple of months ago, and now...." He sighed and looked away, out into the deepening night. "Now, she won't leave me alone. The calls and texts are incessant, and I don't want to be that cowboy, but—"

"You're not interested in her."

Deacon's jaw tightened as he swung his gaze back to

Mission's. He gave his head a quick shake. "I'm really bad at this type of thing."

"And you came to me, because I'm good at it?" Mission rocked back on his heels and settled his weight on his back leg. "At blowing women off? Breaking up with them? Because—"

"None of that," Deacon said, cutting him off. "That's not what I meant, Mission." He exhaled and rolled his neck. "I came to you, Mish, because you're so level-headed. You're great with letting people down in a way that makes them feel like you still care about them."

"I—no one has ever—that's not true."

Deacon offered him a small smile. "It's absolutely true," he said. "Everyone respects you around here, even when you're after them for being late or for missing the entire corner of a field when they're mowing."

Mission could only blink at him.

"I've tried to tell her I'm not interested," Deacon said. "She doesn't seem to get it."

"To her face or through a text?" Mission asked, because messages were never conveyed quite the same via technology.

"Text," Deacon muttered.

"Let me see." Mission held out his hand, and it took Deacon an extra beat for him to fumble in his pocket and pull out his phone. He slapped it into Mission's palm, and he started sliding through it.

He told himself he didn't need to rush off to Stag

Hollow Lodge. As he'd told Kris once before, he could take a minute and think things through.

He found Deacon's text to Judy, and he turned the phone toward him. "Is this it?" The message read, *You should go out with him, Judy. He'd be good for you.*

"Yes," Deacon said.

Mission found his mouth curving up. "Okay, Deac, this is going to be hard, but you're a farm owner, and you have to do hard things all the time, right?"

"Right," Deacon clipped out.

"Okay, so." Mission handed Deacon his phone back. "You never said, 'You're a lovely woman, Judy, but I don't have any romantic feelings for you. I think we're only meant to be friends.'" He tapped Deacon's chest. "That's what you've got to say. I know, it's awful. I know it sounds bad. But if she's not taking the hint—and that, my friend, is not a great hint—the best thing to do is be direct."

"Be direct," Deacon said. "My daddy always told me that too."

"Well, your dad is a great man," Mission said. "Do you want me to type out the text for you?"

Hope entered Deacon's face, but then he shook his head. "No, you were leaving, and I've taken up enough of your time."

Mission stepped out onto the porch with him and reached to pull the door closed behind him. "Yeah, I have to go be a little bit more direct myself," he said.

"Yeah?" Deacon asked. "And not that I care, but I kind

of do, because I care about you, Mish. What happened with Kristie?"

Mission considered him for a moment, but he absolutely wouldn't be disloyal to Kristie. "She had something really hard happen over the weekend," he said. "And she needed some time to herself."

"But you're going to see her tonight." Deacon didn't phrase it as a question.

"Yeah," Mission said, a true smile finally forming on his face. "I'm going to stop and get dinner, and then I'm going to show up and beg her to come home."

"Good luck, Mission," Deacon said, and he followed Mission down the steps. He jogged over to his truck, quite anxious to leave, as Deacon crossed the lawn back toward his house.

Mission got behind the wheel and backed out of his driveway. As he rumbled past the other cabins, which held his friends and colleagues, a sense of calmness came over him.

Don't rush, boy. Take your time and do it right.

Mission listened to his grandfather's voice in his head as he headed first to the grocery store, his ideas taking on a life of their own as he drove.

"Lord, bless me to say all the right things when I get there," he prayed. "Guide me, bless me, help me—and most of all, help Kris to feel the sincerity of my feelings."

God had a couple of hours to answer his prayers, and

though Mission had felt abandoned in the past, tonight, he believed the Lord would come through for him.

thirty-four

The timer on the last batch of chocolate chip cookies buzzed through the cabin. Kristie turned from where she'd been washing dishes to silence the irritating alarm. Baking had been her crutch in the past few years, and she'd needed it more than ever since Saturday.

Really, Sunday morning when she'd packed a bag and left her house in Ivory Peaks for this escape in the city. It wasn't really the city either, but she'd driven almost two hours to the Stag Hollow Lodge, and she'd enjoyed a facial, a massage, and cabin service for the past couple of days.

In all of her quiet downtime, Kristie had had plenty of time to think—and she'd gone down into some *deep* holes.

"You dug yourself out," she told herself as she moved

this latest batch of cookies—a mixture of milk and semi-sweet chips—to a cooling rack. She'd had to run down the road to the store to get the racks, and she wouldn't care if she left them here.

She'd be here for one more night, but she had to go back to work tomorrow, as she had a scheduled cattle immunization day at a ranch north of the city.

She had canceled and rescheduled everything else for the past two days, and for whatever reason, she could hear Mission's grandfather's voice in her head telling her she'd had her pity party and it was time to get back out there.

Out where, Kristie didn't really know, but she knew she couldn't keep hiding at a luxury lodge, ordering expensive food, and pampering herself. She had savings —that wasn't the issue—but she couldn't let one person and his opinions drive her out of her own life.

Regret lanced through her, and it felt like she was being squeezed from both sides. She'd asked Mission for some space, and of course, being the attentive, wonderful cowboy he was, he'd backed right off. She hadn't heard from him in over forty-eight hours now, and her nose and the back of her eyes heated at the thought of losing him.

"I can't," she said, her voice pitching up into a tinny, too-high timbre. "I have to get him back."

She wasn't even sure that she'd lost him, but it felt like she had. In her darkest moments, Kristie had felt like she had lost *every*thing, and after her manicure appointment that morning, she'd made a list of all the things she had waiting for her in Ivory Peaks.

Her beautiful cottage. Her trio of cats. A car that always started, even in the dead of winter. The cookbooks she loved to leaf through. The recipes she'd lovingly cultivated over the past few years.

And then, of course, Jocelyn, Harper, and Lennie. They had been texting for the past day, the frequency and urgency of their messages increasing the longer she went without responding. She'd finally talked to them, and they knew where she was now.

Kristie finished with the cookies and stepped over to the other counter in the kitchen. Her list sat there, and she looked down at it. She'd started listing individual farmers who'd been appreciative to her, and the names of ranches that scheduled her to come multiple times per year. She put down pet names of the cats and dogs and ferrets that came into her home office.

And right there at the bottom, she put Mission's name in all caps, saving him for very last. He certainly wasn't last in her life, though.

He was everything.

She breathed in through her nose and pressed her eyes closed. The scene that formed in her mind came from Saturday at the auction. She couldn't quite see it clearly, because Mission stood in front of her, shielding her from anything coming her way.

Of course, she remembered everything that had been

said, but strangely, it wasn't *what* had been shouted, but the tone of voice used. So much disdain and disgust, and she'd let herself wallow in it, feel it, and experience it before she'd finally been able to dismiss it.

Somehow, tonight, instead of spiraling down into one of those deep black holes she'd been in the past couple of days, she opened her eyes and looked at Mission's name.

Funny how seven letters could mean so much.

Bless him to have a forgiving heart, she prayed. Then she reached for a paper plate and loaded the first batch of cookies onto it as they had cooled already. With three dozen cookies in three different flavors, and almost two hours to the Hammond family farm, Kristie finally picked up her phone with the intent of talking to Mission.

If God granted her prayer, Mission could taste-test the different types of cookies and pick his favorite. Kristie suspected she already knew what he'd choose, as he liked dessert, but nothing overly sweet. He'd spat out the ultra-dark chocolate she'd had him try a few weeks ago, claiming it to be "like chalk."

He wanted something that would melt and give him that sugar high without being cloyingly sweet. And knowing Mission as she did, she suspected him to be a dessert purist.

"He liked his birthday cake," she told herself as she pulled a sweatshirt over her head, tucked her car keys into her purse, and picked up the plated cookies.

The Stag Hollow Lodge had an enormous main

building with four restaurants on-site. She'd gone to the spa there too, and they had three outdoor pools and two indoor, with seven hot tubs scattered throughout the property.

But back behind all of that, even further from the road and civilization, sat a series of cottages. Kristie had been assigned Cabin 712, which boasted two bedrooms, a full living room and kitchen, and her own private deck out the back that faced the wilderness. She'd sat there in the evenings for the past couple of nights, and as she opened the cabin door, she paused.

"Would it be too much to ask Mission to come here?" she wondered.

It was her last evening at the Stag Hollow Lodge, and she wouldn't be able to sit on the back porch with his hand in hers as they simply existed together, the silence between them beautiful and poignant.

"You're not going to call him and ask him to drive two hours here," she said right out loud, and she double-checked her purse for the key to the cabin so she wouldn't inadvertently lock herself out.

She hurried down the sidewalk as night had fallen and the temperature had dropped with it. She balanced the cookies on the passenger seat and rounded the hood to get behind the wheel of her car.

Each cluster of three cabins had its own parking area with a dedicated parking space, but Kristie had ignored the others staying at the cabins near her. Hers sat on the end row, and a pair of headlights came down the one-way road toward her just as she flipped her car into reverse.

The lights sat up higher, probably belonging to a truck, and Kristie ducked her head so she wouldn't get blinded. The truck barely seemed to be moving as it took forever for it to inch closer and closer to her.

Irritation drove through her when the driver didn't turn and continue on his merry way—but stopped right behind her. Her heartbeat hammered at her as she looked in her side mirror, holding up one hand to block the glare of the headlights.

Had she done something wrong? Was this a police officer?

She didn't see any red or blue flashing lights, but she also couldn't make out any distinguishing features of the vehicle. She did notice when the door opened. A boxy, broad-shouldered figure came toward her—a man.

Kristie fumbled with the automatic locks on her SUV, then noted that no other cars had been parked in her little parking lot. Trees, shrubs, and sagebrush prevented her from seeing the other cabins, including her own, and she had no idea if anyone would hear her, even if she could scream.

Just like on Saturday, when she'd been in a tough situation, Kristie felt herself shutting down system by system.

She didn't want to do that, and she'd always been able to stand up for herself decently well. So she took a breath and looked out her window as the man continued his approach.

He finally arrived, and he wore a dark leather jacket with his hands tucked inside. He leaned down, and it took Kristie all of two moments before she recognized the man peering at her from underneath a midnight-black cowboy hat.

"Mission," she breathed.

It took her another few seconds to get her body to move, as such disbelief cascaded through her, rendering her still and silent. He frowned and had just started to lift his hand to knock when Kristie slid her fingers across the door handle and pulled it open.

She spilled into the night, a level of franticness moving through her that she hadn't felt since leaving Arizona.

"You're here," she said. "What are you doing here?"

Mission looked at her, and she cataloged the slow movement as he swallowed. "I miss you, kitten," he said.

Just like that. *I miss you, kitten.*

Those four words undid her completely.

God had been good to her, and kind, in sending this wonderful, attentive, *forgiving* cowboy.

She didn't want to cry in front of him again, so she lunged at him and pressed her face into his chest—the familiar warmth of his body along with the scent of leather and musk and clean cotton clothing smelled like coming home.

She fit beautifully in the space in Mission's arms, and he easily accepted her into his embrace the way he'd always accepted her into his life.

"You're all right, Kris," he said as he stroked one hand down her hair. "I brought dinner, and everything is going to be okay."

thirty-five

"Boy, a man could get used to this view," Mission said as he stepped out onto the back patio where Kristie had said she'd be.

Holding her in his arms meant the world to Mission, but he'd managed to step back and tell her that he'd come to bring her dinner. She'd said she'd provide a dessert, and he'd moved his truck so that others could get by, and they'd both come back into the cabin carrying the things they'd made for the other.

He'd immediately started unbagging the freezer meals he'd stopped at the grocery store to get, and Kristie had stood in front of him, weeping even while she smiled.

She'd picked the spaghetti and meatballs, of course, and she looked over to him now, as Mission passed her a plate with the neatly arranged pile of noodles, the triangle of meatballs, and that extra sprinkling of parmesan cheese.

"There's no garlic bread," he said. "I wasn't sure what kind of place you'd have, but I figured a hotel room would have a microwave."

She'd cleared the evidence of her crying and tears, and she beamed happily at him as she took the plate.

Mission sighed as he sank into the other chair on the patio and looked out into the night. "It's really quiet here."

"Thank you for coming," she said, though she had not asked how he had learned where she was.

"If I'd known there'd be cookies," he said, "I would have been here a couple of hours ago." He gave her a slow smile, noticing the worry in her eyes despite her scrubbed face and smile.

She looked away from him, her nerves clearly on display. Mission didn't want that; he'd come to calm all her fears. Fine, maybe his too.

"I'm not mad," he said.

"You're not?" She twirled up a small bite of noodles and put them in her mouth. "I would be."

"Yeah." He looked into the darkness, able to picture the majestic Rockies through the darkness. "Why?"

"Because I disappeared," she said. "And I told you not to talk to me anymore."

"That's not what you said," he said. "You said you needed some space. You didn't say, 'never call me again.'"

"Well, you didn't call," she said.

"That's because Lennie told me where you were." Mission didn't want to have a rapid-fire back and forth with her, especially not if it felt like an argument.

"I think we're both just reading the same situation differently," he said. "For me, kitten, nothing has changed."

She nodded, her focus solely on her food. "*I've* changed though," she said.

"Have you?" he asked. "Since Saturday?"

She looked up, that blazing fire in her eyes that he loved so much. "Yeah. I have." She almost looked like she wanted him to challenge her, but Mission held his tongue. Kristie just needed to talk, and Mission wanted to listen while she did.

She softened after a moment, and she too looked out into the night. "I haven't had anyone accuse me of anything like that since I left Anthem. It was really hard for me."

"I know that, kitten. I was trying to be there for you."

"I know," she said. "You're wonderful."

With those words, Mission's heartbeat slowed and settled. This was not a fight, and he didn't need to have his defenses sky high.

"Sometimes I need to work through things on my own," she said.

"Yeah, well, I wish you'd have worked through them

on my couch instead of out here, alone," he said. "I don't like how far away you've been."

She nodded and sliced off a bite of her meatball.

"It's okay for me to be concerned about you," he said, thinking of what his grandfather had told him on the drive here.

Dare he repeat it to Kristie? She'd hear everything then, and Mission reminded himself he'd come specifically to say everything, for her to *hear him.*

"Because it's okay to want to help the person you love," he said.

Her head jerked up as she turned to look at him. Then Mission knew she'd heard him loud and clear. A smile came to his face and filled his whole soul.

"That's right, kitten. I'm in love with you. You're it for me, and I want to be at your side while you work through the hard things, and celebrate with you during the good times. I'll give you space if you ask for it, and I'll come running the moment you say you need me."

Kristie sniffled again, and she set her plate of spaghetti on the table between them. She rose and took the few steps to his chair before she settled into his lap and curled into his chest. He wrapped her in his arms, once again marveling at how close he felt to her and how peaceful he became when he held her.

"I love you too," she whispered.

Mission chuckled. "Is that so?"

"Yes." She lifted her head and looked right at him.

"These past few days weren't easy for me either, and I did a lot of soul-searching. And you were part of that."

"In a good way, I hope." He reached up and pushed her hair back off her face, really enjoying the way his love moved through him bit by bit, making him feel warm and comfortable and safe.

"I'm sorry I didn't tell you where I went," she said. "I'm sorry you had to be so far away from your farm."

"It's all right, kitten. I'm sure I'll have bad days too, and you'll have to put up with me."

She searched his face, and Mission wondered what she saw. "You're my anchor." She reached out and cradled his face in one hand. "I started writing down things that would pull me back to the life I have in Ivory Peaks. There's a big list inside that you can look at if you want. Your name is at the very bottom, but I saved it for last on purpose. As I wrote it, and every time I've looked at it since, I knew I only needed one thing on that list to come back to my life there."

"Oh, yeah? What was that?"

"You," she whispered. "If all I had left in Ivory Peaks was *you*, it would be enough."

"*You're* enough for me," he said. "I've been in love with you for weeks, but I was too scared to tell you."

"Scared of me?" she teased.

Mission's smile only lasted a moment, because no, he wasn't truly scared of her. But perhaps a little afraid to admit his only goal had shifted from what he wanted to her happiness and care.

"I was only scared about one thing the last few days," he said. "And that was that I might lose you."

"You haven't," she said. "You won't."

He nodded, fully reassured. "Are you going to kiss me then?" He smiled at her, the moment between them tender and meaningful, despite his gentle tease.

"If I must." Kristie leaned forward and touched her mouth to his. He'd kissed this woman plenty of times in the past several months, but this touch felt new, and different, and exciting.

Fireworks popped through his bloodstream as Mission lost himself in kissing the woman he loved.

thirty-six

Lady's breathing stayed even beneath her stethoscope, steady in the chill of the late afternoon air. Kristie rested a gloved hand on the mare's shoulder as she listened, reassured by the rhythm. She stood tall and patient, coat glossy under the fading sun.

"You're doing great, girl." Kristie gave her a soft stroke down the side of her neck. "I'm so proud of you."

She finished her exam and jotted down a note on her tablet, glancing up to see if Mission was on his way across the field toward her. He wasn't, and he'd always come when she checked on Lady. Usually, by the time she'd packed up her supplies, he'd be leaning against the fence, arms folded, watching with that quiet steadiness that somehow made her feel both safe and seen.

Then he'd carry her cases back to her car, and they'd

make the trek from the administration barn across the farm to his cabin.

She glanced toward the tree line. Nothing. Her heartbeat skipped, and she moved to put Lady away properly. Molly would be thrilled that Kristie could now pronounce Lady fully recovered from her summertime injury, and she fed Lady a strawberry candy from her pocket once she had her back in her stall.

She packed her case and backpack of supplies back to her car, and slightly out of breath, she leaned against the bumper of her car and pulled out her phone. She only had a text from Lennie about this month's dessert night. Still nothing from Mission.

She updated Molly, Hunter, Deacon, and Mission on Lady's recovery, ending with, *So she's good! I won't have to come see her again unless any of you have any concerns about anything.*

Molly responded instantly with, *Thank you so much, Kristie! I am SO grateful!*

Both Hunter and Deacon responded too, but Mission had mysteriously gone radio silent. She tapped over to the thread with just the two of them and sent him a text.

I'm done with Lady and walking your way. We're still on for dinner?

She knew the unpredictability of a farm better than anyone, and perhaps Mission had gotten caught up in something outside of his control. He had promised her breakfast-for-dinner, and her stomach growled as she started along the fence toward the back of the farm.

A slip of nerves moved through her when she thought of Briar getting attacked by a coyote. Thankfully, the woman had been healing really well, at least according to Deacon's second-hand reports.

The sun had dipped behind the mountains, leaving a rose-gold sky painted with streaks of indigo. The air carried that unmistakable Rocky Mountain scent—pine and hay and a hint of snow not far off. Her boots crunched over the path, each step sending up little puffs of dust that caught the last light.

Kristie pulled her coat tighter. The air nipped at her exposed skin, just briskly enough to remind her she better keep moving. Her mind certainly did, reviewing a conversation they'd had since he'd come to the Stag Hollow Lodge

She'd curled up on his couch with coffee, cookies, and Mission, and they'd talked about what came next. Marriage wasn't a maybe. It was a *when*.

Flowers bloomed in her mind, and Kristie wanted to tell him she'd like to be married in the spring, with mountain wildflowers all around them, the two of them and their closest friends. She'd tell him tonight over bacon and eggs.

Her breath clouded as she made it past the pastures and the equipment shed, and Mission's cabin came into view. Kristie froze.

The porch light glowed soft and golden. Tiny string lights wound around the railing, warm against the twilight. String lights that hadn't been there last night. Kristie actually glanced down the road to make sure she hadn't accidentally wandered onto someone else's farm.

She looked back at Mission's house, noting the curl of smoke that came out of the chimney too. That promise of warmth had her moving toward the front porch and those so out-of-place string lights.

She climbed the steps slowly, her heart beginning to tap a faster rhythm. She hadn't knocked or rung the doorbell here for a while, but tonight, she hesitated for a moment. She gripped the doorknob, then reached up and knocked a couple of times as she twisted.

"Mission?" she asked as she walked inside. The scent of salty bacon meshed with the sweeter, distinct smell of peaches hung in the air, making Kristie pause once again.

She'd walked into the wrong cabin—because this one had been transformed. Candles flickered on the table, three vases of flowers sat on the bar, and someone had hung enormous purple ribbons from the edge of the bar.

Most notably, her three best friends worked in the kitchen with Mission.

He wore an apron—a black number that had his name embroidered on it—and stepped over to the stove, where Lennie pointed to something. None of them seemed to have realized she'd entered the house, and Kristie quickly closed the door behind her.

Then Jocelyn looked over to her. She smiled and turned back to the others without even a wave. Kristie almost felt like she'd arrived too early, and she watched as her friends all said something to Mission.

He nodded, the half of his expression she could see the ultra-serious mask he sometimes wore. He finally cracked a smile, and Kristie's heart nearly burst when all three of her friends stepped into him, creating a four-way group hug.

That lasted only a few seconds, and then Lennie, Jocelyn, and Harper stepped back and pulled their aprons over their heads. Harper had to have taken a day off of work to be here right now—and so had Mission, for that matter.

He'd told her he'd make breakfast for dinner, because it was fast and easy, and they could eat within a few minutes of getting off the farm.

"He's so amazing," Harper said as she approached. She hugged Kristie and sighed. "I wish I could meet a cowboy like him."

"There are lots of single cowboys here," Kristie said.

Lennie took Harper's place after draping her apron over the back of Mission's couch. "I hope you know how lucky you are." She moved past Kristie, and Harper had already opened the door, letting in the cooler night air outside.

Jocelyn gripped her tightly, sniffled, and then followed the others outside, the clicking of the door behind her sealing Mission and Kristie in the cabin together.

With wonder wafting through her, she looked over to him, her eyebrows lifted up toward her hairline. "What is going on?"

The low hum of country music met her ears, and Kristie stepped over to Mission. He moved around the island to greet her, positioning himself right next to the third vase of colorful flowers and all those purple ribbons hanging from the counter.

She reached him and traced her fingertip along the letters of her name, then the item that had been stitched right above it—immediately over his heart. "That's me."

"Mm, it sure is."

She looked up at him, his handsomeness everywhere —in his stature, the sexy cowboy hat, the hint of color in his face, and those dark, dreamy, devouring eyes which held hers.

"You baked," she said.

"I did," he said, easing her into his arms. "And I can whip up dinner in only a few minutes."

"You haven't even started on dinner yet?" She wrapped her arms around him and sank into the beauty of this amazing man.

"I've worked hard on this farm every day since I got here," he murmured. "But today, I worked harder than any of those. Because I wanted tonight to be right."

Her breath caught as she pulled back and looked up into his eyes.

He focused on her too. "I'm a simple cowboy," he continued, his voice low, a little rough. He backed up a step and took both her hands in his.

"I've never been good at finding the right words. But I do know this—every prayer I didn't have the courage to speak, God answered when He brought you to me."

Tears stung her eyes, because while Mission didn't say a lot, when he did speak, it was with power, and he said such beautiful things.

Mission dropped to one knee, never looking away from her. "I want to spend my whole life learning how to love you better. Day by day, quiet and steady and...simply. You're everything I've ever wanted, kitten."

"I thought you wanted a dog," she whispered.

He grinned at her. "Besides the dog." He reached up behind him, twisting slightly, to pick up a black, velvet box. It squeaked when he opened it, and Kristie sucked in a breath at the glorious diamond nestled inside.

"This is a real diamond," he said as he lifted it out. "And it's studded with sapphires, because when I look into your eyes, I see the same type of blue stars." He looked up at her again, his smile gorgeous, if somewhat nervous.

"I need you in my life," he said. "Through all the highs and all the lows; through third place losses and purple ribbons; through harvest seasons and long, dark winters and many, many beautiful summers like we just experienced."

Kristie dropped to her knees too, heart so full it felt like it might spill over. Her fingers stroked down his beard, warm and real beneath her touch.

"I love you, kitten," he whispered. "Will you marry me?"

"Yes," she whispered, tears crowding into her eyes now. "Yes, Mission. Of course I'll marry you." And then, without hesitation, she added, "I love you too."

His eyes softened, and his smile filled his whole face. A somewhat nervous chuckle escaped his mouth as he slid the ring on her finger, then placed a kiss right over the gems. He looked up at her then, and Kristie leaned forward, closed her eyes, and touched her forehead to his.

"I made you a peach pie," he murmured.

Kristie lifted her head. "Mish, you're joking."

"With that recipe you love." He grinned at her and groaned as he got to his feet. "Oof. I'm too old to be down on the ground that long."

He pulled her up too, and right into his arms. "Dinner first; pie second."

"Kissing right now." Kristie grinned at him, the world so still and small when she stood in his arms.

"Mm, I think I can do that." Mission lowered his head and touched his lips to hers, and Kristie thanked God Above for the blessing of this amazing cowboy in her life.

He started to sway with her, dancing to the slow

ballad piping through his house—their tenth dance that would lead to forever.

* * *

I love Kristie's friends, and Kristie with Mission, and Mission and his grandfather! I hope you thought so too. If so, **please leave a review for His Tenth Dance by scanning this code on your phone.**

You can read the first two chapters **HIS ELEVENTH HOUR** now! Just keep turning pages.

sneak peek! his eleventh hour, chapter one:

T arr Olson adjusted the collar of his button-down shirt, checked his reflection in the mirror above the sink, and tried not to wonder for the eighth time whether he looked like a man going to Thanksgiving dinner with his friends, or a man chasing a woman who'd made it very clear she didn't want him.

He sighed as he pulled his sleeves down over his fore-arms and buttoned the cuffs slowly, methodically. His knuckles were still a little scraped from trying to fix the busted heater in the RV—something he had yet to mention to Tuck because he wasn't in the mood to be razzed for *still* living in the RV for over two months after the wedding.

He didn't want to live with newlyweds. It wasn't that hard to understand, was it?

So he'd bought an RV, and he parked it at the site

where his house had been under construction for the past nine weeks. He appreciated that Tuck and Bobbie Jo let him shower in the mansion, and he actually liked the coziness of the RV.

He'd never needed a huge house; Tarr much preferred a wide open space, a big yard, a huge pasture with as many horses as he could put on the land. So the RV wasn't a bad place to live—if he was still living in Tennessee.

Colorado had a much different winter season, and Tarr obsessively checked the weather every day to make sure he had the supplies and energy he needed to survive.

Honestly, survival was so hard these days.

He exhaled and rolled his shoulders, loosening the tension that sat across the back of his neck rent-free. From his work around the facility, to keeping himself fed and warm in a shelter that didn't have electricity or running water, to making sure Briar Prescott was taken care of—all of it had combined in the past three months to show Tarr he only had to sleep a few hours each night.

For a moment, he considered texting Hunter, Deacon, and Tucker and telling them he wasn't feeling well and wouldn't make it to the farm for turkey and cranberry sauce.

But if he did that, Tucker would show up on his doorstep.

Maybe he should take a leaf out of Tuck's gameplan when it came to Briar. Tarr had watched his best friend flirt shamelessly with his now-wife. His feelings for

Bobbie Jo had never been a secret to anyone, but Tarr felt smothered by his hidden, repressed feelings for Briar.

"Thanksgiving," he said to himself as he crossed to the small closet and pulled out a jacket. "Time for food, family...and finally drawing the line."

He'd asked Briar Prescott out a couple of times since her encounter with the coyote. She'd turned him down both times. So he'd retreated again—but only when it came to trying to get her to go out with him.

He showed up at her cabin every single day, whether she told him to leave her alone or not. He wouldn't. He couldn't.

She'd healed really well from the attack, to be honest. Her leg only bore a scar now, not that she ever let Tarr see it. He'd seen it when the doctor had removed the stitches, and he could still see the marks all along her abdomen, whether his eyes were open or closed.

That side wound hadn't been as bad as he'd originally thought, though Briar had gotten seventeen stitches to get her skin sealed back together again. He'd sat with her while she slept, ordered or made food, so she could keep her strength up, and set timers to make sure she took her medicines on time. Then she wouldn't wake up in a massive amount of pain.

He'd seen her cry, and listened to her yell at him to get out and never come back, and held her in his arms while he soothed her and his feelings for her deepened and deepened and deepened.

"So not fair," he muttered—what he usually did when telling the Lord he wasn't satisfied with how things were going in his life.

And when it came to Briar Prescott, Tarr was absolutely dissatisfied. He wanted so much more than she'd allowed, and he swiped his phone up from the top of the slim bureau he'd crammed in beside his bed.

He'd texted her a few hours ago, before he'd gone out to do the morning feeding, about the Thanksgiving luncheon out at the Hammond family farm.

I'm good, she'd said. *But thanks.*

He growled, because he *hated* it when she told him *I'm good*. Absolutely hated it.

He looked up, his mind sparking at him, situations between Tucker and Bobbie Jo firing through his memory.

Maybe he really did need to be more explicit with Briar.

At the very least, he was done following her rules. He was done waiting for permission to care. Done waiting for her to recognize how good they could be together—if only she'd let him in.

"I just want a chance, Lord," he whispered. "Is that too much to ask? A real opportunity?" He closed his eyes and forced his mind to go blank, quiet, still. "Not a single date with hardly any conversation, and not me forcing myself on her to make sure she heals up good."

He opened his eyes, seeing the narrow interior of his RV in a whole new way. "A real try."

He felt like he'd thrown out everything he had, but deep down, he knew he hadn't. It only felt like the eleventh hour, because of the miserable way he laid awake at night, dreaming of holding Briar when they were both happy and laughing, instead of when she sobbed into his arms after a painful physical therapy appointment, or wept into his chest at the slow speed at which she'd healed.

But healed she had. Almost all the way now, though Tarr caught her limping for a couple of steps right when she first got up from a table or couch.

His alarm went off, because Tarr did everything by alarms. Then he wasn't late, and he didn't have to think about anything further out than the moment he lived in.

He grabbed his cowboy hat from the hook by the door and walked out into the chilly November air, boots thudding softly on the steps of the RV. The sun had turned weak as they moved into winter, and just because Tarr had lived through a Colorado winter before didn't mean he'd enjoyed it.

He slid into his truck, started the engine, and turned the heat on full blast. The RV hadn't held heat worth a darn since the first snowstorm, and while he could make do, he didn't particularly enjoy wearing a beanie to bed, pulling on down puffy pants, and layering a down sleeping bag over the one he slept in.

"I need a more permanent solution to my shelter problem," he said as he glanced over to the construction site currently covered in white, opaque plastic sheeting. The bad weather the past week or so had stalled the progress on his cabin build completely, and it hadn't been going well before that.

Sighing, he drove away, putting those problems in his rearview mirror for now. Nothing to do about them on Thanksgiving, though he did consider calling a nearby hotel and getting a room there for the next month.

Then, he'd have access to a hot shower any time he wanted, and Tarr could admit he'd already scoped out the hotel options close to the farm where Tuck worked with rodeo stars and Tarr trained animals for the rodeo.

He turned onto the gravel road that led to the far edge of the property, where Briar's cabin sat tucked back against a patch of pines. It wasn't much, but it was homey—one of the original structures on the ranch from way back when—and Briar had made it her own in the time she'd lived there.

He'd been inside that house more times in the past few months than he'd expected. Starting the night of the coyote attack, when he'd dropped everything and sprinted to the barn because she'd called him.

Him.

Not Tuck. Not Bobbie Jo. Not anyone else who worked with them at the facility.

Him.

And from that moment on, it had been *him*, whether she liked it or not.

He'd shown up at the hospital and sat outside her room until they let him in. He'd brought Wiggins in to visit when she was missing her dog so bad it broke his heart. He'd run to the pharmacy for her meds, brought groceries when she couldn't stand upright, and helped her into her bed when the pain flared so bad it left her shaking.

He'd been there when she couldn't sleep.

When the nightmares came.

When her hand trembled too hard to hold a coffee cup, and when she finally—*finally*—walked across the barn without needing to lean on a wall or brace herself against a railing.

And through all of it, she kept trying to keep him on the outside of the walls she'd so clearly built around herself.

But he wasn't going anywhere.

Not tonight.

It was Thanksgiving, for crying out loud. No one should be alone on Thanksgiving.

Tarr pulled into her driveway, eyed the front windows, and killed the engine. The porch light was on, and smoke curled lazily from the chimney. He took a breath, climbed out, and walked slowly toward the front porch.

Wiggins would know he'd arrived, so he wasn't surprised to hear the hound barking inside. He couldn't hear Briar's correction, but he knew she'd hiss at the dog to be quiet.

He climbed the steps—the second one from the top sagging under his weight; that needed to be fixed—and moved right into the door to knock.

Tap, tap.

He tucked his hands into his jacket pockets, stepped back, and waited.

Beyond the door, claws scrambled on wood, and that made him smile. And when Wiggins appeared in the window beside the door, tail wagging wildly, he chuckled. Oh, how he loved that dog.

And the nights when Briar let him bring Wiggins home with him? Heaven, because the dog slept cuddled up next to him and kept him *so* warm.

He'd really like a good woman for that, and of course, Briar was the image in his head whenever he thought about who he'd like to get to know better.

Despite his constant attention to her for the past few months, she'd revealed very little about herself. Tarr hadn't pushed her either, because God had told him to focus on her physical healing. She'd had a lot of that to do, and Tarr simply prayed that God would give him more time with Briar.

Wiggins barked happily and disappeared, only to reappear a couple of seconds later. Briar wouldn't be happy about that, but Tarr had already knocked.

It took a good ten seconds for Briar to pull the door open, and Wiggins came wagging out to greet him.

"Hey, buddy." Tarr crouched down and scrubbed Wiggins's head and jowls, stroking his hands along his neck and down his back.

"I said I wasn't coming."

Tarr looked up at Briar, her hazel eyes captivating him the moment his met hers. "It's Thanksgiving."

"I don't even like cranberry sauce."

"Good thing there are dozens of other things to eat, then." He straightened and took in her bright purple pajamas, this pair one he'd seen before. Yellow and blue stars covered them, but none of their shine had spread to Briar's expression.

Tarr leaned a shoulder against the frame and smiled. "Happy Thanksgiving to you too."

She'd left her hair down today, her curls loose and wild around her face, like she'd just pulled it out of a bun and hadn't planned on seeing anyone. His chest tightened, and not just because of how good she looked like that.

"I'm not going," she said again, softer this time.

Tarr didn't move. "Yeah, you are."

"No, I'm—"

"Briar." He straightened, folding his arms. "You're not staying home alone on Thanksgiving. That's ridiculous. So you can go change and get ready yourself." He pulled his phone out of his pocket, his heartbeat positively pounding at him as he casually checked the time. "We have about ten minutes before we need to leave."

He only moved his eyes as he looked at her again. He swallowed, about to throw gasoline on a live flame, what with her glare kicking up a notch like that.

"So you can go get ready, or I'm going to carry you to my truck wearing those pajamas. Your choice."

She blinked, clearly stunned. So maybe being more like Tuck would play in Tarr's favor. Or maybe Tarr just hadn't spoken to Briar like this since she'd been injured, and she didn't know what to do with it.

Wiggins sat at his feet, both of them facing Briar as they waited for her answer. He panted, closing his eyes halfway as if that would keep Briar's irritation at a minimum.

Oh, to be a dog.

Tarr's nerves ran freely through his body, especially when Briar opened her mouth.

Closed it.

Glared.

But he didn't flinch. In fact, he found himself smoothly folding his arms. "I'll wait right here."

sneak peek! his eleventh hour, chapter two:

Briar Prescott stared at the cowboy standing on her front porch, waves of shock cascading through her. Tarr Olson had rendered her mute like this several times in the past couple of months, but not for the same reason.

Right now, she'd label him belligerent.

No, that's you, she thought.

Tarr glared back at her, unyielding—and that wasn't usually a word she used when thinking about him. Which, honestly, Briar couldn't get this man out of her head on the best of days, and now she'd have to see his dark-haired, dark-eyed good-looks glaring at her as she tried to fall asleep.

He stood there, all calm confidence and quiet steel, like he hadn't just threatened to bodily carry her—*in her pajamas*—to his truck.

And, oh, she believed he would.

He'd told her several times that he wouldn't leave her alone while she needed him, and he'd come back over and over, even after she'd treated him badly. After she'd told him to leave her alone. After she'd rejected his offer to take her to dinner.

Wiggins sat at his feet, tongue hanging out in a dumb, happy pant, as if he was also just thrilled about the idea of her getting dragged to Thanksgiving dinner in flannel and stars.

She blinked, her brain still trying to catch up. Of all the nerve.

"You can't just show up and boss me around," she managed to say, clutching the doorframe like it could anchor her.

"I'm not leaving you home on Thanksgiving. I just can't do it."

"I'm fine."

"I don't think you are—and I just don't care to let *you* boss *me* around anymore." Electricity zipped between them, the energy striking her straight in the heart even as her jaw dropped open.

Tarr deflated, those broad shoulders holding up that sexy black leather jacket sinking. "Briar, sweetheart," he murmured. "It's *Thanksgiving*. No one should be alone today, and I just...God wouldn't let me drive away while you were still here." He reached out and brushed the tips of his fingers along hers. "Please, go change your clothes and brush your teeth. We're down to eight minutes."

Him and his timers.

"I don't want you to be alone."

She hated how those words hit her right in the soft and quiet parts of her heart, which sat far too close to the place she didn't let anyone touch. Not anymore, at least.

But if there was someone she wanted to let in, it was Tarr.

"I like being alone," she lied.

Tarr arched one eyebrow and waited, steady as a fence post, the kind of cowboy who wasn't going to budge until something gave.

And for once, it wasn't going to be him.

Briar exhaled hard through her nose, turned, and stalked back into the house. "Come in and close the door, then. It's not warm out there, cowboy."

She stormed down the hall and slammed her bedroom door behind her. Not because she was mad—well, she *was* mad—but mostly because she needed to breathe without the heady scent of Tarr's cologne infecting her rational brain cells. If she looked at him for one more second, she might do something foolish, like let him see her vulnerability. Or that it meant a lot to her that he cared, that he wouldn't give up on her, that he *saw* her.

In her bedroom, Briar turned in a full circle, trying to get her bearings. She really just wanted to go across the hall to her painting studio and use the good light coming in the west windows to create something amazing.

After that, she'd planned to bake off the homemade mac-and-cheese she'd bought from Shelley, a woman Briar bought food from all year. She was a good cook and was trying to support a daughter on a highly competitive dance team.

Briar liked lemon zucchini bread she didn't have to make, and chicken tamales, and Shelley's mac and cheese couldn't be beat.

"I was going to watch that romance with the sled dogs," she grumped as she pulled her pajama top off and reached for a dark purple sweater. She sniffed it first, found it fresh enough, and pulled it over her head.

She wanted to leave her teeth unbrushed just to show Tarr that she didn't have to do everything he said. But in the end, Briar hated leaving the house with dirty teeth, and she scrubbed as fast as she could before sitting down on the bench beside her bedroom door and pulling on a pair of cowgirl boots.

She sighed as she stood up, her anger blown out. She now wore real clothes, and her very-near future held sitting at a table full of people who actually liked each other. People who had *families*.

People who weren't broken.

Because she still felt broken, though she looked pretty normal on the outside.

It had been almost three months since the coyote

attack. Twelve weeks since she'd woken up in a hospital bed with Tarr Olson sitting in the corner, watching her like she was something fragile and precious at the same time.

He'd never left, not really. He was there the next day. And the next. And every day after that.

He brought all the foods she liked. Medicine. Wiggins. Movies. Her favorite soda pop.

Himself.

And Briar, who had lived so long with no one to rely on but herself, had let him in. Not all the way, but more than she ever meant to.

She'd cried in front of him. Clung to him when the pain got too sharp. Let him lift her into her own bed, help her with zippers, bring her ice packs, and distract her with dumb, cowboy-dad jokes and dog stories when she couldn't sleep.

Tarr Olson had become her *person*—and she hated how easily it had happened. How much she wanted to reach for him sometimes, even when she didn't need the help. How, when something happened, he was the first person she wanted to call and tell.

She joined him out in the living room, where he barely glanced up from his phone. "Ready?"

"Yes." She watched him as he stood, his demeanor much calmer and slower than she'd expected for him demanding she spend the holiday with him.

Because he didn't want her to be alone.

Because he cared, even though he'd literally said he didn't care what she thought or wanted.

"Let's go, sweetheart." The smirk on Tarr's face—half-satisfied, half-something else entirely—made her want to punch him and kiss him in equal measure.

And she had no idea what to do with that. So she simply said, "Okay," dumbly, and let him put his hand on the small of her back and guide her out of her own home with pure magic sparkling down her spine from his touch.

The Hammond family farm looked like something from a greeting card. Soft white lights hung along the wrap-around porch. A festive wooden turkey welcomed everyone to the farmhouse. Laughter spilled out the front door as they approached, because someone had already opened it.

Tucker, of course. Briar would recognize his loud laugh anywhere.

Briar hesitated at the bottom step, and Tarr automatically slowed with her, though Tuck said, "Hey, you guys made it," with his smile as wide as a mile.

Tarr took her hand and dang near pulled her up the steps, laughing as he did. "Hey, brother." He released her to hug Tuck, and Briar put a smile on her face and did the same.

Wiggins bounded into the house like he belonged

there, but Briar let the two cowboys go ahead of her before she followed.

Inside, the warmth hit her like a hug. So did Bobbie Jo, immediately wrapping Briar in an embrace that nearly knocked her sideways. "I'm so glad you came," Bobbie Jo said, grinning. "We're just putting out the place cards right now."

She led her down a hallway past a formal living room and into the back of the house. An ornate table had been set with candles, autumn leaves, and more soft lights. Two of Molly's teenagers squabbled over who should sit where while Molly and Hunter bustled around in the kitchen together.

Things this busy and loud usually overwhelmed her, but today, it didn't. Deacon nodded at her with a warm smile, and Jane and Cord waved from the couch where they were trying to wrangle their son into a bib. But oh, Clint wasn't having any of it.

A table positioned against the wall groaned under the weight of the food. Turkey. Rolls. Three kinds of potatoes. Even as she watched, Molly set a bowl of salad down on the end and turned to ask, "Baby, where's that butter?"

"It's on the table, Momma," Lisa said. "The turkeys? Daddy said to put them on the table."

"They're on the table," Hunter said, his grin infectious. He trained it on Briar, wiped his hands on his apron and came toward her. "Howdy, Briar."

"Hey," she said, almost cowed by his height and presence. "Thank you so much for having me."

"I'm glad Tarr convinced you to come." Hunter shook her hand and turned as his younger kids started to argue over where their older siblings had placed them at the table.

Tarr came to her side and nodded to another woman in the living room. "That's Alaska Whitby," he said, his voice low enough to be meant just for her. "She's a riding instructor here at the farm and didn't have anywhere else to go."

Another stray, Briar thought, but it comforted her that she wasn't the only one there. She also noted how Tarr had found out who she was and come to tell her, knowing that she wouldn't like sitting down to a meal with someone she didn't know.

She remained on the sidelines, Tarr's steadiness at her side. She'd forgotten what this felt like. People passing plates. Joking. Teasing. Talking over each other. The scrape of chairs, the clink of silverware, the scent of hot, baked bread.

"We're ready!" Hunter yelled as he pulled a tray out of the oven. "Molly's finishing up with the gravy, so it's time to sit down."

"Everyone has a place card with their name on it at their spot," Ryder, Hunter's oldest, said. "You can trade places if the other person is cool with it." He exchanged a look with his daddy, who smiled at him like Ryder was made of gold.

What would that feel like?

Briar hadn't had anyone look at her like that in so long.

Wrong, shouted in her mind, and her eyes migrated to Tarr as he once again took her hand and led her over to the table. Tarr didn't look at her right now, but he'd definitely looked at her with that soft, loving edge in his eyes that only confused her more than anything.

"You're here, sweetheart," he said, pulling out her seat. "I'm right next to you."

Bobbie Jo sat on her other side, with Tucker next to her. Across from Briar sat Alaska, with Cord and Jane down on this end of the table too, and Deacon and the kids flowing down and around the end of the table where Molly and Hunter sat.

She blinked fast and sat very still, letting the glorious, familial energy wash over her.

"Let's pray," Molly said into the settling silence at the table, and everyone seemed to know what to do. They joined hands, and Briar quickly latched onto Bobbie Jo's on her right and sighed silently as Tarr once again secured her smaller hand in his much larger one.

"Ryder, buddy, you're up," Hunter said.

"Please remember it's Thanksgiving," Molly said. "It's not a race to see how fast you can say the prayer, okay?"

Her son grinned at her, and Briar bowed her head as

everyone else did. These movements, this thing they all knew, it grounded her. She found herself exhaling as Ryder started with, "Dear Lord, we are so grateful for Thy bounteous blessing in our lives."

He spoke at a normal speed, and he went through his gratitude for the farm, the horses, the cattle, and their friends and family before he asked for a single thing.

Like a lightning bolt to her mind, Briar knew she needed to be more grateful. Even the little things needed to be recognized, and she lifted her head after Ryder had said, "Amen," properly chastened.

Tarr took her plate as he stood. "Be right back."

She stared after him as others queued up to get food too. Tuck and Bobbie Jo remained at the table, and only Cord went with Clint to get something to eat, leaving Jane behind as well.

"You look amazing in purple," Jane said kindly, and it took Briar a moment to realize she was talking to her.

"Thank you," she blurted out. "This is one of my favorite sweaters."

Jane smiled and nodded. "So, are you and Tarr seeing each other?"

Briar reached for her glass of ice, and then the sparkling apple-grape cider. "Uh, no," she said. "He's just persistent and irritating and wouldn't let me stay home today."

Jane's smile faltered completely, and she glanced over

to Bobbie Jo. "And I thought you were salty," she said good-naturedly.

Bobbie Jo turned toward them. "Is Briar being thorny?"

"It's Tarr," she said by way of explanation.

Bobbie Jo grinned and nodded. "He rubs her the wrong way." She got to her feet as Tucker did, and she squeezed Briar's shoulder as she passed. Bobbie Jo was a bit salty from time to time, but she and Tucker were also the cutest couple in the whole world.

He treated her like royalty, and she respected him like a king.

Tarr returned with their plates, and he set a fully loaded one in front of her with the words, "I'm going to go snag the strawberry jam."

Jane got up as Alaska returned, and Briar wasn't sure if she could pick up her fork and start eating or not. Despite her reservations about coming, the turkey steamed in front of her, looking juicy and delicious with the gravy and mashed potatoes alongside it.

No cranberry sauce, she noted, but plenty of bread and butter. Tarr really knew how to earn gold stars, that was for dang sure.

"How long have you and Tarr been dating?" Alaska asked as he returned with his coveted jam.

Briar stared at her now, wondering what everyone else saw when they looked at her with him. "I'm sorry, what?"

Alaska sighed. "He knew exactly what to get you—and not to get you. He's so sweet, the way he took care of you." She beamed over to Tarr as he tuned into the conversation. "I so need a boyfriend like him." She grinned, her blue eyes brightening. "Do you have any brothers?"

Tarr, to his eternal credit, blinked at her in apparent surprise. Briar sat frozen, throat tight.

"So, how long have you been together?" Alaska finally put a bite of cooked carrot in her mouth, and Briar almost wished she'd choke on it.

Briar's heart beat so loud she could barely hear the noise from the rest of the Thanksgiving crowd, most of them returning to the table now, the chatter increasing in a dull roar that made zero sense to her.

Tarr turned to look at her, brows drawn down slightly. "How long have we known each other?" His eyes searched her face, and horror washed through her, because she didn't know what to say. She didn't *have* words for the way he made her feel sometimes. The way he made her *want* to feel.

Tarr smiled, gentle and sure. "We'll have to work it out tomorrow, while we're on our breakfast date." He scooped up a bite of creamed peas and put them in his mouth.

Briar stared at him. "Breakfast? Tomorrow?"

Together? screamed silently through her mind.

"Just say yes," he said quietly, tapping her fork with the tines of his. "We're eating now, sweetheart."

She wanted to argue against a breakfast date tomorrow morning. And snap at him that she knew how to pick up her fork and start eating. She couldn't, not with so many people around.

Oh, this Tarr Olson. Smart and handsome, he'd brought her to a Thanksgiving meal to show her that some families were normal, and then asked her out in an environment where she couldn't say no.

She put her hand on his knee, satisfied that he flinched and that his gaze flew to hers. "Yes, I can't wait for breakfast tomorrow. Should be a real *scream*."

She gave Alaska a tight smile she hoped didn't come across as too manic, then she picked up her fork and cut a piece of turkey. Laughter rose up from the other end of the table, leaving Briar to stew as she put that first juicy bite of turkey and gravy in her mouth.

Thoughts flew from one side of her mind to the other, things like, *Why does Tarr make me feel like I'm on fire?* to *What do other people see when they look at us?* to *How did he know to get me double mashed potatoes, no peas, and extra bread?*

In short, when had Tarr Olson snuck into her life, and why couldn't she seem to kick him back out?

Worse, why didn't she want to?

Yes, she had a lot to talk about at breakfast tomorrow —assuming she didn't cancel between now and then.

Even if you do, she thought as the salted butter melted over her tongue. *Tarr will just stand on your front porch until you agree to go with him.*

She glanced over to him, and blast him all the way to the moon, he gifted her with a small smile, the kind meant only for her.

He knew he'd won, and she knew she'd be dining with him tomorrow morning whether she wanted to or not.

* * *

Oh, tomorrow's breakfast is going to be ON FIRE - and I can't wait!

Preorder **HIS ELEVENTH HOUR** so you don't miss a moment of life in Ivory Peaks with the Hammond family!

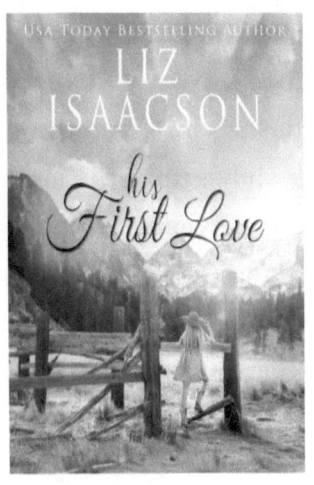

His First Love (Book 1): She broke up with him a decade ago. He's back in town after finishing a degree at MIT, ready to start his job at the family company. Can Hunter and Molly find their way through their pasts to build a future together?

His Second Chance (Book 2): They broke up over twenty years ago. She's lost everything when she shows up at the farm in Ivory Peaks where he works. Can Matt and Gloria heal from their pasts to find a future happily-ever-after with each other?

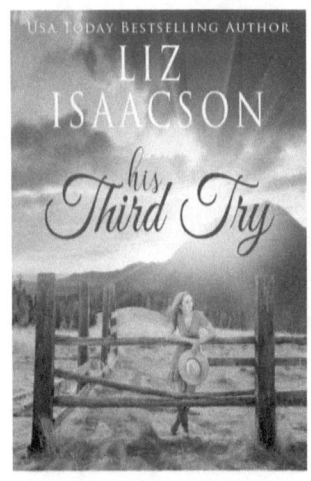

His Third Try (Book 3): He moved to Ivory Peaks with his daughter to start over after a devastating break-up. She's never had a meaningful relationship with a man, especially a cowboy. Can Boone and Cosette help each other heal enough to build a happily-ever-after...and a family?

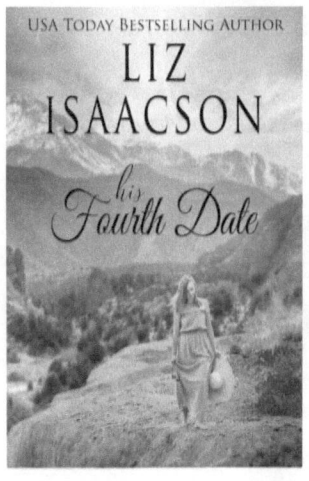

His Fourth Date (Book 4): Their relationship has been nothing but loose goats, a leaking roof, and her complete humiliation after he pays her mortgage so she won't lose her farm. Travis wants to go back in time and start over with Poppy, but he doesn't know how. Can a small town speed-dating event get their second chance off on the right foot?

His Fifth Kiss (Book 5): They once had a few summers together. Now, Michael Hammond is back in town after a devastating injury over-seas. He's looking to reset and recover...not to fall in love. But with Gertrude Whettstein also back at the farm, can Gerty and Mike make their second chance romance into a happily-ever-after?

USA Today Bestselling Author
LIZ ISAACSON
his Sixth Sweetheart

His Sixth Sweetheart (Book 6): She's had a crush on him for decades. He's finally in a place where he feels ready to date the boss's daughter. Can Cord and Jane take their relationship to the next level without getting burned?

His Seventh Stop (Book 7): He's a seasoned cowboy on a delivery mission. She's a resilient hobby farm owner braving the winter storm. Can Keith and Lindsay forge a bond in the heart of a tempest and find love in the calm that follows?

His Eighth Ride (Book 8): Tag has secretly admired Opal from afar. He even went so far as to ask her out, but the timing was all off, and now he's just awkward around his best friend's little sister. Can their unexpected reunion mend the fences between them and finally lead them to the forever love they've been waiting for?

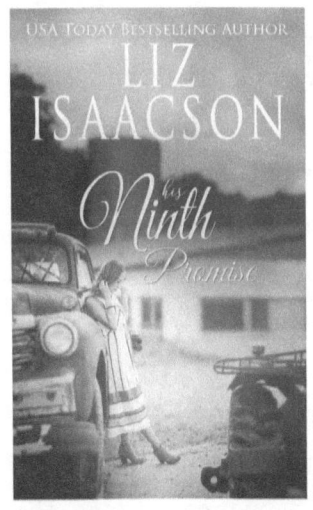

His Ninth Promise (Book 9): At home on the Hammond Family Farm, where gypsy souls and rodeo dreams collide, Tucker's heart has been beating for Bobbie Jo. But with her heart set on a distant love and Tucker searching for something more, their paths seemed destined to cross but never converge. Can he stick it out for another ride if the promise is coming home to Bobbie Jo?

USA TODAY BESTSELLING AUTHOR
LIZ ISAACSON
his Tenth Dance

His Tenth Dance (Book 10): Mission has carried the weight of his past for a long time, and letting someone in feels like a risk. But maybe, just maybe, Kristie is worth it. When his granddad tells her about his secret crush, sparks fly between them, walls come down, and love might just get a second chance to take the lead... if Kristie and Mission are willing to take a leap of faith.

christmas at whiskey mountain lodge in coral canyon™

Colton (Book 1): All the maid at Whiskey Mountain Lodge wants for her birthday is a handsome cowboy billionaire. And Colton can make that wish come true—if only he hadn't escaped to Coral Canyon after being left at the altar...

Wes (Book 2): She broke up with him to date another man...who broke her heart. He's a former CEO with nothing to do who can't get her out of his head. Can Wes and Bree find a way toward happily-ever-after at Whiskey Mountain Lodge?

Gray (Book 3): She's best friends with the single dad cowboy's brother and has watched two friends find love with the sexy new cowboys in town. When Gray Hammond comes to Whiskey Mountain Lodge with his son, will Elise finally get her own happily-ever-after with one of the Hammond brothers?

Cy (Book 4): A cowboy billionaire beast, the woman he asks out in front of everyone, and the family traditions that softens his heart and bring Cy and Patsy together.

Ames (Book 5): A cowboy billionaire who's rough around the edges, the woman he ghosted last Christmas, and their second chance at happily-ever-after.

Graham (Book 1): Graham Whittaker returns to Coral Canyon a few days after Christmas—after the death of his father. He takes over the energy company his dad built from the ground up and buys a high-end lodge to live in—only a mile from the home of his once-best friend, Laney McAllister. They were best friends once, but Laney's always entertained feelings for him, and spending so much time with him while they make Christmas memories puts her heart in danger of getting broken again...

Eli (Book 2): Since the death of his wife a few years ago, Eli Whittaker has been running from one job to another, unable to find somewhere for him and his son to settle. Meg Palmer is Stockton's nanny, and she comes with her boss, Eli, to the lodge, her long-time crush on the man no different in Wyoming than it was on the beach. When she confesses her feelings for him and gets nothing in return, she's crushed, embarrassed, and unsure if she can stay in Coral Canyon for Christmas. Then Eli starts to show some feelings for her too...

Andrew (Book 3): Andrew Whittaker is the public face for the Whittaker Brothers' family energy company, and with his older brother's robot about to be announced, he needs a press secretary to help him get everything ready and tour the state to make the announcements. When he's hit by a protest sign being carried by the company's biggest opponent, Rebecca Collings, he learns with a few clicks that she has the background they need. He offers her the job of press secretary when she thought she was going to be arrested, and not only because the spark between them in so hot Andrew can't see straight.

Can Becca and Andrew work together and keep their relationship a secret? Or will hearts break in this classic romance retelling reminiscent of *Two Weeks Notice*?

Beau (Book 4): Beau Whittaker has watched his brothers find love one by one, but every attempt he's made has ended in disaster. Lily Everett has been in the spotlight since childhood and has half a dozen platinum records with her two sisters. She's taking a break from the brutal music industry and hiding out in Wyoming while her ex-husband continues to cause trouble for her. When she hears of Beau Whittaker and what he offers his clients, she wants to meet him. Beau is instantly attracted to Lily, but he tried a relationship with his last client that left a scar that still hasn't healed...

Can Lily use the spirit of Christmas to discover what matters most? Will Beau open his heart to the possibility of love with someone so different from him?

Todd (Book 5): Todd Christopherson has just retired from the professional rodeo circuit and returned to his hometown of Coral Canyon. Problem is, he's got no family there anymore, no land, and no job. Not that he needs a job--he's got plenty of money from his illustrious career riding bulls.

Then Todd gets thrown during a routine horseback ride up the canyon, and his only support as he recovers physically is the beautiful Violet Everett. She's no nurse, but she does the best she can for the handsome cowboy. **Will she lose her heart to the billionaire bull rider? Can Todd trust that God led him to Coral Canyon...and Vi?**

Liam (Book 6): Rose Everett isn't sure what to do with her life now that her country music career is on hold. After all, with both of her sisters in Coral Canyon, and one about to have a baby, they're not making albums anymore.

Liam Murphy has been working for Doctors Without Borders, but he's back in the US now, and looking to start a new clinic in Coral Canyon, where he spent his summers.

When Rose wins a date with Liam in a bachelor auction, their relationship blooms and grows quickly. **Can Liam and Rose find a solution to their problems that doesn't involve one of them leaving Coral Canyon with a broken heart?**

Finn (Book 7): Her sons want her to be happy, but she's too old to be set up on a blind date...isn't she?

Amanda Whittaker has been looking for a second chance at love since the death of her husband several years ago. Finley Barber is a cowboy in every sense of the word. Born and raised on a racehorse farm in Kentucky, he's since moved to Dog Valley and started his own breeding stable for champion horses. He hasn't dated in years, and everything about Amanda makes him nervous.

Will Amanda take the leap of faith required to be with Finn? Or will he become just another boyfriend who doesn't make the cut?

Zach (Book 8): When Celia Abbott-Armstrong runs into a gorgeous cowboy at her best friend's wedding, she decides she's ready to start dating again.

But the cowboy is Zach Zuckerman, and the Zuckermans and Abbotts have been at war for generations.

Can Zach and Celia find a way to reconcile their family's differences so they can have a future together?

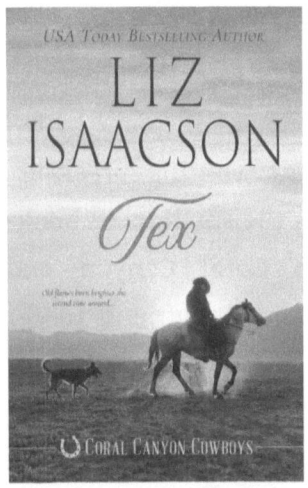

Tex (Book 1): He's back in town after a successful country music career. She owns a bordering farm to the family land he wants to buy...and she outbids him at the auction. Can Tex and Abigail rekindle their old flame, or will the issue of land ownership come between them?

Otis (Book 2): He's finished with his last album and looking for a soft place to fall after a devastating break-up. She runs the small town bookshop in Coral Canyon and needs a new boyfriend to get her old one out of her life for good. Can Georgia convince Otis to take another shot at real love when their first kiss was fake?

Morris (Book 3): Morris Young is just settling into his new life as the manager of Country Quad when he attends a wedding. He sees his ex-wife there—apparently Leighann is back in Coral Canyon—along with a little boy who can't be more or less than five years old... Could he be Morris's? And why is his heart hoping for that, and for a reconciliation with the woman who left him because he traveled too much?

Trace (Book 4): He's been accused of only dating celebrities. She's a simple line dance instructor in small town Coral Canyon, with a soft spot for kids...and cowboys. Trace could use some dance lessons to go along with his love lessons... Can he and Everly fall in love with the beat, or will she dance her way right out of his arms?

Blaze (Book 5): He's dark as night, a single dad, and a retired bull riding champion. With all his money, his rugged good looks, and his ability to say all the right things, Faith has no chance against Blaze Young's charms. But she's his complete opposite, and she just doesn't see how they can be together...

...so she ends things with him.

Gabe (Book 6): He's a father's rights advocate lawyer with a sweet little girl. She's fighting for her own daughter. Can Gabe and Hilde find happily-ever-after when they're at such odds with one another?

Jem (Book 7): He's still healing from his vices, and Jem has dedicated everything he has to his two kids. At least he's not mourning his divorce anymore, and in fact, he might be ready to move on. She's his former best friend, and once he breaks his wrist, his nurse. Can Sunny somehow rope this cowboy's heart?

Luke (Book 8): He swore off women when his ex told him he might not be their daughter's father. But a paternity test confirmed he is, and Luke Young has dedicated his life to his little girl and his brothers' band. There hasn't been time for a girlfriend anyway. He's tried here and there, and the women in small-town Coral Canyon are certainly interested in him.

But he's been thinking about his massage therapist for a while now. Can he ask Sterling out when all they've ever been is professional? Oh, and there's the fact that she's seen practically every inch of his body... Awkward, right?

Bryce (Book 9): Bryce Young has been broken and drifting for years. After giving up his son for adoption, he left Coral Canyon and hasn't returned...until now.

Harry (Book 10): He's a country music star who doesn't live in town. She's a Missing Persons Investigator with strong ties to her community... and she's not so sure about Harry's T-shirts... But Belle knows her heart sings whenever she sees Harry - if only that were more often.

about liz

Liz Isaacson writes inspirational romance, usually set in Texas, or Wyoming, or anywhere else horses and cowboys exist. She lives in Utah, where she writes full-time, takes her two dogs to the park everyday, and eats a lot of veggies while writing. Find her on her website, along with all of her pen names, at feelgoodfictionbooks.com.

www.ingramcontent.com/pod-product-compliance
Lightning Source LLC
Chambersburg PA
CBHW020518110726
47899CB00004B/1152